CW01574485

Sisters & Lovers

Sisters & Lovers

Jeanne Montague

PIATKUS

Copyright © 1992 by Jeanne Montague

First published in Great Britain in 1992 by
Judy Piatkus (Publishers) Ltd of
5 Windmill Street, London W1

**The moral right of the author
has been asserted**

A catalogue record for this book is available from the British Library

ISBN 0 7499 0102 0

Phototypeset in Compugraphic Times 11/12pt by
Action Typesetting Limited, Gloucester
Printed and bound in Great Britain by
Butler & Tanner Ltd, Frome and London

For my very good friends:
Monica, Paul, Di, Margaret,
Maryam, Sandie and Cyndie, with love.

Book One

Innocence Drowned

Bye, O my baby,
When I was a lady.
O then my baby didn't cry;
But my baby is weeping
For want of good keeping,
O I fear my poor baby will die

The Oxford Dictionary of Nursery Rhymes

Turning and turning in the widening gyre
The falcon cannot hear the falconer;
Things fall apart; the centre cannot hold;
Mere anarchy is loosed upon the world,
The blood-dimmed tide is loosed, and everywhere
The ceremony of innocence is drowned;
The best lack conviction, while the worst
Are full of passionate intensity.

The Second Coming, by W.B. Yeats

Prologue

London, 1890

Lottie knew that her mother was dead. For one thing, she was silent, no longer wracked by that tearing cough; for another, she was cold. The child's fingers recoiled as they searched over her face. It was like marble – the icy marble of the angels poised above graves in the local churchyard.

The room was cold, too, but Lottie was used to that. Rarely did coal smoulder in the dusty iron fireplace. Once, when her father was alive, there had been coal and food and comforts, but this was months ago, a lifetime to a five year old. She could barely remember his face. She knew, with that solemn inner awareness of hers which her mother had once smilingly termed 'old-fashioned', that she would soon forget her face as well. Even the memory of her voice was fading.

'You're a funny little old-fashioned thing, ain'cher, Lottie?' That smile, that warmth and love, cuddles, kisses, the occasional scolding slap – all gone for ever.

Lottie had awakened as a sullen dawn struggled through the uncurtained windows. They were layered with dirt; fumes from the factory stacks, the London fogs, all the smoke that belched from a thousand city chimneys. She had been aware of chill and had shrugged the thread-bare blanket over her narrow shoulders, curling into her mother's side, a little animal seeking warmth, but then realised that there was no heat in the body. For days it had been hot and damp with sweat and fever, but on that dire dawning it was like a block of ice.

'Mam,' Lottie whispered. 'Mam, wake up.'

No answer, only the breathing of the toddler, Tweeny, locked in slumber on the other side of the bed. Lottie clambered to her knees, leaning over the still figure, shaking it, gently at first then more violently as panic seized her. Tears began to crawl down her dirt-streaked cheeks. She rubbed them away with the back of her hand but gave up as more followed. Mam's face was grey, pinched about the nose, with brownish half-moons under the staring eyes. Her long red hair, once her pride and joy, lay in greasy twists about the soiled pillow.

'Mam! Mam!' Lottie coiled her fingers in the hair, tugged it.

Tweeny woke and sat up, rubbing her eyes. She yawned widely, then stared at her sister. 'Why you cryin'?' she asked, and crawled across the body, worming her way into Lottie's arms. 'Want some bread,' she demanded. 'Me 'ungry.'

'Don't be a damn nuisance,' Lottie exclaimed impatiently. 'There ain't no bread. There ain't nuf'fin. Get off me. You've pissed yerself again.'

Tweeny began to cry noisily. She always did when reproved or unable to get her own way, having quickly discovered that it was a useful weapon. Adults usually jumped to her bidding when she cried.

'Mam!' she bellowed. ''Ottie bein' nasty ter me.'

Lottie was already up, smoothing down the tattered dun-coloured dress she had slept in, running her fingers through her tangled ringlets. She was aware of grinding hunger pangs, too. There had been nothing to eat for several days – she couldn't remember how long. She struggled with her thoughts – three days, four? The last time Mam had had money was after she had brought that man back to their room.

'I'm goin' out, pet,' Mam had said, dragging herself from the bed where she had lain prone for hours. 'You be a good gal an' look after Tweeny.'

'But Mam, it's so cold out there an' you're ill,' Lottie had protested.

'I gotter go, lovey. We need food. I need medicine. Christ, I need a drop of gin and a penn'orth of opium. How else am I goin' ter get through the night? Just shut up an' do as I says.'

Lottie hated it when her mother put on that red dress with the frilly skit. It was the signal for a miserable, lonely evening locked in the attic, culminating in Mam returning accompanied by a man. Hated it when her mother sat before the cracked mirror, dabbing rouge on her cheeks and lips, pinning up that flaming curly hair and placing a huge hat on top, that horrid, gaudy wide-brimmed hat with the drooping purple feathers. Mam always looked different then – hard, somehow, like the cats prowling in the alleys. And on that particular night her face had shone waxen under the rouge and a coughing fit had interrupted her preparations. She had hung over the chamberpot, choking and retching, her forehead beaded with sweat. When Lottie needed to use it later she found the contents haloed with blood.

Mam had captured her prey, coming back very late, with him stumbling after her. The fumes of gin had hit Lottie's nose as she was lifted from the bed and placed, with her sister, on a mattress in the corner. Though more than half asleep, she did not complain, accustomed to this procedure. It meant food and a few knubs of coal, the means of boiling the kettle and brewing hot tea. Sometimes Mam put a slosh of gin in it for the girls.

Being hustled from bed was a small price to pay for these luxuries, but she resented the men who provided the money – fat men, skinny men, old or young. Through slitted lids she would watch them in the light of the single candle, see them doing strange things to her mother – witness the wonder of her stripping naked, her body painfully thin – so beautiful, her mother. She shouldn't be doing this, Lottie would think indignantly. She's like a princess. They should be on their knees before her, not running their hands over her, touching her breasts and legs – between her legs, saying such dreadfully rude things. It never happened when Pa was alive. Pa looked after her, cared for us. Why did he have to die?

Sometimes she wanted to jump up and hit them when they seemed to be hurting her mother, mounting her like dogs she had seen in the streets, grunting like animals as well. She had done it once, hurling herself, spitting and clawing, at a beery-breathed sailor, but Mam had shouted and fetched her a clout, and she had never dared repeat it.

'Don't you never do that again, Lottie, or I'll tan your 'ide!' Mam had said when the man had gone. 'Frighten 'em off and we'll starve ter death! You just keep your eyes shut tight an' go ter sleep. Take no notice. You're right. Men *are* brutes, but we can make 'em pay! That's all that matters!'

Sometimes her customers were kind to the children, giving them pennies, petting Tweeny who played up to them, but backing off from her stony-eyed sister. She would hear them remarking to her mother first thing in the morning as they idled in bed with her, 'She's a rum little thing, Meg, not like t'other. A pretty piece, that one. In a few years you'll be able to put her on the game and take it easy yourself.'

They did not always stay, mostly slipping off when they had finished that peculiar ritual which Lottie could not understand. Then Mam would have the girls in beside her again and sometimes she cried into her glass of gin, desperate, inconsolable. Crying and coughing, praying: 'Dear God, 'elp me. Save my babies. Oh, what am I goin' ter do?'

Now Lottie wondered the same thing. She could hear sounds rising from the dingy street far below the attic windows: the rattle of carts, the slow footsteps of people dragging themselves to work, a woman's strident shout, raucous laughter. Then the hawkers set up their clamour, crying their wares. If only I had some money, Lottie thought, I could nip downstairs and buy milk for Tweeny, and maybe a loaf of bread. Then she froze, knowing she would have to run the gauntlet of Mrs Baggot or her son, Albert. Mrs Baggot was the landlady and they owed her rent. Mam had told Lottie to keep out of her way, and under no circumstances let her into the room. Lottie feared Mrs Baggot above all things, and avoided Albert.

He was an ugly, uncouth boy, with gap teeth and pimples. Always trying to catch her when she went out to the privy in the backyard or in a dark angle of the stairs, trousers unfastened, fingering himself and then wanting to touch her. She had so far managed to squirm free. Child of the streets, and precocious, she knew what he was after and had no intention of giving in to him, no matter what he offered her. But this was in the past. Supposing he said he would buy them some food. Would she change her mind?

Tweeny was making a terrible racket. She stood by the bed, mouth open wide, face red with temper, hair standing up in spikes. Her tears ran down to mingle with the mucus from her nose, then drip to the stained bodice of her cotton frock. She was bare-legged, bare-footed, and chilblains turned her toes into little red sausages.

'Shut that row!' Lottie ordered, giving her a hard smack.

This served only to increase the noise. Tweeny looked behind her to make sure the way was clear and then threw herself on the floor, kicking and screaming.

The commotion had the effect that Lottie had been trying to avoid. She heard footsteps thumping up the stairs and a woman's harsh voice raised in anger. 'What's goin' on? What you young limbs o'Satan up to? Meg! Can't you keep them brats quiet? Gord, it comes ter somethin' if a body can't sleep on of a mornin'. Damn kids. Any more of it an' you'll be seeking other lodgings, m'lady, punters or no soddin' punters!'

The door crashed open and a figure in a filthy old dressing-gown stood there. She was a fat, slovenly woman, her greying hair tumbling over her broad shoulders, horny feet thrust into a pair of down-at-heel carpet slippers. She took in the room at a single glance, saw the still body on the bed, the two weeping children.

'Jesus Christ,' she said, 'What's up wiv' your ma?'

Lottie ran to the bed, planting herself between it and the landlady. 'Leave 'er be!' she hissed fiercely. 'Don't you touch 'er!'

'Get away, you silly little bitch! Maybe she's dead.'

Hard hands gripped her, shook her mercilessly. She was thrown across the room. Tweeny was hysterical, taking advantage of the drama to storm and shriek. Mrs Baggot pressed her ear to their mother's chest, then straightened up, shaking her head. She rounded on the now silent Lottie.

'She's been an' gorn an' snuffed it. Well, 'ere's a go. Not that I'm surprised, mind you. Didn't think she'd see another spring.'

'What's goin' on, Ma?' Albert poked his head round the door, leering at Lottie. His sandy hair was cropped short and his ears stuck out. A bully, a coward, ever ready to pick on the defenceless, but running home snivelling when the tables were turned.

'You'd better go an' tell the work-'ouse people.' Mrs Baggot gave a contemptuous sniff. 'There's no money ter bury 'er. It'll 'ave ter be a pauper's grave. Good enough fer the likes of 'er, any road. An' she owes me.'

She began to ransack the room, going through their few belongings, getting ever more angry at finding nothing of value. Albert lounged against the wall, picking his nose ruminatively. 'You won't find nof'fin' 'ere, Ma. She ain't 'ad no customers fer ages.'

His mother regarded him with a jaundiced eye. 'Tell me some'fin' I don't know. I'd 'ave 'ad me cut if she'd struck lucky, but she were too poorly ter go out. Anyway, who'd want to hump a sick 'ore? 'Fraid of catchin' the pox.'

He joined her in her greedy search. Lottie cringed, seeing them tossing aside her mother's clothes, rifling her possessions. To her horror, she saw Mrs Baggot approach the corpse and strip the wedding ring from the left hand. She had a struggle for the body was already stiffening. Why can't she leave it? Lottie mourned. Her mother had not sold it, even in their worst hour, clinging to that symbol of marriage and decency, maybe remembering the days when life had promised hope.

'An' the brats?' Albert sat on the side of the bed, scuffing the bare floorboards with his hob-nailed noots.

A crafty look crossed his mother's flabby features. 'Aye, the brats. Well, Lottie's big enough ter start work, and Tweeny's a good looker. She's got them big cow eyes that'll bring in the gelt when you takes 'er out beggin'.'

'I ain't thieving fer you!' Lottie shouted, glavanised into life. 'The rozzers'll get me! I'll be flung in'ter nick. I won't do it!'

Mrs Baggot loomed over her. A rank, unwashed odour crept from her body. She yanked at Lottie's arm. 'You'll do as I says. An' later on, there'll be gentlemen willin' ter pay a good price fer you. Your ma owed me money an' I'm goin' ter get it some'ow. I ain't lettin' you off or feedin' you if you don't work.'

Lottie gave a desperate glance round the shabby room, at her dead mother, at Tweeny. The child was sobbing piteously and this was no longer pretence for she sensed that something was wrong, something dreadful that threatened her security. Though Lottie had often been impatient with her, now a pang of woe struck her heart. Tweeny looked so small and helpless, tears streaming, nose streaming, trickles of urine inching down her short legs.

It was no use, Lottie could not stay. She stamped her foot hard on Mrs Baggot's toe. The women let her go, hopping about, cursing. Lottie hurled herself through the door and hurtled down the dark, winding staircase. She could hear Albert clumping in pursuit. She ran on, streaking through the dingy hall with its cracked linoleum and damp walls, then she stopped, unable to reach the doorknob. In an instant she had abandoned the front way out and doubled back, plunging down the rickety basement steps to the kitchen. Firelight flowed from the bars at the front of the range. An oil-lamp punctured the gloom. Lottie made for the backdoor and freedom.

There was a high wall on both sides of the yard and a fence edging the neglected garden. She raced down the path, climbed on to some bricks and peered into the lane which separated the identical row of houses beyond. By craning her neck, she could see a portion of the street. The gas-lamps were still lit, long amber avenues of mellowness containing movement from which rose the dull, uniform rumble of wheels, the clop of hooves.

The drop on the other side seemed immense but she could hear Mrs Baggot shouting. She scrambled over and let go of the fence. She landed on her feet, skidded, then was up and off. Blood oozed from her grazed knee. She pelted down the street, panting for breath, a stitch clawing at her side. On she ran and on, terrified to stop lest the awful apparition of Mrs Baggot grab her from behind. The street was busy, filled with hurrying people, and the small girl was soon hidden in their midst. Dingy streets, shops already open – they were familiar to her at first but then, as they gave way to a broader thoroughfare, she realised that she was hopelessly lost. She had never been so far from home before.

Terror of the Baggots forced her on. The crowd was thicker here and her ears rang with the noise and confusion of it all; the cries of vendors; the cheapjacks in the side-alleys with their stalls of gaudy goods; the costermongers hawking fruit. Their voices rose above the jingling tradesmans' vans, the trot-trot of horse-trams, the heavy thud of patient, feathery-heeled Shires hauling drays, their great bodies steaming. Above all and through all, came the smell of hot, crusty bread drifting from a baker's shop.

Lottie paused, leaning against the wall. Her fear and exertions had warmed her but now the penetrating cold began to bite, stinging her face and nipping her naked feet. Her knee started to hurt and tears welled up in her eyes. In her mind she still saw Tweeny. I shouldn't have left her, she thought guiltily.

'Look after, Tweeny,' Mam had said. 'You're a big gal now an' she's only a babby. Don't you ever leave 'er when I'm gone.'

But I had to! Lottie argued, sobbing quietly, tiny and ragged, a grubby urchin. The pedestrians, immune to such a commonplace sight, passed her without a second glance. Lottie ground the tears into her cheeks with one grimy fist, sniffing loudly. I'll come back for you, Tweeny, when I've made my fortune. I'll find work. Come and get you in a fine coach. Just you see, I'll never forget you – never –.

Hunger gripped her. Oh, the smell of that bread! She stepped closer to the shop-front. It was unglazed and the contents were temptingly on view, luring purchasers. Long brown loaves; plump cottage loaves with an extra coil on top; round rolls, glazed and crisp; flat plaited loaves; iced cakes and currant buns, a tribute to the baker's art. It was unendurable. Lottie had stolen before, though she had indignantly refused Mrs Baggot's plans for her future. Now, unable to resist, she reached out and grabbed a loaf.

She was not quick enough. Even as she turned to run, the shop-keeper was hollering, 'Stop, thief!'

Lottie fled, barging into people, dodging and weaving. Aware of the increasing uproar in her wake, she ran blindly, terrified when she heard the shrilling of a police whistle. She dropped the loaf, darted across the road, was momentarily aware of vehicles advancing on either side, lost in a maze of wheels. A powerful equine head hung above her, with blazing eyes and a frothing mouth. She saw the glittering harness, heard the trampling of mighty iron-tripped hooves and the squealing of brakes. Then something struck her a violent blow.

I'm going to die, she thought in a rush, as her body was flung under the carriage. In a moment I'll see Mam in heaven! I'll understand everything. And, for an ecstatic instant, it seemed that she *did* understand – fleeting impressions – the moon and planets dancing, putting on a dazzling firework display for her alone, too beautiful to grasp.

The coach juddered to a halt and Lottie lay trapped beneath it, her eyes wide open, blank, staring, as she delved deeper and deeper into unconsciousness.

Chapter One

A gentleman stood before the fireplace, broadly built and of distinguished appearance, legs spread as he rocked on his heels, hands clasped lightly above the tails of his black frock coat. He looked down at the woman seated on the couch close by, a concerned expression on his handsome, bearded face.

'My dear Eva,' he said, 'you know that I'd do almost anything in the world to please you, but really! As your lawyer it's my duty to tell you that this could cause considerable complications, and as your friend I must warn you that it's a trifle mad, to say the least.'

Eva Pendral smiled, exclaiming, 'Oh, Freddy! Don't be so stuffy! Look at the poor little thing. How could I possibly let her go now? After all, it was my carriage that ran her down. She's so tiny, so helpless and alone. I want to keep her.'

Frederick Haldane glanced towards the brass bedstead wherein lay a motionless child. Following that glance, Eva rose and beckoned him closer till they both stood beside the bed. He was touched by the tenderness that softened her features as she gently smoothed a curl back from the child's brow. Once again he was swept by an emotion which, as a logical man of the law, he firmly controlled. It was a mixture of respect, affection and something stronger which he would never admit, not even in the nightly privacy of his solitary pillow, very much resembled love.

He cleared his throat and murmured, 'Her arm is mending?'

'Yes. Dr MacArther is pleased with it. A clean break, fortunately. He tells me that children heal with remarkable speed.'

A frown drew his bushy brows together as he brooded on this urchin who had turned Eva's world upside down, showing a side of her diverse nature which he recognised. A friend of the family, he had know her for years. Once he had nurtured the hope that she might return the warmth he felt for her but, with a sinking heart, had seen how she avoided romantic associations, almost recoiling from them. He knew she was an intellectual with a conscience who had developed a sometimes embarrassing interest in social reform. It was as if by devoting herself to such matters she successfully blocked any natural urge for a husband or children of her own.

'Is she still suffering from concussion?' he asked, aware that she expected him to show interest. Indeed he was not a heartless man and wished the brat no harm, but he would have preferred Eva to have sent her to one of the hospitals.

'She's more lucid every day, Freddy.' A radiant smile lit up her face and, though many considered her plain, he thought her beautiful. 'Despite your dire warnings, I shall keep her with me, educate her, give her all the things she could never have known had she remained in the slums.'

With a rueful grimace, Frederick eyed the muslin drapes of the bed, the satin quilt, all the fine furnishing that comprised this gracious guest-room on the second floor of Albion House, Eva's magnificent home in a select Mayfair square. The child would be treated like a princess, of that he had no doubt. His doubts lay not with *her* welfare, but with the long-term effect of Eva's impulsive action.

She was a young woman, just turned twenty-three, and for the past eight years had been the inheritor of the Pendral banking fortune. She was immensely rich, and a respected member of the close-ranked upper classes. The bank had been established by her ancestors one hundred and fifty years before. Its clientele was exclusive. Among its many duties was the task of dealing discreetly with the monetary considerations of Royalty. Eva's grandfather, Thomas Pendral, had been given a title by Queen Victoria for services rendered. Frederick was one of the lawyers attached to this considerable organisation, and it was he who advised Eva on her own expenditure. Thus he was party to every aspect of her business interests. It was natural that he should show concern when she announced her intention of taking this waif under her wing.

As for Eva, she was aware of little save the glow of happiness which had been with her for days. If the child proved to be an orphan, then no one could take her away. There were advantages to being one of the richest women in England. It conferred power. Till now, Eva had wielded that power for the good of others. Now she intended to use some of it for herself.

She had been horrified when she leaned from her carriage window after the coach had braked so abruptly on that momentous morning almost a week since. She had seen the swiftly gathering crowd drawn like wolves to any accident, heard the indignant mutterings rising to a roar of rage as the scruffy bystanders realised that one of their own kind had been mown down by an aristocrat.

Eva had flung open the door, ordered the footman to lower the iron step and, heedless of danger to herself, had alighted on to the muddy road and pushed through the angry mob to where her coachman was soothing the startled horses. His companion had just lifted a small crumpled body away from further damage by stamping hooves. It was that of a bare-footed girl in a filthy dress.

She had lain limp in the liveried arms, and for a moment it had appeared that she was dead. Then she had stirred, moaned, and something had come alive in Eva, an emotion long stifled. At her brisk order, the child had been carefully placed across the padded seat inside the coach. Eva had whisked off her fur cape and wrapped it round her. Then she had addressed the crowd, assuring them that she would be given immediate medical attention. Her coachman had made enquiries as to the parents, but no one seemed to know to whom she belonged.

Their attitude towards Eva had changed dramatically when they heard her name. More people had poured out of the public houses to see what all the noise was about, reacting with typically outspoken comments. Word had spread.

'It's Laidy Pendral, 'er what 'elps the poor. She opened that 'ostel fer fallen gals down Mile End Road.'

'Did they want to be saved?' one cynical oaf had asked, lounging against the coach, clad in a torn suit, muffler and greasy cap.

'Bloody 'ell, I'd 'ave gorn there meself if I weren't so set in me ways.' This had come from a blowsy slattern in bedraggled finery. 'It's gotter be better than findin' some dirty sod willin' ter cough up 'is money to poke yer. You just try it, Bill, an' see 'ow you likes it!'

'Three cheers fer 'er Laidyship. Me an' me ole man'll be movin' in'ter one of them apartments soon. Them what she 'ad put up down Bethnal Green,' another woman had added, her rusty black skirt trailing on the ground behind, her battered hat anchored to her bun by long, dagger sharp pins.

'An' what about the 'orspitals? Given money to them an' all, she 'as,' others had shouted, then their attention had turned to her servants, mocking their smart green livery and dignified stance.

Easily moved to laughter or rage, their good humour had returned. All agreed that the nipper, whoever she was, had struck lucky. She could hardly be in better hands. Then, like magic, the outer fringes of the crowd had dissolved as a policeman shouldered his way througth the circle. Within minutes an open space had been cleared, and Eva had found herself in conversation with this blue-uniformed guardian of law and order.

Now, remembering the incident, she stroked the child's curls that spread across the lawn pillow. They were lank and matted but, despite the fact that she probably had head-lice, the doctor had advised against washing her hair or giving her a much needed bath till she had recovered. So, apart from carefully removing the rags that covered the bruised body and slipping her into a white nightgown of her own (too large, but no matter), Eva had followed his instructions to the letter.

She longed for her patient to awaken again. The child had opened her eyes momentarily hours after the accident, but had been very confused. By that time the doctor had set the broken arm, and Eva had insisted on being present, holding the pad of chloroform to the small nose, while clasping the lifeless fingers in her free hand.

Though she had engaged a nurse she had refused to rest, seated by the bedside during the long vigil, obeying an impulse that demanded she be the first person the child saw when she regained consciousness. She recalled her joy when those lids, so fragile and almost transparent, had lifted to show a pair of pewter grey eyes still misted by the dreamy realms through which she had been roaming.

'It's all right,' Eva had whispered, leaning over her. 'You are safe with me. Can you tell me your name?'

The answer was so low that she could hardly hear it. 'Lottie Drummond.' Then the child had become agitated as fragmented scraps of memory returned fleetingly, tears making clean streaks down her dirty face. 'I wants ter go 'ome. I must find me sister.

She had seemed inconsolable and Eva, frightened for her, had sent for the doctor again, even though it was the middle of the night. He had come, of course; she was too generous a patron to offend. He had his charity wards to consider, besides which Eva's sincerity commanded the respect of her acquaintances. He had administered a soothing potion and said that Lottie must be kept quiet. Eva had restrained her natural impatience to get to know her.

Soon, she had promised herself, her lonely heart yearning towards the little girl, soon she'll be able to tell me everything.

Though Eva had had every material advantage, she had never been blind to the discrepancies between her own life-style and that of the less fortunate. The sole offspring of a middle-aged man of radical political persuasion who had sought consolation for his wife's death in his daughter's company, her education had been above average for a girl of her station.

He had engaged tutors, given her the benefit of his own considerable knowledge. Old for her years, Eva had grown up to be outspoken and unconventional, bored by her contemporaries who thought of nothing but fashion and flirtations, with no ambitions beyond netting a well-heeled, titled husband. She had been presented at Court when she was eighteen, and officially 'come out', but had caused a mild scandal by announcing that she had no intention of looking for a mate. Friends had done their best to dissuade her, then, defeated, had left her to her own devices.

Now by taking in this waif she had the chance to put her ideas into practice closer to home. It was all very well being a philanthropist, but the child would provide a deeper insight into the problems afflicting so many of the working-class. Also, though she was unaware of it, her frustrated maternal instinct was demanding satisfaction.

Wake, oh wake! she begged silently, conscious of Frederick at her side, sensing his disapproval, resenting his interference. Sweet though he was, Freddy was a man, and men seemed to imagine they had the God-given right to have women obey them. Eva's beloved father had been the only one to whom she was prepared to bow her proud head. Since his death she had cherished her independence. The gentlemen seated at the long, highly polished table in the boardroom of the bank had learned this to their cost when she swept in to their meetings.

Though pretending otherwise, Lottie was conscious, peeping through the dark lashes that made fans against her cheekbones. She lay motionless in the huge, comfortable bed, as she had often lain lately, half awake and half asleep, too dazed to decide which. She knew where she was, and during the increasingly frequent moments of lucidity had begun to recognise the things she could see from the pillow. She was in a light, airy room with flower-patterned wallpaper and white paintwork. A fire blazed in a marble surround, and a gilt-framed settee upholstered in pink brocade was drawn close to it. Rain hurled itself against the windows and trickled down the panes. It would be raw outside, she thought, cold and horrible, but here it was deliciously warm. And, above all, there was the lady who was always hovering over her like an angel.

At first Lottie had thought she was dead, had gone to heaven, and that the lady was indeed one of God's angels. She knew about these, having seen them when Mam had taken her to church, stone ones flying from the buttresses, others shining from the stained glass windows – glorious creatures in vivid greens, reds and blues. But after a while she had decided that this couldn't be one of the Heavenly Host as she didn't have wings and was wearing a tight-waisted dress with a high collar and leg-o'-mutton sleeves. This conviction was confirmed when the blue-clad nurse, frighteningly efficient in her white starched cap and apron, addressed the vision as 'Lady Pendral'.

No one, to Lottie's knowledge, ever called an angel 'Lady'. How could they when angels, so she understood, were male? Like the Angel Gabriel who Mam had said came to tell the Virgin Mary that she was going to have Baby Jesus. It must be so because Mam was always right. Then Lottie remembered that Mam was dead. Mam was gone. Tweeny was gone, too, and she had broken her promise to Mam to look after her.

Unable to keep up the pretence any long, Lottie began to cry quietly, despair, pain and fear washing over her in waves. With a rustle of silk, Eva sat on the bed and held her close, murmuring, 'There, there. Don't upset yourself.'

Lottie's resistance melted, and she yielded to the sensation of soft arms, resting her cheek against the burgundy ruffles of Eva's bodice, breathing in the perfume that emanated from the lace. Unaccustomed to affection from anyone save Mam, a hard core of suspicion inside her refused to go away. What did this lady want? She had learned early that there was always a hidden motive behind people's pleasantness. She trusted no one, as wary as a feral kitten.

She looked up into Eva's serene and listening face. Hazel eyes smiled at her from that pale oval, light brown hair puffed out becomingly on either side. Why was she being so kind? Lottie wondered. Was it possible that she had been mistaken, and there was beauty and goodness in the world after all?

Held in an enchantment, she drew in a deep breath and her sobs quietened. Then a shadow fell across them and she froze, seeing the man. He had been in the room several times before, and Lottie had watched him. Fading in and out of focus, he had constituted a threat. She had heard their voices and, though never raised in anger, his had held a tone which she knew meant that he was disagreeing with the lady and that the dispute concerned herself.

Now he spoke again in that refined accent which she recognised as belonging to a 'toff'. The lady spoke like it, too, but her voice was low and musical. 'Eva,' he said rather sternly, 'are you quite sure this is the right thing to do? She'll be like a fish out of water. Wouldn't it be more compassionate to return her to her own people.'

'Perhaps we should let her decide for herself,' Eva replied, and taking Lottie by the shoulders as carefully as if she was made of spun glass, she asked solemnly, 'Don't be afraid to tell the truth, dear. Would you like to stay with me?'

Lottie was not sure. She ached for Mam, but nothing would bring her back. But there was Tweeny! If only this lady would look after *her,* too, then everything would be wonderful – a dream come true. She tried to put this into words, tried to explain about the little sister left in the hands of that awful Mrs Baggot, but her thoughts were muddled and her tongue would not work properly.

Several days passed before her delicate eggshell of a head mended sufficiently for her to be able to tell Eva what troubled her, and her saviour promised that she would do her best to find Tweeny. She was as good as her word, sending her servants down to the docklands, enlisting the aid of the long-suffering Frederick. They searched the areas to the east, north and west, asking questions in Hoxton, Limehouse and Wapping, even crossing the River Thames to Bermondsey, but it was as if Lottie had appeared from nowhere, without kin or friends. Eva was secretly delighted. The child was hers now, and to make it an even more immutable reality, she began to call her Charlotte, and she accepted this, eager to put the nightmare behind her.

Physically she recovered quickly, her skinny body filling out with the good food lavished on her, the unhealthy pallor replaced by a peachlike bloom, the dullness disappearing from her eyes. After a while the doctor pronounced that her arm was healed and the splint was removed. The next day Eva came into the guest-room, followed by her personal maid, Lambert, who carried garments draped over one arm.

Charlotte had seen Lambert before, met her steely eye and known that she did not approve of her. She may have adopted her full Christian name but would never lose her streetwise awareness and had quickly gathered that Lambert had been in Eva's service for many years, was devoted to her and very protective. Charlotte found her alarming, rather like a sergeant major in her black dress. Tall and thin, flat-chested beneath the pristine bib of her apron, her mousey-coloured hair was so neat that it might well be a wig. On top was set a small white cap from which two streamers floated. Lambert never seemed to relax and seldom smiled.

'Right, Charlotte dear, up you get.' Eva began, brimming with excitement. 'We're going shopping this morning.'

Lambert spread the clothes on the bed, lips tight. Charlotte ignored her and beamed at Eva. She flung the quilt aside and hopped out, no longer wearing a borrowed nightgown but one of her own, for Eva had already ordered garments to be sent to Albion House for her.

'Right-o! Where're we goin'?'

'You'll see. Come on, have a wash and then we'll get you dressed. Don't forget to clean your teeth.' Eva's eyes sparkled as Lambert conducted Charlotte into the adjoining bathroom and turned on the taps of the flower sprigged porcelain basin on its ornamental stand.

'I can do it meself,' Charlotte snapped, as Lambert began to lather the flannel with lavender-scented soap. 'I don't want no one 'elpin' me.'

Lambert had washed her before, deliberately heavy-handed, scrubbing away at neck and behind ears till Charlotte's skin tingled. She was harsh with the hairbrush as well.

'Just you keep still, gutter-snipe!' Lambert hissed through gritted teeth. 'You'll do as you're told.'

Charlotte writhed and protested, making it as difficult as possible, then miraculously Lambert's handling changed. She became almost gentle. Eva was standing in the doorway, watching them. Though Lambert was as faithful to herself as she could be, she did not trust her with the child. Her intentions were of the best – her mistress's welfare – and she would never dare to criticise openly, but Eva was tired of her broad hints about the folly of trying to make 'a silk purse out of a sow's ear', as she put it. Eva had other plans for Charlotte and was already putting these into operation.

'The nursery upstairs is being redecorated. It will soon be ready for you,' she said, and unbuttoning her cuffs and folding back her sleeves, took over from Lambert. 'I've already written to Nanny Pendral. She was my own nanny, you know, and she's agreed to come back and look after you.'

'Is she your sister?' Charlotte looked at her in the big mirror behind the basin.

Eva threw back her head and laughed heartily. 'Good gracious no! Whatever gave you that idea?'

'You called 'er Nanny Pendral,' Charlotte protested, hating to look foolish or ignorant in front of Lambert.

'Ah, well, you see, most nannies like to take on the name of the family they work for,' Eva explained, dabbing Charlotte dry with a fluffy towel. 'I can't tell you her real name. She's always been Nanny Pendral to me.'

'Can I 'ave some scent?' Charlotte asked. The exotic perfume that drifted about Eva was a thing she admired and envied.

Eva looked down into the small pointed face which, once the

dirt had been removed when she dared wash her, had proved to be a very pretty one. 'Not yet, dearest. When you're older,' she promised, then lifted a slender enamelled tin from a top shelf. 'But you can have some talcum powder.'

'Corblimey!' Charlotte exclaimed happily, taking a long sniff at the round perforated lid. 'I'll smell like a bleedin' rose!'

Lambert gave an indignant snort, then said frostily, 'Forgive me for saying so, my lady, but you should make her rinse her mouth out with soap! Swearing like a navvy! Whatever next?'

Eva subjected her a sharp, warning stare, put an arm round Charlotte and led her back to the bedroom. 'Nanny will teach you how to speak properly,' she said.

'What d'you mean? I speaks proper, don't I?' Charlotte bit her lip, giving way to the feelings of inadequacy of which she had been painfully aware lately. Her great grey eyes swam with tears. 'Ain't I good enough fer you?'

Eva hugged her, her voice choked with emotion. 'Of course you are, darling! But it will be less embarrassing for you if you speak like us, act like us – stop using swear-words.'

'Don't you like me cussin'?' Charlotte loved Eva, wanted to do everything to please her, even if it meant forfeiting the richly pungent oaths which were part and parcel of her vocabulary.

'I don't mind,' Eva assured her. 'But others will. It's impolite to upset people and make them feel uncomfortable.'

'All right. I'll try ter remember,' Charlotte promised, staring Lambert straight in the eye over Eva's shoulder, while she thought, I'll never stop cussing you – you sour-faced old bag!

She was not yet used to the clothes Eva had provided. There seemed to be so many of them. A vest, and fleecy-lined liberty bodice with rubber buttons and suspenders to which were fastened black woollen stockings. Cambric knickers trimmed with lace, a flannel petticoat topped by another of finest lawn threaded with blue baby-ribbon, then a tartan frock with a full, calf-length skirt and fancy collar.

Remembering Eva's words, Charlotte restrained her lurid comments as she was fastened and laced into all this cosy covering. It was a novelty as yet, though she wondered how it would feel in the hot weather. Used to having only one patched dress and no underclothing, running barefoot through the snow and slush of winter as well as the heat and dust of summer, she found the clothes restrictive. Even so, she twirled around, making the skirt fly out, every latent feminine instinct enjoying the spectacle of herself reflected in the cheval-glass on its mahogany stand.

'Cripes, ain't I the swell?' She gave a cheeky, irrepressible grin.

Lambert sighed inwardly, thinking, she's a Cockney brat to the marrow. Pure East End. Whatever is the mistress thinking of? She'll never be able to pass her off in polite society.

Eva had no such qualms. She found the child adorable, a tiny elf-like creature, gamine and irresistible, filled with animal high spirits. Her quickness of wit was remarkable; even her vulgarity and sublime ignorance of the conventions was charm itself. She was accustomed to her friends' children, only brought down from their nurseries on special occasions, rather prissy little girls and pompous boys on their best behaviour. By contrast Charlotte was like a breath of fresh air blasting through a hothouse. Eva was looking forward to seeing how she reacted when she met some of them. It would be entertaining to say the least. Heaven only knows what Nanny will make of her, she thought. But Nanny had always been the soul of kindness, though no fool. Few children could deceive her.

Eva managed to catch the imp, seating her on a stool before the dressing-table. 'Let me brush your hair. You look like Shockle-Headed Peter.'

'The boy in the fairy story. Will you tell it me again?' Charlotte sat cross-kneeded, schooling herself to be still.

'Maybe tonight, when you're in bed. Now, be patient, and we'll soon be off in the coach.'

'Like a princess?'

'If you say so.' As they talked, Eva worked on the mass of tumbling curls.

Once cleansed of dirt, Charlotte's hair had proved to be a rich shade of brown with a touch of auburn. It was thick and curling, falling across her shoulders. Eva soon tamed it, drawing the side pieces back and fixing them with a pink bow.

'That'll get in the way of me 'at,' Charlotte reminded, her eyes on the lace and straw creation adorning the milliners' stand to one side of the table. 'I loves that 'at!'

She did indeed adore it, having sat there spellbound when Eva had lifted it from a round cardboard box the day before. Now Eva smiled and, taking it up, placed it squarely on Charlotte's head, tucking the bow away inside the crown. 'Don't move,' she warned as she pierced the brim with amber-headed pins, fastening it securely. 'There. What d'you think of that?'

Charlotte was rendered momentarily speechless, her eyes widening, her lips forming into a whistle. 'I looks like a – ' she was going to say 'bleedin', then remembered in time – 'duchess,' she said.

A coat came next, made of crimson velvet trimmed with white fur, and her outfit was completed by a matching muff, gloves and black high-buttoned boots. Quality stuff, she mused. I wonder how much I'd be allowed on these if I was to take them to the pawn-shop? No need ever to do that again. No more having to sell things to buy a bite to eat. I wish Mama and Tweeny could see me. As she thought of them, it seemed that a giant fist was squeezing her heart.

Lambert came with them to the front door where the brougham waited. Eva and Charlotte were soon installed within it and although her mistress was clad in a sensible morning costume and long coat, the maid insisted on spreading a fur carriage rug over their knees, while listening intently to last minute instructions.

'We shall be back for lunch, Lambert.'

'Very well, milady.'

Soon the vehicle was bowling along Regent Street, and Charlotte pressed her nose against the steamy window glass, drinking in the scene, then she got bored of the seemingly endless stream of traffic and started to draw a face there instead – a round face with dots for eyes and a wide, smiling mouth.

'Don't do that, dear,' Eva corrected her. 'Now you've made your gloves wet. Ah, we've arrived. Time to get out.'

The coach rocked to a halt and a footman leapt down to open the door. Charlotte was agog, forgetting that Eva had told her it was rude to stare. There was so much to see, so many people milling around her. She was hemmed in by long flowing skirts and neatly trousered legs. It was a handicap being small, and she was glad when the footman made way for them, creating a path towards the doors of the large, imposing store.

Then she could see that there were children among the grown-ups. A boy wearing a blue velvet suit stuck his tongue out at her. Charlotte responded by lifting the stiff forefinger of her right hand. He flushed and averted his eyes, the gesture understood even in his refined circle.

'Why're all these kids shoppin'?' she wanted to know, trotting along at Eva's side, one hand tucked securely into her.

'It's late November, and they've been brought to choose the toys they want,' Eva answered. 'Then they'll add them to their list of requests to post up the chimney for Santa Claus.'

'Santa Claus? . . . ooes 'ee when 'ee's at 'ome?' Charlotte wanted to know.

Eva was annoyed with herself for her stupidity. Charlotte had always been deprived. Of course she would be unaware that Christmas joys were every child's right. Not this year, she vowed.

We'll go down to Greyfriars and she shall have a Christmas she'll never forget. The old house will ring with merriment.

Charlottle listened solmenly while Eva told her about the saint who visited every child on Christmas Eve so that no one went without a gift to help celebrate the birth of Jesus.

'I never 'ad none, nor did Tweeny, but I knows all abaht Baby Jesus,' Charlotte declared, leaving Eva in a dilemma as to how to explain this injustice.

'Sometimes he can't reach eveyone, though he wants to,' she said rather lamely, thinking, bringing her up is going to be more difficult than I anticipated. It's as well that Nanny Pendral will be here next week.

'My birf'day's in December, on the twenty-second, but 'ee never come to that neither,' Charlotte vouchsafed. It was the first time she had mentioned this and Eva made a mental note, wondering what else she remembered but was keeping to herself.

'Is it, my love? So you've not had it yet? Well, we'll have to do something about it, won't we?' She smiled, then changed the subject. 'Come along, Chatterbox. Time we were going.'

Charlotte continued to eye the children, suddenly realising that she now looked very like them. She still could not quite believe that it was real, half expecting to wake in the attic with Mam. For a while she and Eva joined the window shoppers, until welcomed by a burly commissionaire with gold epaulettes on his red jacket, a peaked military cap and sparkling white gloves, who ushered them through the revolving glass doors.

The interior seemed like a palace to Charlotte. She would not have been surprised if someone told her that Queen Victoria lived there. Brilliantly lit by electric chandeliers, it was filled with all the gorgeous luxuries that money could buy; big hats extravagantly garnished; gloves of varying size and colour; paste jewellery that looked every bit as valuable as the real thing; artificial flowers, ribbons and furbelows. The counters displaying this artistically arranged merchandise were presided over by genteely spoken shop-girls smartly clad in black, their hair tonged and combed and pinned up in fashionable high styles.

Eva, instantly recognised, was accompanied by a floor-walker who fawned on her while snapping imperious fingers at the assistants, demanding that they pay attention to such an important customer. Charlotte hated him on sight, distrusting his superior air, his impeccable suit, cravat and shiny tie-pin. She objected to the way in which he ordered the girls about, could see right through him to the rather shabby soul beneath.

He's a bully, she decided, and thumbed her nose at him behind Eva's back. He glared at her through his pince-nez, would have loved to smack her backside but dared do nothing about such rudeness. Chew on that, mate! she thought gleefully. And I hope it chokes you!

He takes me for a toff, she mused, quickly catching on to the situation. Blimey! I really shall be a toff if Eva's going to keep me with her for ever and ever. This thought buoyed her up during the long time her benefractress spent in the department displaying ladies gowns. A toff, she kept repeating to herself, I'm a toff now.

It all seemed unreal and her head began to swim, that tender spot in her skull throbbing. Dazed, she stared at a shawl pinned against the wall like a tapestry, its two great flower-embroidered wings unfurled, long fringes shimmering. Flounces of lace hung each side of it like garlands, a lavish stream of every kind of lace. This formed a frame for the centrepiece – a dummy, draped in a yellow silk cape lined with squirrel. Eva was examining the gowns and asking Charlotte's opinion as seriously as if she was addressing an adult.

'What d'you think of the dresses, my dear? That one over there is lovely, isn't it? I must confess to being tempted.'

Charlotte mumbled a reply, but her head was aching in earnest now and the colours flashed before her eyes – gowns of every conceivable hue and fabric in Chinese silks, French satins, moiré, panne, taffeta. Such dresses! The dummies' round bosoms swelled out the tight bodices, their ample hips exaggerating the narrowness of the waists, the skirts swirling into yards of material at the hems, all draped and arranged and magnificient. Charlotte, seated on a gilt-edged chair, feet swinging in her new leather boots, wished they could go home.

It was so frighteningly strange. She had never been to the West End of London before, her infant world consisting of narrow, shabby streets, and rooms crawling with bugs rented in dingy lodging-houses, with barely enough food to keep one alive. Without warning she had been plunged into a life where money flowed and everyone had everything they wanted, or so it seemed.

When they left two hours later, they were followed by a porter staggering under a selection of cardboard dress-boxes, for Charlotte had been equipped with everything she could possibly need, and a few extra things besides that Eva could not resist because they were so charming. Worn out by it all, Charlotte slept during the short journey home, her head resting against Eva's fur-clad shoulder.

The nursery at the top of the house was ready within a few days, and she was installed there in the care of Nanny Pendral. At first suspicious of this small determined lady, Charlotte gradually began to trust her, in the same way that she did Eva. Of course, she could not know that Eva had already discussed her at some length in letters to Nanny who had mentally rolled up her sleeves and prepared to do battle with her dear ladyship's waif.

Battles there were and plenty. Nanny was kind but strict, and quite implacable when it came to obedience. Charlotte, a wilful, undisciplined creature, could rant and rave to her heart's content but Nanny always triumphed. Gradually she won Charlotte over. Consistent, scrupulousy fair, kindly, humorous and warmly loving, she became the stable rock in a sea of uncertainties, but no one could oust Eva as the pivot upon which Charlotte's world revolved.

Although Nanny did not countenance spoiling, Charlotte had only to wish for something and it was immediately granted, as if Eva was indeed a Fairy Godmother with a magic wand. Toys filled the day-room of the nursery; a dappled rocking-horse on hoops; a family of beautiful china-headed dolls; books, games – everything a child's heart might desire. But in the midst of knowing that she need never be hungry or cold again, Charlotte did not forget that somewhere in the teeming, squalid London slums there lived her baby sister, Tweeny.

It was icy cold in the room to which the two girls had been taken. Not their usual garret where the rain dripped through holes in the roof, but a place set aside for a special purpose.

The youngest of them, curled up on the bed, was day-dreaming, temporarily unaware of her miserable existence. In her imaginary world she was no longer an ill-used slave, but someone rich and famous. Maybe an actress, like the pictures she had seen in the crumpled newspaper wrapping the h'apporth of chips and penny piece of cod that Mrs Trimby sometimes brought in for her own supper. Not for the children, of course. A crust of stale bread and a lump of scrag-end was good enough for them.

I must be an actress, she thought, everyone knows that they wear fine clothes and I'm dressed up to the nines. Lost in this dream, her chapped fingers encountered the cotton dress that covered her thin body, but she pretended that she was smoothing velvet, relishing the feel of the silky pile.

When I'm grown-up, she thought, when I've got away from this place, I'll never wear anything but velvet. It won't be long now. I'm nearly ten. I'll run away soon, like I did from the orphanage. That old bitch won't see me for dust! Now I'll go back to my dream again and find a prince. He's got to be handsome, though that doesn't matter just as long as he's rich! Rich! Rich!

Suddenly she was wide awake, hearing sounds below, and Mrs Trimby's voice, followed by footsteps mounting the creaky stairs. She pictured her coming nearer, accompanied by that man.

He had been expected, of course. This was not his first visit. It was Saturday night and he usually came then. Jennie hated Saturdays. When Mrs Trimby had locked her in the bedroom earlier, she had experienced a sickening drop in her stomach, knowing that he would be arriving soon. She had heard others come, their furtive knocks, their voices conversing with Mrs Trimby in the hallway, heard them being ushered into other rooms where the other children waited. A couple of girls and a boy lived there, as well as herself and Ada.

She remembered Ada gratefully. She wasn't alone, not quite. She poked her elbow into her sleeping companion's ribs.

'Wake up!'

'What's the matter?' Ada muttered. ''Tisn't 'im comin' in yet, is it?'

'Yes,' Jennie hissed on a tense whisper. ''Ees on 'is way.'

'Blast an' bugger it,' Ada complained, wriggling down under the cover. 'Now we shan't get no bloody sleep for ages. It's your turn to get up an' serve in the shop, remember?'

'I wish God would strike 'im dead!' The vehemence in Jennie's curse startled Ada into full consciousness.

'That's a wicked thing ter say,' she protested. ''Ees not a bad old geezer. An' we gets ter wear our Sunday dresses. 'Ee likes ter see us all dolled up, prim an' proper as 'oly nuns.'

''Ees rotten. She's rotten. This whole damn 'ouse stinks!' Jennie grated.

He was at the door. The handle turned and he came in, bringing with him a blast of cold damp air, overlaid with the smell of smoky bars, suggestive of noise and the uncontrollable forced gaiety of such places.

Mrs Trimby was there, too. Jennie could see her framed in the doorway, a dark figure in a bombazine dress ornamented with jet, her hair strained back and dressed high. She loomed there, a big, gaunt woman holding a candlestick. Entirely lacking in bodily beauty, her soul was just as ugly. Her mouth was large, thin-lipped and twisted, flanked by bulging cheekbones. Her eyes, set deep beneath a low forehead, glared warningly at the girls who crouched on the bed.

'You behave yourselves,' she said. 'This nice gentleman has come to see you.'

She was using that mock-refined voice that Jennie despised so much. It was reserved for dealing with vicars, do-gooders, customers – and clients. Normally she was as common and foul-mouthed as her neighbours. Jennie stared at her contemptuously through the gloom. She was afraid, but the torments of hell would not have made her show it. She hated Mrs Trimby with all the force and energy of which she was capable, and would gladly have watched her being crucified, even seized the hammer and driven in the nails herself.

The procuress went out, closing the door carefully behind her. The room was dark again, Jennie waited. The man came on, tripped over a stool, swore, then reached the bed. It sagged under his weight as he collapsed on it. He was breathing heavily, his face turned towards the girls. Faint light from the window gleamed on the bottle he raised to his lips. Jennie could hear him swallowing, see the indistinct bob of his Adam's apple.

His speech was slurred as he said, 'There you are then, my little lovelies. Time for games. It's all right. The wife don't know about it.' He broke into a tuneless singsong, waving the bottle. '"When the cat's away, the mice do play."'

Ada eased forward. She was a year older than Jennie. Passionately devoted to her friend, she admired her, loved her, knew that she was different from anyone she had ever come across. She was prepared to shield her, as she had already done many times before, offering herself almost cheerfully.

He caressed her for a few seconds without much enthusiasm. He was feeling the effects of the evening spent careering round the public houses. Part of him wanted to slump down and sleep – but the other, that crimson, nagging, aching devil in his loins – insisted that he satisfy his urges in his accustomed fashion. His hands crept under Ada's blouse, but when they fastened on her firm round breasts he hesitated. They were getting bigger. The touch of that developing flesh repelled him and he lost interest. Ada was very nearly a woman. Soon her hips would broaden, like his wife's. Like his mother's. Big women, bossy women, devouring women who threatened even though they were desirable. Desirable and forbidden. Mature women scared him to death. When with them, visions of his mother would arise to torment him.

'Can't fuck women,' he mumbled to himself. 'Daren't touch 'em. Bloody cows! Bloody mares!'

'I don't know what you're on about,' Ada giggled, squirming from under him.

How can she do it? Jennie wondered, arms clasped about

her body, knees drawn up and pressed close together. He's disgusting!

When she had first arrived at the house a year before she had not paid much heed when he visited Ada. There was usually some sort of sexually based transaction taking place for, at the back of the shop, was a room that Mrs Trimby hired out to prostitutes. Adults seemed big and strong and incomprehensible, while Jennie was small and weak and clear-minded. Her world was more logical than theirs. At times they seemed insane. They did such strange things. This man had wanted to do strange things to Ada. Jennie had not thought much about it, too worn out by long hours spent minding the shop and doing housework, though knowing she must keep her mouth shut and not tell anyone.

Her life had been comprised of secrets for as far back as she could remember. Don't tell! Keep your trap shut! Bert had taught her how to thieve. She had learned fast with Mrs Baggot beating her nearly senseless if she came home empty-handed. There had always been fear and dirt and hunger, yet she had survived, became tough and resilient. Hard, too, all the sensitivity knocked out of her. Besides dodging the police, she had learned much more in the streets – how to fight, how to swear, lie and cheat.

When she was six she had almost been caught picking a gentleman's pocket and, too old to elicit much sympathy by begging, Mrs Baggot had turned her over to the workhouse authorities, giving them her real name of Jennie Drummond. The nickname of Tweeny was a thing of the past, soon forgotten, as were memories of either mother or sister.

The orphanage, a hideous, red-brick building, had had a clincial air. She never forgot the smell of carbolic soap and polish, ever after loathing the sight of brown linoleum and tiled walls. A certain amount of learning had been forced into her – reading, writing and arithmetic, coupled with fear of that terrible vengeful God they worshipped, who would send you to the fiery pits of hell if you misbehaved. She had endured the harsh discipline, brutal punishments and strict régime for three years, then run away.

Mrs Trimby had found her, near dead from cold and hunger, and taken her home. Her lot had improved, but only marginally. Mrs Trimby had several means of making money. Her unlawful activities were carried out behind the screen of a respectable tobacconists' shop in a narrow street near the East India Dock. Sometimes she received stolen goods, while another of her sidelines was arranging illegal abortions. She also provided minors to satisfy the desires of perverts.

Jenny had not yet been called upon to make money for her in this way, though Ada did. She did not know the name of this man who paid heavily for the privilege of being alone with them. He was a weedy person, his head balding save for a piece in front where it was oiled and trained into a quiff. He was tidily dressed, wearing a collar and tie, and he had an air of affluence about him. Maybe he was a shop-keeper or a clerk, but whatever he did for a living, Jennie had never seen him sober.

It was Ada to whom he had always turned in the past, content to have Jennie watch, but Ada was growing fast, and he pushed her away. She was not the one he had come for tonight.

He heaved himself from the bed. 'Got to have a piss. Can't see a bloody thing. Light the damned gas, girl. Where's the pot?'

Jennie did not move. She heard Ada fumbling and that very instant the scrape of a match and light gleamed suddenly from the incandescent mantle, showing up their faces. Jennie wished it was still dark, did not want to see the room with its cheap furnishings, the empty fireplace and bare boards. There was a washbasin with a marble top in one corner, and the man felt about under it for the chamberpot. It clanged as he grabbed it awkwardly before urinating into it. Then he came back to the bed with his trousers unbuttoned.

'You going to be nice to me, little pet?' he was crooning, swaying there, a foolish, happy smile on his face, his eyes misting as he looked down at Jennie.

He had wanted her for a long time. Mrs Trimby had promised him that she was still a virgin. Oh, she'd made him wait, the cunning bitch. Played on his desire week after week, refusing to let him have her.

'I could get a fortune for her up West,' she had said repeatedly, seated in her parlour as they drank gin together. 'Why, some of those fine gentlemen would fall over themselves to have a ten year old, especially now that the law's been passed raising the age of consent to sixteen. But she ain't ready yet, and when she is – it'll cost you.'

Cost him it had. Tonight she had yielded to his pleading, eyes glinting greedily as he poured a stream of gold sovereigns on to the oilcloth covered table, almost grovelling in his eagerness. 'Is that enough? D'you want more? Come on, dear lady. I've always been a good customer, haven't I?'

Now he looked at Jennie as if from the top of a mountain, from the peak of his inflated imagination. A child still, and how lovely. She's perfect, he thought, and wanted to enjoy that perfection, the muscles in his groin responding. She hates me, he realised, and knew a moment's regret. She doesn't want to do this. But she must! She must! I must have her – want her hands – and, Christ, her mouth!

It was a kissing mouth if ever God made one, the upper lip drawn in giving a demure expression, the lower one heavy, full-blooded. She had the mouth of a lover, the eyes of a cat, the body of a child, an irresistible combination.

He edged closer. His knees were pressed against the edge of the mattress. 'Pull up your dress, sweetheart,' he whispered hoarsley. 'Let me look – '

Jennie sat there like a stone statue, while her mind was whirling with plans of escape. She made no move to obey him and he wanted to see her desperately, needed to view her thinness and immaturity, imagining her sex like a pale, smooth almond, hairless and delicate – her tiny breasts, no more than muscle as yet.

Strange feelings and fantasies poured through him, love and longing for the innocent, the unsullied, the children he would never have. His wife was barren. He was rendered impotent when with her. He longed to fondle Jennie, to do the unthinkable with her – his make-believe daughter, his tiny mistress.

'Let me take a peek, darling,' he implored.

'No!' Jennie's voice was low but determined. 'Leave me alone.'

'Don't be shy.' He was frantic, her refusal whipping up his lust to an unbearable pitch. 'I'll give you a shilling for yourself, if you will.'

Jennie alerted. A shilling was a fortune to her. She had never owned so much money in her whole life. Her brain was working fast, cold and calculating. Maybe, if she hesitated a bit long, he would offer more.

'A shillin'? Just fer lookin'?' she asked levelly.

'Aye, just for that.' He was panting, face shining with sweat in the gas-light. Jennie stared at him disdainfully, nausea in her stomach but the pale glimmer of hope radiating her mind.

'All right,' she agreed, and with an expression of complete indifference she raised her dress, exposing the chest, the waist, the long, gawky legs of hers. So frail, so young, so vulnerable.

'Good girl – lovely girl,' he murmured and, mesmerized, leaned over her, hand outstretched.

Jennie rolled out of his reach and covered her body. 'Where's the shillin' you promised?' she said, her voice shrill, eyes like chips of ice.

'I'll give it to you in a moment. Please, let me touch you – just a little bit. It won't hurt.'

Jennie's arm shot out, hand raised, palm upwards. 'Now! I want it now! Don't you welch on me, you bastard, or I'll go an' tell the rozzers you're a dirty old man!' She meant this threat, though she had the street-child's fear of policemen.

Ada, curled up on the far side of the bed, eyed her friend uneasily. There was a frightening quality about her. She had already recognised that there were depths to Jennie impossible to fathom. She was rebellious and disobedient, but quietly so, often severely punished by Mrs Trimby for her insolence.

The man drew some coins from his waistcoat pocket. 'Tell you what, Jennie – I'll give you the shilling, like I said, but if you're good to me, I'll make it half a crown and –' he could hardly contain his excitement, afraid that if she did not give in soon he might spend himself without even touching her – 'and if you let me do exactly what I like, then I'll make it *five* shillings. How about that?'

Jennie had not been reared by brutality for nothing. She was shrewd, merciless. It was the only way to survive. She cast a quick glance round the room. The door wasn't locked. The night was bleak outside but she had slept rough often enough. Time to move on, she decided.

'Give me the money first,' she snarled.

He grunted with relief. What was money compared to the delight he envisaged? He almost threw it at her, trembling from head to foot. Coins rained down on the blanket. Never taking her eyes from him, Jennie snatched them up, held them tightly in her fist. He lunged for her. She was off the bed like an eel, sprinting for the door. It opened wide and she was away, her feet hardly touching the bare treads of the stairs.

It was dark there, but she knew the way. She had kept her shoes on and was glad of it. They clacked as they contacted the tiles in the hall. Her fingers found the front door. She was across the threshold, closing it quietly behind her, and out into the anonymity of the streets. She was free! From now on she would be her own master. No more slaving for anyone. Damn them all to hell!

Chapter Two

Lady Bernice Frewston draped herself elegantly on the couch in Eva's boudoir, placed a cigarette in a slim ivory holder, and touched the tip to the flame of a tasselled pocket lighter. After blowing smoke rings through her aristocratic nostrils, she said, 'Well, you've done it. Congratulations! Fancy turning a slum child into a lady, *and* having the nerve to present her at Court, no less!'

'It wasn't so hard,' Eva replied from the dressing-table where she was putting the finishing touches to her toilet. 'Charlotte has always proved quick in every respect. She's better educated than most girls of our class.'

'That wouldn't be difficult,' Bernice broke in. 'Lord knows parents don't bother much with a daughter, just as long as she can speak French, play a piece on the piano and paint a water-colour.'

'I think such an attitude shocking,' Eva answered, glancing across at her. Bernice was attractive and vivacious, a perfect example of the mature woman so much admired in the circles in which she moved.

'You take life far too seriously, my dear.' Bernice twisted one slender wrist this way and that as she talked, watching the diamonds flashing in the bracelet she wore over her elbow-length white glove. 'That's what comes of never encouraging beaux. You should have married, like I did.'

Eva stiffened, cross with Bernice for mentioning this. She could not analyse precisely why it annoyed her, but blamed it on lack of confidence, well aware of the contrast they made. Though she was wearing an equally expensive gown and her jewels were even more valuable than Bernice's, she knew that she could never, with the wildest stretch of imagination, be called beautiful.

I'm plain, she thought, staring relentlessly at her reflection in the mirror. My face is what is classed as 'homely'. Every time a man has shown interest in me I've been unable to trust his motives, haunted by the knowledge that he's probably only after my wealth. Unable to settle for a money oriented marriage I've recognised that I'm unlikely to find the love I want for simply being *myself*, not because I own the bank.

It had not always been so. Eva had fallen in love once, and once only. There had been one man to whom money meant nothing compared to the fire of genius that consumed him: Victor Dalbiac. It had happened when she was sixteen. He was an artist who had been commissioned by her father to paint her portrait, a charismatic individual the like of whom she had never met before. He, in turn, had found that her aloofness concealed a painful shyness. He worked his magic on her and, though twice her age, had succeeded in stealing her heart and possessing her body.

No one had known about the affair, or so she had thought, until learning from him later that he had taken on a wager with some of his feckless colleagues who had dared him to melt the ice maiden. Deeply wounded by this careless admission which had come when he was tired of her, she had neither reproached him nor let him know how much she had been hurt. She could have put pressure on him, insisting that he marry her to save her reputation, but knew that wealth and convention meant nothing to him, daemon-driven as he was and oblivious to much else. When he had departed for the South Seas, Eva had come to her sense with a jolt, thankful to the bottom of her soul that she had not fallen pregnant.

She had buried the incident in a remote corner of her mind where it lingered like an unwanted acquisition that cannot be sold or given away. Mortified by her own gullibility, and bitterly regretting having yielded her virginity to a rogue, she had, nonetheless, tasted physical passion, and was sometimes tormented by memories of it, yet had exerted iron self-control and never fallen prey to desire again. Sexual congress had become a tainted thing in her mind; it meant pain and shame and disillusion. She wanted no part of it ever again, and yet on occasions – when the nights were warm and flower-scented – she would toss in her lonely bed, aching for the fulfilment she had experienced so briefly. Then she would curse Victor Dalbiac, reflecting sadly that what one has never know one doesn't miss.

She thrust these unhappy images from her, directing her mind down other pathways. I'm unsophisticated, and far too earnest, she fretted. Oh, I give the occasional party, hunt at Greyfriars, entertain in much the same way Bernice does, though my chosen companions are very different.

Eva found the smart set tedious with their everlasting preoccupation with fashion and clandestine love-affairs, and preferred the more stimulating talk of men of letters, artists, sculptors, musicians, actors and radicals. Her peers considered her odd, though they were too polite to show it.

But I know what they're thinking, she continued her inward monologue. I'm a spinster. I go around unchaperoned but there's never been the slightest hint of an indiscretion. I worry about injustice, spend hours in the slums about my 'good works'. How I hate that expression! It sounds so self-righteous, and I don't feel like that. Once my equals looked at me askance for such behaviour. Getting older has made it easier. Now they accept me as an eccentric maiden lady. Men, even those with an eye on my fortune, have stopped trying to persuade me to marry them.

This was a relief and yet, lately, she had been restlessly sensitive to the fact that the years were rolling by. I'm thirty-six, she thought, and a panicky feeling gripped her. Why is this worrying me? I didn't care once. After Victor abandoned me I prayed for the peace of middle age.

Maybe it was because Charlotte was now eighteen and on the threshold of life. Eva had wrapped herself around her, lived through her, taken pride in her achievements, instilled her own principles into her. As she had said to Bernice, she had proved a more than able pupil, warm-hearted, brave – and exceptionally beautiful.

What shall I do if she falls in love and wants to leave me? The notion stabbed Eva like a knife. I can't stop her. It wouldn't be fair. Would she give up our work? Devote herself to her husband? A dreary vista of empty years ahead yawned before her. And yet I'm giving her every encouragement to do this, she thought. Above all, I *want* her to be happy.

Bernice's sweetly modulated voice dragged her back to the present. 'I always knew you were clever, Eva,' she was saying, stubbing out her cigarette in a brass ashtray shaped like a leaf. 'But this beats all! Such colossal cheek! When the King came to supper with me last night I told him all about it – even bet him that he wouldn't be able to guess which of the girls dipping curtsies to him in the Palace this afternoon would be the imposter. You know how Eddy likes practical jokes, and this is the biggest one of all. He found it highly amusing, and I think I've won the wager. I'll find out when I see him later.'

Eva roused herself from her gloomy speculations, aware that she must pull herself together. This was a great occasion for Charlotte, and for her, too, for she had proved to the scoffers that her experiment had been successful, but she was exhausted. The build up to the evening had been hectic with so much to arrange.

'Charlotte has done well. I'm pleased with her.' She managed to keep her voice level, and herself controlled.

'And so you should be! You've worked a miracle. Won't it be a hoot if she nets an eligible peer at the ball tonight?'

Everything was a hoot to Bernice, and Eva often envied her insouciance. They had come out in the same year, been friends ever since, though Bernice had married a marquis, given him three children and then, as was customary amongst couples in the group that circled King Edward VII, she and her husband had gone their own ways, but most discreetly. No one minded affairs, but it was a sin to commit the unforgivable folly of bringing them into the open. As for divorce? This was out of the question. Those unfortunates who had attempted it had found themselves ostracised, whether they were the guilty party or no.

Recently Bernice had, through conniving and careful planning, reached that enviable pinnacle of every political hostess's ambition – she was now Edward's mistress. One of many, it was true, for the newly crowned, sixty-year-old king had always had a weakness for ladies, but Bernice, with her wealth and experience had proved a formidable rival to other aspiring Royal whores. As for her husband, Quentin? The amiable marquis had quietly accepted that his wife should receive regal favour, welcoming this distinguished guest to house parties and grouse shooting organised at great expense at Bishop Combe, his estate in Berkshire. That his lovely wife had caught the eye of England's beloved reprobate of a ruler he felt to be a singular honour.

Eva knew the details, Bernice had always confided in her, but she found it hard to stomach the double standards demanded amongst the élite. Despite her knowledge of life in the raw gained through her association with the poor, Eva was a romantic – a little cynical perhaps, a bit frayed round the edges, but finding comfort in poetry and music, and the biggest joy of all in the girl she had accepted as her ward. In Charlotte she had found a sister, a daughter – someone on whom to pour out her love.

The clock on the marble mantelshelf chimed seven times and Eva rose from the padded stool. Lambert, who had changed little through the years, stood behind her, holding a fan and a silk bag which she handed to her mistress. Pride softened her flinty eyes as she looked on fondly. To Lambert, her dear Lady Eva had never seemed anything but a lovely, gracious woman. Though she might consider that she wasted her time trying to improve the lot of the under-privileged, she did not approve of such characters as Lady Bernice, with her extravagance and loose morals.

'Why, Eva, what a gorgeous gown! The bead-work is exquisite.'

Bernice was full of admiration, her blue eyes running down the tightly-fitted creation of oyster satin which flared out from the hips to the floor, richly encrusted with sequinned embroidery. 'You've a figure like a girl, whereas I've put on weight.'

There was a touch of complacency in the way in which she posed before the pier-glass, smoothing her well-corsetted waist and inching the neckline lower across her white shoulders and full bosom. It was the fashion to be well-built, and she was of superb proportions, with the tall figure and fine features of a woman of breeding. She was wearing a shade of deep rose which suited her blonde colouring and cameo complexion. Her hair had been dressed high, smoothed over pads to give it the required volume, and teased into curls at the brow. A diamond tiara echoed the gems at her throat, ears and arms.

Always uncomfortable if anyone paid her a compliment, Eva blushed as she said, 'Thank you, Bernie. I fear I'm a little bony for present taste, though you're right about the embroidery. It was worked by a seamstress I know. Her name is Alice Brooker, and she is very skilled indeed.'

Bernice dimpled at her. 'One of your waifs and strays, I suppose.'

'Alice is poor, yes, and handicapped by a baby whose father ran off and left them. She's not robust, but you should see her spirit. These women make me feel ashamed. You've no idea of the appalling conditions they work under, and their pay is a pittance.'

Bernice looked pained. 'I don't want to know, Eva. You may charge through disgusting hovels playing at knight-errant, but I'm certainly not inspired to do so. I've given you that Gainsborough portrait of one of Quentin's ghastly ancestors for your auction sale, but you won't drag me into the slums with you, not for all the tea in China! Why can't you simply throw a party without it entailing some event to swell your charity fund?'

Not only was the ball an opportunity to have Charlotte accepted; when Eva entertained on a large scale she always contrived to include something with which to augment assistance. Tonight there was to be an auction and for weeks she had badgered her aquaintances to donate valuable items.

'I can't take life lightly,' Eva began, wondering how best to explain her feelings. 'Why was I born with so much when there are thousands of others living at starvation level? I'm no more worthy than they.'

Bernice slipped an arm about her, smiling warmly. Despite her faults, she was sincere and essentially kind-hearted. 'Dear Eva, always running yourself down. You should have more faith, darling. My God, you've everything to be confident about! I hear you make those dull old things at the bank jump through hoops to please you. And you've cocked a snook at everyone by insisting on bringing up your little waif to be a lady.'

'I suppose I haven't done badly, have I?' Eva could not help asking the question, though impatient with herself for needing her friend's approval.

'Of course you haven't, silly goose.' Bernice gave her an encouraging squeeze. 'But I do wish you'd let your hair down once in a while. Come to Bishop Combe when the Season is over. I'm going to invite all sorts of interesting people. Say you'll come! And bring Charlotte. If anyone harbours doubts about her, they'll vanish when she's in the saddle. I've never seen such a girl on horseback. Hands like gossamer, and what 'seat'! She's a natural, my dear. I'm very fond of your Charlotte. I only wish she was really your daughter.'

Eva backed away, for once launched on her favourite topic, Bernice was likely to continue for ages. 'Don't start that again,' she pleaded.

Bernice refused to be silent. 'You should have married, pet. Think what fun we could have had. Now you're neither fish nor fowl. Being married gives one total freedom, you know.'

'I have total freedom.' Eva's face clouded and she retreated into dignity.

'No, you haven't – never will have till you've a ring on your finger. Take notice of what your old Auntie Bernie tells you. I *know*, knew it from the time we were put on the marriage market. Why d'you suppose I accepted the first man who proposed, and when I'd only met him a couple of times at dinner-parties? I wanted to be mistress of my own establishment, wanted to be free to follow my fancies, once I'd filled the nursery for him. He's never bothered to look closely at my last two babies, and even if he noticed that they don't resemble him in the least, he's much too much of a gentleman to say so.'

Lambert stood quietly in the background, listening, well aware that Lady Bernice had forgotten her presence. Servants were beneath her conscious notice and this applied to most ladies of her ilk. Thus in every one of the Big Houses, the staff knew exactly what their masters and mistresses were up to, and used this knowledge to their own advantage.

Eva could not help smiling at her friend's uninhibited remarks. 'I remember that the only instructions one of my elderly great-aunts gave me when I entered London society was to tell me never to comment on a likeness,' she said.

'Quite right,' Bernice nodded. 'This is a tactful rule to remember when admiring friends' offspring.'

Eva laughed at that, relaxing as Bernice intended she should, and, arm in arm, the two women made their way downstairs to where the guests were starting to arrive.

Standing in her bedroom, Charlotte heard the rumble of coaches, and knew that it was time for her to take part in the biggest event of her life. Yet she delayed, though not exactly nervous, well able to hold her own among the guests. Eva had made sure that she had absorbed learning under the care of teachers who had educated her in mathematics, science, literature, music and languages, while poise had been acquired from dancing and deportment masters.

Why then am I holding back from sweeping down the grand staircase to meet my fate? she wondered. Perhaps it was because it put a seal on the day. There was a finality about stepping over the boundary between girlhood and womanhood. She looked different, had done so since early that morning when, like a sacrificial victim, they had prepared her to meet the King. Her dark locks, glittering with fiery tints, no longer fell freely about her shoulders. The hairdresser had practised his art on her. Indeed, he had returned to check on his masterpiece before the ball took place, fussing as he twirled his comb, taming stray fonds that had escaped, bending them to his will.

Now he had gone, leaving a faint trail of perfume in his wake, and she stared at a stranger in the mirror, a woman, not a child, hair up in a sleek style with a cluster of ringlets at the crown. She was alone, having dismissed her maid, supposedly fully equipped to handle the taxing evening ahead. Her image stared back at her, and it was difficult to believe that it was herself. In the same way that she had hardly credited reality when she entered the Drawing Room of Buckingham Palace and curtsied to the King and Queen, this disembodied feeling gripped her again.

The girl in the silvered reflection was lovely. Charlotte had always recognised that her looks were arresting, not with conceit, but more as a fact of life. She wished she could recall her mother's face. Where did I get those features and a skin that turns golden brown at the first touch of the sun? Was it from her or from my father?

she wondered, and not for the first time. Maybe he was a foreign sailor, yet his name was Drummond. That's not very exotic.

She knew about the dockside area where Lascar sailors lingered in their blue denims and round red caps, where Chinamen with pigtails pattered by, and seafarers of all nationalities left their ships for a brief spell of pleasure in the public houses or the arms of women ready to accept payment for their services. Though she had been brought up as a West End child whose feet had trodden the green grass of Kensington Park where the air was always clean, in recent years her work with Eva had taken her back to the slums.

Back to our roots, she said to the girl in the mirror. It's no use you pretending otherwise, with your grand manner and fine clothes. That's where we came from, you and me. Dipped a courtsey to the King today, did you? So what? He's a randy old sod from what I hear.

The mirror girl gave her a haughty stare. Charlotte shrugged and turned her back. There was something distinctly disturbing about looking at herself. I'm playing a part, she thought. This isn't really me. But what is? I'm happy, aren't I? Eva is wonderful and makes me feel useful when we're visiting needy families, taking food, clothing, medicine – anything to ease the suffering. How she remonstrates with the drunken husbands of sickly wives, offering regular employment if they'll stop wasting their money on alcohol. They stand before her, shuffling their feet, thoroughly ashamed, but she knows that if she gives them money it will find its way into a publican's pocket. She's fighting a losing battle, but won't give up.

I like going with her, know that I'm doing something to help, but my main motivation is the hope that somewhere, someday, I'll meet Tweeny. But how would I recognise her after all these years? Eva and Freddy tell me that it's useless, ever since the day we came across that communal grave of orphaned children wiped out by a diphtheria epidemic.

Charlotte closed her eyes, hands clenched so tightly that the nails bit into the palms. Transported back in time, she saw that dismal spot on the dim screen of memory; a burying-ground dominated by an ugly, square-towered church, one of many built in the late-seventeenth century.

It lacked the grace and sanctity of earlier places of worship, somehow imbued with the cynicism of that era. It could have been a temple dedicated to any deity, even to the forces of darkness. She had stood there in the rain gazing down at that large, pathetic mound of earth sparsely covered by rank, yellowing grass. Uncared for, unkempt, though a little bunch of flowers had been laid on it by an anonymous mourner. A compassionate passer-by, maybe? They were long withered. The church had seemed to come closer. She had felt its presence like a weight on her spirit.

Frederick had held a large black umbrella over her and Eva which had made the atmosphere even more claustrophobic. She remembered him saying, 'Your sister probably ended up here, Charlotte, if indeed she survived infancy. It was a terrible scourge and swept like the plague through the slums and work-houses.'

Her head had told her logically that this was true. Her heart had denied it, irrationally and painfully. She's not there under the sod, she had thought, convinced of it and moving away from shelter, leaving Frederick and Eva looking after her in puzzlement. Lifting her face to the weeping skies, she had faced the church defiantly, that monstrous monument, so powerful and dominating, using fear to control those who entered its precincts. You haven't got her, she had shouted inside herself. She's still alive, I know it!

She was roused from her thoughts by a gentle tap on the door. At her call to enter, a tiny, grey-haired lady stepped into the room. Charlotte forgot her worries, running over and hugging her.

'Nanny! Oh, Nanny, I didn't know for sure that you'd be able to come,' she cried, careless of creasing her gown or ruffling her hair at seeing that familiar, much-loved face that had been of such importance in her world before the advent of governesses, teachers and her personal lady's maid, Tilly.

'Tut, tut! You must have known I'd not miss viewing my precious in all her glory!' Nanny scolded, embarrassed though pleased by such a display of affection. She stood back, ran a critical eye over Charlotte. 'Humm – not bad,' she conceded grudgingly, while her twinkling eyes were unable to disguise her pride.

'When did you arrive? Why didn't you come before? I needed you here!' Charlotte found that she wanted to burst into tears, to stamp her foot and rage because Nanny had neglected her. How childishly absurd, she chided herself. A great girl like you behaving like a spoilt baby!

Nanny viewed her with customary calm. She had always been so sensible, reassuring, eminently realistic. 'The train was late at Paddington. I couldn't get away sooner because young Master Clifford has whooping cough. I'm someone else's Nanny now, you know – not yours!'

'I'm sorry, of course you are,' Charlotte mumbled, thinking how strange it was that this person, so small now against her own tallness, still had the power to make her jump to attention.

'You seem to forget that I left you years ago, Miss Charlotte,' Nanny continued.

'It was the saddest day of my life. I cried for you night after night.' Charlotte was remembering how bereft she had felt, inconsolable for months.

'What nonsense, you were perfectly all right.' Nanny was smiling, for Charlotte had always been the favourite amongst her many charges. Self-willed and difficult to be sure, but well worth the effort.

They had met since from time to time, as Nanny passed from one household to another when the children entrusted to her care outgrew her. Eva had never lost touch with her, and it was she who had suggested that Nanny came to visit during the celebrations. Now, looking at her, Charlotte realised with a pang that Nanny was getting old.

A hundred memories came crowding in: of nursery tea by the open fire protected by a brass edged guard; of walks through the parks with bright summer sunshine or a touch of frost in the air; of a reliable presence, always around when needed – a soothing figure in a white winceyette, no-nonsense nightgown, hair in plaits each side of that wise face, there when Charlotte woke from some frightening dream. Comforting and comfortable Nanny, that mine of information, of stories and saws and platitudes. A forthright woman who was not above teaching her to sew on buttons and use the flat-iron, though in her position she would hardly be called upon to practise such skills.

Seeing her was just what Charlotte needed to steady her nerves. She pirouetted in her white satin and lace so that Nanny might view her from every angle.

'You think I look the part? Will I be the belle of the ball?' she asked.

'Who's fishing for compliments?' Nanny snapped. 'Any more of this and you'll end up on the stage!'

Charlotte wanted to shout with joy. Nanny most definitely approved, but nothing would have made her admit it. At one time this reference to ending on the stage had baffled Charlotte, for she had often been taken to see the ballet at Covent Garden Opera House and the Pantomime at Drury Lane Theatre so had been unable to understand this threat. Later she had come to realise that many actressess, singers and dancers were still regarded as ladies of easy virtue.

She beamed at the short, stout figure in a neat charcoal grey costume and plain hat. 'You'll be here, when the ball is over?'

'Oh, yes, my lamb. I'm not going further than my old room upstairs in the nursery,' Nanny promised.

'And you'll peep at me from the top of the staircase, like we used to when grand company was expected?'

'I may, so you'd better behave yourself,' came the trenchant reply. 'I expect perfect comportment, as becomes a genteel young lady.'

Charlotte leaned down to place a kiss on the wrinkled cheek. 'I promise,' she whispered.

'That's a good girl,' Nanny said crisply. 'Now off you go. Mustn't keep people waiting.'

Albion House had been built around the middle of the last century, a solid Victorian mansion set in specious gardens. Its architecture was of the popular Gothic style. It even had a conical turret with a red-tiled roof shaped like a witch's hat. The interior was romantic in the extreme, the rooms festooned with moulded garlands designed by William Morris, the pre-Raphaelite artist who had used his talents to provide lovely homes for those who could afford them. With the sentimental revival of things medieval, he had included colourful leaded windows and painted panels depicting knights and damsels, while the furniture was made of intricately carved wood with much emphasis placed on leaves, ferns and writhing vines.

The music-room was of such proportions that it could easily be used for dancing and, on this night, the Persian carpets had been rolled up and taken away, the floor waxed and polished, and a small orchestra installed at one end. This was playing a selection of light melodies when Charlotte arrived to stand by the door with Eva and receive their guests.

The company was a distinguished one and Frederick, on hand to assist Eva in any way possible, watched them enter after being announced by the butler, Hopkins. He eyed them with wry amusement, noting how they smiled on Eva and her ward, hearing their effusive compliments, and wondering what they were really thinking. Each of them must be aware of Charlotte's history, yet they treated her as if she were indeed one of the Pendral family. And why should they not? he thought with a flash of pride. By Jove, she looks the part!

He had grown fond of her over the years, come to share Eva's enthusiasm, felt almost fatherly towards her, though unable to stop himself from dwelling on what might have been. If only he and Eva had married and Charlotte was their child ... Stop it, you old fool! he lectured himself. This is very nearly as satisfying – more so, in many ways. It's good to beat them at their own game, that motley crew, powerful and rich, who are England's ruling class.

He noticed that Eva had carefully selected her guests, inviting not only her particular cronies, but also those who were influential and had unattached sons. Is she seeking a husband for Charlotte? he wondered, and a shadow settled over his mind. Surely not. Eva had never accepted a proposal herself and it was doubtful that she would insist her protégée do so. Yet there was no denying the effect the girl was having on the young men. They were clamouring to have their names added to the dance-card that dangled from her wrist. He saw how gracefully she bent her head to write them down with the tiny pink pencil attached by a silk cord.

When everyone had arrived, Eva signalled to the conductor of the orchestra and the first dance was announced – a quadrille, which Charlotte led partnered by a dashing soldier in scarlet dress uniform. Frederick had already claimed the privilege of leading Eva on to the floor, and he gave her hand a congratulatory pat. She looked up at him with shining eyes.

'It's going rather well, don't you think?' she asked as he slipped his arm about her waist and they moved through the intricacies of the dance.

'Splendidly,' he answered.

'Dear Freddy, you've always been solid as a rock. I don't know what I'd do without you,' she murmured with that candour so characteristic of her.

He knew that she was absolutely sincere, but the pain refused to be dulled. She regarded him as her dearest friend, ever supportive, but did she really see him as a man? He was, as it were, part of the furniture. Frustration worked like yeast behind his polite façade. He wanted her, longed to breath life into the slumbering fire he sensed lay in the core of her, so damped down that he doubted if she acknowledged it existence. Would she ever yield to bodily passion? Was her life to be wasted when she had so much to give? A womanly woman if ever he'd seen one, a woman designed to love, to bear children. He prayed that she would wake to this fact before it was too late. He was prepared to wait, but for how much longer? He had reached his late forties. There was no lack of suitable ladies willing to take him as their husband. He owed it to himself to pluck up the courage to convey his feelings to her.

'Eva, there's something I want to talk to you about,' he said, and she was startled by the urgency of his tone.

'Not tonight, Freddy. The auction will take place after supper, and we've been given lots of lovely things. As well as the Gainsborough, there are a pair of Ming vases, some jewellery that once belong to the Tsarina of Russia, a set of drawings by Reubens, and much more besides. Interest is running high and the auctioneer says that people are bound to bid against one another. If it's a business matter you want to discuss, then can't it wait till tomorrow?'

'It's not business,' he muttered, sweating under the tightness of his stiff white collar and formal evening suit.

'I'm sorry, it will have to be much later, when everyone has gone home,' she replied, a frown gathering between her finely arched brows. He knew a pang of regret, hating himself for alarming her, yet no longer willing to spare her.

The quadrille finished in a burst of applause and Eva was whisked away by a ruddy-faced squire, one of her hunting companions from Greyfriars. She was lost to Frederick in the crowd as the strains of a waltz rang out.

'Our dance, I believe,' cooed a soft voice close to his ear, while his nostrils responded to a sultry perfume that betrayed the presence of Lady Bernice. 'Come along, Freddy dear. Your beloved has given herself up to other arms.'

He bowed and then clasped her lightly round the waist, though his guard was up. Bernice was a woman of great experience to whom few explanations were necessary, yet he would not let her breach his defences.

'Our Eva, you mean?' he prevaricated. 'A lovesome woman in every sense. Almost a saint, wouldn't you say?'

'Nonsense, Freddy. She's made of flesh and blood like the rest of us,' said Bernice as they twirled to the strains of the *Blue Danube*. She spoke briskly, but Freddy was sure that her briskness was neither unkind nor unsympathetic.

'That may be so, yet she drives herself beyond the bounds of mortal strength,' he demurred.

Over his shoulder Bernice was flirting with a cavalry officer who sported a fiercely pointed moustache. Rumour had it that she often entertained him to tea alone and, though it was never openly discussed, everyone knew what *that* meant. Many a liaison had been consummated in a drawing-room during the circumspect tea-time hour. When she looked into Frederick's face again it was with an unusually serious expression.

'It's time she stopped being the angel of the poor and found herself a man,' she remarked. 'It may not be the done thing for a woman of her rank to marry her lawyer, but Eva has never cared a pin for the opinion of the world. In any case, you're awfully well connected, aren't you?'

Frederick would have resented this coming from anyone else, but they understood each other very well. Only Bernice would have dared sound him out, and he admired her courage. She was a free spirit who behaved with true magnificence, like a courtesan of the Renaissance period. She never did things by halves. It was all or nothing with Bernice. Now she was the King's latest love – of course she was – nothing less would have sufficed. Oh, she might amuse herself with handsome boys but she was ambitious on a grand scale, and if fate had trouble in store for her, then it would be in the nature of a spectacular tragedy. There was nothing petty or mean about Bernice Frewston. They said no more on the subject of Eva, but Frederick derived comfort from this brief chat with her.

By the time supper was announced, Charlotte was tired of being introduced to so many people whose names she had no hope of remembering, and such a succession of unattached males hovering in attendance. The guests consisted of people of rank – nobles, Members of Parliament, officers, ladies of every age and temperament – some rustling as they danced, some moving heavily, some laughing like clear bells, others speaking in low tones. She was aware of them watching her while appearing not to do so, though there were several who made no secret of it, staring openly through their lorgnettes.

She shared Eva's suspicion of these women who dominated society. They fell into two camps: those who were married, had reached maturity and were game for adventures (no man liked to tangle with an unmarried girl, it was too compromising) and those starchy, dignified dames of the older generation who deplored the laxity of King Edward's Court. There was no doubt that the former were the most entertaining, and Charlotte was fond of the glamorous Lady Bernice.

She managed to make her escape, carrying a dish of ice-cream and finding a quiet nook in the conservatory, a glass-structured addition to the house filled with plants of great size and impressive foliage. The air was pleasantly damp, spiced with the fragrance of tropical flowers. She sat down on the raised stone rim of a pool where bronze mermaids frolicked beneath a gushing fountain, and spooned the sweet into her mouth. She knew that this creamy pink confection had been made from fruit sent up from the gardens of Greyfriars, frozen into a strawberry-shaped mould, then turned out on a silver salva, decorated with fresh, ripe berries, and borne in to take pride of place on the buffet table.

She felt vaguely uneasy, remembering the children with whom

she was in almost daily contact. They never had enough of the basics to eat, let alone indulge themselves in treats like this. Had Tweeny ever tasted such a wonder? Sometimes she disagreed with Eva who, though attuned to the grim poverty abounding, saw no reason why she should not have the occasional party, particularly if by so doing she could make people reach for their cheque-books. Sometimes she would hold a raffle, at others simply have large tubs placed in prominent positions with notices requesting contributions, and tonight it was the auction.

Indeed, she gave employment to a whole army of servants, both in London and Wiltshire, people who were devoted to her, proud of their association with Albion House and Greyfriars, that ancient manor in the heart of the country. Eva was a generous mistress, and no one went without, yet Charlotte could not shake off her sense of guilt.

She had not been in the conservatory long when she was tracked down. The young man's name was Archie Stapley, and she had met him several times before – a pleasant enough fellow but, for her, lacking in any form of attraction. Not that she had had much experience with men. For one thing, Eva took up most of her time, and for another she possessed a natural reserve, unable to flirt and express big-eyed admiration just because they were males. She suppressed a sigh of exasperation as he stood there uncertainly, giving her a bashful grin.

'I s-s-say, Miss Charlotte – ripping p-p-party, what?' he stammered, suffering from the curious disability of being nearly tongue-tied until mildly drunk.

Charlotte took pity on him, casting an encouraging smile in his direction. 'I'm glad you'r enjoying yourself,' she rejoined, placing the empty dish on the low wall and disturbing the golden carp browsing lazily under the lily pads. They dived deeper with a flash of iridescent fins.

Archie leapt forward, almost knocking the dish in amongst them. 'C-c-can I get you some m-m-more?'

'Oh, no, thank you.'

He hesitated awkwardly. He was not long out of university, fair-haired, with a sprinkling of freckles across his nose. His pale blue eyes watched her eagerly, but when she caught that glance he hurriedly looked away. It struck her that he was as awkward in this artificial atmosphere as herself.

'I'd rather be in the country, wouldn't you?' she asked, and patting the space beside her, added, 'Sit and talk to me, Archie.'

He needed no second bidding, but did not seem to know what

to do with his hands so she suggested that they might light up cigarettes. This surprised him.

'You s-s-moke?'

'I enjoy one now and again,' she admitted. 'But never in public, of course. Even Lady Bernice doesn't do that.'

He fumbled for his cigarette case, opened it and offered her one from among its fellows lying neatly against the metal, held in place by a narrow elastic strap. There was a delay while he searched through his pockets for his lighter, apologised, eventually found it, lit her cigarette.

It was pleasant there with the splash of the fountain, the talk and laughter coming from the ballroom, the overall sound of music. Later, Charlotte was to remember this moment of peace spent in the company of such an unassuming lad, looking upon it as the lull before the storm. They had something in common – a love of the countryside. Soon Archie stopped stuttering, even though he had had only one glass of champagne, forgetting to be shy in his enthusiam for horses and the hunt.

Charlotte adored Greyfriars, part fortress, part manor house, buried deep in Wiltshire, its boundaries edging Salisbury Plain. It had appealed to her from the first moment she set eyes on it. There was so much freedom to be had, no rules to adhere to – just a round of riding, of accompanying Eva when she visited her tenants, and taking the dogs for walks in the woods. There one could slop around in cardigans and easy, calf-length skirts, sensible shoes or riding boots. One didn't have to dress for dinner or even partake of it in the dining-room if one didn't feel inclined. The lack of even that small amount of formality which Eva could not avoid in town was refreshing in the extreme.

'You'll come and hunt in July?' she asked Archie, noting how he flushed with pleasure, wondering if she was giving him too much encouragement and if he would think she was considering him as a prospective bridegroom. She wasn't in the least, had no ambitions to marry anyone. I'd better make this quite clear from the start, she thought, and said aloud, 'Let's get one thing straight. I may be mistaken in your interest in me, but I want you to know that I've no intention of marrying for ages, maybe not at all. I look upon you as a friend, nothing more.'

He was silent for a moment, then he gave her a smile that transformed his boyish face. 'That's all right, though I must admit I find you dashed pretty. It would be nice if you'd give a chap a chance should you change your mind. Mater and Pater would be over the moon if we got spliced.'

I expect they would, Charlotte thought, for though his father was as blue-blooded as could be, she had heard that the family were in financial straits. There was no doubt at all that they would overlook the fact that they were taking a nobody into their noble House, provided she had the Pendral millions behind her.

'We don't want to raise their hopes, do we, Archie?' she said sweetly. 'So we'd better go back to the ballroom now or people will begin to speculate. I'll lose my reputation if it's thought you had the chance to seduce me out here.'

'Really, Miss Charlotte! I'd never try to do that,' he protested.

Charlotte stared him straight in the eye. 'Of course you wouldn't. Not the done thing, is it? But supposing I was one of the maid-servants? What then, Archie? Don't you and all the other chaps look upon these girls as fair game?'

'W-w-where did you hear that?' Archie was nonplussed for it was perfectly true. The fellows thought it sport, but their sisters were not supposed to know anything about it.

His ideas about women were confused. He had been taught that upper-class girls did not know about sex, unlike common women who were thought to be different physically. Shy he might be, but he had already had his share of servants and prostitutes. It was his nanny who had initiated him into fleshly delights at a very early age. But to hear such words dropping from Charlotte's lips completely threw him, until he remembered the rumour that she came from a humble background. She had mentioned seduction. Should he try to kiss her? One glance from those clear grey eyes made him think better of it.

The ballroom was more crowded than ever, and the noise swelled with chatter and laughter, the swish of silks, while the air was heavy with the scent of French perfumes and hair pomade. Charlotte was sensitive to something different in the atmosphere – an excitement and stir absent till then. Weaving through the throng, she realised that it was centred on a group near the door. People were staring, whispering, while Eva and Frederick moved forward to speak to the man who had just come in.

Seeming perfectly indifferent to the gaping around him, he bent to kiss Eva's hand. He was above average height and erect as a lance, with great width to his shoulders and an unforgettable face – too hard to be romantically handsome but rivetting nonetheless. Charlotte found it impossible to keep her eyes from him. At the same time she saw that Eva looked pale and strained as she beckoned to her.

'You'd better obey,' advised Archie.

'Who is he?' she asked.

'Don't you know? That's Phelan Charteris. He's Lady Eva's cousin.' Archie's lips tightened and there was a slightly envious look on his face. 'He's the most sought after man in the Kingdom at the moment. Every hostess is lionising him. He has just returned from excavating ancient tombs in Egypt – an odd fish who mixes with rather controversial people. His father was a renowned archaeologist, and his mother a famous beauty. The father is dead but the mother still holds court in Florence, or so I've heard. Surely you've already met him, haven't you? Or have they guarded you from him? I gather that he has a rather unsavory reputation.'

Had he indeed? This raised her interest even further, but she asked, 'Who are those other men with him?'

Two strangers were also talking to Eva, and it seemed that they had arrived at the same time as Mr Charteris. One was a bulky individual with keen eyes and an impressive grey-streaked, reddish beard, while the other was a slight young man with hair the colour of ripe corn. All three of them were bronzed, as if they had lived under a tropical sun for months on end.

'That tough-looking chap is Andrew Tyler, the explorer,' Archie said. 'Haven't you read about him in the papers? He's been charting unknown areas of the Riff Mountains, and is much in demand for his lectures on said subject, illustrated by magic-lantern slides. I think the fellow with him is a distant relative or somesuch. Name of Julian Leigh. I've seen them both at my club. I expect Charteris met Tyler abroad, but when you get to know him you'll find out that he keeps company with all sorts.' He noticed that Eva was glancing at them impatiently, and added, 'I say, I think you'd better go to her.'

Charlotte did so and, as she reached her side, Phelan Charteris noticed her and smiled faintly. Something passed between them, and though she couldn't tell what, Charlotte felt it shock through her to the bone.

Now Eva was introducing her. She found herself being scrutinised by a pair of deep-set eyes – dark and piercing. 'Ah, so *you* are Eva's protégeé. I've heard so much about you,' he said, as he took her hand.

She felt his touch burning through her glove. It was unnerving. There was no doubt that he was a striking person. Curly hair holding the blue-black sheen of a raven's wing framed a narrow, tanned face, and his smile was brilliant though it did not reach those peculiar eyes. There was arrogance in the way he carried his well-proportioned body, and he was dressed with extreme care.

Whiplash lean, there was not an ounce of spare fat on his frame. He looked what he was – an adventurer, but an aristocrat, too. Charlotte hazarded a guess as to his age, and came up with the notion that he was a little younger than Eva.

She rooted about in memory. Eva had spoken of her cousin once or twice but never elaborated more than to offer the information that he had been born in Greece and spent much of his time abroad, though his family home lay not many miles from Greyfriars. Charlotte had sensed that she did not want to talk about him, had thought it rather odd, then dismissed it as of little consequence. Meeting him at last, she was doubly intrigued.

Andrew Tyler was bowing to her, and so was Julian Leigh, both attentive and polite, though the former seemed a little uncomfortable, as if he would rather be riding a camel over sandy dunes or treating with Bedouin tribesmen than taking part in a coming-out ball. It appeared that he knew Phelan well. They talked to one another in the easy, joking way of men who have spent much time together, living rough. Julian, on the other hand, hovered on the periphery, party to some, but not all, of their apparent intimacy.

'Do you intend to spend more time in England, Phelan?' Eva was saying, and her dislike of her cousin continued to perplex Charlotte. No one else could possible be aware of it, for on the surface she was politeness personified, but then no one knew Eva as well as Charlotte did.

'Yes, I'll be returning to Hawksdown Hall just as soon as the Season is through,' he replied. 'But I'm staying in London at the moment and, when Andrew mentioned that you'd asked him and Julian to this party, I couldn't resist coming along, assuming that you'd accidentally omitted to invite me.'

'It was no accident, I assure you,' Eva said levelly.

'No? You surprise me, Cousin Eva.' The look he cast her was glacier cool.

'I assumed you'd not find such a gathering amusing.' Eva neglected to tell the truth. She had known he was in town, but had deliberately left his name off her guest list. I was right to do so, she thought. There's something about him that sets my teeth on edge. As a boy he was strange, and this hasn't improved with the years.

'Not very kind to leave your only surviving relative out in the cold,' he chided gently, but there was a sarcastic tinge to his voice. 'You must have realised I was eager to meet your adopted daughter.'

'Charlotte is hardly that.' I don't owe him an apology, Eva

thought angrily, yet he is almost demanding one. 'I'm not that long in the tooth yet.'

His laugh held carefully veiled mockery, and he raised one strongly marked eyebrow significantly. 'Don't be so prickly, Eva. Truth to tell, this auction you're holding was one of my reasons for coming. The Tsarina's jewels, a remarkable set of eighteenth-century gems, and the Gainsborough also. It would look well in the Long Gallery at Hawksdown. Don't you agree?'

'I can't say, never having entered your house,' she retorted pithily.

He lifted his shoulders and spread his hands wide in a gesture that betrayed his foreign upbringing. 'This must be rectified at the earliest possible moment. I invite you there – Miss Charlotte, too.'

Charlotte like the sound of her name coming from his lips, but was bothered by the conversational undertones. As she listened, half her attention was focused on Julian. He was more than merely handsome. His finely chiselled features were flawless, and he had a smooth, golden-brown complexion, tawny hair streaked lighter by the sun, and green eyes. A touch shorter than Phelan, he was slim-waisted and slim-hipped, and his exquisitely tailored evening suit fitted like a glove.

The appearance of these three interesting men had caused a flutter among the newly 'out' girls who stood quietly in their demure white frocks, chaperoned by their parents. The older ladies were also eyeing them, and it was not long before Bernice came over, angling for an introduction.

Phelan's eyes met Charlotte's again and again, and it seemed as if his glance drew her into a kind of intimacy, as if he was saying 'These tiresome people. When can we be alone?'

The opportunity came during the auction which was held in the drawing-room where chairs had been positioned for the comfort of those who wished to participate. Charlotte found herself in a window embrasure with Phelan. The crowd was thick around them, and his wide shoulders boxed her in. Window glass behind her, damask curtains on either side, Phelan blocking her view – unless she was downright rude there was no way she could escape from him.

'Don't you want to be near the front to join in the bidding?' she suggested, holding her wide-spread ostrich feather fan between them like a shield.

'I've an agent doing it for me,' he answered, as if it was the most natural thing in the world that everyone should obey his orders.

He was standing very close to her, and she could not avoid the masculine smell of him, a combination of perfumed shaving soap, brandy, Havana cigars and something else which she could not quite define. Her sense of humour came to the fore as she thought to herself, It's danger I can smell and, if what Archie hinted is true, the whiff of decadence. Oh, wicked Cousin Phelan! Is he like that notorious milord of Regency days – Byron, the poet and rake? Mad, bad and dangerous to know?

Whatever it was she was decidedly interested, and he seemed to be equally intrigued by her. It was flattering to be the centre of his attention when so many of the other women were turning green with envy, all mad about him. Yet Charlotte was much too sensible to be swept away. 'Handsome is as handsome does,' Nanny had always said, though refusing to elucidate on the meaning of such an ambiguous statement.

Eva had taught her to take her time before forming judgement of peoples' character. Living in a mostly female environment her knowledge of men was limited. While better informed than many girls of her age and status, all she knew about sex had been culled from books or through talking to her maid, not by actual groundwork in the field of combat. She was no match for someone as experienced as Phelan. She sensed this, was wary but excited. He challenged her, and she was not the sort of person to ignore a challenge.

'I can't see the auctioneer,' she complained, wanting to get away from him, to think about him calmly without that disturbing chemistry working between them.

Phelan did not move, and his lips curved into a smile. He's laughing at me, she thought indignantly. He takes me to be a silly schoolgirl bowled over by his charm. He had told Eva that he'd heard about her. What had he heard? That she was an East End brat? For once Charlotte found herself regretting that she was not a genuine member of the nobility. Phelan had an advantage over her and she did not doubt that he would use it, if he could.

She could hear American voices in the crowd, knowing that Eva had invited several couples visiting England from overseas, humbly born but now millionaires. They had daughters with them and were seeking aristocratic bachelors who would be willing to trade, offering to marry the girls and give them titles in exchange for living the rest of their existences in the lap of luxury. Eva knew they were big spenders, eager to ape the élite, buying mansions on both sides of the Atlantic and stuffing them full of antiques. Dollars were as equally acceptable as sovereigns by her fund.

'Ah, I think my man has outbid rivals for the item I wanted,'

Phelan said, looking across the room to where the auctioneer stood on a rostrum, whilst his assistants, a couple of stalwarts in brown cotton coats and flat caps, hefted in the larger pieces.

Charlotte saw Andrew talking to one of them, and he was soon elbowing his way through the crowd, carrying a flat leather case.

'Here you are, Phelan,' he shouted, even before he reached them. 'They've cost you a packet though. That damned chap, Vanveeren, was determined to have them for his fat wife.'

Phelan took the case in his narrow, beautifully shaped hands and flicked the catch, then opened the lid. Charlotte could not restrain a gasp. There, against the black velvet lining, sparkled a magnificent ruby and diamond necklace, with matching bracelet and pendant earrings.

She had seen them displayed before the auction, registered that she would like to own them, then dismissed this as sheer vanity on her part. When on earth should I wear such things? she had argued sensibly to herself. They are for Court occasions and I'm certainly never going to be an ambassador's wife. Yet she could not deny her longing for those gems that had once graced the Tsarina of Russia. Now Phelan had bought them and, she supposed, he would give them to his wife.

'She's a very lucky woman,' she sighed.

'Who?' he enquired blandly, closing the lid again and handing the box back to Andrew with instructions to ask Lady Eva to place it in her safe for him.

'Your wife,' she answered, relieved to see that the auction was over and the throng thinning.

'I'm not married.' He was looking at her gravely and she wondered what went on behind those secretive eyes.

'Oh, I see. Then you'll present them to your fiancée.'

'I have no fiancée.'

'Why did you buy them, if not as a gift for a lady?' He has a mistress, she decided. That must be it.

'Oh, but I do intend to present them to someone.'

'May I ask who?'

Why doesn't he move? she was thinking. There's plenty of room. No need for him to keep me trapped here. She went to pass him but his hand closed round her bare upper arm. His unsmiling lips were close to her own, and for a moment she thought he was going to kiss her. She was unable to stir a muscle or pull away.

'You may ask, and I'll tell you,' he murmured. 'I bought them for you, Charlotte.'

Chapter Three

'You can't accept such a gift! Tell him so at once!' Eva's face was white, her eyes blazing with rage.

Charlotte was shocked to see her thus – the cool, controlled Eva who rarely lost her temper. 'I haven't said I'll accept, merely that I'd consider it and ask your advice,' she countered, feeling suddenly older than her guardian somehow, wiser, too. Maybe it came from being slum-born where one thought very carefully before refusing an offer of any kind.

The ball was over and they were in Charlotte's bedroom, that wonderful room with its Art Nouveau decor. She had always loved it, each fulsome, sensuous ornamentation delighting her. But now she could find little comfort there for this was the first serious disagreement they had ever had.

Eva was only too aware of this, even more upset because they had fallen out over a man – Phelan, with whom, on the rare occasions they had met, she had never seen eye to eye. He was the son of her father's sister, Augusta. The only children of Thomas Pendral, they had been fiercely jealous of one another, and this had not lessened as they grew older. Augusta had been beautiful and something of a rebel, but had eventually married well, though her husband had squandered his fortune on his obsession for digging up the past – removing her and their son to Greece and Italy.

For nearly twenty years Hawksdown Hall had been unoccupied as a residence, neglected and deserted, with the exception of a portion of the east front that had been used by a caretaker. Eva had deplored this wasted space, wondering if she might buy the house from Phelan and turn it into a haven for the pathetic, battered wives whom she had encountered during the course of her work. She yearned to protect them from their brutual husbands, and had written with this suggestion to Phelan at his address in Florence. His refusal had been adamant. He had no intention of selling and was planning to return soon to claim his own.

Phelan and she were the only ones left of the Pendral brood. In an age when large families were the rule, the Pendrals had been singularly unproductive. And it will end with me, Eva thought. If Phelan is an example of the modern man, then I'm even more determined not to marry. I've already named Charlotte as my heir. She's a level-headed girl whom I can trust to continue with our projects when I'm dead.

This being so she found it hard to understand why she was even contemplating keeping the Tsarina's jewels. It was out of character. But then, dislike him though she might, Eva was not insensitive to Phelan's magnetism. She regretted that he had arrived in London at this juncture, flashing like a sinister comet over the scene; Phelan, of the devilish reputation and undeniable fascination. Unfortunately he had the power to touch that inherent trace of evil lurking in every human heart.

Eva had responded to it when they were in their early teens and the east front of Hawksdown Hall had housed him on a brief visit. Details of their first meeting had been deeply imprinted in her memory. It had happened when she was riding on the hills, seeing him in the distance, realising that he was the mysterious relative whom her father was loath to mention.

As she had reined in her mare close to his horse, she had seen a dark youth with a smile that hinted at carnal knowledge. An angry youth, swishing his whip as if he would stike her as his eyes raked over her features, figure and severe riding habit.

'So *you* are my Cousin Eva,' he had drawled, the wind tousling his curls, and she had drawn in a quick breath, having never seen anyone so handsome. 'I've been wondering about you. They tell me you're a blue-stocking, most scholarly and bookish. Now that I've met you I can well believe it,' and his peat-brown eyes had slid impudently over her.

Eva had risen to the bait. 'You think I'm not good at anything else?' she had asked haughtily. 'You're wrong. I'll bet I can beat you to that coppice over there.' She had indicated a clump of trees on the horizon.

'You're on!' he had shouted, digging his spurs into his horse's sides.

'There you are! I told you I could do it,' she had declared, triumphantly when she reached the target first, beating him by a head.

'Very good – for a girl,' he had answered scathingly. 'Do you also accept dares?'

'Sometimes.' There had been something about him that had made her want to throw caution to the winds.

'Will you accept one from me?' Again, his eyes had held hers, making her think of adventure, of feats of arms, of swashbuckling escapades such as she had read about in the novels of Alexandra Dumas.

'What is it you're asking me to do, Phelan?'

That moment was stamped on her memory for ever, the breeze rustling the beeches overhead, the sharp tang in the air, that sense of isolation. There had been no one within miles, only herself and her cousin. He had leaned across to rest a hand on her knee. It was the first time any male had touched her, with the exception of her father.

'You spend a lot of time in the library at Greyfriars, don't you?' His question had surprised her.

'Yes,' she had replied slowly, aware of a chill when he removed his hand, wanting him to replace it.

'Well, then, I've been told that your father owns some rather rare books, ones that he keeps locked away. Is that so?'

She had pictured that large room, with its row upon row of glass-fronted shelves, and its little inner sanctum which she was never permitted to enter, and her father saying, 'You wouldn't be interested in the books there, child. I have to keep them under lock and key because they are immensely valuable.'

'What is it you want, Phelan?' she had asked.

'I'm not invited to Greyfriars,' he had answered. 'Seems that my family aren't welcome there, but I want to see those books. My father told me about them, and they're unique. Why don't you get the key and let me in when no one's about?'

Completely under his spell, she had allowed herself to be persuaded against her better judgement. As it happened, her father had been away, and it had been an easy matter to creep downstairs at dead of night, unbolt the front door, take Phelan into the library and use the keys stolen from her father's bedroom. By the light of a candle, the two young people had opened the inner room, opened the bookcase, and drawn out Thomas Pendral's priceless collection.

Eva vividly recalled the shock when the first large volume had given up its contents. It was a book of eighteenth-century pornographic drawings, explicit in the extreme. Phelan's face had taken on a strange expression as he turned the pages, smiling, glancing at her from under his heavy eyelids. He had whistled softly, nodded and flipped to another, and yet another.

'These are wonderful, Eva. Don't you think so?' he had whispered, while her face had flamed with embarrassment. 'My God, look at *this* one? Is it possible to get into that position? I'd like to try, wouldn't you?'

The experience had been horrible, yet exciting, too. They had got away with it, undiscovered, and Phelan had promised to meet her again next day. But he wasn't at the trysting place and, later, she angrily sought him out in the stable of Hawksdown. She had found him in the loft with one of the farm girls, a flighty lass who already had a bad name. Phelan had been at his sneering worst, and Eva had quickly climbed down the ladder and left, his mocking laughter ringing in her ears.

It was then that she had determined to have nothing more to do with him. Family loyalty? Clap-trap! He deserved none. A share in the Pendral fortune? He could whistle for it! In some way she blamed him for her throwing herself at Victor Dalbiac less than a twelvemonth later. She had been trying to prove that she was not so undesirable after all. She had not seen Phelan since that moment of anguish in the Hawksdown stable, until tonight, and here was Charlotte arguing with her over him.

'The nerve of the man!' she continued to rant, though partly voicing a grievance many years old. 'How dare he? If you'd told me you wanted the gems I would have bought them for you!'

'But that's illogical.' Charlotte began to pace the room, driving her fist into the palm of her left hand. She had already kicked off her high-heeled satin slippers, glad to feel the floor under her stockinged feet, wanting to get out of her tight, hampering gown, more agitated than she had ever been in her life. 'If you'd done that, you might as well have never held the auction, and poured more of your own money into the fund. I didn't want them – well, I *did*, but knew them to be unpractical.'

It was three in the morning and everyone was tired. Eva recognised that she should have left this discussion until after they had slept, but Phelan's abrupt arrival had unsettled her, and now this!

The first thing she had known about it was when Hopkins sought her out while she was talking to the Vanveerens about the Gainsborough they had purchased. The butler had paused by her side, waiting for her to finish her conversation, his bulky, dignified presence impressing the Americans. They hinted later that, if she could spare him, they would just adore to take him back to New York with them. Politely refusing, Eva had passed on the name of an employment agency which would probably be able to help them find someone almost as stately.

Hopkins had said that Mr. Charteris had bought the jewels and requested permission to house them in Eva's safe for a few hours. She had unlocked it herself and stowed the leather case within, innocent of the reason for her cousin's acquisition of such expensive items. It was only now that the truth had come out.

'Where is he?' she asked, passing a hand across her throbbing temples. She could feel a migraine starting, those warning signs of flashing lights at the corner of vision and creeping numbness invading the right side of her body.

'In the library with Freddy. He's waiting for my answer.' Charlotte stopped her restless prowling, eyes meeting Eva's defiantly.

Phelan! Phelan! His name was ringing in her brain over and above everything else, so strange when, until that evening, she had hardly been aware that he existed. Now her every nerve tingled as she recalled how he had looked at her, how his hand had brushed hers as he handed her the jewel-case. She had not sought this encounter. It had come to her unbidden. The most striking man at the ball had singled her out for notice. It had been satisfying to watch the envy of the other women, seeing how their lips parted and their eyes became deeper and more desirous as they stared at him.

Eva drew herself up, though the effort made her feel sick, pain tightening around her forehead like a steel band. 'Then we'll go and see him together,' she stated.

'Why do you hate him so much?' Charlotte had never used such a cold tone to Eva. This is silly, she lectured herself. I'm quarelling with my dearest friend and I don't want to – don't truly wish to go any further with Phelan – but she's dictating to me and I don't like it.

Eva's reply was equally icy. 'He humiliated me once.'

'That's all? Can't you forgive him?' The ground seemed to be shifting under Charlotte's feet. An entirely new aspect of Eva's personality was being revealed, a vengeful woman whose vanity had been piqued by some real or imagined slight.

'It's hard to do so.' Eva softened, smiled tremulously. 'You'll think this an unworthy emotion, but I sensed then and am now convinced that there's something unwholesome about him. People talk – '

'You never listen to gossip and have taught me to ignore it.' Charlotte was already shaping excuses for him in her mind, but she could not help asking, 'What do they say?'

Eva looked away. Though she and Charlotte had discussed many aspects of life, she could not bring herself to mention the rumours that circulated concerning Phelan.

'I'd rather not repeat it at the present time.'

'Very well. I'll give the jewels back. After all, it's your right to have the last word on the matter, I suppose,' Charlotte said angrily, voice muffled as she searched for her shoes under the sofa.

'My dear, I've never made you do anything you really haven't wanted to, have I?' This conversation was hurting Eva more than she had ever dreamed. 'You are your own woman, mistress of your own destiny. I can only advise from my observations, and I warn you that Phelan is too worldly a man for someone like you to tangle with.'

'That's for me to judge, surely?' Charlotte spoke with far more confidence than she was feeling, seated with one leg crossed over the other as she pushed a foot into a satin pump.

The migraine triumphed. Eva groaned, pressing the heels of her palms against her temples. 'All right, you deal with it. I must go to bed. Ring for Lambert and tell her to have my tablets ready.'

At once Charlotte was contrite, placing an arm about her and helping her to her room. Eva was often the victim of these criplling headaches brought about by stressful situations. She gave Lambert her instructions and waited until Eva was in bed, then she ran along the corridors and down the staircase. There she paused, aware that someone was playing the piano in the music-room, and it was not a piece she recognised, nothing from the limited repertoire which she struggled to perfect. A loitering guest whiling away the time till a carriage arrives? she wondered, then paid it no more heed.

The library contrived to be cosy despite its size and grandeur. It glowed – the maple walls showing pastoral scenes in marquetry of pearwood, tulipwood and amboyna reflecting the discreet lighting. Bookcases ranged from the maroon-carpeted floor to the sumptuously decorated celing, their doors of stained glass, each holding a heraldic device. This was no musty, unused apartment designed to give a false impression of learning for Eva and Charlotte were frequent visitors to its peaceful seclusion. More often than not the bookcases stood open, as one or other of them drew forth volumes and curled up to study on the petrol blue velvet of the inlaid settle.

One glance showed her that Phelan was not there. Frederick rose from the deep armchair where he had been listening while Andrew regaled him with tales of derring-do in the dessert. Julian, seated on the edge of the desk, lounged to his feet. He eyed her in a friendly fashion and, even in the midst of her disappointment, she was again struck by his appearance. It was impossible not to admire him – he had the face of an angel. But where was Phelan?

As if in answer to her unspoken question, Julian said, 'He got tired of waiting. He's in the music saloon. Listen.'

Once more, from the distance, she heard the liquid notes of a pianoforte played by an expert. So it was him! Frederick heard them, too. He had been wondering about Phelan, and sounding Andrew out. Apparently, they had been at Oxford together in their youth, and had later met up in Egypt. As for Julian, he had joined them in Florence, where they had gone to recuperate from the rigours of Eastern travel. On the surface, all seemed well, but Frederick could find little to like about Phelan. What mischief's brewing here? he wondered. Why this sudden arrival? And why, in the name of Heaven, does he want to give those jewels to Charlotte?

He could not fault his manners or obvious breeding. An aristocrat to the bone, he was austere yet overpowering, with something in his personality so dazzling that wherever he went he would command notice. But Frederick, who always kept an ear to the ground, had picked up bits and pieces of information about him. The gossips usually exaggerated, of course, but there was never smoke without fire.

That lovely mother of his, Countess Augusta, for example. It was said that she held court like a queen in Florence and that her appetite for pretty boys was insatiable. She had always been the centre of some scandal or other, and her son seemed to follow suit. So, this being the case, why had he returned to his homeland? Had he thought it wise to abandon foreign climes for a while? Had they grown too hot for him?

'Is that Phelan playing?' Charlotte breathed, and Frederick noticed with a sinking heart that she was staring at the door in round-eyed awe.

'Yes,' Julian answered, flicking back a blond lock that had strayed across his brow. 'He's good, and has studied in the European *conservatoires*. If it were not impossible for a man of his standing to appear in public, then he could well be a concert artiste.'

'That would be a crying shame, a waste of a good man!' Andrew grunted, a glass of whisky in one hard, calloused hand. 'There's no one I'd rather have around in a tight corner. He has nerves of steel. You should see him dressed in Arab costume, Miss Charlotte. He looks the part, by God, and speaks their lingo. I wish I'd had him with me in the Riff Mountains, could have done with his gun on more than one occasion, I can tell you.'

Charlotte smiled at him vaguely, but drifted toward the door, unable to help herself, lured by those cascading notes. She was in a daze – following the music – entering the saloon where servants were tidying up, sweeping the floor, putting chairs to rights, leaving everything in order before they ended their eighteen hour day. Charlotte passed by without seeing them, going to where Phelan sat at the black Steinway grand.

He ignored her presence, his mouth set in concentration as he thundered out stormy cadenzas or lightly drew forth limpid, fluid notes. Charlotte had not dreamed of the existence of such beauty of piano sound. What had seemed dreary scales and trills during her unwilling hours of practice became transformed into ethereal harmonies, tales, fancies and idylls expressed in music instead of verse.

Suddenly he stopped, sitting back with his hands on his knees, lifting his eyes from the keyboard. Charlotte had not realised that she had come so close, her elbow resting on the silk shawl draped across the piano lid. She met his look and, as when they first met, it seemed that his eyes probed into her very soul.

'You play brilliantly,' she stammered, utterly disconcerted.

He nodded gravely. 'Thank you.'

'What was it you were playing?' I'm so hopelessly ignorant, she thought. Oh, I know some of the works of Chopin, Mozart and Beethoven, but this music is unfamiliar, disturbingly so.

'The composer is Debussy,' he answered, flexing his hands, those long, strong fingers touching the keys again. 'He's French, and most innovative. His pieces are tone poems. Whatever the technical explanation may be, I always seem to hear the dropping of fountain water at twilight in a dark forest peopled by Corot's nymphs. Listen to this. It's called *Le jardin sous la pluie*, and one can imagine the gurgle of rain-water as it rushes along a stony path during an April storm.'

He began to play again, and she was entranced, watching his hands in the mystical light of early dawn, the greyness lifting outside, the electric bulbs within the room rendered garish in comparison. Phelan paused once to request that they were extinguished. The servants complied, and then departed, leaving them alone in the empty, echoing room. Phelan played from memory, he had no need for sheet music. Gradually she was able to distinguish his features more clearly, the dark eyes under the heavy brows, the thin, haughty face with pronounced cheekbones, the black hair tumbling across his forehead.

Debussy's music distilled its essence into her being, sometimes mysterious and sombre, sometimes tranquil, always rich and sensual. Phelan changed from one piece to another, saying at one point, 'You like this? It's *Clair de lune*, the essence of moonlight. Do you see it in your mind's eye?'

'Oh, I do! I do!' she exclaimed, her hands clasped to the lace at her breasts.

'You show true appreciation,' he went on, never ceasing in his masterful interpretation. 'I believe that music is the greatest of art forms. Exalted states of feeling, unrelated to anything in the material world, lose much of their strength when confined to word or form. Adequate expression is only possible by the rhythm and sound of music.'

Charlotte reeled under the impact of his words. How could Eva dislike such a man? He was intelligent, understanding and supremely sensitive. Eva must be unaware of this side of his nature, she concluded, and longed to run upstairs and tell her. She'll change her mind. I'm sure she will.

'I only know that it speaks to me, moves me deeply,' she said, her voice ringing with passionate intensity.

'That's all you need to know,' he said softly, finishing with a final flurry of chords. 'Let your emotions run riot. Don't be afraid if it makes you cry with sheer happiness. Don't struggle if it rouses uncontrollable yearnings for love.'

She looked at his hands, seeing the lean, tanned backs of them, showing veins and sinews and long strong fingers. Had he really held a rifle and killed people?

'Andrew told me you're a fighter,' she said.

He smiled. 'I'm a Jack-of-all-trades.'

'And master of none?'

'On the contrary. I'm master of every one.' Coming from anybody else this would have sounded boastful, but Phelan was simply stating a fact.

The room was filling up with light and he left the piano stool, coming round to stand near her. A thrill of fright and something else as yet unnamed raced through her veins. I shouldn't stay here with him, she thought, but I can't leave. He had mentioned love and she wanted to hear more, wondering what really happened when a man and woman had intercourse. To read of it made it seem an almost ridiculous act. Why should people want to do such a thing?

It was all very well discussing it sensibly with Eva, but the only other person with whom she had been able to talk was her maid servant. When Tilly was assured that it was proper to go into details with her young mistress, she had plunged into graphic accounts of her dallyings with various swain, the most recent and ardent of whom was the chauffeur, Wilkins. Charlotte had listened like an obedient child learning a lesson, though she still could not quite grasp the significance. Why should Tilly risk pregnancy for the sake of such peculiar activities?

''Cause it's such a lovely feeling, miss!' Tilly had replied, as cheerful as she was capable, laughing loudly, showing pink gums and large white teeth. 'Makes me go all – I dunno – wobbly at the knees. He's a real masher is Wilkins. Goes at it like a rabbit, he does.'

Wobbly at the knees? That was how Charlotte was feeling, alone in the dawn with Phelan. She wanted to touch him, to let her arms creep up around his neck and draw his face down to hers, to feel his hands caressing her, and the touch of his lips on her mouth. She pulled herself together sharply, shocked by the hot ache stabbing her loins.

Phelan was looking at her as if he knew of her arousal, and this confused her even more. 'It's late –' she began.

'Or early?' His shoulders lifted in a shrug. 'Hardly worth bothering to catch up on sleep. Let's go into the garden and watch the sun rise.'

The terrace still bore traces of the party; a forgotten plate holding fragments of lettuce or greenish-brown caviar; a champagne glass that had rolled beneath a bench; a woman's discarded shawl; a dance-card that fluttered in the breeze. The outdoor staff would be coming on duty to put all to rights.

Charlotte allowed Phelan to lead her down the broad shallow steps to the pathway between velvety lawns bordered by flower-beds. The gravel crunched under their feet. The birds had begun their hymn of welcome to the sun. There was a faint, faraway hum as London woke to life. With the dawn came colour. It made Charlotte hold her breath as she gazed up at that cloudless sky where faint stars gleamed until extinguished by the rosy glow from the eat.

As if by silent accord they turned across the grass toward the summer-house. The dew was soaking through Charlotte's thin shoes but she took no heed. When they reached the charming thatched building, she sat on the bottom step and Phelan leaned against the rail.

'Do you mind if I smoke?' he enquired politely.

When she shook her head, he lit up a cigar, drawing on it reflectively for a moment before saying, 'Would you like to come to Italy and meet my mother?'

She was not yet accustomed to his habit of snatching extraordinary statements out of the blue. Almost everything he said left her dumbfounded. 'I can't do that!' she cried.

'I didn't ask you if you could or could not do it.' He stared at her through the fragrant smoke. 'Answer my question. Would you like to meet her?'

'Well, yes – I suppose so.

'Good. Then we'll see what can be arranged.' He spoke as if it was a foregone conclusion that whatever he decided upon should be done.

'Even if Eva would agree, I can't drop everything just like that and go off with you.' His arrogance amazed and irritated her. 'I've work to do.'

One peaked eyebrow lifted slightly in sceptical amusement. 'Work? Young ladies like you don't work, do they? What are you – a typist – a shop-assistant? I take it that you're joking, aren't you?'

Charlotte could feel her cheeks flaming under his taunting regard. 'I'm not talking about paid work.'

He sank down beside her, resting back on his elbows, long legs in tight black trousers stretched out before him. 'Ah, I see. You refer to Eva's obsession with charities.'

Charlotte remembered Eva's kindness, her courage and concern. Helping people was her dominant passion, the reason for her existence. She would not have classed it as an obsession, and resented Phelan's flippant use of the word. Suddenly her enjoyment of the rapidly warming garden, her tingling excitement at being there with him, took a downward plunge. She was aware of the light-headed feeling brought about by a sleepless night. Her eyelids felt gritty, and she needed to rest.

'I'm going in now,' she announced. 'I've a call to make this afternoon.'

She stood up while Phelan remained seated, looking at her through hooded eyes, the cigar to his lips. A virgin, unawakened to passion as yet, he decided, an earnest girl whose beauty should be exalted, not wasted on devotion to duty. 'Can I drive you there in my car?' he asked with that charm which, at his mother's knee, he had learned to use when it suited him.

'No, thank you. I shall ride my bicycle.'

'Do you wear a divided skirt and porkpie hat?' he asked, mock-serious. 'I'm sure it causes a stir when you arrive for tea at some duchess's soirée. I'd love to be a fly on the wall.'

'I'm not doing the rounds of social visiting,' she said firmly, wishing that he did not make her feel such a fool. 'I've an appointment with a vicar concerning one of his parishoners and the shop Eva is about to open for her in Bond Street.'

His lips quirked. 'So Cousin Eva has turned to *trade*. Good Lord, soon London may see a countess behind a counter! A shop, indeed. Ladies don't run shops.'

Try not to rise to the bait, she cautioned herself, but could not resist it. 'She's not running it, and neither am I. This girl handstitches the most exquisite embroidery. Thanks to Eva, orders are now pouring in and we have to have somewhere to expand production.'

He sighed and tossed away his cigar butt, then rose in a swift, agile movement. 'All right, Charlotte. I'll drive you there and wait outside. I must admit I find churchmen tedious.'

She shook her head. 'It's better to travel by bike. Large cars and carriages smack of the toff, and tend to scare off the inhabitants.'

He pulled down his mouth and accepted defeat. 'Well, then, what about my calling for you later? We could go to a concert.'

'You're very persistent.' Still nervous of him, she felt that she had scored several points. Now he would see her as she liked to imagine herself, an independent, strong, free-thinking person who did not hesitate to cycle round London, capable of organisation, and holding her own with men of the cloth.

'I usually get my way.' He made to take her hand, but she pulled back.

She found that her urge to surrender to his wishes was proving stronger than her will to resist. It would be lovely to hear an orchestra, to be escorted by such a man, to indulge in some light-hearted fun after her trip to the slums which was bound to be depressing.

The words popped out of her mouth before she could stop them. 'Maybe I could manage a concert.'

'Capital!' He smiled broadly as if she had just given him a great boon. 'I'll pick you up around seven.'

Eva is not going to approve, she thought, then rebellion flared up. Eva's condemnation of Phelan had roused a stubborn devil in her, strengthening her resolution to have no preformed opinion thrust down her throat. There's no harm in my accepting an invitation to a concert, she fumed. I can see that he's prejudiced against our work, but I'll soon change that. He's not an unreasonable man and, when he sees what we are achieving, I'm sure he'll offer his help.

The garden was ablaze under the swiftly climbing sun. She could seen the groundsmen commencing work, carrying hoes and forks, or trundling wheelbarrows. The notion of a breakfast tray brought to her bed before she slept was an appealing one. She was about to bid Phelan goodbye when Andrew came out on to the terrace, shading his eyes with his hand, then seeing them and shouting,

'Phelan! The car's here!'

'I'm coming.' He sounded cross at being disturbed, and his brows swooped down in a frown. He succeeded in grasping Charlotte's hand, his eyes burning into her. 'The trip to Italy?'

'We'll see.' It was hard to concentrate under that direct gaze and with her fingers linked with his. Then she added, 'We've got to get a few things clear. You want me to meet your mother. D'you know where I come from?'

'I know a great deal. Don't worry, my beloved mama is open-minded. She won't condemn you for clawing your way to the top of the tree.'

'I've hardly done that. You make it sound so mercenary. I was a victim of circumstances.' She was angry at his tone.

'Very fortunate circumstances, I'd say.' There was a hard slant to his mouth that hinted at a barely controlled temper. His grip tightened and he pulled her closer to him. 'What of the jewels?'

'Take them away with you,' she said, her body rigid to prevent her breasts from brushing his chest. 'I can't have them.'

He relaxed his grip, and that firm, beautiful mouth hovered over hers for an instant before he released her. 'Not now, perhaps, but you will. I'll give them to you on our wedding day.'

Surprise rooted her to the spot. 'Our what?' she gasped.

Though he had withdrawn to the far side of the steps she felt that he had come suffocatingly close. 'Our wedding day,' he repeated, casually brushing a smear of dust from his jacket. 'Oh, yes, my dear – we shall be married, come hell or high water. There's no doubt about it. I've made up my mind.'

'Come in, Charlotte. Welcome, welcome! Careful you don't trip over the toys. Oh, those children – what a muddle! You can see why I won't let them rampage in my study, can't you? Young savages,' said the vicar of St Mark's as Charlotte stepped over the threshold into an untidy hall with a brown-painted dado surmounted by wall-paper of sprawling leaves and cabbage roses.

It was not unusual for the imperious clanging of the frontdoor bell to be answered by him or his wife, for Stephen and May Savill had trouble with their servants. They were too kind and considerate, and though loyal to a fault, their meagre staff, consisting of a maid, a cook and a nanny, would hardly have been human if they did not take advantage of such leniency.

'Don't worry about it,' Charlotte said, pushing aside a small wooden fire-engine, a dolls' pram and a pair of rubber galoshes. 'You know I don't stand on ceremony.'

She had left her bicyle leaning against the rickety gate, and walked up the path. The air was hot and breathless, full of dust and a myriad stinks. Plane trees drooped over the sour earth where a few flowers straggled. The smell of cats was overpowering. The vicarage squatted alongside the church. It was a gaunt-looking house, the doors and windows hiding beneath pointed stone arches, whilst a hedge of struggling privet rendered the downstairs rooms darker still, even on such a sunny day as this.

Stephen Savill was a little over forty, and had been an athelete in his youth. He still insisted on exercising, riding round the parish on his bicycle in preference to the car recently purchased for this purpose. His features were regular and pleasant-looking, dominated by an angular nose and a lofty brow from which the hair was receding. Though quiet spoken, he was able to frame his thoughts with force and clarity, and he had an air of latent authority about him. Strong he was, and he needed to be with the duty of caring for the physical well-being of his flock and attempting to instill Christian doctrines into people whose main concern was finding the wherewithal to keep their bodies alive, never mind their immortal souls.

Charlotte liked visiting the Savills, that overworked, devoted couple and their eight energetic children whose ages ranged from six months to sixteen years. May was such a fragile-seeming, diminutive woman that Charlotte never ceased to marvel at how she had managed to produce such a large, boisterous family.

'They're all out,' Stephen continued, holding open the door of his study that she might enter. 'May and Nanny have taken them down to the docks.'

'Is Gwen at home?' Charlotte took off her hat and shook out her hair.

It was such a relief to wear it loose after the restrictions of yesterday, and good to be in the easy atmosphere of the vicarage again. Though Phelan dominated her thoughts, excitement knotted her stomach as she wondered if Gwen had done what she had requested. Maybe today I'll learn something about my parents, even find a clue that may lead me to Tweeny, she thought.

Gwendoline was the first-born, a big, splendidly handsome girl who resembled her father. All the Savill children seemed to thrive in that overcrowded neighbourhood. The atmosphere was polluted by soot from hundreds of chimneys and the chemicals belched from a score of factories, yet they did not appear to have suffered through living there. On the contrary, they were the most healthy and well-balanced of youngsters.

'She'll be back soon. Just popped out on an errand for me.' Stephen stuck his head through the doorway and shouted down the passage in the direction of the kitchen. 'Annie will bring in some tea but you know what she's like – it may take ages.'

The study had always been a source of fascination to Charlotte for it contained so many interesting things. The walls were papered in red flock and there was a threadbare carpet of faded Oriental design; also a great deal of oddly assorted furniture for although the vicarage was dull and unlovely, May was an expert on antiques, always haunting the second-hand markets and filling the rooms with fine pieces bought for a song.

She had come from a long line of middle-class clergy, while Stephen was of the upper echelon, sometimes returning to the family seat in Shropshire to indulge his passion for riding. His curacy had been spent in a fashionable West End church, then he had been offered the ministry of this rough parish, a spot reputed to be a haunt of vice, populated by criminals and drunkards. He had jumped at the chance of doing something worthwhile, bored by the superficial routine of a prosperous area.

Annie entered, bearing a tea-tray. She was disgruntled, having been awakened from a nap, and plonked it down on the table unceremoniously. Even though dressed in her afternoon uniform of black silk, she failed to look either clean or tidy.

'Thank you, Annie,' Stephen said pleasantly. 'You may go now, and could you tell Miss Gwendoline to come here as soon as she gets in?'

'Yes, your Reverence,' Annie muttered grudgingly, and took herself off.

Stephen poured the tea, and handed Charlotte a cup. 'Now then, tell me about your visit to the Palace, and the ball last night. Why aren't you wearing your hair up? I thought this was the acme of every girl's ambition. Gwen is giving me hell because I won't permit it yet.'

For a while they discussed these events, and then went on to the shop, and Alice Brooker's part in it. Charlotte felt more at ease in that cheerful, shabby room than she had been since meeting Phelan. Though she had slept the morning away, he had been in her mind on waking. Marriage? He wanted to marry *her*? It was unbelievable and she was sure he had been teasing her. She had refrained from mentioning him when she looked in on Eva, who was sitting up in bed, blue smudges beneath her eyes. No need for a further row, she had decided, and had steered the conversation in the direction of the instructions she was to give Alice.

The cushions of the sagging armchair were feather-filled and comfortable, the tea hot and strong, the fruit cake superb. 'May made it herself,' Stephen commented with a grin. 'Our cook can be counted on to produce the most incredible stews, but she burns everything else, her pastry's like concrete and she can't bake a cake to save her life.'

'Eva would dismiss her,' Charlotte said, hiding a sleepy yawn behind her hand. 'There're some things she won't tolerate and wasted food is one of them.'

'Oh, we don't waste anything. Can't afford to. We eat what Cook provides, but sometimes May takes over and gives us a treat.' Stephen took out a pipe and pressed tobacco into the bowl from a round soap-stone jar, then suggested, 'Shall we go and see Alice?'

Charlotte knew that they should, but the bike ride had been a tiring one and last night's lack of sleep was catching up on her. More than anything else she wanted to talk about Phelan Charteris, but could not bring herself to do so. How could Stephen understand such a complex character? She was certain Phelan *was* complex, even though she did not know him well.

She caught sight of the pianola placed against one wall, its closed top supporting photos of college groups including a very young, fresh-faced Stephen, and various shields mounted on dark oak which he had won for his prowess at sport. Memories would not be suppressed, no matter how hard she tried – Phelan at the piano at dawn, while snatches of music teased her ears.

She sat up abruptly and leaned forward. 'Do you know the works of the French composer, Claude Debussy?' she asked.

Stephen was startled by this question but he gave no indication of it, puffing at his pipe lazily. Something has happened since last we met, he thought, watching her. It's more than all this business about coming out. Heavens, but she's developing into a beauty, a lovely, graceful creature. He studied her, trying to pinpoint the difference. Her eyes were still wide and clear and honest, but they were unusually bright, almost feverish, and her lips were slightly parted from some inner excitement.

Eva Pendral's waif. He knew the story, and had often wondered if Eva had been wise in bringing her up in totally different circumstances to those into which she had been born. How much truth was there in the theory of nature as opposed to nurture? Would blood out in the end? Stephen had known Eva for several years, ever since he moved to the slums and became involved in her improvement schemes. Charlotte had been a frequent visitor to their house, giving him the chance to observe her growing up, filled with compassion coupled with an almost scientific interest in the experiment. So, why this sudden question about music?

'I know of Debussy's works, but am not over familiar with them. I'm a Bach man myself. Why?'

'I heard someone playing his Preludes last night,' she replied, and he noticed that her warm facial tones had deepened across the cheeks.

He was about to probe further when there was a commotion from the hall: children's voices, and the harassed accents of his wife attempting, unsuccessfully, to hush them. The door of the study burst open and Gwendoline hurtled in.

'Charlotte!' she shouted happily. 'It's good to see you! I thought you wouldn't deign to visit a scruffy lot like us now you've curtsied to the King. What did he look like? Is he as fat as they say? What was Queen Alexandra wearing? Did she have a crown? Was the Countess of Warwick there?'

'Really, Gwennie, calm down, do!' This came from her mother who had followed her in. She was bothered by her daughter's reference to one of King Edward's mistresses. Sometimes the precocity of her brood made her feel uncomfortable, though it was Stephen's policy to discuss a wide variety of topics with them, believing that few subjects were unsuitable and that knowledge was all important.

The older ones crowded the doorway, vying for Charlotte's attention, the girls in brown Holland pinafores over print cotton dresses, sun-bonnets on their heads, the boys in knickerbockers, shirts and caps. Their nurse, in a blue and white striped blouse, grey flannel skirt and straw hat, held one of the youngest who squealed incessantly. May picked up a toddler who hid his face in her full sleeves and then peered shyly out. The baby in the enormous black, boat-shaped perambulator parked in the hall, began to yell lustily until someone swooped him up.

Stephen winked at Charlotte. 'The menagerie has arrived. Goodbye to our quiet chat.'

'What shall we do about Alice?' Charlotte asked as she was handed the baby. He made a damp patch on her skirt. She lifted him against her shoulder and patted his little back to bring up the wind, but he began to bawl again. May took him from her, said that he was hungry, and left the room.

'I'll talk to Alice later.' Stephen could see that the women needed his help with the children. 'You stay with Gwen. I expect you've a lot to chew over.'

How did he guess? she wondered uneasily. Does it show in my face? The study was empty once more, the noise dying away in the distance, but it was Gwen who spoke first.

'Kids, kids, kids! I'm fed up with them! Now Mother says she's expecting another. She must be mad! I'm never going to have any. Babies come in two types, I've decided – the batter-pudding kind, and the little old men who are born looking like their own grandfathers. Not my cup of tea at all.'

She flung herself down on the couch, blew out her cheeks in exasperation, then reached for the last slice of cake on the tea-tray. Gwen never simply sat anywhere, she sprawled; she never walked, she ran. She had always wanted to be a boy. Stephen was partly to blame for he had been convinced that the first child would be a male who would fulfil his thwarted athletic ambitions. Instead May had presented him with a baby girl. He had loved her from the start and, nothing daunted, ahd taken her to cricket matches as soon as she could walk and there instilled into her his own passion for sport of any kind.

No, Charlotte decided, looking at her affectionately, I can't tell her about Phelan. She wouldn't understand. Maybe she's too young just yet, too full of boats and bicycles, of going to Shropshire and riding her grandfather's hunters. But there was something else, a project they had started some time before, which was the main reason why Charlotte visited the vicarage.

'Did you look through the church archives?' she asked, capturing Gwen's attention with her earnestness.

'I started, but – phew! There's hundreds of them!' Gwen said, drawing her legs up inelegantly, showing a great deal of brown lisle stocking, arms about her hunched knees. 'Why don't we go down into the vaults and have another go?'

'Could we? Won't anyone object?'

'No, Dad's busy and the verger will be having his tea.' Unable to stay still for long, Gwen jumped to her feet. 'Come on.'

A dozen thoughts chased through Charlotte's head. Phelan was calling for her at seven and she had not told Eva about it yet. But somehow since meeting him it had become even more imperative that she discover something about her parents. It had occurred to her a while ago that there must be some record of their marriage somewhere, maybe of her birth, and Tweeny's too. Perhaps a few lines in some musty old book which would reveal where that lost father and mother were buried. Stephen's church was as good a place as any to start searching.

She had confided in Gwen who, with her taste for mysteries and adventure, had promptly offered her help. She had access to the underground areas of the church where such ledgers were stored. So Charlotte followed where she led – along the corridor, through a door leading to the back regions and, eventually, to a covered passage which connected with St Mark's.

Outside the streets were hot, crowded and noisy, but the church was cool, deserted and still. It acquired a mystery absent when the pews were filled with people and Stephen held sway in the heavily carved pulpit. Charlotte and Gwen spoke in whispers, their footsteps sounding irreverently loud on the stone flags. Sunlight filtered in from the highly decorated windows, and one in particular struck Charlotte, for it depicted the devil's head in detail at the Day of Judgement. His Satanic Majesty reminded her of Phelan.

She had a feeling of sadness that was not real sadness. It was an enjoyable melancholy, a poetic self-indulgence, the same feeling as when she listened to Debussy's music. She shivered, keeping close to Gwen, uneasy in the echoing nave. Gwen, however, was of the earth earthy and did not possess a vivid imagination. Her father's church held no fears for her. She did not expect to be confronted by a cowled figure with skeleton fingers beckoning her into the crypt to take her place among the dead.

She found the vestry, flicked on a switch and the room was bathed in the glow from shaded lamps. Then she advanced to a small door set under an arch, opened it briskly to reveal a set of steps winding down.

'What's the matter?' Her eyes sought Charlotte's, and, reading the hesitation in them, she smiled widely. 'Not afraid, are you? It's as safe as houses down there. Not a ghost to be had. It's not a burial place, you know, only a deposit for dusty tomes. Don't be such a ninny. I'd be much more scared of meeting the King, and you did that without turning a hair.'

The chilly air gave Charlotte goose-bumps, but there was nothing else for it. She had instigated this business. Down the stairs then, one foot placed carefully after another on the sharp turns where the stone was worn smooth. Gwen bounded ahead. Disappeared from sight, then her shadow was flung, huge and grotesque in the harsh light as a bare bulb swung crazily.

'Is this it?' Charlotte glanced about her apprehensively, but no terrifying apparition lurked there. It looked as ordinary as an accountants' office. Tables, cupboards, shelf after shelf of large folders, tied with tape, papers poking out of them. Births, deaths and marriages. Generations of them. So many hopes and fears and untold stories buried away forever in the vaults.

Gwen was running a thumb along the rows of files. 'Let's see. I've already scanned through several but didn't find anything. What did you say your mother's name was?'

'Margaret, and he was Simon.'

'Are you sure they were married?'

Charlotte closed her eyes against the bright flash of memory. A thin, dead hand – the left hand with a gold ring on the wedding finger. A woman pulling it off – a fat bully, her mouth open on a glare of teeth, like a savage beast.

'Yes, I'm sure,' she said.

'How far back d'you think you'll have to go?'

'Twenty years. Say eighteen eighty-three or four.' Charlotte had worked it out. She had been five when Eva found her, so possibly her parents had been married for one or two years before her birth.

Gwen heaved a massive volume from its resting-place and on to one of the tables. 'Here you are. I must admit I was in a bit of a rush, and didn't know for sure where to look. You have a go.'

Charlotte lay the book flat and opened the thick cover with a puff of dust. A smell of musty paper and ink filled her nostrils. It was a record wherein were registered every marriage service, each christening and funeral taking place at St Mark's during the years she had mentioned. There were a surprisingly large number and Charlotte's heart sank as she realised that this was only one book among hundreds stored in churches all over London. Her task seemed to be impossible. What faith had her parents followed? This was an Anglican diocese, but maybe they had been Roman Catholics, Methodists, Baptists – anything!

Phelan's features were superimposed across the neat rows of faded, copperplate writing. She saw his eyes, his mocking smile, heard his voice whispering in her imagination, 'Perhaps they were pagans, like me. Did they worship Dionysus, or the great god Pan? Maybe they made blood sacrifices on the altar of music – like I do.'

She shook off that tantalising vision and concentrated. Page after page revealed nothing. She closed the book with sad finality. 'It's hopeless. I'll never find them,' she sighed.

'Don't despair, comrade,' Gwen urged. 'Maybe we've got the wrong years. Let's search further.' Then she added as an afterthought, 'Why don't you ask at the Records Office? Everything that's ever happened to anyone is supposed to be kept there, isn't it?'

Charlotte pushed her hair back from her eyes. 'I've thought of it, of course I have, but if I start making official inquiries, then it might upset Eva. I think she's almost forgotten that I don't really belong to her, and has furnished me with papers and things, to use if I want to go abroad, or get married – or even buried!'

She sounded so edgy that Gwen gave her a sharp glance, then said, 'All right. Let's have another rummage, shall we?'

The clock on the church tower began to chime, its sound reverberating through the building. Charlotte glanced hurriedly at her watch. 'I can't. It's six now, and I'm due to go out at seven.'

'Ooh, somewhere posh?' Gwen's round face lit up. 'Is some man you met at the ball coming to whisk you away in his carriage?'

'I'm going to a concert at the Queen's Hall,' Charlotte answered airily. 'Yes, I did meet him last night, but he's no one of importance.'

They walked back through the church and Charlotte was close to tears, bitterly disappointed because their mission had been fruitless, though she had known that the odds were against her. Gwen was enthusiastic and she knew that she had only to call on Stephen's aid and he would help her, but his time was limited and she felt she had no right to bother him.

'Say goodbye to your parents for me,' she said, as she found her bicycle and mounted it.

Gwen stood on the pavement, impervious to the scene outside the pub on the other side of the road where stood a collection of prams in which pale-faced babies, dummies in their mouths, slept fitfully while their mothers were drinking in the dim interior. This was part of her life. She accepted it along with so much else, the quarrelsome drunks, the domestic fights, the beggars, the markets, the hurly-burly of the streets.

She was much more intrigued by Charlotte: the romance of her adoption by Lady Eva, the assignation to which she was hurrying, the unsolved riddle of her birth. Charlotte began to pedal slowly, and Gwen walked alongside.

'Sorry we couldn't find out about your parents,' she said, her mop of bright hair shining in the evening sun. 'I'll go on looking, but are you quite sure they were married. They weren't living in sin, were they? Cook calls it 'living over the brush', but it means the same thing. D'you think you're illegitimate? I've always wanted to be illegitimate – so much more exciting than being born into a respectable family like mine. Lots of famous people were bastards.'

The shadows were lengthening now, the western sky like amber-coloured flame bathing everything in beauty. The distant factory chimneys and church spires stood out black against it, and a hush had fallen as if the city was drawing breath before the activities of the night. Charlotte saw it all, responding to its ethereal quality, even as she looked at her friend, running along at her side.

'I can't tell you for sure they were married,' she said. 'She wore a ring, but I suppose that doesn't prove anything. I had a little sister, and I don't know what happened to her.'

She turned to cycle along a road which would eventually return her to Albion House, waving farewell to Gwen, and her thoughts were deep. Gwen spoke blithely of being a bastard, but then she was secure in her identity. She knew that she was different from the people of her father's parish. They were poor, but the Savills had money – not a great deal but enough. They did not have to worry about being out of work, or paying the rent, or where the next meal was coming from.

Charlotte was not faced with these problems either, but she worried about her parentage. Eva had done all she could for her, more than enough, but she could not shake off this longing to be part of a family, *her* family, linked by ties of blood. If only I could find Tweeny, then I'd be whole. This insistent idea occupied her throughout the journey, so that her wheels span over the road's surface and Albion House appeared before her in no time at all.

Tilly was waiting for her in the bedroom, and her evening dress was already spread out on the bed. Charlotte tore off her clothes and relaxed in a warm bath, yet she could not quiet those tormenting thoughts. Phelan would soon be there, and she must inform Eva of her intention to go out, yet uppermost in her mind was the rememberance of that tiny, forlorn figure from her past. She saw the tears making clean rivulets down Tweeny's cheeks, heard her outraged cries.

I've not forgotten, Mam, Charlotte vowed inwardly. If she lives, I'll find her. If she's dead, then I'll pray for her and put flowers on her grave.

Chapter Four

The West End of London – the heart of that great, sprawling city which, since the time of the Romans, had gradually thrust out like some giant amoeba, absorbing the surrounding countryside. The capital of the British Empire, where immense wealth rubbed shoulders with dire poverty. The playground of the chosen few, where lay the mansions of the mighty, the seat of Government and the main residence of the King. It was also the haunt of numberless vagrants who hung around outside the theatres, the clubs, the expensive restaurants, in the hope of scrounging a few coins.

Jennie stared about her with wide eyes as she climbed from the bus at Piccadilly Circus. It was a world of horses, carriages and motor cars, with pedestrians everywhere, each busy about their own concerns. Forgetful of the purpose that had brought her there, she wandered along, drinking it all in, responding to the surging life, the dare and danger of London, where young girls like her could vanish without a trace.

Oxford Street was a Mecca for shoppers. Ladies in cart-wheel hats and skirts that brushed the ground, their shoulders swathed in luxurious furs, their hands buried in matching muffs, stepped from carriages or limousines. They were driven by cockaded coachmen or liveried chauffeurs as upright as soldiers, and the doors were opened with a flourish by poker-faced footmen. Their escorts handed them out, influential men, wearing top-hats and double-breasted overcoats, but it was not only the well-to-do who were lured by the brightly lit shop windows. All manner of folk crowded the pavements.

There were women flaunting cheap imitations of the massive headgear worn by their superiors; men in sober suits and bowler hats, complete with the almost obligatory moustache and walking-stick; Cockney lasses in fringed shawls and straw bonnets, sharing tubs of whelks as they chattered and laughed loudly, their men clad in flashy checks, spotted neckerchiefs and flat caps; tightly-collared clerks and neatly costumed typists on their way to a nearby corner tea-shop, snatching a lunch break.

Out-of-work musicians scraped away on fiddles or put flutes to chapped lips in the hope that hearts might be softened and pennies drop into the upturned hats lying at their feet. Every so often they were moved on by pairs of policemen in high helmets and navy-blue uniforms with leather belts from which truncheons swung, who paced through the crowd with measured tread, hands clasped behind their backs. Even so, as in all such throngs, the rag, tag and bobtail of minor criminals took full advantage of this golden opportunity to pick pockets and reap a bountiful harvest.

Jennie thrilled to it all, as she always did when journeying 'up West'. She loved the crowds, the bustle, the voices of the street traders rising above the clatter of traffic. She paused when her ears caught the unmistakable tinkle of a barrel-organ coming from a side-alley, feet tapping in waltz-time as she joined the group of people gathered round the owner who was busily engaged in turning the handle of his machine. She heard the sparkling notes, was aware of cold, of her breath masking her face like smoke, but at the same time her mind was divided, at one with the shivering monkey in his crimson jacket and fez with the tarnished gold trim. He crouched on the lid of the instrument, his tiny face like that of a wizened child, his eyes bewildered.

What is he thinking about? she wondered, as the spectators laughed when his master prodded him into activity, thrusting an open-topped pouch into his paw that he might hold it out for contributions. Did he dream of his native country, far away from this misty land and mocking faces?

His owner showed no pity although he was from Italy and must also yearn for olive-groves, blue skies and heat. Yet Jennie knew all too well the brutalising effect of poverty. If the monkey amused the fickle public, then the Italian's wife and children would eat. What price the little creature's well-being compared to this? He was only a monkey, after all. Another could be purchased cheaply as a replacement when he finally pined to death.

She turned away, spirits sinking, losing that sense of optimism that had brought her there. It would be just the same with me, she thought unhappily. I entertain the punters in the pub where I work, dance for them, belt out songs, yet if I suddenly disappeared no one would notice and the landlord would get another girl to replace me.

On the bus she had felt happy and hopeful, really believing that the chance meeting with Albert Baggot a few nights since would give her the opening she desperately needed. It was incredible that he had recognised her after all this time.

'Well, stone the crows! If it ain't Tweeny Drummond!' he had exclaimed, catching her by the arm as she jumped from the make-shift stage in the public bar of the Bell and Crown.

She had shaken his hand off, well able to take care of herself against amorously inclined customers. 'Who the 'ell are you?' she had demanded, standing with arms akimbo at the tightly-laced waist of her shoddy dress. 'My name ain't Tweeny Drummond – it's Jennie Blossom!'

Albert had laughed, displaying a mouth full of uneven teeth, a smartly dressed young man, his hair gleaming with macassar-oil. He looked prosperous, an imitation gold watch-chain spanning his waistcoat. Before she could protest he had bought her a beer, urged her to sit with him, 'for old time's sake'.

Jennie had reluctantly complied, though unsure if she really wanted a reminder of those early days. Albert had a glib and able tongue, however, though she did not trust him, listening dubiously as he boasted of his success.

'You're a corker, Jennie, and no mistake,' he had insisted, going over her figure with experienced eyes. ''Blimey! What a stunner! What you doing wasting your time in a dump like this?' He had jerked a contemptuous thumb at the dingy interior of the pub.

Jennie had looked round, seeing it afresh though she had accepted it as home for many months, glad to find a haven where the landlady needed help behind the scenes, and the landlord did not try to take advantage of her. Above all, she had been given the chance to try out her skills as an entertainer.

Yes, she had thought, it's a ramshackle hole to be sure, the floor sprinkled with sawdust, the marble-topped tables ringed from countless glasses of liquer. As for Vi, the barmaid . . . what a bitch! And she had stared through narrowed lids to where Vi stood before an array of bottles – Vi with whom she waged continual warfare. The barmaid glared back, crimped hair stuck full of ornamental combs that glittered as she pulled swiftly at the row of handles in front of her.

The crowd had been their usual intoxicated selves, stamping their feet, shouting for Jennie to sing again. She had stood up, saying to Albert, 'I must go. Can't keep my public waiting.'

His grip on her wrist had been vicelike. 'Come to my office in Soho. I'm always on the look-out for talent and can get you a better gaff than this. 'Ere's where you'll find me,' and he had pushed a business card into her palm.

She had decided to forget it. Albert was definitely not to be trusted, but after yet another row with the jealous Vi, she had felt unable to endure her lot further. She would take Albert up on his offer, see if he could find her a job at one of the theatres. I don't care what it is, she thought. I'll be a dresser, sweep up, scrub out the lavatory, anything so long as I can breathe the atmosphere of grease paint.

She read and re-read Albert's address, 'Number 6, Old Compton Street, Soho. Second floor', then without giving herself time to hesitate further she had escaped from the pub.

It had still been dark, but the streets held no fears for her – she was their tough offspring. Often she had had no other resting-place. It was a damp day, a smoke pall hanging over the city. Normally Jennie scrambled up the treacherous winding stairway of the bus, elbowing others aside so that she might sit on the front seat with the driver. Like the cabbies, they were big, experienced, confident men who, if they liked the look of you, might exchange a cheery word or even let you hold the whip. But she was wearing her best hat and did not want to risk damaging it, so had occupied a wooden bench in the interior.

The streets they had passed through had been of uniform dullness until they reached the fashionable squares, parks and roadways of Mayfair. She had immediately sat up and taken notice. This is where I should be living, she had thought, and elated by her dreams, she had jumped from the bus when the driver braked at Piccadilly, head filled with hope, telling herself that people were not so bad.

She had smiled at a postman in his funny hat with a peak at both ends, a huge sack on his back as he delivered mail, and grinned at the errand boys on bicyles whistling the latest music-hall songs as they trundled their way between the traffic. But the sight of the monkey had brought her down to earth with a bang. It was as if her own frivolity alarmed her, as though to be anxious, expecting the worst, was the only true state of mind. She was so weary of poverty, tired to death of unhappiness of loneliness and insecurity. Surely sometimes – *sometimes*, good things happened, didn't they?

She entered the main thoroughfare again and wandered along until suddenly catching a glimpse of herself in a shop window. It came as a shock. She had washed at dawn and put on her one set of tidy clothes, thinking that she looked quite presentable, but now –

Could that sorry thing really be herself? she wondered despairingly.

Smart? She looked like a tramp! She was filled with pity for that bedraggled creature, almost as if she was looking at a stranger.

Her coat was out at the elbows, though she had tried to patch it, secondhand when she bought it off a market stall, and her shoes, someone's castoffs, had rubbed a hole in her stockings and chaffed her feet. Her nose was running and she wiped her sleeve across it as she stared beyond her reflection at the wonders in the emporium window. Then she forgot that she was shivering with cold, and that hunger pangs were grinding in her belly, gazing wide-eyed at the goods glittering beneath the electric lights.

She drew in a long, shuddering sigh. It hurt her ribs, caught in her throat, brought on a fit of coughing. She recovered her breath, aching with the desire to own such things. I must have them! she thought feverishly. I'll do anything – anything just as long as I'm not poor any more. The lights whirled as if to phantom music, and she wanted to dance with them, to show onlookers that she was just as good as the actresses who drew the crowds in the Leicester Square theatres.

'You aw' right, gal?' A voice drew her back. The scene steadied itself and she was in touch with reality again.

It was a coster who had addressed her, a scrawny person with a cap tilted over one eye. He was standing behind her with his donah. Pearls adorned his suit, and his lady's hat was heavy with the sweep of colourful ostrich plumes. They were both regarding Jennie anxiously, quizzically, ready to help, eager to send their warmth towards her, a warmth engendered by their own good nature, and the gin they had been consuming.

Jennie shrank back, shook her head, warded off their concern, unable to bear their kindness lest she crack. They were happy. She could read it in their faces. They knew love. Their arms linked, he carrying parcels – parcels for the children waiting for them back home in their lodgings. A happy family, with him working hard to support them, and her, too, no doubt selling flowers at the base of the graceful statue of Eros in the middle of Piccadilly Circus.

The plinth always blazed with flowers sold by the 'girls' to the blades of the town. It was they, cheerful, saucy, who brought the first real news of spring every year. Soon it would be mistletoe and holly, bargained for in Covent Garden Market in the chilly small hours before dawn. Why wasn't she on duty there? Jennie wondered. Did flower-girls have time off?

'You looks all in, ducks,' the woman was saying. ''Ere, take me shawl – goo on, take it, there's a love.'

Jennie put up her hands in protest. 'No! No!' she gasped. She couldn't bear it. Kindness hurt her, no matter how she longed to experience it.

Turning, she ran blindly back the way she had come, down Oxford Street, dodging through the crowd, not stopping till the narrow alleys of Soho closed about her. This was better. Dirty streets, rundown shops and, as she penetrated further, whores loitering in doorways – painted young ones, toothless old ones. Touts and pimps, thieves and vagabonds, misery that settled round Jennie like a familiar pain. Drunks reeled up the middle of the road, shouting abuse at passing carts. Outside the pubs knots of women stood, gossiping and drinking their stout. If they wanted to relieve nature they did so by lifting their tattered skirts and straddling the gutter, the conversation and drinking uninterupted. The air reeked of booze and bad sanitation.

People sat on their doorsteps, a few oddments offered for sale, pathetic household things, the flotsam and jetsam of their lives: old clothes, picture-frames, chipped china – stuff which it was useless to lug to the pawn-broker. 'Uncle' would have merely look down his prominent nose, lifted his shoulders in an ironic shrug, spread wide his hands in an Oriental gesture, and refused with a deep, mournful sign. Jennie knew this well, having often resorted to the 'pop-shop'.

Old Compton Street was a shade more respectable. Here was commerce of a different kind. Jennie found number six, and climbed a flight of stairs to Albert's office. She stiffened her spine and knocked on the door boldly. A voice told her to come in. She entered a cluttered room where Albert was seated at a deal table. The atmosphere was full of the stale odour of used cigars.

'Ah, there you are,' he cried, and swung his feet down from the table's stained surface.

Jennie was again aware of how unattractive he was: sandy hair parted in the middle and plastered with pungently scented oil, sandy brows and lashes, yellowish teeth in a sharp face. He's like a ferret, she thought, but said aloud, 'Decided I might as well. Nothing to lose, 'ave I?'

'Indeed you ain't. I can do you a bit of good. The boss ain't 'ere at the moment. I'm in charge.' Albert preened himself, thumbs hooked in the waistcoat pockets of his brown suit. There was nothing subtle about him – he was brash and decidedly common, from his slicked back hair to the pointed toes of his patent leather shoes.

Jennie glanced round the room with its filing cabinet, large Imperial typewriter and scabby walls covered with faded play-bills and photographs of girls. They stared back at her roguishly, some displaying their hour-glass figures in frilly gowns, others coyly showing bare shoulders with, here and there, the glimpse of a breast.

'What *is* your business, Bert?' she asked.

He indicated a cane-seated chair. 'Sit down, Tweeny – sorry, Jennie. I'm in the entertainment line, as it were. My boss acts as an agent for singers and dancers. I might be able to get you on 'is books and, for starters, you'll need some pictures took.'

'Like them?' Jennie nodded towards the girls on the walls.

'That's the ticket. I'll introduce you to this bloke what I knows. Very good with a camera, 'ee is. What d'you say?' he gave her a wink and seated himself on the desk next to her, swinging a foot. He was wearing cream spats buttoned over his shoes.

'I ain't got no money. I can't pay for photos,' she protested, wishing she had not come, wanting to get away from this cocky individual who so obviously fancied his appearance and its effect on females, young or old.

'Don't worry abaht that, love. 'Ees a pal, a mate of mine. 'Ee'll do it, if I asks 'im. What d'you want to drink? What abaht a nice port with a dash of lemonade?' He was already rummaging in a cupboard and bringing out a couple of bottles and some glasses. 'We got to drink to the future, you and me – and to the old days, too.'

Jennie took the glass, more to give her hands something to do than because she needed a drink. She did not like the way Albert was smiling at her, so sly and knowing. He wanted to talk about the past, did he? Very well. ''Ow's your ma?' she asked crisply.

His face darkened. 'The old bitch is dead! I've looked after yours truly for years now. Done all right for myself, considering. I wanted to find you, Jennie. You was my first love, you know. Went to the orphanage to see 'ow you was getting on but they said you'd scarpered. You could've knocked me down with a feather when I saw you in the pub the other night.'

'I'm surprised you knew it was me,' she replied, slowly sipping the port, and wishing that he hadn't.

'Oh, come off it! I'd 'ave known you anywhere. You always was a bit different to the rest, and you've growed into a lovely gal, Jennie – look like real class, though we knows different, don't we? You're no more class than me, ain't that so? Two of a kind, us. But we're going to make it to the top, you just see if we ain't.'

Encouraged by her silence, he reached out and grabbed her. She tried to disengage herself without offending him. Maybe he really could help her and she did not want to ruin the chance. His hands were hot and unpleasantly moist. He drew her up from the chair and caught her between his thighs. She could see every detail of his acned skin, the pallor of his face, the watery protuberant eyes.

'And the photographer?' she reminded, enduring his embrace.

'I'll fix something up. Leave it to me. You don't 'ave to go back to that pub, do you? I can get you a room near 'ere, dirt cheap.'

'I can't afford anything.' Her eyes held his. They were strange eyes, amber flecked with green, and filled with a warning light that prevented him from trying to insinuate a hand into her bodice. 'I get my board and lodging at the pub. I skivvy there and, when I'm tarted up of an evening, people give me money for singing, not much but enough to buy a few things. I can't chuck up my job, just like that.'

Albert was not accustomed to refusal. Many was the aspiring young actress with whom he had had his way by promising to make her a star. He had no scruples, taking his cue from his boss though this man did, in fact, do all he could for his clients, if he thought they had talent. As for the ninety-nine out of a hundred applicants who had no gift at all – well, who was to blame him if he took advantage? It was one of the perks of the trade.

Jennie knew when someone was trying to deceive her. Fifteen years of street living, and she still retained her virginity. This had taken some doing. She had achieved it with her trenchant tongue, quick fists, spread claws and swift feet, fighting off any lecher who propositioned her, able to attack and ridicule him, spitting out profanities. No man had ever tried it a second time – except for Albert, and he had never been able to keep his hands to himself. But then, much water had flown under the bridge since they last met. It was inevitable that he would attempt to use her – him being what he was, and men being what they were. It's the nature of the beast, she thought cynically, but he's in for a shock.

'You don't 'ave to 'urry off, do you?' he whispered, his mouth against her ear, sour breath brushing her skin. 'The boss won't be back yet, and when 'ee does come. 'ee'll be three sheets to the wind. Give us a kiss, Jennie.'

'Show me what you can do for me first,' she answered, her hands against his chest, putting space between them. There was challenge in her eyes, challenge in her smile. Young though she was she had learned early that men would do a lot for you in the hope of the return they wanted.

Albert groaned, angry at her refusal but compelled to control his low-grade lust. 'Dammit, I'd love to show you – up 'ere on the table, if you'd let me.'

She had escaped, putting the desk between them. 'I'll bet you would, but nothing doing, Bertie boy.'

Albert glowered and lit up a cigar. 'You're an 'ard-'earted piece, ain't you?' he grumbled. 'Don't you like a bit of 'ows-your-father?'

'What d'you take me for?' Her brows shot up in indignation and rebuke. 'Did you think I'd drop my knickers for you first go off? No thank you. I got 'em firmly tied on, I can tell you. Got to with mucky buggers like you about. I want a bit of respect, if you please.'

Those shining golden eyes presented a sight that Albert found both intimidating and entrancing. His desire for her was pressing. He needed relief but accepted that he would have to wait. Jennie was calling the tune, and he could do nothing but grit his teeth and ache. Jesus, he raved within himself, I'll have to find a whore when she's gone or I'll go barmy! But his cunning brain was working overtime. He could see that Jennie was ambitious, probably greedy, and vain too. This, he told himself, will be her downfall.

'All right, my precious. Don't get mad at me,' he said with an unctuous smile. 'I'm a red-blooded male and you're so gorgeous. Only natural that I try it on, ain't it?'

'What about my voice? What about my dancing? I know I'm good at it.'

'You are! No doubt abaht that. But photos first, then I can trot 'em along to the powers that be. I know a bloke at the Gaiety Theatre who'll give a talented girl the chance of an audition. What d'you say to that?'

Christ Almighty, she's going to be a hard nut to crack, he gloomed. But he was telling the truth about her gifts, genuinely impressed when he had heard that sweet, true voice and seen the grace and allure of her movements on stage. Maybe he would have a star on his hands after all. That would be one in the eye for his boss if she was successful and it was *he*, Albert Baggot, who had discovered her.

Jennie gathered up her bag, ready to leave, having judged Albert's frustration to a nicety. 'Proof of the pudding,' she answered lightly. 'You knows where to find me if you've any news.'

Albert was desperate, cursing her for a teasing bitch. 'Tomorrow morning, early,' he blurted out. 'I'll fix up a sitting with my mate. You leave the pub. I'll 'ave found you a room by them.'

'And what do I do for money? Does it grow on trees in Soho?' she asked cuttingly.

'If you do a few extra pictures what 'ee can sell, then you'll be all right for a bit of cash,' Albert insisted, accompanying her to the door, hardly able to resist touching her again.

She brushed his advancing hand aside. 'Don't push your luck,' she advised. 'Tomorrow it is, but no tricks, Bert. I'm warning you.'

With the dignity of a duchess she swept past him and out of the door. Waves of heat laved her, the sweat breaking out at her armpits and trickling down her back. She really did feel strange. I hope I haven't picked up 'flu, she thought. That bloody damp room of mine! But not for long, perhaps. Is Bert genuine? Will he really help me? I've got to do it – know that I can! One day my name will be top of the bill and everyone will want to come to the theatre and see me.

She hurried down the stairs. The landing was lit by a spluttering gas-jet that cast a small circle of yellowish uncertainty around itself, but no further. She stopped on the ground floor, more disturbed by Albert than she cared to admit. Was he behind her? She thought she could hear him stumbling in pursuit, that stupid, almost drooling expression on his face. She was coughing again, needing to rest. There was a door to one side, bearing a dog-eared sign. Without stopping to read it, she seized the handle and let herself in.

The first thing that struck her was a sweet smell. She breathed it in, eyes tight shut. It reminded her of the Chinese laquered box in the pub parlour. Sometimes, when dusting, she had lifted the lid. It had smelt like that, sandlewood and spices, the odour of the mystic East. When she ventured to open her eyes, it was as if she had indeed been transported to an exotic country far beyond seamy Soho.

Candles lit the room with a soft radiance, and the place distilled its own glow from the varying tones of Indian rugs covering the floor and hanging against the walls. There were shelves of books, and curious ornaments, or perhaps not just decoration for they were weird – statuettes of gods, brass chalices, coloured tapers unlit and living in bundles. Incense smouldered in strangely wrought stands, their bases consisting of coiled metal snakes. Was this a shop? Jennie mused, and wanted to ask the woman seated at a table that was draped in a midnight blue chenille cloth.

'Hello, my child,' she said, as if Jennie was expected.

She spoke with a foreign accent, and she was most unusual, her ebony hair wound into thick plaits about her handsome head, held in place by tortoise-shell combs. Her face was ageless; she could have been twenty or twice that age, there was no way of telling. She seemed youthful, and yet when Jennie looked into her black eyes they held a wisdom as old as time itself.

'I'm sorry,' Jennie fumbled for words, then lied to excuse her rudeness at bursting in. 'But I was being chased by 'im upstairs.'

A smile lifted the thin features. 'He's a poor thing, isn't he? A fool. I've warned him not to deny his potential, but he won't listen. Too gross and uncouth.' Then she rose, tall in a robe of some rich stuff woven with gold thread. 'Come to the fire. Would you like some toasted muffins?'

So easy, so casual, as if they were old friends. Jennie nodded and moved to the fireplace set across one corner. She felt she should say something, tell her what she was going there, but the woman did not appear to expect an explanation. She simply pointed to a big square tapestry cushion and Jennie sank down into its feathery softness. A sofa was set beside it, along with an embroidered footstool. The sleek black cat on the hearth-rug stopped worshipping the flames and subjected Jennie to the unblinking scrutiny of his emerald eyes. He was introduced to her as Set.

Jennie had never before experienced such tranquillity. The atmosphere was that of a church – but no, too vibrant. A temple, perhaps – a shrine. But which god was worshipped there?

'Who are you?' she asked.

The woman took the kettle from the trivet and poured boiling water into a silver teapot. 'I'm Zena,' and she nodded to a poster pinned against one wall.

It was a print designed to catch the eye of fairground crowds, a crude portrait that did not do her justice: a gypsy scarf binding her hair, gold hoops in her ears, hands cupped around a crystal ball as if to coax out an image, playing cards drifting like autumn leaves. Round the edge of the poster were painted the Signs of the Zodiac. Gilt lettering stated boldly: 'Madame Zena, the World Renowned Fortune-Teller. Patronised by the Crowned Heads of Europe'.

'You tell fortunes? Is Zena your real name?' A note of awe crept into Jennie's voice.

Zena laughed. 'It's one of my names. Yes, I'm what is known as a fortune-teller, though I'd rather look on my talent as God-given. As for the Crowned Heads? Well, a prince did come to see me once and my manager exaggerates.'

'Are you a real gypsy?'

'I am.'

'And you've travelled with fairs? How exciting.'

'Not as exciting as you may imagine. I follow the road in the summer, but during winter I've this consulting room for just as long as I can bear to be confined in a brick building.' She handed Jennie a toasting-fork. 'Cook the muffins, please. We'll eat, and then talk more.'

Here's a rum go, Jennie thought, the fire scorching her cheeks as she concentrated on the toasting. The cat, alerted, received his share of the feast then washed his whiskered face in appreciation. Zena drew up another cushion and curled up on the floor beside the cat, tickling him in that sensitive spot under the jaw. His eyes closed in ecstasy, while Jennie watched her from beneath lowered lashes. She did not fear her but had the Eastender's suspicion of gypsies, though could not help being impressed. Zena's lithe figure, her fingers ablaze with antique rings, the way her robe opened at the throat to reveal her olive skin, made her seem like a queen.

'I'd like to stay 'ere forever,' Jennie heard herself saying, without realising that she was thinking aloud.

'And I'd love to have you, but it isn't to be.' Zena slanted her a glance. 'Not yet, child – not yet.'

'But you'll let me come again?' This seemed terribly important to Jennie.

'Hush, be patient. Tell me, when were you born?'

'In October – the seventeenth, I think it was.' Jennie had been given these details at the orphanage.

'As I thought, an air sign. You were born under Libra. I'd like to know where and at what hour, but I suppose it's no use asking you that.'

She took one of Jennie's hands in hers, staring down at the roughened palm. She sighed as she stared, and let the hand drop abruptly, then she stood up and walked to the table.

'What is it?' Fear rippled through Jennie, though she tried to hold on to the feeling of warmth and contentment. It was slipping away like sand running between her fingers. 'What did you see?'

Zena controlled herself, sat down in the carved chair and lifted the square of black velvet shrouding a crystal ball cradled on a wooden stand. 'Matters that I'll confirm with this,' she said solemnly. 'Take the chair opposite me.'

'I ain't got much money,' Jennie said bluntly, though doing as she was bidden. 'If Royalty comes to you, then it must cost a packet.'

'I don't charge friends,' Zena answered simply. 'I'm not expecting any clients till after dark. They come by hackney cab, and slip in here like criminals, afraid their friends will mock them. Yet, later, they whisper of my predictions to intimates who, in their turn, make appointments with me.' She smiled encouragingly. 'Hold the crystal. Don't be frightened.'

'I've never done nothing like this before.' It's all tricks, Jennie was thinking, tricks and lies. She won't take me in with her mumbo-jumbo.

'It may be your first time, but it won't be your last,' Zena said, fingers playing with her talismanic necklace as if it were a rosary. 'I know your life has been hard. I feel sorrow all about you, but there's courage, too. You're a fighter.'

Jennie wanted so much to tell her, to let it pour out like pus from a suppurating wound but something was stopping her, and she realised that it was Zena herself who did not wish to be influenced before scrying.

'The world is an 'ateful place!' she burst out, clenching her fists till the knuckles shone chalk-white. 'That bloke upstairs. 'Ees a part of it, but I'm going to use 'im to get on.'

Zena held up her hand, silencing her. 'Take up the crystal so that it can absorb your vibrations, then pass it to me.'

Jennie hesitated, till Zena lifted the shining ball and placed it in her hands. It was smooth and filled with the reflections of the room, images grown small to fit within the globe. It generated a curious warmth. Not quite sure what was expected of her, Jennie held it between her palms. After a few moments Zena took it, replaced it on the rest and drew it closer. Then she held her hands around it, not touching, merely hovering, and stared over it at Jennie, struck by her beauty.

She was more than merely pretty – a memorable girl, despite the cheap clothes, the accent, the total lack of polish. Hers was not a face easily forgotten, and she held her head proudly on that slim neck. She was too thin, but her body had the promise of a glorious ripening. Her hair was dark red, thick and ringleted, her eyebrows a shade fairer, arched in an expression of mute questioning above the amber eyes which burned in echo of the fury that had possessed her since the moment of her birth. Zena felt the blast of this rage and trembled over the shiny ball. Who was this girl? Child, angel or devil? There was a hard inner self buried deep within her that no amount of kindness could reach.

She looked into the sphere. It became opaque, and she knew the swaying, moving motion within it foretold the coming of a vision. Zena was a true seer. She was gifted with the 'sight', though at times she faked it, when customers bored her and she could tell them nothing good. This is what most of them paid their money to hear – tales of riches and luck and love. Now she stared steadily into the crystal's depth. A black mist gathered, then, slowly, the darkness divided. Forms and figures appeared.

She saw a face that reminded her of Jennie, but wasn't her. A girl in a fashionable gown was searching for something – or someone. Zena saw a great mansion, servants, knew that this fortunate creature lived in luxury and yet she was in danger and would be unhappy soon. Then she was obscured by other pictures, seeming to rush back in time like a child's flicker-book. Jennie grown young again, ragged, abused – a man filled with unnatural lusts in a dark room – the child running in disgust, sleeping in the cold streets, seeking work, any work in order to keep body and soul together. Unending toil, humiliation under which her proud spirit smarted – then above all and through all, her voice singing . . .

Forward in time to the future – that voice would make her a fortune, but at what cost? Zena was fascinated yet repelled by the rapdily shifting images. Tears ran unheeded down her cheeks.

'What is it you see?' Jennie's anxious questions brought her out of her trance.

Zena looked across at her with eyes that were filmed over, and the expression on her face was terrible to witness. 'I can't explain, only describe what I see. What I *feel* is more difficult to define. There are trials ahead of you, trouble beyond anything you've yet experienced.'

'Gawd! Is that all you can say?' Jennie shouted scornfully, disappointed because she had been expecting to be told of a handsome prince coming to save her, at the very least. 'Ain't I suffered enough? All them damn people bossing me around – damn men trying to fuck me! Cold, hungry, tired out! Can't you promise me something better than that?'

'Oh, yes – you'll get everything you've ever dreamed of, but the price will be high.'

'I don't care! When will it 'appen?' Jennie tossed her head defiantly, thinking: Bert's going to help me. I'll use that nasty little turd, then tell him to go stuff himself!

'In a year, maybe two. Your life will change beyond imaginging.'

'Shall I be rich. Shall I dance and sing on the stage?' Jennie demanded in a loud, strong voice. She was filled with energy. This room, this woman, had healed her and given her hope. It was as if she was drawing on the gypsy's life force, sucking it into her own body.

Just for an instant Zena's eyes held hers over the scrying-ball, then she looked down, as if seeking solace in the crystal. When she spoke again, she sounded alarmed. 'Yes, you 'll be rich. All will come to you: wealth, power, the stage, the limelight – even love, though not in the way you expect it. But, my dear, be careful!'

'I don't understand –' Jennie began.

'Listen to me!' The urgency of Zena's request forced her to pay attention. 'I see such things here, incredible things. They come thick and fast. You'll travel, and in the travelling your fame will increase. Power as well, but it will be material power, not spritual. I see you covered in jewels, wearing silk and furs – everything that money can buy shall be yours. Men will love you – adore you.'

'But that's wonderful!' Jennie exclaimed, clapping her hands together 'I've always known some'ow that it'll be mine.'

'There's no doubt about it, but if you're not careful you'll become ruthless in the process.' Zena's expression was one of foreboding. 'Is this what you really want? Would you trample on other to get your way?'

'No,' Jennie answered quickly, but she was lying. 'I'll be good and kind. I'll give money to them what needs it. Why should riches made me bad? Oh, tell me some more.'

Zena pushed the crystal away, and sagged in her chair, suddenly old. 'Not now.'

'Please look again. Please!' Jennie could see that she was exhausted, was aware that Zena had already done more than enough for her, but something remorseless within prompted her to argue.

'I can't. But I'll tell you this – there is a woman somewhere who is very close to you. I saw her at the beginning of the sitting. I think you're related to her.' Zena placed a hand on either arm of the chair and sat straight, eyes closed, breathing deeply and regularly.

'I ain't got no relatives,' Jennie said, going to her side and gently touching her on the shoulder. 'Mam died when I were a nipper. Dad, too – so Ma Baggot told me. She were the woman what took me over, and that geezer upstairs is 'er son.'

'Watch him,' Zena warned, moving stiffly from the chair. 'He could harm you.'

'I can deal with that mucky lizard, don't you worry! I'll eat 'im for breakfast!'

Zena gave a rueful smile and shook her head as she settled on the couch. The cat leapt on to her lap. She caressed his silky fur, and his rumbling purr joined the pop and crackle of the fire. Jennie felt herself dismissed but delayed the moment of leaving, saying, 'Does it always tire you out? This crystal gazing, I mean.'

'Not always. You're special, child. I owe you a debt. I'm not sure what, but it is to do with our past – the wheel of rebirth – karma.'

'I don't understand.' Jennie was confused, making a note to look up that strange, foreign word in the scruffy, coverless dictionary she had unearthed from a neighbour's dustbin. 'You looks all in. Can I make you another cup of tea?'

Zena shook her head. 'I just need to rest a while. I'm better already. I try to do good, and good always filters back to the giver. Although I'm at the beck and call of my fellow creatures, I can truthfully say that I love my work. All the riches of the world wouldn't tempt me to barter the gift I've been blessed with.' She held the cat against her breast, looking down into his adoring eyes. 'Isn't that so, my wise one?'

Jennie put on her hat, though she was reluctant to leave. 'I'd better be going. Thanks for everything. Can I come again?'

'If you wish, though I can't guarantee that I'll be here. The Romany never stays long in one place. But we'll meet again, I'm sure. It's written in the Book of Fate,' Zena answered dreamily. 'Remember, little one, the darkest hour is always before the dawn. Be wary, for you could destroy yourself. May the Blessed Virgin watch over you.'

Jennie's feet dragged as she went towards the door. She looked back once. 'Thank you,' she whispered.

Zena appeared to be asleep. Only the cat observed Jennie's departure. Very quietly, she let herself out of the door.

Chapter Five

'Coffee, *monsieur*?' the waiter asked, bowing slightly from the waist, immaculate in black, a damask napkin over one arm.

'Yes, and a cognac, too.'

The man seated on one of the long, red plush-covered seats ranging the walls did not look up as he replied. He was engrossed, using the back of the menu to make a sketch of the woman at the next table who was wearing an outrageous hat. A bird-of-paradise had been slaughtered for its adornment, the brilliant plumage spreading across the huge brim. Women! he thought, half irritated, half amused. They'll go to any lengths in the name of fashion.

It was early evening in the Café Royal, and the sound of Regent Street traffic was muffled. Through the frosted opacity of the windows he was dimly aware of a passing horse-drawn bus, and the shadows of men and women trailing like ghosts through the rain, but within those opulent precincts it was easy to forget the damp, greasy pavements, the dreariness of London in winter.

The café was noted for its comfort and impeccable service. It had a reputation of being the centre of the capital's Bohemia, and within its lofty, spacious rooms artists and writers gathered, men of the turf and boxing-ring, too. One might bump into actors, jockeys, pugilists, accompanied by their managers or trainers. There was always a selection of women. Some were society ladies who considered themselves to be *avant garde* and liked to fraternise with the racy Chelsea crowd, boasting about it to their friends over tinkling tea-cups in sedate drawing-rooms next day. Then there were artists' models and actresses with an eye on the main chance, some employed and some not. It was the haunt of perfectly respectable people as well, drawn there by the superlative French cuisine.

In the upstairs dining-room with its medallioned walls, those who understood about good food and good wine delighted to eat. The café had a wonderful cellar of wine, the brandies were superb, and the Burgundies equalling them. But tonight Richard Sinclair did not feel like eating. A coffee and drink was all that he required. He had not dressed for the occasion either, wearing a tweed suit and soft-collared shirt, a cravat instead of a tie. His curly-brimmed felt hat lay on the seat beside him, along with his Ulster overcoat.

He held the menu away from him, critical of the caricature. It wasn't bad. He swiftly added a caption: 'From the Café Royal Zoo. Fine feathers don't necessarily make fine birds!' He knew an editor who would take it for his scurrilous radical magazine. Richard had already had several sketches and photographs printed there.

He could almost hear his mother's voice saying, 'It's a dreadful publication. Why do you mix with such people? I can't understand you.'

He smiled to himself as he sipped the excellent coffee. No, the Honourable Lady Sinclair, widow of Sir Donald, never could and never would understand her youngest son. There had been an almighty rumpus when he had announced his intention of taking a room at the top of a rambling house in Holland Park, instead of residing with her in Berkeley Square. She had stormed and protested in vain, for when Richard made up his mind nothing would shake him.

'An artist! You want to be an artist? Ha! A disreputable pack!' she had cried, rustling about her drawing-room in an agitated manner.

Richard, very nearly as angry, had glared back at her, loving and despising her, this faded beauty who still had her train of admirers. She was dictatorial, snobbish and, in an effort to make herself look younger, dressed in styles that did not suit her. He thought her jealous, touchy and acquistive, and was heartily sick of the empty courtesies and meaningless formalities with which she screened herself from reality.

'What do you know of them?' He had swung round on her from the window where he had been staring out at the vista of bare trees and wet grass set behind railings in the centre of that elegant square – a secluded oasis of green – for the use of residents only.

'Plenty!' Her answer had taken him by surprise. 'Have you forgotten that when I was a girl I had my portrait painted by Dante Gabriel Rossetti? Oh, yes, I was one of his languid damozels, and he made me look wan-faced and consumptive! He tried to make love to me, too! Imagine that?'

'Did he succeed?'

'Oh, you – you! You're useless! Worthless! Why couldn't you have gone into the army, like your youngest brother?'

There had been several such scenes before she realised that argument was pointless. Richard had moved into his studio, set up his easel and his photographic equipment, and had never been happier. To be able to come and go at will, answerable to none, offered him a freedom unknown till then. Since he was born his life had been organised by nannies, then teachers, and finally, by the dons at Oxford, though there discipline had been more relaxed. Now he was twenty-six, and taking his first step towards the fulfilling of his ambitions. He wanted to draw, but more than this was a desire to make use of the camera as a means of creative expression.

Richard had always been a rebel. Born into power and status he had, much to the consternation of his mother, sought the company of the lower orders. He loved the simple people who worked on the family estate, enjoyed hobnobbing with grooms and servants, appreciating their wit, their native cunning, their knowledge of how to survive in a harsh world. At university he had met up with other earnest young men who chafed at the injustice of a political structure that insured the rich remained rich and the poor remained poor. Though cushioned by an allowance which he could not afford to spurn, he ached to earn money by his skills, a concept that his mother found incomprehensible. In her book gentlemen did not soil their hands with work of any kind.

Richard had finished his coffee and gone on to the brandy, holding the balloon-shaped glass between his palms and inhaling the bouquet. The café was filling up, and his attention sharpened as he saw a group enter the room. Their leader waved his cane in greeting and guided his companions among the chairs and tables until they reached him.

'Richard, old chap! I thought we might find you lurking here,' he said in a rich, rolling voice.

'Sit down, Everett. D'you want a brandy? Waiter!' Even as he called for service Richard rose to his feet, for one of their company was a girl. No lady by the look of her, but it had been drilled into him that a gentleman did not remain seated while any female, with the exception of a servant, was standing.

Everett pulled out a chair for her, then, after a short consultation regarding their drinks, began the introductions. 'You already know Albert Baggot, I believe, but let me present Miss Jennie Blossom. She has ambitions to tread the boards. Isn't that so, my dear? Jennie, meet Mr Richard Sinclair.'

'How d'you do,' Jennie said, looking around her in wonder whilst trying to give the impression that she went to places like that every night of the week.

'I'm 'er agent,' Albert put in, bracing his thighs to rock his chair on its back legs as he glanced round the room with a self-satisfied smirk, convinced that he fitted in perfectly. He had spent a long time in preparation and was wearing his newest suit and brown boots. The barber had oiled his hair till it was glossy, and shaved him closely. He reeked very high of eau-de-Cologne.

'I'm pleased to meet you, Miss Blossom.' Richard looked at her gravely, wondering where Everett had found her.

He had intended to do no more than acknowledge her, but discovered that he could not look away, suddenly aware that she was something more than one of his friend's little cocottes. Despite her tasteless gown, feather boa and flamboyant hat, she carried herself regally, and her figure was enchanting with rounded hips, a tiny waist and full bosom.

He could see that her hair was remarkable, even though she wore it piled up and covered by that vulgar hat. Desire tingled through him to his fingertips: the desire to unpin it, to see its curling mass coil about her shoulders, to have those heavy, gleaming waves fall over him like a russet curtain, and he knew a sudden spasm of jealousy against the men who had already had this experience. There was little doubt in his mind that she was a prostitute.

She's young, he reflected, and felt pain and pity, very young, under sixteen most likely. Forbidden fruit. Jail-bait. Yet her eyes held wariness and wisdom and hardness beyond her years. Who the hell was she? And from which sleazy child-brothel had Everett extracted her?

Shyness was a failing from which Jennie had never suffered and she held his searching stare, registering a personable man with brown, crisply waving hair and a moustache and clipped beard several tones lighter. His eyes were deep blue and diabolically clever, burning, energetic eyes, shaded by long lashes, and the peaked brows above them gave him an ironic, quizzical expression. He was tall and muscular, his supple shoulders suggesting that he enjoyed strenuous sport – tennis, rowing, or something similarly taxing.

Everett Braithwaite was pleased at the effect she was having. Every man in the room was goggling, and it was *he* who had first claim. Albert had introduced her to him several days ago, suggesting her as a model, but so far she had refused to take her clothes off, neither had she yielded to him. Such modesty was challenging, for Everett was unused to modesty, especially from women of her class.

He had plenty of money and a certain swaggering attraction, and played at being an artist whereas in reality he had chosen this occupation as a means of enjoying the free and easy life it offered. He had a certain talent for designing pictures which could be reproduced for the mass market, and his father was a North-country industrialist who provided him with a generous allowance and funded exhibitions of his work. Braithwaite the Elder was proud of his son, proud of the education he had given him, proud that he mingled with the right people and was doing well for himself.

'Our Everett's come up in the world,' he was fond of boasting to his partners in the boardroom of the steel works he owned. 'Aye, the lad's living in London, mixing with the nobs. No, he didn't want to come into the business and that's all right by me. I've plenty of brass, and nothing will stand in the way of him and his sisters having the best of everything. We weren't born quality, but we'll be quality afore we're through, by God. I want grandchildren who'll take precedence over me, even though they may laugh at my thick accent and rough manners.'

Everett hardly bothered to remember his background these days, except when he was forced to go to Sheffield now and again to take part in some tedious family reunion held in the hideous red-brick monstrosity of a mansion his father had had built. It was as if he had always lived in London, his voice bearing no tell-tale Northern trait, on equal terms with men like Richard.

Yet even though to all intents and purposes he wore the mantle of a gentleman, beneath the surface he was as ruthless as his father, particularly when it came to women. With the stubborn arrogance inherited from a self-made man, he rode roughshod over anyone who stood in his way. Jennie's haughtiness had made him doubly determined to have her, by fair means or foul.

She was sitting next to him at the table. He reached out and took her hand in his. She did not resit, and the feel of those fingers was strange to his touch, being both cold as ice and yet, in some peculiar way, suggestive of hidden fire. It was odd, and not entirely pleasant, neither was the watchful expression in her eyes.

'Enjoying yourself?' he asked, trying to fight that feeling, then he looked across at Richard. 'I think we should have some champagne, don't you?'

Jennie did not withdraw from him, but neither did she respond when he squeezed her thigh. She sat there aloof while a heady sensation of power surged through her. These men all wanted her! She could tell that by their hot glances, their smiles. She would have them eating out of her hand before long! Gentlemen they may be, but they were fools, every one – as foolish as the labourers who had lusted after her in the pub.

She'd already started with Everett, playing him like a fish on a hook, and she glanced at him sideways from beneath her lashes, a tiny, secretive smile hovering over her carmined lips. Yes, he'd do, to begin with. He was a large man, not tall, but heavily built with broad shoulders held well back. Coarse-featured, already running to fat, he had two incisive streaks running from the sides of his nostrils to the edge of his mouth and a dark beard forming a sharp wedge on his chin. Attractive? Not to her. She felt no more than a sort of dubious respect for him because he had money and knew his way around.

The champagne arrived in its ice-bucket. The waiter made a great show of pulling the cork. The wine frothed out, spilling into their glasses. Jennie had never tasted champagne before, the bubbles tickling her nose, the sweet liquid trickling over her tongue and down her throat, settling warmly in the pit of her stomach. It was good. She drank another glass. So this was what the swells drank, was it? I'm here, in the Café Royal, drinking champagne! Not bad for a girl who's just starting her career, she thought, and even managed to smile at Albert Baggot.

He had done what he promised: found her a room, introduced her to his boss, John Sefton and taken her to have her photograph taken, footing the bill with a dismissive wave of his hand. He had also paid for new clothes, insisting that she must dress well or she would never make her mark. At first she had demurred, hating to be indebted to him, but Albert would have none of this. A loan, that's what it was. She could pay him back when she started making money.

Sefton had been encouraging when she sang for him, though suggesting that she really needed more experience and should take dancing and singing lessons. This had depressed her, but Albert refused to share her gloom. He'd soon find her work, he had declared. The artists were always on the look-out for models. She could pose for them and pay for her lessons out of her earnings. The photographer had been raving on about her, too. He wanted to take more pictures, though it would be helpful if she'd consent to show a bit more leg. She had nothing to worry about. She was to leave everything to Albert.

Maybe he's not such a bad stick after all, she thought through an alcoholic blur, resting her elbow on the table and cupping her chin in her hand. A pal, that's what he says he is, my pal. He hasn't touched me since that time in his office, behaving like a regular gent. Zena must have been wrong about him. Where is she? I called on her again but she wasn't there. The room was locked and no one seemed to know anything about her. Taken to the road again, had she? Restless feet, gypsy feet. I miss her.

Tears filled her eyes. She wanted to lay her head down in her arms and cry. Someone, she was not sure who, filled her glass again. She drank it, felt better – so this is how wine will taste when I'm a star, she thought. I'll have champagne for breakfast, dinner, tea and supper! Won't drink anything else!

The circle round the table had grown larger – male faces, male eyes, male smiles. She heard titles being bandied about – Lord This and the Duke of That – saw evening suits, trailing white silk scarves – heard cultured, drawling accents. They clamoured to talk to her, slapped Everett on the back, told him he was a lucky dog. All except Richard – she was aware of this – how he just watched her, saying little, his compelling eyes speaking volumes. She was offended by what she read there. He thinks I'm a slut! Damn him, I'll show him. I'm a singer, an entertainer – not a tart.

'I want to dance!' she announced, swaying to her feet.

A cheer went up. This seemed to delight them, and she smiled widely, happier than she had ever been before. They wanted to see her dance, to hear her sing.

'Of course you shall dance, sweetheart!' shouted Everett, and she saw that he had an arm about Albert's shoulders. They were both grinning. 'But they don't permit dancing in the Café Royal.'

'I *want* to dance!' she stamped her foot, staggered, felt arms supporting her. It no longer mattered who owned those arms. She snatched up one of the bottles and raised it to her lips, swallowing deeply, then repeated, 'I want to dance *now*!'

The manager of the café was at Everett's side. She could not hear clearly what he was saying. It was something about too much noise, and would *monsieur* very kindly leave? A pity, and he hated to ask, but the other customers – there had already been complaints.

'That's all right, sport,' Everett assured him, swinging his scarlet-lined opera cloak over his shoulders, and picking up his top hat and cane. 'Call us a couple of hansoms, there's a good fellow.'

'Don't want to go,' she grumbled, lower lip rolled out in a pout. 'Want to dance.'

'So you shall,' Everett murmured reassuringly, clipping her about the waist. 'Can you do the cancan?'

''Course. Any bugger can do the bloody cancan,' she replied with drunken scorn.

'That's fine. We'll go back to my place. And Billy will play the piano for the lady, won't you, Billy?' Everett demanded of a thin youth with a monocle and receding chin. Billy nodded eagerly.

'Count me out,' Richard said as he got up from the table and picked up his overcoat.

'No?' Everett cocked an eyebrow at him. 'It's going to be a good night, I promise you. Who knows what may happen before it's over?'

'That's what I'm afraid of.' Richard's strong mouth turned down at the corners. 'I've some work to do, and have had quite enough to drink as it is.'

'Suit yourself, but you'll miss out on the action. Ain't that so, Baggot?' And he winked at Albert who was leaning on the back of a chair for support, eyelids reduced to slits in his flushed face.

'That's so, guv.' His speech was thick.

'It better be.' Everett's bonhomie turned to sudden menace and he seized Albert by the lapels, dragging him up and pinning him against the wall. 'I've paid you enough, you shifty sod, and I want something for my money!' He set him down on his feet with a force that made his teeth rattle.

Jennie heard the manager say the cabs were waiting outside. She found that she had lost a shoe somehow, and everyone crawled around searching. It was held aloft triumphantly. She was too drunk to put it on, or walk, so two gentlemen made a chair of their arms and wobbled to the door, amidst hectic cheers from other patrons. Cold, drizzle, the kindly, bewhiskered face of a cabby . . . Then there was the musty interior of the hansom, a body against her, hands groping her. Everett's or someone else's? She wished it was Richard's, and wanted to weep because he had refused to come. The wheels rumbled and the streets flashed past. In the fleeting light of a lamp she saw that it was Everett.

'Oi! Leave off! Stop pawing me!' She pulled away, huddled in the corner. God, I must be careful! Too much to drink. He'll take advantage. No, he won't. He's a gent. They're all gents. I shall be safe with them.

'Don't be silly. No harm in a cuddle. Can't you see that I'm madly in love with you,' he whispered hoarsely.

'That's what they all say,' she retorted, but wondered just the same. It was the first time anyone had declared love for her. She couldn't take him seriously, could she?

The motion of the cab was that of a stormy sea. Her stomach rose, and sour saliva ran into her mouth. Swimming flecks of blackness almost blinded her. 'I'm going to chuck up,' she warned, and was sick over the floor.

He gave her his handkerchief, but coldly, as if dismayed by this turn of events. 'What you need is some more champagne. You'll feel fine when we get to my house.'

The cab stopped. She was helped out, her legs quaking, still queasy. There was much noise from her companions. They were banging on a door with their canes, hallooing loudly as when catching sight of their prey whilst hunting. The house was one in a terrace of five dwellings in a quiet Mayfair cul-de-sac. A footman let them in.

Jennie floated across the threshold, lights dazzling her, a hall tiled in ochre and white chequered square, like an enormous chess-board, stretching before her. Stairs winding up and up, a landing, more stairs and then a room that appeared to go on forever, with a vast uncurtained north-facing window. Standing beneath it, she could see the stars twinkling between scudding clouds. They seemed to be touching the glass.

Corks popped, a fusillade of miniature artillery. Everyone had brought bottles of champagne with them. Billy, she thought his name was Billy, began to play the upright piano, its fretwork front backed by green satin. He thundered out a popular song and she heard herself singing, the gentlemen roaring the chorus and banging on the floor, in much the same way as her erstwhile customers at the Bell and Crown.

Her glass was forever brimming, no matter how often she drained it. Everett had been right. She didn't feel sick any more, just light-headed and oh so happy. They liked her! Albert's face materialised out of the dimness beyond the shaded light standing on top of the piano. Then she saw him slide slowly, almost gracefully, to the carpet. He lay there prone, oblivious to people stepping over him. Was it then or later that she ceased singing and began to dance? The sequence of events was not important. Jennie's mind was like a book with scattered pages that night, and nothing made any sense.

She wanted to lie down but the gentlemen were shouting for the cancan. Another glass of champagne and she was ready to please them, as arch and suggestive as any brazen Paris hussy, hitching up her skirts and frilly petticoats, displaying cambric drawers, black stockings and stilt-heeled button boots as she kicked her legs head-high. She was dreaming that she was on a stage, under the spot-light, listening to the tumultuous applause of an admiring audience – then she blacked out.

Later she was lying on her back on a divan, feverish and dry-mouthed. Her bodice was open, her breasts naked. Someone was kissing them. She felt his weight on her body, wanted to protest, to get away, but was unable to speak or move a muscle. At that moment a man's voice came from behind her head. She didn't know who spoke but he said,

'She's coming round, Everett. Have another drink, Jennie,' and he poured champagne between her lips. It dribbled down her chin, her throat, her breasts. Someone was licking it off.

She could not see him, or anything else, clearly for more than a moment at a time. The light of awareness kept flickering, as if some sort of shutter passed intermittently over her brain. She was so tired, no longer wished to go home, merely to sleep.

'That's a good girl. Now don't struggle. We're not going to hurt you. Hold her arms, chaps, and grip her ankles. That's it. You'll get your turn later.'

She was certain that this was Everett talking. His hands were on her thighs. There was cold air on her skin where her underclothes should have been. His fingers were searching, invading. Had he suddenly grown four hands? She felt them on her breasts, too, stroking her nipples.

No, she wanted to scream, don't – I can't – I *won't* – but her tongue refused to work. There was something else, not just his fingers, something large, hurtful, thrusting into her. She shut her eyes and the light through the lids was scarlet scratched with purple.

'My God! She *is* a virgin!' Everett exclaimed, panting with exertion. 'Baggot wasn't lying after all!'

Pain shot through the haze, violent agonising pain. Then it faded into blackness as Jennie plunged, whirling, into oblivion.

Twin rows of lamps hung over the river from Battersea Bridge, reflected in the dark, oily surface. There was no sound but the tide ebbing from the Thames mud with lapping, sucking noises against the Chelsea Embankment. A hush held London in thrall, that dead time just before dawn when the world seems to be in suspension, slung between night and day. Vapour drifted over the surface of that busy river which had kept its secrets for centuries. The sky was clear and the moon, having nearly finished her course, lay in the black cushion of the heavens, pallid, ghastly, like a dying thing.

Jennie saw its pock-marked face staring down as she lifted her weighted lids. She closed them again with a groan. Her head felt as if it had been kicked by a mule. Her whole body had its own particular smart, then the pain centred, pulsed, throbbed in the region between her legs. Where was she? What had happened to her? It was no use hiding behind the darkness of her eyes. The will to survive refused to be disobeyed, no matter how much she longed to die.

Yet she lay on the bench for a while longer, curled up into herself, arms clasped about her against the cold, trying not to think, but struggling to remember, fragments of the night's events drifting like a mirage, difficult to grasp, fading, coming back. The pain squeezing remorselessly at her temples could not be ignored, a skull-splitting, thumping headache. She wanted her bed back in the lodging-house, needed desperately to crawl into its womblike softness, to shelter there for ever, never stirring, never walking the streets or facing human beings.

Public transport would be running soon, though the streets were still deserted. I'll get a bus home, Jennie thought, then, panicking, felt around in her pocket. Her purse was still there, thank God! Whatever else had taken place under cover of darkness at least she had not been robbed. She sat up, though the effort cost her dear. The Embankment stretched away on either side of her, electric bulbs strung along its length like a giant's necklace. She knew it well, with its elaborate wrought-iron railings, and benches placed at regular intervals so that people might rest while admiring the view. There was a row of Regency houses behind their neat gardens on the other side of the road.

The lamps were losing their brilliance, and a kind of greyness began to creep over everything, the stars going out, one by one. A restless trilling filled the air as the sparrows awoke. Second by second the greyness lightened and the curve of the Embankment grew clearer. With daylight and the return to consciousness came anger, and bowel-churning fear. Cold drops of seat broke out on Jennie's brow.

They'd dumped her there, those villains, and the ringleader was Everett! How could they be so cruel, callously leaving her where anything could have befallen her in that deserted spot? I could have been murdered, she thought with growing indignation. Murdered and thrown into that sinister, uncaring water to end up, a rotting corpse, at Greenwich or further. Maybe hauled out with a hooked pole by the river police. What an end to my career!

There was a sluggish pink glow in the sky now, a smouldering pinkness which quickly faded into dirty grey. The day had dawned and reality could no longer be delayed. Jennie examined her wrecked self very gingerly. Her jacket was intact but her bodice was ripped. The hem of her skirt had come down in one place as if her heel had caught in it during a struggle. Her petticoats were intact, stockings wrinkled down about her ankles, but there was no sign of her underwear. They raped me, she thought, riven with dread. Got me drunk and raped me. Jesus Christ, I'll kill them! I swear I will! I don't care if I swing for it!

Images of vengeance burned in her brain as she got up and limped unsteadily towards a bus stop. Time held no meaning, though it was half an hour before an omnibus came into view, the enamelled signs on its sides glowing. The driver saw Jennie and pulled on the reins, in command from the vantage point of his high perch at the front, bowler hat placed firmly on his head, a mackintosh cape about his burly shoulders, big hands in gloves controlling the pair of sturdy horses between the shafts who were snorting and blowing impatiently.

Jennie climbed aboard, edging along the slatted seat. It hurt to sit, she discovered. The small oil-lamps were still burning, and there were very few passengers, only an old man in a frayed overcoat who coughed continually and spat on to the floor. A young couple at the back sat holding hands as they pretended to read a newspaper. Jennie gave them a glance and then looked away, more desolate than ever because they were in love and saw nothing more than each other's eyes.

The conductor jumped on the running-board and cried a cheerful, 'Fares, please!' as the bus jerked into motion.

When Jennie reached the rundown apartment house, she dragged herself up the short flight of steps, into the hall, and ascended the stairs to her room. Her heart was beating like the wings of a trapped bird in the cage of her ribs. She forgot that she hated her dingy lodgings. Now its decaying walls offered sanctuary. Even the ever-present smell of cooked cabbage overlaid with fried kippers was welcoming. Jennie fumbled for her key, dropped it twice, then managed to insert it in the lock. The door swung open and she was inside, slamming it shut, leaning back against it.

She closed her eyes with a sigh. Privacy, a space in which to examine the damage, though it would not be possible to assess its far-reaching effect yet. Jennie was not a church-goer and hardly ever said a prayer, but now, from the depths of her soul – Dear God, she prayed, don't let me be pregnant.

The room was damp and cold. She went to the single sooty window and pulled the curtains aside, then turned to the mirror hanging above the wash-stand. Hatless. They hadn't bothered to put on her hat. Her hair-pins had gone, too, and the long curls covered her shoulders, tangled, untidy, framing the white mask of her face. There were dark circles beneath her eyes.

She took off her jacket and began to undress, tugging at buttons with trembling fingers. She returned to the mirror when she was naked. There were bruises on her arms, bruises, already purpling, on her breasts – and deep imprints left by harsh fingers on the insides of her legs. Blood, too, blood that had run down and dried on the delicate skin.

Her eyes widened in horror as she saw not only blood but another substance also, sticky, sickening. She flinched as she touched her pubis, slid her fingers lower finding soreness and swelling. It was true. Her virginity had been wrested from her without her knowledge or consent. You idiot! she raged against herself. How could you have been so stupid, so vain, silly and gullible!

Cold rage settled around her, and feelings of disgust and guilt. Albert had arranged it. She could see it all now clearly and pitilessly. How much had Everett given him to deliver up the sacrificial lamb? Jennie could almost hear his whining voice,

'She's pure, guv. No, straight up! Would I try to con you? No bloke ain't fucked 'er yet. Take my word for it, squire, you won't catch no nasty disease from 'er. She's clean as a bloody whistle.'

Bastard! Bastard! she raged, beating her fists against the scabby wall. He must be stamped out, exterminated, blotted from sight, swept from the earth! Despair made her pray again, on her knees at the bedside as she had been taught in the orphanage. Oh God, dear Lord, don't let me be pregnant! Please – please –

Exhausted by weeping, she clutched at the quilt, and her sobs subsided. Her teeth were chattering with cold and shock. A bath. This seemed the most important thing in the world. Water to cleanse her body of their filth, those foul men who had violated her. Filled with purpose, she fetched her tatty dressing-gown from its hook behind the door and wrapped it about her body. Then she took up her sponge-bag and a towel. Money. She had to have coins for the gas which heated the copper geyser in the one communal bathroom.

On the landing she met a fusty old woman whose gnarled toes stuck out of holes in her slippers as she waddled in the same direction. Jennie reached the door first and spread her arms across it, almost snarling. Her wild-eyed aspect stopped the woman from arguing. She contented herself with cursing vilely and backing off.

Trembling with haste, Jennie inserted the coin in the slot and turned on the geyser. It coughed and spluttered, then steaming water gushed from its silted interior into the cast-iron bath, rust red at first, then clearing. She let it run, its torrent joined and cooled by cold from the verdigris-coated tap at the end of the tub. Steam arose, thick as a November fog, soaking into the stained wallpaper which was already hanging off in strips.

Water, so warm, so comforting, so clean. She sponged her abused body then lay back and closed her eyes. Peace lapped her, but it was a momentary respite. A thought slashed through her like hot steel. Albert Baggot. Had he taken his turn with her? She shuddered, nauseated by the idea of him satisfying his lust in her unconscious flesh. This was, perhaps, the greatest horror of all.

She leapt from the bath, pulled out the plug and was gone before the water had drained away. Dripping, towel wound round her, she sped for her room and began to dress as rapidly as she was able.

Albert was skulking in his Soho office, having found his way there at daybreak after coming out of his drunken stupor on the floor of Everett's studio. There had been disorder everywhere: bottles, smashed glasses, the smell of flat champagne and cigar smoke. He had let himself out of the front door. Soho was nearer than his lodgings so, like an animal seeking the nearest bolt-hole, he had gone there. He felt ill. Was he wearing his own or someone else's head? He could not be sure.

He filled the aluminium kettle from the tap above the sink, placed it on the gas-ring and waited for it to boil, then he made himself a cup of black tea, sipping it morosely. He regretted overdoing the champagne. Seems like he had missed his chance with Jennie. He had intended to take the masters' leavings, but the wine had defeated him, as far as he could recall. Jennie, Jennie ... maybe that proud little bitch would be more amenable now.

As if conjured by thought, she appeared in the doorway, saw him, marched straight up to him without a word and slapped him hard across the face. He staggered back.

'What's that for?'

Her eyes were alive with fury. Even her hair seemed to spark. 'What d'you think? You vile, slimy, disgusting piece of offal! You sold me. Pretended to be my pal, and then sold me to those bastards!'

Albert retreated to safety. 'I did you a favour.'

'Some bloody favour!'

'No, it's true. Listen, Jen, those toffs, they got plenty of money, more'n you and me'll ever 'ave,' he began, eyes darting shiftly about as he looked anywhere but at her. 'I know you wants to go on the stage, but you can't do it yet. You need cash for lessons, clothes, and you should be seen in posh places – the Café Royal, Romano's. Braithwaite 'as the necessary – I thought you'd see this and get in with 'im, but you wouldn't, so I thinks to myself: 'Ee wants 'er – 'ee'll see her right. What 'arm in softening 'er up so she's more willing?'

'Sod! Greedy little sod!' Jennie ground out. 'Don't try to tell me you did it for my sake. You're a pimp, Bert, a thieving, mother-fucking pimp!'

His face darkened. Really, this row was doing nothing for his liver, and it was like a bit of raw cat's meat that morning. 'Hoity-toity!' he sneered. 'You're a fine one to talk! You come from the gutter. You'd still be there if I 'adn't found you. Even the clothes on your back were bought by me.'

'That's right, and I wish it weren't so,' she fired at him. 'But that don't make me your property, free to do with as you like.'

Albert ventured closer, though keeping well out of arm's reach. 'You ain't my property, I knows that, gal. But did you please Braithwaite? Does 'ee want to see you again?'

'I don't know, but even if 'ee does, I'll tell 'im where to go!' She was spitting venom. 'I suppose you knows what 'appened, bastard! I don't, but I guess 'ee wasn't the only one what dipped 'is wick when I'd passed out with the booze. Did they all 'ave a go? Did *you*, you bloody creep?'

Albert cringed before this raging termagant, trying to explain that he also had been unconscious, and the studio deserted when he woke. Then, in a frantic effort to placate her, he babbled on about the advantages of her becoming Braithwaite's mistress. 'Just for a while, Jen – till you've 'ad your voice trained.'

'Piss off!'

'Aw, Jen, be reasonable,' he pleaded, nearly crawling to her. 'Cripes, but you looks lovely this morning. Getting 'umped don't seem to 'ave 'urt you. Quite the contrary. I've never seen you looking so good.'

It was true that Jennie had raked through her scanty wardrobe, casting aside most of the garments she had once thought smart. Instead she had selected a white blouse and black skirt, off-the-peg but reasonably well-cut. Over this she wore a black overcoat, waisted and full at the back. Her hat was new, of a moss green shade and slightly turned up at the side. Altogether the effect was of a modest middle-class girl. It had originally been purchased on Albert's advice in case she happened to get that audition at the Gaiety Theatre, for the boss, George Edwardes, expected likely candidates to give the impression of refinement.

It was the first time Albert had seen her in it, and even he was impressed by the change it brought about. I hope Braithwaite realises that she's a cut above the rest of the tarts, he thought. Worth far more than the ten guineas I got for letting him have her.

Jennie had gone there intending to give him a piece of her mind and then leave, never to have anything to do with him again, but commonsense was gradually prevailing. She knew that without Albert her chances of success were nil. She would be forced to return to the Bell and Crown and beg for her old job back. She was too uneducated to apply for office work, a typist or secretary perhaps, and employment in a shop was out of the question, again because of her accent and lack of polish. Apart from a determination to spit on Everett if he ever crossed her path, depression loomed as her rage lessened. She no longer cared what happened to her.

Albert could see that some of her fire had died, and he quickly took advantage. She was too fine a piece of merchandise to let slip through his fingers. 'Tell you what,' he began, moving towards the kettle again, 'let's 'ave a cuppa, sit down and talk it over. What d'you say?'

'I'm not going on the game.' She was adamant on this point, but she took a chair and accepted the tea.

'Nobody's asking you to,' he protested. 'All right, you don't want Braithwaite, so what about posing for my friend, the photographer? We can get a good deal out of 'im, and you'll be able to stay in your digs and get in those dancing lessons.'

Weary to death, Jennie reluctantly agreed. Albert was a snake and needed watching constantly, but she had little alternative. What did posing matter now? Stark naked? It no longer seemed important. She had been raped by men she trusted, gentlemen who had seemed so fine, so mannerly and courteous, people she had looked up to. The secret parts of her body had been exposed for usage in ways she could not even begin to imagine. They had had their way, careless of the damage they had done both physically and mentally. She felt she could sink no lower. There was no point in reporting them to the police. No officer would take her word against those of gentlemen. She would be humiliated and ridiculed.

So Jennie began to work for Albert's friend, a smooth operator called Ford Dobbs who had a photographic studio behind his shop in Waldour Street. There, during the week, he took pictures of family groups, businessmen in stiff collars standing by a spreading aspidistra plant, chubby babies lying on white fur rugs or nervous young women wearing their best dresses and chaperoned by a proud mother. A small, neat man with a waxed moustache and relaxed manner, he was polite, helpful, and conveyed complete respectability, but Jennie knew this to be a front. At the weekends he used his skills to produce photographs which would command more money than all the rest put together, if sold undercover in the right quarters.

He took many of her, overjoyed to find someone so compliant, and his favourite one was the first she posed for, thrilling to her expression of utter boredom and indifference. She was like a doll, the epitome of every man's fantasy – with her sulky mouth, her contemptuous, heavy-lidded eyes, the way she stared straight into the camera as she sat there clad in a skimpy chemise. Her breasts were bare, the lacy hem of the shift barely reached the tops of her spread legs, the slim expanse of her thighs exposed, and the tempting dark triangle of hair at their apex. Black stockings covered her from ankle to knee, held in place by fancy garters.

They tried other positions. Jennie on her stomach, propped on her elbows, one leg out straight, the other bent, as a child will lie on a rug reading a story-book. It was charming, innocent even, until the eye travelled to her firm naked buttocks. Jennie bending over to fasten her high-heeled shoe, glancing provocatively over her shoulder, as if to catch the voyeur staring up her short skirt. Jennie resting on a cushion-heaped couch, skirts hitched high to show suspenders and stockings, head back, tongue circling glistening lips, eyes half closed in mock ecstasy, one hand slipped between her legs. The viewer could easily imagine he had caught her indulging in a secret vice.

But this wanton, shameless creature was not Jennie. She followed Ford's directions, lay as he told her, placed her hands where he directed, did as he commanded, but in reality she was miles away, high above the studio, in clear spaces far removed from reality. At the end of each session she dressed behind a screen, put on her neat coat and hat, took the money he gave her. Albert always met her at the door, expecting his cut. She handed it over without a word and went back to her lodgings.

Christmas was near but she did not celebrate, locked in her room, eating her frugal meals, going to bed early to keep warm and save gas, spreading her money on the coverlet and counting it. There was not much, but it was mounting steadily. There would soon be enough for her to seek out a competent singing teacher, and a retired ballerina who would initiate her into the mysteries of the dance.

Two months had passed since her encounter with Everett and his friends, and it was then that Jennie turned her back on God. She had never felt Him to be her friend anyway. Now missed periods, sore breasts where the nipples had changed from pink to brown, and sickness when she lifted her head from the pillow each morning, told her more plainly than any midwife that He had ignored her prayers.

Chapter Six

'I can't agree to it, Charlotte,' Eva said to her rebellious ward in the study at Greyfriars.

'But it's my birthday tomorrow! Surely I may invite whom I please to dinner?' Charlotte stood before her with stormy eyes.

She had expected this reaction, fully prepared to do battle, Eva's obstinacy infuriating her. Throughout the journey to Wiltshire she had been rehearsing this scene in her head and the silent stating of her case had seemed perfectly reasonable then. This was the twentieth century, not the dark ages. Such family feuding sounded like something out of a Bronte novel. But coming face to face with Eva was daunting, and it took every ounce of courage not to waver.

Eva was seated deep in a chair, her back to the window, gazing steadily at the roaring logs set between iron firedogs in the wide stone hearth. The ruddy light of the flames played on oak panelling dark with age, on book-lined shelves, portraits in gilded frames and comfortable leather-upholstered chairs. Watery sunshine filtered through the quaint little oriel window angled in a corner, throwing bright patterns from coloured glass on to parquet flooring. The narrow, recessed casements overlooking the expanse of lawn were hung with crimson velvet drapes held back by thick cords with tassels a foot long. It was a pleasant room where once Tudor ladies had sat sewing. Now it was Eva's study, and Charlotte had passed many a happy hour there – but not today. The atmosphere was tense with the force of their disagreement, both strong-willed women who loved one another, but who had come to the parting of the ways because of Phelan Charteris.

Eva had preceded her to Greyfriars, going early to ensure that all was prepared for Christmas. It was also Charlotte's birthday a few days before the twenty-fifth of December, and Eva had desired to be there alone to plan this celebration. Charlotte had welcomed the separation, taking advantage of it to spend more time with Phelan.

Wilkins had met her and Tilly off the train, and they had covered the distance between the country station to the manor by car. Charlotte had been lost in thought, her nervousness increasing as they reached the uplands. The bleak, exposed roads were bounded by smooth, sculptured fields which caught every change of light, nestled behind dry-stone walls thick with cress-green moss and lichens shaded from rust to black. She had made Wilkins stop for a moment on the hill overlooking the house, never tiring of this first glimpse. Greyfriars lay in a dip in the parklands, an Elizabethan mansion of great size and magnificence. Throughout the centuries additions had been made, but it retained most of its original architecture.

Its long stone façade with regularly placed mullioned windows and slate-tiled roof was mellow with age. A series of fantastically ornamented chimneys reared towards the sky, and some of the walls were enveloped in ivy, giving the impression that the house itself had evolved from the soil like some natural growing thing.

Feasting her eyes on it, Charlotte had been aware of a lump in her throat, for this place was very dear to her and it had looked particularly beautiful that day. The clouds were moving fast, driven by a strong wind, and there had been showers all the way from London. Now the sun had appeared, making Greyfriars' windows and weather-vane glitter before it vanished, hiding behind cloudy veils again.

Charlotte had told Wilkins to move on. Soon the gravel of the drive had showered up beneath the car wheels and, in a short time, she had been running up the stone steps where the dignified Hopkins, unable to control a broad smile, waited to welcome her. Reluctant to see Eva but knowing that she must speak her mind, she had hardly spared a glance at the tall, sparkling Christmas tree in the Great Hall, the piles of presents beneath it, the holly and mistletoe garlands, going straight to the study and into the attack. As she had anticipated, her suggestion that Phelan be invited to dinner had been met with point-blank refusal.

'I'm sorry, Charlotte, but I've sworn never to have that man in my house again. London was bad enough, and he entered uninvited. It was dreadfully rude! Continuation of this friendship is most unadvisable.' Eva hated denying Charlotte anything, especially on her birthday, but she could not reconcile herself to her liking for Phelan.

'Unadvisable for whom? For you? I'm not asking you to make a friend of him, though I can't for the life of me see what you have against him.' Charlotte sat on the arm of a chair, one leg crossed over the other, her full beige shirt draped to the floor.

Once again Eva attemped to explain, though she had no actual damning facts to go on, just a gut feeling. 'He's not suitable – and he moves in a very fast set.'

Charlotte leapt to her feet. 'You don't know him, Eva. If only you'd talk with him, then you'd understand that he's not as black as he's painted.'

Eva tried another approach. 'Look here, Charlotte, we've so much to do. The shop. Have you been there recently? How's Alice?'

'She's well, though tired. They've been inundated with orders for Christmas presents. It seems that every lady in London wants her lingerie made by Alice and her team now.'

Charlotte was proud of their success, and did not neglect this delicate girl and others who had joined the venture. Eva had done a wonderful thing, ignoring the mockery and contempt levelled at her, running the shop at considerable cost to herself, enabling the girls to earn reasonable salaries, striving to create work that had nothing to do with charity.

But she had to admit to herself that she could no longer give it her wholehearted attention. Phelan occupied her thoughts. He had introduced her to a wonderland of delights: symphony concerts; the theatre; the opera house where she had thrilled to the passions of the music dramas. They had gone to the British Museum where, in the Egyptian Room, treasures which he had unearthed in the Valley of the Kings, were already on display. Then there had been intimate evenings spent in his Sloane Square house, where he had captivated her with stories of adventures in the East, and entranced her with his piano playing.

Passion? Oh, yes, she was learning what this meant. Passionate music that ran like fire through her veins; Phelan's kisses that made her ache for more; desire which had never bothered her till she met him, and which now gave her sleepless nights, aching, yearning, beginning to understand why Tilly could not resist Wilkins.

It was bewildering, and she hated herself for permitting this emotional upheaval, but the truth was that she only felt really alive when with him. Gwen was arriving next day to spend Christmas with her, a very excited Gwen who had never before visited Greyfriars and was almost delirious with joy, but even this failed to prevent Charlotte from creating disharmony.

Eva was not insensitive to Charlotte's turmoil and, despite this, she was happy to see her. Life was dull when they were not together. She made an effort, smiled at her and said, 'Why not ask Bernice about Phelan? She's much more in tune with the latest gossip than I? She and Quentin came yesterday with a whole retinue of servants. That woman simply can't travel light! She's brought the children and their nanny. I've opened the nursery for them.'

'Has Freddy arrived yet?' Charlotte needed to see this kindly man who always acted the benign uncle. She, too, wished that Eva would acknowledge his devotion and marry him.

'Yes, so all in all, it should be a splendid Christmas,' Eva said and thought she did not voice it, Charlotte knew that she wanted to add: If *you* behave yourself!

'Phelan's at Hawksdown,' she replied, and wondered why she had not kept silent.

'I know.' Eva's voice hardened. 'For the first time in years the old house will celebrate Christmas.'

'We've been invited over. Andrew Tyler's with him, and Julian,' And what difference does this make? Charlotte questioned inwardly. Eva likes them no better than Phelan.

'I would be surprised if they weren't. The three of them are as thick as thieves – gambling, womanising. Oh, I know they're popular at the moment, public heroes in fact, but their morals leave much to be desired.'

'You hate Phelan, don't you? And anyone associated with him.' Charlotte's lower lip was trembling. She was on the verge of tears, suddenly weary of battling.

'Hatred is too strong a word. I don't go around hating people,' Eva protested, but she wondered if this was strictly true. Phelan had the power to disturb her profoundly and, in return, she wanted no contact with him.

Charlotte had taken to a worried pacing, reminding Eva of a caged tigress with her long strides. So lovely a thing, so young, and in the eyes of someone like Phelan, so innocent. Eva feared for her. But I can't protect her for ever, she thought. I can't shield her from hurt. What am I to do? Frederick sprang to mind. They had already discussed Phelan and his interest in Charlotte. I'll see him again, just as soon as she'd gone to her room, she decided.

'And that's your last word? You refuse to ask Phelan?' Charlotte's mouth felt stiff with fury and she had trouble forming the sentence.

'Yes,' Eva said.

Charlotte flung away from her, making for the door, unsure where she was heading, only knowing that she had to escape. Eva's voice halted her for an instant. 'Where are you going?'

'I'll be back for tea,' she answered coldly, and stalked out.

The Great Hall was deserted. The others must have retired to their rooms or were sitting in the drawing-room, drinking sherry. She did not want to talk to anyone just then. Her only thought was escape, and she fled up the ornate staircase. The beauty of the house permeated the anger that tormented her, forcing itself on her awareness – panelling, antiques, oil-paintings and priceless ornaments, things of which she had always been conscious as part of the comfortable background.

Tilly was in the bedroom, and she looked up with raised eyebrows as Charlotte slammed the door, recognising the storm-signals. Tilly was a loyal girl who had been her maid for three years. She was canny, observant and dependable, loving Charlotte and keeping watch over her. She turned from unpacking garments from suitcases and hanging them in the large wardrobe, noting Charlotte's gesture of exasperation. She waited for the storm to break and it was not long delayed.

'What shall I do, Tilly?' Charlotte demanded, walking across to kneel on the padded seat that followed the length of the bay window, staring at the garden below. 'I've had a row with Lady Eva.'

Tilly nodded, having listened to her grumbling all the way down in the train. Her plumage had been ruffled and no mistake. Eva would be in a bad mood as well. Such a pity for it might spoil the dinner party. She sighed, though appearing to be absorbed in placing undergarments, scarves, stockings and gloves in the drawers of the tall-boy. For some time she had been increasingly worried about her mistress, sharing Eva's suspicion of Phelan and his cronies.

'No doubt she's upset, too, Miss,' she said tactfully, that large-boned girl who was not exactly pretty, but who had, nevertheless, a devastating effect on the opposite sex.

Charlotte ran a finger along the beaded woodwork of the windows frame, eyes nearly black with anger. 'That's not the point, Tilly. She refuses to ask Lord Phelan to dinner tomorrow evening. It's absolutely awful. I want to introduce him to Gwen.'

'I expect she has her reasons. Indeed, he does seem to be wooing you a mite fast, Miss, if you'll pardon my frankness. You don't know much about men, but I *do*. Slippery customers every one, be they workman or toff.' Tilly's broad features were anxious, for she could see that Charlotte was ripe for loving, deny it though she might, and she longed to see her safely married, dreaming of the morning when she might help her don her wedding gown, and then join the other servants in the church to watch her become a bride.

'Why do you all think Phelan's a villain?' Charlotte sprang to her feet, impatience in every movement. Even Tilly appeared to have joined the conspiracy. 'I'm going riding. I don't want to think about it any more.'

For once the perfection of her room failed to console her, though such a lovely place, redolent of history with its fluted panels surmounted by the crests of former occupants. The whole house was like an enchanted castle where it would come as no surprise to encounter people in period costume, even warriors in clanking armour. But Charlotte's pleasure in it was soured, and she ignored the silk needlework hangings glowing with colour, and the four-poster bed with its green brocade curtains.

In a couple of swift steps she reached the wardrobe, yanking her riding-habit from a hanger, searching for her boots. A gallop on Juniper would clear her head, and she was soon ready, the skirt worn over breeches clinging to her hips, the tight-fitting jacket outlining her waist. It took but a moment to pile her hair into a net and clap on her low-crowned topper. She used the servants' stairs to reach the stable-block at the rear of the house.

It was good to be rid of smoky London skies, and the air, though frosty, was warmed by weak afternoon sunshine, good to feel the mare's rippling movements beneath her, and when they passed through the gate Charlotte let her have her head. Almost without thinking she made for the spot which, to her, was the embodiment of Greyfriars, cantering across the park towards the stretch of downs beyond. Juniper knew the way and needed little guidance. The park dropped below them and the wind whipped over open country.

Charlotte reined in, looking down into the valley and across to the opposite slopes. The wintery browns and ashgreys blurred the view, seeming to enfold the rooftops of the cottages. It was satisfying to be up there where the aspect was always breathtaking, no matter the season. Rolling hills, secluded dales, and just outside the village she could see the church, tiny as a toy, with its jumble of tilted headstones. Memories of childhood welled up: harvest festival services, the wonder of the Nativity. Charlotte could almost smell the interior – cool, musty, with its memorial tablets, the latest of which bore Pendral names.

Damn the Pendrals! She wasn't one of them, not really. But who was she and where had she come from? Gwen had not been successful in helping her find out. She dug her heels into Juniper's sides, breasting a rise where, like a beacon, stood one single huge stone, relic of a forgotten age. It dominated the skyline, known as the Black Knight. Charlotte had played in its shadow when a child, unaware then that this monolith had been erected long before the church, village, barns or cottages – before the Romans, before the Druids, before recorded history.

She loved this eerie, isolated spot. Even in midsummer there was always a faint, keening wind whistling round the Knight. She slid from the saddle, letting the bridle trail while Juniper lowered her head to crop the yellowing tussocks. The pitted stone was cool to the touch, and Charlotte rested her cheek against it, seeking reassurance from this timeless monument whose origin and purpose had been lost in the mists of antiquity. She turned so that her back was supported by it, gazing into the distance. The spread of chocolate and ochre fields was like some vast patchwork quilt. Here, a snowy flock of sheep dotted like stars against the green there, the silvery band of the river.

Her attention sharpened as she saw a rider following the path she had taken, now disappearing behind a clump of trees, now reappearing purposefully. As he came nearer, she recognised Phelan. Excitement coupled with annoyance flicked at her raw nerves. Her peace was about to be disrupted. He saw her and waved, the wide-spread stride of his hunter bringing him closer.

'I knew I'd find you here!' His voice reached her faintly, almost obscured by the singing of the Black Knight.

Too late to make a run for it, and did she really want to? Charlotte glanced at Juniper, measuring the distance and deciding that it was not worth the effort. Her respite could only be of short duration for duty demanded that she return to the manor soon. There would be guests arriving that evening, gentry from the surrounding area, farmers and their womenfolk gathering in the Great Hall, following tradition. The carol-singers were due to come, to sing their ancient lays and be rewarded with hot punch and mince-pies, after which the village children would each receive an orange, then a gift from the tinsel-trimmed tree.

Phelan was alongside her now, and her heart skipped a beat. He was at his best in the saddle, seated their like an emperor, back straight, muscular thighs guiding his horse, firm hands on the reins. The melting sensation in her knees angered her, also the fact that she was forced to look up at him.

'Why did you follow me?' she snapped rudely. 'Heavens, there's no peace to be had anywhere!'

Phelan appraised her coolly, then cocked a foot out of the stirrup and dismounted. 'I told you I'd know when your train pulled in to the station, didn't I? I had my spies posted. What's the matter? You're troubled, my angel.' His hand came out to grip her by the upper arm and draw her towards him, roused by her resistance. 'Had a row with Eva about me, I suppose.'

That bloody nuisance of a woman, he was thinking, remembering how he had first met her when they were young, in a spot very like this one. To amuse himself during that boring spell in the country he had talked her into disobeying her father, and then spurned her. He had always resented her, and now took delight in luring her beloved waif away from her.

'Oh, Phelan, I hate quarrelling with her!' Charlotte cried, allowing his arm to settle around her waist, yet pressing her hands against his chest to wedge a space between them. She was aware of the strong beat of his heart beneath her spread fingers.

'I know, darling,' he whispered, while her pulse leapt with that odd combination of fear and excitement.

Heat spread upwards into her cheeks and her brain whirled in confusion, her distress making her vulnerable to his sympathy. She rested her face against the coarse tweed of his hacking jacket. The light touch of his hands burned through her coat, causing an unsatisfied ache within her. Warning bells rang in her head. She could feel herself sliding toward dark and dangerous depths which terrified her.

She looked up at him, the breath catching in her throat. He was so powerful, possessing such easy assurance, and an overweening pride betrayed by the set of his square jaw. Why shouldn't she accept his proposal of marriage? Why not take him as her lover now? For one crazy moment she visualised sinking down on to the grass and letting him do what he willed with her, then she could confront Eva with a *fait accompli*, foiling her plans to keep them apart.

But even in that moment of temptation, she turned her face aside when he sought to capture her lips with his. He cursed quietly, then his mouth travelled on to explore the sensitive area just below her ear. Weakness spread through her limbs, and she was even more frightened.

'Phelan – please!' she begged, tone rising in panic.

He lifted his head and flashed her a devastating smile, the confident smile of the conqueror. 'Charlotte, lovely Charlotte – don't fight it,' he urged, breath warm on her cheek.

She came to herself, stiffened, tried to withdraw, but he held her firmly. In her heart she recognised that he spoke the truth. She was fighting her own nature as much as him, that deeply passionate part of her that she had controlled for so long. She was well aware of its existence, a sweeping tide of hungry yearnings pulling her this way and that.

Phelan's hand cupped her breast, the shock of it forcing her into a renewed effort at escape. If she stayed in his arms a second longer there was no knowing what her eager body might trap her into doing. She pulled away, her hair falling free of the restraining net. They stared into each other's eyes, with the Black Knight as a silent chaperon, and the patient horses nuzzling the grass. Above, a mackerel sky was beginning to streak with fans of pink, mauve and palest green as the sun settled behind the brow of the hill. Evening clouds were piling up fast, and the air was cold. Charlotte shivered, horribly afraid that the friendship she had hoped for would now be at an end.

'Don't rush me,' she pleaded. 'I'm so muddled. I want to see you, want to have you come to Greyfriars, but there's Eva. She's done so much for me.'

'Too much, I fear,' he answered grimly. 'She smothers you.'

She hoped he would not see how close she was to breaking down. 'I thought you understood – were my friend.'

'I am.' He came up behind her, his hands at her waist. 'So much of a friend that I can see you need freedom. Eva or no Eva, I want you to come with me to Italy in a few week's time.'

'It's impossible. Can't you see that? If Eva won't invite you to dinner, then how do you suppose she'll let me go abroad? I can't disobey her, can't hurt her.' She moved her head from side to side, unable to put her jumbled emotions into words.

'But you want to come, don't you? Want to be introduced to my mother as my fiancée? Don't you? Don't you?' He took advantage of that uncertain gesture to bury his lips in the tangle of curls at the nape of her neck. Her sense leapt, every nerve tingling down her spine to her toes at that seductive caress.

'I can't think properly when you do that,' she whispered, then groaned at the full realisation of her position. 'And I've got to think, Phelan –'

'Forget it for now,' he chuckled, pushing the soft tendrils away from her ear and gently nibbling at the lobe. 'Let's go into the copse. No one will see us. I want to show you what love's all about.' His arm tightened, pressing her back against his body, making her aware of his need.

Just for a moment she saw the dark mass of the spinney at

the edge of the moorland, but then her interest was caught and held by the sight of Greyfriars cupped in its hollow far below. Twisted chimney-pots lifted towards the surrounding tree-tops, its walls melting into the background. Wisps of smoke spiralled from some of the stacks, coiling like incense into the evening air, speaking of warm fires, warm food, warm rooms, of home and safety. Phelan offered adventure, the unknown, but was she brave enough to take it yet?

She jerked herself free, ignoring the angry darkening of his brow, and ran for her mare, shouting over her shoulder, 'I'll race you back!'

She did not hear his snarling rejoinder, vaulting into the saddle, heels bobbing against Juniper's belly. Then the ground was racing beneath the flying hooves, her hair tossed across her flushed cheeks, all thought numbed by that pounding beat. One swift glance behind showed Phelan in pursuit. His face was set in grim lines as he gained on her, but the gates were in sight and he could not enter. One final burst of speed and she had reached them. The hard ride had brought relief, but as she slowed the mare to a trot that brief elation died like a snuffed candle.

Phelan was beside her. She gave him a sideways glance, uneasy at his glowering looks, that classic profile turned sulkily away. Her heart sank. She had blundered badly, alienating him, and she now thought this a foolish move. Why was life so difficult? Lord, what a birthday this was going to be!

'I'll not give up,' he muttered, turning his horse's head in the direction of Hawksdown Hall. 'Eva has no right to deny me. Who the hell are the Pendrals anyway? Their ancestors were traders – common money-lenders. Mine were Norman knights who came to England with the Conquest. Greyfriars has only been in their hands for a couple of generations. Hawksdown Hall has always belonged to the Charteris family. She's a jumped-up nobody, and should be glad that I want you.'

'Don't talk about her like that! She's a fine woman, a real lady, no matter what you say. I expect your damned forebears were nothing more than robber barons! You certainly behave like one sometimes.' It was awful to feel so angry with him when all the time Charlotte longed to be back in his arms, experiencing the warring emotions he infused throughout her mind and body.

'Touché!' he jeered, with his sinister smile. 'If the oh-so-noble Eva changes her mind, then send word and I'll come tomorrow.'

'She won't,' Charlotte answered.

He shrugged. 'Who knows? Women are strange beings, even one

as serious-minded as Eva. I shall continue to bombard her with invitations to Hawksdown. Good night, Charlotte.'

'Good night, Phelan,' she said very low, then rode between the gates towards the stable, already bereft because he was no longer with her. It was as if ill-omened stars were gathering force against them.

In the twilight she handed Juniper over to a groom and trudged towards the house. For a moment she gazed up at the pointed gables and uneven rooftops, then the view wavered, fractured across by tears. She fought them off, squaring her shoulders and making for the backstairs, but it was no use. She could feel them, hot and salty, running down her face.

Gwen, usually so talkative, was reduced to 'oohs' and 'aahs' when Charlotte took her on a tour of the house. This happened almost as soon as the car pulled up and Gwen, all excitement, tumbled out. The morning was crisp, cold and sunny, and Charlotte considered Greyfriars to be even more beautiful in winter than in summer, but then, whatever the season, she always decided that it suited the manor better than any other.

Clad in a Shetland wool cardigan and thick shirt, Charlotte had seized her friend by the hand, very nearly dragging her under the archway of the front door. 'Pay your respects to Lady Eva, Gwen, and we'll be off. There's so much I want to show you. Don't worry about your trunk. Hopkins will see to that.'

It was not that Gwen was a stranger to stately homes. She had often visited her paternal grandparents, and their house was massive. Unlike the vicarage, money was never short here, and their holidays at Mapleton Grange were ones of unusual luxury. On the other hand her mother's home, though comfortable and also situated in the country, was a far cry from the Shropshire one. Her people had always been associated with the church, and the atmosphere there was in complete contrast to Mapleton Grange – quiet and tranquil, with no frivolity allowed. Gwen and her siblings preferred the bustle of Mapleton, where something was always going on, but neither house conveyed anything like the grandeur of Greyfriars.

Now the two girls wandered the state rooms together, and Gwen was overcome by the splendour surrounding them. They spoke in murmurs out of respect for the hushed apartments, some of which were never used, keeping their secrets in the dim silence. At last they reached a room rumoured to have been used by Queen Elizabeth on one of her progresses through her kingdom. Gwen paused on the threshold while Charlotte threw back the shutters. The sun streamed in, poking impudent fingers among the sumptuous velvets, the room suddenly filled with light. The figures on the tapestries seemed to dance, and the great four-poster towering towards the ceiling was no longer a gloomy cavern, its formidable faded purple drapes rendered human and friendly.

'I'd love to sleep here!' Gwen exclaimed, and flung herself upon it, bouncing up and down on the silver-embroidered quilt. 'Why doesn't anyone use it?'

'It's the Master Chamber,' Charlotte answered, smiling with pleasure at her friend's delight. 'There's no master at present, only Eva, and she prefers her room in the tower.'

'But there will be one day, when you get married.' Gwen's rounded face stared up at her from the bed's depths, a child still, although she was almost seventeen and filled with romantic notions. 'You'll marry Phelan, won't you? And then he'll be master here.'

Charlotte frowned and drew the woollen jacket closer about her, conscious of how cold these abandoned apartments were, echoing and full of ghosts. Who had suffered there amidst such glory? The women, dominated by harsh husbands or fathers. What agonies had unwilling brides endured in that monstrous bed? Had some of them died within it after giving birth to yet another child? Somehow the idea of Phelan lording it at Greyfriars struck her as unpleasant.

'Nothing's settled, Gwen. Eva doesn't know anything about it, so please don't mention it.'

Gwen nodded solemnly, sitting cross-legged on the bed, still wearing her fur-trimmed hat and outdoor coat for Charlotte had given her no time to change. Her brown eyes were wide as she promised to keep this important secret. 'Do you love him?' she asked.

'I don't know,' Charlotte answered, wishing she was as naive. Gwen always saw matters in black and white, there were no grey shades in between.

'You *must* know. It's most awfully thrilling. I'm dying to meet him tonight, and his friends that you've told me so much about. Aren't you just crazy with impatience? I couldn't be so calm, cool and collected. How d'you do it?' Gwen could not keep still and now she was up, clasping Charlotte's hands, swinging her round and round.

'I don't really believe it's happening yet.'

It had come as a shock when, on joining Eva for tea after her ride, she had handed her an unsealed white envelope. Perplexed and wondering, Charlotte had drawn out the deckle-edged card, unable to credit the evidence of her own eyes as she read: 'Lady

Pendral requests the pleasure of the company of Mr Charteris, Mr Tyler and Mr Leigh to a dinner party tomorrow evening at 8 pm. RSVP.'

She did not need to thank Eva, her radiant smile had been enough, and the invitation had been dispatched without delay. Apparently she had Frederick and Bernice to thank for Eva's change of heart, as she learned over tea in the drawing-room with Bernice wearing a satisfied expression and Frederick paying special attention to a somewhat subdued Eva, though Charlotte was not told what had taken place between them. At bedtime she had kissed Eva, and said that this was the best possible birthday gift she could have had.

Gwen had been given a room next to Charlotte's, and as parsons could not generally afford personal maids for their daughters, Tilly was serving them both. It was a cosy arrangement and suited them admirably. They rested in Charlotte's room during the afternoon. It was the rule that young ladies should spend at least two hours in their beds if an exciting evening was in the offing. Charlotte and Gwen did not sleep, sitting under the puffing eiderdown, half hidden by the curtains, drinking hot chocolate and catching up on news.

Though appearing calm, Charlotte was churning with anxiety as she visualised Eva's meeting with Phelan. She prayed that he might be on his best behaviour, curbing his sarcastic tongue, but was relying heavily on Julian to smooth over any awkward moments. The more she got to know Julian, the more she liked him. He radiated elegance, slim and supple as a palm, a wonderful source of fun, with his angelic smile and rapier-sharp wit. She had never met anyone more kind and considerate, but was wary of the hard-bitten, sometimes brusque, Andrew.

The hours crawled by, but finally it was seven-thirty and the girls were ready to go down, taking a final peek in the pier-glass. Charlotte was wearing a rose chiffon over-robe that partly covered her pink silk gown. Slit at the front from belt the hem, it was lavishly embroidered with seed pearls. Her hair, brushed high, was also interwoven with pearls. Gwen was more simply attired in white muslin with a blue sash, and though the dress had been bought for the occasion, she had given her mother a hard time, complaining that it was too childish.

'You're so beautiful, Charlotte,' she said wistfully, feeling gauche and unsophisticated, sighing outwardly because of the edict against putting up her hair until she was eighteen.

'So are you,' Charlotte replied sincerely, sighing inwardly because she was no longer as innocent as Gwen. The world had touched her through the agency of Phelan.

'The pair of you are as pretty as a picture,' Tilly agreed, standing back to view them proudly, hands folded over her lace apron. 'A credit to my handiwork, if I do say so as shouldn't. All that pressing and goffering! I thought I'd never be done with the smoothing-iron. Now don't you go getting into any scrapes, Miss Gwen. We've got to look after you for your pa and ma, or our lives won't be worth a tinker's cuss.'

'I promise to be good,' Gwen smiled at the maid-servant, finding it highly entertaining to think of her with Wilkins. Though he was sturdy and very masculine with his handle-bar moustache, Tilly topped him by several inches.

Tilly nodded, satisfied, then she fixed her eagle eye on Charlotte. 'So, Mr Charteris is coming, after all? Everyone's talking about it belowstairs, Miss. Just you watch out. Take my advice and keep him in his place. That's what I do with Wilkins and its works a treat. Got to start as you mean to go on.'

Charlotte remembered this when she met Phelan in the Great Hall. Keep *him* in his place? Impossible! I wouldn't want to, she thought. Phelan is Phelan and I'd not change him. Eva greeted him cordially, and he was very polite, but Charlotte felt their animosity, and was relieved when Bernice came over, making a beeline for Andrew on whom she had set her sights.

She had worked hard to make Eva change her mind. During the talk she and Frederick had had with her while her ward was out riding, she had advised Eva not to oppose her as this would make her all the more determined to encourage Phelan. Now, having done her duty by the girl, Bernice concentrated on her latest victim. The King had gone to Sandringham,, there to play the devoted husband and model father. Her services were not required, so she was free to amuse herself.

At first she had wanted Julian. He was charming and attentive, and knew about fashion, a refreshing change from other men who talked only of horses, war, politics and the Stock Exchange but, on a recent deer-stalk in Devon, her wayward fancy had been captured by Andrew.

The climax of the hunt had been exciting, with the beast at bay and Andrew, ahead of everyone else, running and leaping through the heather, keeping up with the hounds. The doomed stag had come to rest in a stream, the hounds baying from the bank, the rest of the party straggling in the rear. Bernice had elbowed her way to the fore and seen everything. Andrew had not carried a gun, but had unsheathed his knife, double-bladed and a foot long. He had splashed into the water, seized the stag by its lowered antlers and driven the knife into the cornered animal's shoulder, his strength forcing it into the heart. Bernice had decided, then and there, that he was the man for her.

'What about Quentin?' Eva had asked when she told her that she intended to have him over the Christmas period.

'*What* about Quentin? He'll spend his time eating, sleeping and hunting. You know Quentin, a dunderhead when it comes to things that really matter.'

Now she slipped her arm through Julian's, giving him a flirtatious smile to goad Andrew into action. She noticed that Gwen was goggling at the boy in wide-eyed admiration. Wherever he went the women were drawn to him as by a magnet for he was very much the dandy, fun-loving and debonair.

'Be nice to Charlotte's little friend,' she said, while he grinned down at her and nodded, aware that Andrew was her chosen quarry.

'Anything to oblige,' he said, his good humour and romanticism a welcome contrast to the more or less obligatory cynicism that prevailed in her cramped world.

Eva, though slightly disapproving, had ensured that Bernice sat next to Andrew at the dinner table, with her husband on her other side. She liked Quentin and was rather sorry for him, but he seemed to ignore his wife's cavaliers, a countryman at heart who was more concerned about his hunters than her amours.

While dinner was in progress, she stared down the table to where Phelan was seated between Charlotte and Gwen. She had done as Bernice suggested, bowing to her superior knowledge, but she liked the situation no better than before. To see him there stuck in her craw, yet if by encouraging him she caused Charlotte to grow weary of the relationship then, no matter how painful, this was the right course.

She looked away, unable to bear the sight of his dark head bent toward's Charlotte's, and concentrated on her guests. There were forty in all, but the long refectory table accommodated them easily, its polished surface shining with Georgian silver, cut glass goblets, branching candle-sticks, and a gilt epergne from which hot-house flowers spilled, artfully arranged to simulate nature.

The talk was light and frothy, laughter rising to the central chandelier with its sparking crystal drops. Greyfriars relied on oil-lamps and candles for illumination and the glow was softer than electric light. Bernice was glad of it as she leaned an elbow on the table and glanced at Andrew through her lashes, wondering if Eva followed the rule adopted by considerate hostesses who always slipped the names of the occupants into little brass holders on the bedroom doors, thus avoiding confusion. She doubted it, and wished her friend was a little less straight-laced. No matter. Such trifles would not deter a lady like herself. Andrew, hardened warrior that he was, would be hers before long.

Course after course appeared from the depths of the kitchen, served by footmen who, because they were in the country, had been allowed to dispense with the knee-breeches and powdered wigs protocol demanded for dinners in town. Instead they wore trousers with a crimson cord down the seam, and waistcoats of the family livery. Most of the food had been produced on the Pendral farms, the vegetables and fruit grown in the kitchen garden. Charlotte would have felt guilty about such an abundant variety of dishes had it not been for Eva's generosity towards the needy. Every poor person that she knew of had been given turkey, pork and beef, besides cakes, puddings, and such essentials as bread, butter, sugar and tea.

Charlotte toyed with the courses which appeared before her in rapid succession. It was unnerving to be sitting there surrounded by people who were busily engaged in eating, yet glancing in her direction. Obviously Phelan's inclusion in the party was causing much speculation. By now, few were ignorant of Eva's feelings towards her cousin. Phelan seemed sardonically amused, commenting on the excellence of the cuisine, his eyes on her face as they made small-talk.

Later Eva conducted the ladies to the drawing-room, leaving the men to port and cigars. Gwen was in a ferment. There had been so much to see, hear and taste. The glittering dinner-table set with rare wines and tempting dishes, the beautiful bejewelled women in costly dresses, the cultured men talking easily of gay and harmless things, had captivated her. Above all, there had been Julian, and she had sat with eyes glued to him. Never had she seen a more handsome man and once, to her horror and delight, he had winked at her. Gwen thought she would never stop blushing, hugely embarrassed.

It was better to be with Charlotte and the ladies in the drawing-room, though she found the latter intimidating. She envied their élan, their coiffures and expensive gowns, their manners. They were so secure. She could not imagine them being upset or confused, and longed to be like them.

Much of their talk went right over her head; innuendoes about people she did not know; the latest dance steps; the most recent theatrical performances; gossip concerning the Royal family. She noticed that Eva did not join in, sitting quiet and aloof, though smiling now and again at some remark Bernice made.

'Are you enjoying yourself?' Charlotte asked as they sat together on the scroll-backed sofa.

'I should just say I am!' Gwen answered with a quick smile. 'My goodness, I have to keep pinching myself to make sure I'm not dreaming.'

After half an hour they were joined by the gentlemen, and Julian immediately made his way to where Charlotte and Bernice were sitting. Gwen was tongue-tied, entranced by his golden beauty. To her, he seemed perfect in the black dinner-jacket that emphazised his fine shoulders and narrow waist.

To her disappointment, Phelan kept his distance, leaning an elbow on the overmantel, deep in discussion with Quentin and some of the members of the local hunt. She nudged Charlotte, and whispered, 'Why isn't he speaking to you?'

'Oh, Phelan's mad on horses,' Julian heard this aside and answered for Charlotte. He was sitting on the floor at Bernice's feet and looked up with his dazzling smile. 'He's decided to play the countryman for a while, all smelly tweeds and muddy boots. It won't last long. He gets these fads and fancies. Last year it was Egypt, but soon he'll be itching to get back to Tuscany again.'

'Ah, Tuscany! I've not been there for ages,' sighed Bernice, giving Andrew an encouraging smile so that he came to sit beside her.

'Florence! *La Bella*! The City of Flowers!' Julian rolled up his eyes, hand on heart. 'There's nowhere more beautiful than the Villa Alinari, home of Phelan's mother, the Contessa.'

Bernice tapped him playfully on the cheek with her fan. 'You speak so warmly that I suspect you have a sweetheart there – some olive-skinned girl with melting brown eyes who adores you.'

'D'you think so?' he answered, smiling.

'Of course!' She turned to Gwen who was listening, all eyes and ears. 'I'll bet there's a lovelorn female waiting for him, don't you agree, Gwen?'

Julian lay back on his elbows, fingers playing idly with the fringe of her shawl. 'It's true. Every girl in Florence is dying of love for me.'

Bernice gave him a hard stare. It was impossible to tell if he was joking or not. That was the trouble with him, an elusive prankster who never took anything seriously, then she leaned across for an ashtray, pressing her thigh against Andrew's and saying, 'Do you like Florence? Or is it too tame for you? Not enough action, perhaps?'

'Florence is fine,' he answered, a smile on his keen brown face with its strong nose and full lips. He was amused by her games, and found her delicious, never turning up the opportunity to enjoy a fine woman.

'Well then, if you're not off on another expedition soon, maybe we could all go there next year,' Bernice suggested, one hand resting lightly on his shoulder.

'As a matter of fact, I'm booked to give some lectures in Europe,' Andrew said. 'That would work out quite well.'

'Lovely!' Bernice exclaimed, then glanced across at her hostess. 'What d'you say, Eva? Will you come? I think you need a holiday, my dear. You work too hard.'

Eva shook her head. 'It doesn't appeal to me, Bernice. I'll go to Brighton if I need a rest.'

'Brighton is a bore,' Bernice declared, making a kissing mouth at Andrew. 'One can't rely on the weather, and I long for blue skies, the heady perfume of flowers, the clear radiant light that is only found in Italy.'

'It sounds wonderful,' Charlotte added hesitantly.

'If you're not keen, then why don't you let Charlotte go with me?' Bernice suggested and Charlotte could have hugged her. 'Gwen could come along as well.'

Gwen's face fell. 'Oh, but Daddy couldn't possible afford to send me, though I know he'd think it good for my education. He always says that travel broadens the mind.'

Bernice brushed this aside as of no consequence. 'It will be my treat, child. Ask him when you get home.'

Eva decided it was time to put a stop to this nonsense. Bernice was being completely irresponsible, blinded by her latest infatuation. Couldn't she see that if Charlotte accompanied her, it would be tantamount to throwing her into Phelan's arms? Bernice was looking straight at her, as if the say: Remember what I told you yesterday? Give her full rein, my dear. Let her discover for herself if he really is her Prince Charming.

'We'll speak of it again later,' she said coolly.

She decided it was time to break up this bothersome conversation and suggested that if anyone wished they might to into the card-room and play bridge. Some seized upon this, whilst others declined. Bernice was pleased to see Quentin disappearing through the door. He never could resist the lure of gambling. Frederick took the opportunity of a word with Eva.

'Well done,' he said, sitting beside her and resting an arm along the back of her chair. 'I know how much it cost you to take our advice and invite him here, and I hope we shan't regret giving it.'

Eva shook her head. 'I hope so too, but I'm very much afraid Charlotte is besotted with him. I'm cross with Bernice. Now she's talking of a trip to Italy, and Charlotte's fretting to go with her. Bernice and her passions! I could slap her at times!'

'Don't worry,' he advised. 'Charlotte's a sensible girl, and if Phelan doesn't come up to the high standards you've set her, then I think she'll lose interest. As for Italy, let's get Christmas over before we start worrying about that, shall we?'

He was muddled in his thinking. One part of him wished Charlotte well and did not want to see her hurt, while the other, more selfish part could see that if she disappointed Eva then perhaps he might step in and console her. His heart contracted as he looked at her. She had never seemed more queenly or more gracious. Perhaps because of Phelan's presence she had dressed with special care, wearing black velvet, very simply cut, the rich pile setting off her fine alabaster skin. Her hair was dressed severely, drawn back from her austere features, and she wore a magnificent diamond choker around her throat. She made every other woman present seem tawdry in comparison.

The bridge-players were utterly absorbed. Eva was talking with Frederick, and Julian continued to engage Gwen in conversation, while Bernice and Andrew were engrossed in one another. Phelan leaned over the sofa and murmured, 'Is there somewhere we can go? I've not had a moment alone with you. Show me the wonders of Greyfriars.'

Charlotte knew that she shouldn't, but went with him all the same. Phelan opened the door for her, and she passed through it into the dim corridor, hoping that the other women had seen them go, hoping that Eva had not. She carried a candle-stick. It lit up her face, planing hollows under the cheeks, throwing up the spiky shadow of lashes against the brow bone. When they reached the Long Gallery he took it from her and placed it on a coffer. They paused, hand in hand, and she thought how well he fitted into such a surrounding.

'I'm hunting tomorrow,' he said. 'Quentin has asked me. I'm being accepted by the county gentry. Soon Eva won't be able to exclude me.'

'Won't she?' Charlotte was not so sure.

'No, she won't, and I think she may have to agree to your visiting Italy. How can she object if Bernice is your chaperon, and the little Gwen person is with you, too?'

'They were talking about it just now.'

'I know. The seeds have already been sown.'

'You're a very devious person, aren't you?' She was half admiring, half condemnatory.

'I'm used to getting what I want.'

'I haven't said that I'll marry you.' He was taking a lot for granted, so certain of her answer that she found it displeasing.

'No, you haven't, but I hope you're giving it serious consideration.' His hand gently smoothed her bare arm, but he did not try to kiss her, and such hesitation surprised her.

'Yes, I am.' She wondered at his soft voice, his calm control.

'That's fine. And I can come here and see you again?'

'If Eva says you may.'

He took her back to the party, holding her hand gently, making no attempt at kisses or caresses. The change in him from the man she had met on the downs was extraordinary, making her even more aware that he was an enigmatic and baffling person.

They had been gone for such a brief while that no one had missed them. Phelan went straight to Eva and said, 'It's time we were leaving. Thank you for a most enjoyable evening. I hope you'll come to dinner at Hawksdown Hall very soon.'

'It's nearly midnight!' Julian exclaimed, jumping up and bowing to Gwen. 'If we aren't gone before the last stroke of twelve, Cinderella, then your lovely gown will become rags and we'll all turn into pumpkins!'

The icy fist of winter had London in its grip. Several factories were on short time and men had been stood off. As always during periods of extra hardship and distress, May Savill opened up her soup-kitchen, using the large room designed for parochial meetings, and church functions such as rummage sales.

This was situated at the back of the vicarage, a sparsely furnished area with rows of hard wooden chairs against the walls. A trestle table stood at one end, behind which hung a notice board where bits of paper and posters of forthcoming events were attached by rusty drawing-pins. One advertising a Boxing Day pantomime given by amateur players at the parish hall was still there, though this performance had come and gone several weeks before.

Gwen glanced at it, remembering that exciting Christmas spent at Greyfriars, though it now seemed an eternity away. Only the thought that her father had given his blessing for her trip to Florence kept her going. Would she really be leaving all this behind in a short time? How different it would be to the tasks now allotted to her.

For days she had run down to the market at dawn, to stand in the cold, watching the butcher in his blue coat and striped apron sharpening his long knives, then purchasing and dragging home pounds of the cheapest cuts. And every morning, on her return, Cook fell upon the haul, hacking the tough meat into segments and tossing them into the great cauldron bubbling on the range. May would be there, too, busy at the chopping-board, slicing root vegetables to add richness to the stew she was providing for the hungry who queued every morning, until admitted to shuffle along the corridor to the room where Gwen helped serve them.

She disliked this work, though understood that it was a necessary part of her father's care for his flock. It was depressing to see so many people beaten down by poverty and reduced to accepting charity, their thin, dirty hands outstretched for a free meal. The place stank of unwashed bodies and clothes that had been worn too long. There seemed to be an endless line of people: old ones who coughed and hawked; hollow-cheeked mothers clutching runny-nosed babies pinned into faded rags; urchins in cast-off clothing, bare blue feet swollen with chilblains; sunken-eyed drunks who had spent their last penny on gin. They were a silent crowd, humour gone in the face of such adversity. Even the babies were too weak to cry, for crying used up energy and there was none to spare.

Gwen and the sisters old enough to help, toiled ceaselessly through the morning, helping their mother and Annie. It was not that these people were vagrants. In the normal way they earned a modest wage but times were hard, work short, money even shorter. The soup-kitchen was their last resort, the only thing between them and starvation.

The final spoonful was ladled from the big black pot. 'That's all, I'm afraid. Come again tomorrow,' May called out in that falsely cheerful voice she reserved for such occasions, wishing that the pan was bottomless or that Christ would appear to perform a miracle. The desperate disappointment on the faces of those who would not receive a portion was heart-rendering to witness.

Gwen had one bowl left, and she handed it to a girl who stood waiting by the trestle. She was clad in an old skirt and thin blouse, a moth-eaten shawl flung over her hair. Her burning eyes stared into Gwen's as her hand shot out to grab the stew with all the ferocity of a hungry wolf. Gwen started back, shocked by the sudden thought that it was Charlotte who faced her. There was something about the girl, the way she held her head – her eyes – something –

By the time Gwen had recovered the girl had gone, slipping out of the door like a phantom. At that moment, a voice spoke at her elbow and she started round, the expression on her face causing Charlotte to exclaim, 'What's the matter, Gwen? You look as if you've seen a ghost. I'm sorry I couldn't get here before. I'll be earlier tomorrow morning.'

Gwen gasped with relief at seeing her friend there, warmly clad, well fed, not haggard and animal-eyed. 'Oh, Charlotte! Thank goodness! I've had a funny sort of experience. There was a girl here just now – and she reminded me of you. Don't ask me why or how, for I can see now how wrong I was. She was filthy, a sluttish creature – the dregs –'

Charlotte gripped her by the arms, shook her violently. 'Where is she?'

'She snatched the food and legged it out of the door. Why? What's up?'

Tweeny! Charlotte's thoughts raced. Could it have been Tweeny? She pushed through the crowd trailing reluctantly away from the comparative warmth of the room, elbowed them aside, made cruel by her frantic need to reach the door. There was no one in the back porch and she ran out into the street. Oh, be there! she prayed to that unknown girl. Be there. Be Tweeny, my sister!

But the street was empty. Only a mangy dog nosed about amongst the frost-hardened rubbish in the gutter. Whoever the girl had been, London had sucked her into its maw again.

Book Two

The Dawning

But one man loved the pilgrim soul in you,
And loved the sorrows of your changing face.

When you are Old by W.B. Yeats

My heart is like a singing bird
Whose nest is in a watered shoot;
My heart is like an apple tree
Whose boughs are bent with thickset fruit;
My heart is like a rainbow shell
That paddles in a halcyon sea;
My heart is gladder than all these
Because my love has come to me.

Because the birthday of my life
Is come, my love is come to me.

A Birthday by Christina Rossetti

Chapter Seven

The Pendral Bank was situated in the Strand. Designed by John Adams, the dignified, harmonious building inspired confidence in investors and clients alike, a confidence that had never been misplaced.

Eva's private office was on the second floor, overlooking the street. It was a large, impressive apartment once used as a residence by the founder of the bank. Reached by a curving staircase of superb teak, the corridor leading to it was thickly carpeted, the walls bearing portraits of the strong-featured Pendral men whose astute perception had developed such an enterprise from modest beginnings as shipping insurers, through to importers and, finally, to being the most important merchant bankers in England.

There was William Charles, financial adviser to King George III; his son Robert, who had steered the bank through the turbulent years of the French Revolution and the long, drawn-out war with Napoleon; Edward Thomas, who had managed the affairs of the Prince Regent, later to become George IV, and when he died without legitimate heirs, those of his brother, William IV; then Thomas Mark in whom Queen Victoria and her beloved Consort, Albert, had placed their trust. The last portrait of all was of Eva herself, aloof in mourning-black for her father, her eyes staring into the distance. An observer who was a stranger would not have guessed that beneath such a calm exterior lay a strong will, fierce independence and implacable determination.

On a mild day toward the end of March, the man traversing that hallowed pathway to the inner sanctum paused before Eva's picture, but only momentarily. He did not dare lag behind the lean, round-shouldered gentleman in black jacket and pinstripe trousers who had met him at the head of the stairs. His handshake had been firm, at variance with his somewhat vague manner, as he had introduced himself as Mr Barford, Lady Eva's secretary.

'Dr Armstrong? She is expecting you. Please follow me,' he had added, a perfect example of the bank's image of quiet gravity. Now a smile warmed his cadaverous face and he nodded towards the portrait.

'Is that her?' Dudley Armstrong asked, keeping his voice low in that atmosphere of hushed decorum.

'Yes, sir. You've not met her yet?'

'I've not had the honour.' Dudley's thoughts were racing, thanking his lucky stars that he had been able to obtain this interview. 'The Reverend Savill asked her if she would see me, and she graciously agreed.'

Mr Barford said no more, walking ahead of Dudley until they came to a massive cedarwood door whose architrave was crowned with carved acanthus leaves. It was opened by an efficient-looking woman wearing a high-necked cream silk blouse and navy blue skirt. Her broad bosom gave her the appearance of a pouter pigeon, her waist was tightly belted and her hips ample. Dudley met a shrewd, gold spectacled gaze as she stood back so that they might enter.

'Good morning, Dr Armstrong,' she said brightly. 'My name is Miss Jarrold, and I'm Lady Eva's assistant.'

Dudley stepped into a reception room, tastefully decorated in blue and gold. There was a further delay while Barford slipped through a further door and Dudley stood smiling nervously and exchanging platitudes with Miss Jarrold. Yes, it certainly was unusually mild for the time of year. Yes, he had seen the crocuses in Hyde Park and agreed that they made a colourful display. Yes, it did certainly seem as if they might expect a hot summer.

Miss Jarold, very composed, was obviously accustomed to delivering this smooth patter, trained to be polite yet distant, working her way up to her present enviable position via the hard road of junior clerk, teller, then under-assistant. She had adhered to the bank's strict rules where every moment of every day was carefully planned and the beginner was expected to work on Sundays, as well as throughout the week.

At last Mr Barford returned on noiseless, careful feet, reminding Dudley of a Malibu stork he had once seen at Regent's Park Zoo. Then, filled with curiosity to meet this lady of whom he had heard so much, he accompanied him into her room.

My God! he thought to himself as he glanced round. I've come to the right place. It oozes money. Can I get her on my side? I hope Stephen's paved the way. Just as well I put on my only decent suit. I think it's presentable. The material dark, matt, and neatly pressed, not shiny and the worse for wear like his working one, or crumpled like his beloved tweeds. And he was glad he'd taken Beth's advice and invested in a new white shirt.

He had never seen such luxury, though everything was in perfect taste, without the slightest hint of ostentation. He was struck by the richness and elegance of the magnificent Chinese wallpaper, the Turkish carpets, the sheen of intricately carved, craftsman-made mahogany furniture, the water-colour landscapes, the porcelain, the plush drapes framing the windows.

He registered it in a flash, then his eyes went directly to the woman standing near the broad, leather-topped Empire desk. She was slight, straight-backed, holding her head with regal dignity on a long, slender neck. Her gown was beautifully cut, but plain – leaf-green moiré with matching velvet trim – no frills, no furbelows, eminently suitable for any weighty business discussion that might occur during her busy day.

Eva looked up, smiled, gave him her hand. 'Stephen has told me about you and your work, Dr Armstrong. You're most welcome.'

Dudley could have kissed her with relief. Good old Stephen! Would that all churchmen were as caring, he thought, taking the chair she indicated, while she seated herself opposite him on the other side of the desk and asked Mr Barford to arrange for coffee to be sent in.

Dudley lifted his briefcase on to his lap and clicked the catches. 'I've brought some plans to show you,' he began, bringing out a sheaf of papers and, shyly at first then gaining confidence, he started to tell her about the dispensary that he wanted to open in Wapping. 'A clinic, if you like,' he went on, encouraged by her interest. 'A place where the poor can come to be treated and receive medicine free of charge.'

Eva perused the plans carefully, at ease with this big, gangling man with the slight Scottish accent, honey-coloured hair and brown eyes alight with enthusiasm. He was just the sort of person she liked dealing with: direct, articulate and dedicated.

'Is it not possible to use your surgery?' she asked.

'I've thought of this.' Dudley was recalling the discussions he had had with Beth, and how they had racked their brains to find a way of stretching their small house for the further use of his patients. 'It can't be done, I'm afraid. I have a consulting room there, of course, but I'm thinking in terms of something bigger, with a dispensary and a decent-sized, warm waiting-room. Beth – that's my wife – and I have two little children and need every scrap of space at home for our own use, so I've been looking around and found this empty shop in Canyard Street which will be ideal, if it's decorated and done up.'

Eva tapped the desk with her pencil, already taking fire from him. She knew all too well the difficulties those with a very limited income had in finding the money for doctors and drugs. Often people died through lack of proper medical care. She helped the hospitals in every way possible, but the occupants of the slums hated going to them, remembering the old days when their kind had been experimented on by surgeons, with sometimes dire results. To them, entering the fearsome portals of such establishments was tantamount to signing their own death warrants. It was not like that now, but old habits of thinking die hard among the uneducated.

Eva came straight to the point. 'You'll need money.'

'Oh, yes, a great deal,' he answered, aware that the palms of his hands were sweating. 'For a start, we'll have to rent the place.'

Her arched brows shot up. 'Rent, Doctor? It's never wise to rent a property. You put yourself in your landlord's power if you do.'

'I know that, but I can't afford to purchase it. I've only been in practice for three years, did my training at Guys Hospital before that, and I spent every penny I possessed on buying into the partnership. I was the junior partner, you understand, but Dr Phillips retired recently, so now I have more freedom to follow my own ideas.'

'Tell me more about them.' Eva rested her elbow on the table, cupped her chin in her hand and gave him her undivided attention.

Dudley ruffled his hair in an unconscious gesture, mind filled with concern for his patients. 'It's the pregnant women, nursing mothers and their infants, that bother me most. They need special care, and lots of advice. But you already know about this. Stephen has told me of your work, so I don't have to elaborate, do I?'

Eva heaved a sigh. 'I'm worried about them, too. Sick women bringing sick children into the world. I've already endowed several cribs in the Infant's Hospital, Westminster.'

It was on the tip of Dudley's tongue to confess his real reason for wanting the clinic, but he was not sure whether it would be proper to discuss such matters with a lady like Eva. Double standards prevailed, and although anything relating to sex occupied the minds of most, it was rarely talked about in mixed company. He prevaricated, deciding that it would be unwise to risk her disapproval by an out and out declaration of his intention to advocate contraception.

'The trouble is that they have too many babies in too short a time,' he ventured, waiting for her reaction.

'I know,' she replied.

Dudley tested her out, it was now or never. 'I can help them to prevent this.'

She considered him steadily, and then said, 'Do I understand that along with dealing with their ailments you want to teach them how to limit their families?'

'This is one of the reasons why I want the clinic, yes.' Oh, dear, I've done it now, Dudley thought ruefully, there's no turning back. So he launched into his crusade. 'As you may be aware, the rich in most civilised countries have used methods for preventing conception for years, though without the approval of church or state. I can't speak for Europe or America, but in England statistics show that there's been a dramatic drop in the birthrate among middle-class couples as well, but the poor, whose need is greater than all the rest put together, are still governed by lack of money, ignorance and fear.'

'Some of the women I've met in the slums talk vaguely about being careful,' Eva replied, recalling their desperation, embarrassment and crying need to put a stop to repeated pregnancies.

Dudley shifted restlesly, the energy pounding through him making it hard to remain seated when he wanted to leap up and pace the floor. Even as they deliberated, he knew that somewhere yet another woman was dying in childbirth or poisoning herself with noxious substances in an effort to procure a miscarriage. Schooling his impatience, he contented himself with making expansive gestures with his arms as he talked on.

'Some of them know about anti-conception but only through seeing advertisements in chemists' shops and by talking with their friends, so it's still a very hit-and-miss affair. Most women rely on backstreet abortionists, or getting rid of unwanted pregnancies by swallowing pills of lead-plaster, sometimes the liquor in which copper coins have been boiled, or quinine crystals. A large percentage lose their lives. It's criminal! I want to be able to substitute reliable, well-fitting appliances for furtively bought devices whose failure all too often leads women to resort to dangerous drugs or the services of some dirty old hag who'll insert an instrument into the uterus to disturb the foetus. I've heard of knitting-needles or crochet-hooks being used. Diabolical! So, I'd like to substitute the trained adviser for backyard gossip, and the well-equipped clinic for the bumbling quack.'

He sat back, knowing that he had shot his bolt, waiting for her reaction. She could show him the door or support his cause. There were no other alternatives. He was given a breathing space as Miss Jarrold brought in the coffe, and Eva poured the steaming, fragrant liquid from the silver pot into bone-china cups and handed one to him, along with the cream-jug and sugar-bowl.

Eva was wishing that Charlotte was present, but she had gone to Europe. Letters received from her had been disquieting. It seemed that she was totally besotted with the high-life, and Phelan. They were on their way to Florence and there had been no talk of an early return. Eva missed her dreadfully, felt hurt and rejected, yet refused to acknowledge that she was suffering from the base emotion of jealousy.

She had kept herself busy, spending hours with Alice in the Bond Street shop, busy with her money-raising schemes, but even this and Frederick's constant companionship had failed to lift her spirits. Albion House was too big and too empty. She would catch herself turning to make some comment to Charlotte, only to remember that she was not there. They had never before been separated for such a lengthy period. But this morning's meeting with the young doctor had proved to be a god-send. Here was something really worthwhile into which she could pour her resources, time and energy. It would keep her mind occupied, prevent its constant fretting as to whether Phelan had succeeded in seducing Charlotte, if she was in love with him and would accept a proposal of marriage should he ask her. The very idea of either of these possibilities made her skin crawl.

When she spoke again it was to ask, 'What do other members of the medical profession say about this?'

Dudley almost knocked over his cup, enraged by the blind complacency and obstinacy of his fellow doctors. 'Tshaw! Most of them are influenced by the opinions expressed in *The Lancet*,' he barked. 'Scathing articles have appeared there condemning the chemists who sell anti-conception devices, and pillorying magazines such as the dress-making periodical *Myra's Journal*, who insert what *The Lancet's* editors term 'filthy advertisements' in their publication. They say that if women read such things they'll soon acquire knowledge that will place them on the same footing as experienced prostitutes. It's all too ridiculous! They even demanded that the chemists and publishers should be arrested, tried and given penal sentences. This has already happened several times in the United States.'

'*The Lancet* doesn't give its blessing to Dr H.A. Allbutt's *The Wife's Handbook*, either?'

Unbeknown to Dudley, Eva had made a study of the problem and, for some time, had been wondering what she could do about it. She had even considered joining the Malthusian League which, since eighteen-seventy-seven, had been ceaselessly battling against bigotry, hypocrisy and hostility in their fight to spread contraceptive knowledge.

'Good heavens no! They think the book should be burned. I've had many an argument with colleagues about this. Dr Phillips, for example. *The Lancet* is his bible! He was elated when it categorically stated that to advise on the control of birth was as distasteful to the medical practitioner as to the most fastidious churchman. I couldn't do anything while he was senior partner, but now ill-health has forced him to give up.'

'Speaking of churchmen, where do Stephen's sympathies lie?' Eva was thinking of his own large family. May was expecting another baby in June.

Dudley had forgotten her rank, forgotten that it would be considered immoral in most quarters for them even to be thinking about such a controversial subject, let alone mentioning it. All he could see was that she was an ally, the clinic no longer an impossible dream.

'Stephen is for it, one hundred per cent. No doubt there will be trouble with his bishop if this leaks out, but he doesn't care.' He grinned at her, aware of the question forming in her mind. 'I know he has lots of kids himself, but that's through choice. May loves babies and is never happier than when pregnant. She's positively blooming at the moment, but he has told her quite firmly that this is the last child. In any case, their circumstances are rather better than those of his parishioners. I can't see either of their families letting them go short, can you?'

'Stephen wouldn't accept charity from his parents, or hers,' Eva demurred, but she knew that Dudley was right. The Savills were in an entirely different category from most of the other residents of the East End.

'I'm not worried about the Savills.' Dudley dismissed them brusquely, made impolite by his eagerness. 'Will you help me, or do I have to look elsewhere? Something *must* be done. If you could only be there when these women venture to visit me, creeping into the surgery as if they're committing a crime. It's heartbreaking to see the eager expressions on their anxious faces as I tell them a few simple facts about cleanliness and hygiene. I know they're dying to ask me how not to get pregnant but daren't, and I'm hamstrung until I move into other premises.'

'Do their husbands ever speak of it to you?' Eva's voice rose and her eyes hardened. 'Why is it always the women who worry themselves into the grave? The men want the pleasure, so they should do something about it.'

Dudley raised an eyebrow at her, a wry smile twisting his lips. 'Lady Eva, can you honestly believe that the labourer coming home drunk on a Saturday night would bother to use a sheath or practise *coitus interruptus*? No, if the women want protection, then they'll have to take the responsibility.'

'As ever – for everything.'

'That's right.'

Dudley knew of many cases where the husbands refused point-blank to countenance their wives attempting to use any form of contraception. Superstitious and bull-headed, they looked upon it as an insult to their masculinity. The more children the 'old woman' produced, the more it added to the myth of their virility. These unfortunate females would have to seek advice in secret, and keep that secret at home or be beaten black and blue. Very occasionally, when he was tired, having been up all night fighting to save a mother's life after a bad delivery or a bungled abortion, witnessing yet another example of man's inhumanity to woman, Dudley wished that he had opted for a less troublesome practice in some select suburb where, if these things happened at all, they were brushed under the carpet.

'You realise that you could be in danger if what you're doing becomes known? Some people look upon family limitation as a monstrous evil, threatening unity, the church, even the Government. Poverty and overcrowding keep the masses subjugated. You might even face imprisonment and be kicked out of the profession,' Eva warned, though she could see that he was quite adamant.

'I'm not daft, Lady Eva. I've a wife and family to support and can't afford to offend my paying patients. Don't worry, I'll be discreet, and I'll certainly not be concentrating entirely on this problem, but open the clinic doors to anyone who needs treatment.'

'Very well,' Eva said, and smiled at the expression of intense relief that lit up his craggy features. 'I'll buy the premises, and make sure you have money to equip them. I'll also fund it, for you can't run a free enterprise like this without financial backing.'

Dudley could no longer contain himself. As he got to his feet his chair went crashing. He ignored it, leaned across the desk, scattering papers and pens, clasped Eva's slim hands in his massive ones and wrung them. 'Thank you – thank you! You'll not regret it. Will you come and see the premises?'

Eva gently released herself. 'I must speak to Mr Haldane, my lawyer. He'll have to sort out the deeds and suchlike.'

'Not now! Not yet! Come with me at once – this moment – there's no time to lose!' Dudley urged. 'Please, Lady Eva. I want you to see exactly what you're buying. Share my vision. Know that you'll be giving hope to hundreds of people.'

It was impossible to refuse him, and Eva rang for Miss Jarrold, instructed her to cancel appointments for the rest of the day, put on her hat and coat, and soon found herself in Dudley's battered Ford car, rattling away from the peace of the bank into the noisy, smelly confines of Poplar.

Canyard Street was typical of the area, an alley situated off the main road which was filled with old, sagging houses, small stores, grim factory buildings, a multitude of pubs, open-air markets and a number of steamy fish and chip shops. Dudley pulled up outside a particularly depressing-looking building. The windows were boarded up, the roof in desperate need of attention, but as he talked, pointing out this or that advantage, so it was transformed in Eva's eyes into the clean, brightly painted and restored building he visualised so strongly.

He had no key, but she followed him round to the back door which yielded easily when he leaned his broad shoulder against its rotting wood. Inside it was even bleaker – dirt, cobwebs, the daub and plaster ceilings collapsed in several rooms where the rain had penetrated the cracked tiles, inching its way down to the lower stories. The floor boards were missing in some places, pulled up and used for firewood by vagrants, so Dudley explained, happily rummaging among the rubbish.

Eva picked a path through the debris, taking heart from his optimism, forced to agree in the end that if money was lavished on it, the dilapidated house with its shop-front could possible be turned into something useful. By the time they left, he had managed to convince her and, in celebratory mood, they drove to his house where they sat in the kitchen while his wife, a lively woman with a fine intelligent face, gave them cups of hot tea and slices of cake that she had baked herself.

They treated Eva as one of the family, in no way awed by her title, and soon all three were on Christian name terms. I've made some new friends today, Eva realised happily, surprised to find that she had not thought about Charlotte for hours. There was no sign of the children; they were out with their nanny, Beth explained.

'We can just about manage to employ her,' Dudley added, lighting a cigarette and relaxing in the informal atmosphere of his own domain. He had left the two women alone for a brief while, going off to change his suit, reappearing wearing a pair of baggy corduroy trousers and a Fair Isle sweater. 'And a maid, too, though she has to double up in the kitchen. That leaves Beth free to help me in the surgery when we're busy.'

'I was a nurse before we married,' she said, casting him a loving glance. 'I'd like to pursue my career later on, when the children are older. I intend to work at the clinic regularly. Did Dudley tell you that we want to do something for childless couples, too? Infertility can be as misery-making as having more babies than one wants.'

Eva shook her head. 'No, he didn't mention this, but I think it's a good idea.'

'It's Beth's notion really. She has a friend who can't conceive, no matter how hard she tries.' He looked at his wife with a respect which Eva found refreshing. He really does want her to shine in her own right, she thought. He's a large-hearted tolerant man, and she's much to be envied.

'It's pitiful to see her,' Beth continued earnestly. 'She simply adores our children, and has begged Dudley to tell her if there's any way in which she can become a mother.'

'And is there?' Eva sipped her second cup of tea, enjoying herself more by the second. A vast new world of questing and knowledge was opening up before her, and it was exciting.

'Oh, yes. I've examined her and suggested a minor operation which may put matters right. If Beth works with me it will be invaluable. Women are often shy of discussing intimate matters with a man. There's an awful lot of prejudice about anything associated with reproduction. Funny, really, when it's of such vital importance to all of us.'

Is it? Eva wondered, and it was as if a cloud had darkened the sunny kitchen. Will it be to Charlotte? Charlotte and Phelan in the rutting heat of the bed. What a horrible thought!

Victor Dalbiac sprang to mind, and her own unhappy experience with him; the adulterous Bernice and her many lovers; a whole welter of bored cynicism among a set who sneered at the concept of true love; the down-trodden wives in the slums who avoided intercourse with their husbands if they possibly could. Yet there was May and Stephen, and now Dudley and Beth, married couples who were comfortable together, who shared their hopes, dreams and fears, who curled up in their big double beds at night, knowing ecstasy in each other's arms. It made Eva feel bleak, more conscious than ever of her own solitary state. There would never be any call for her to worry about conception or anti-conception, and she tried to cheer herself with this thought, but failed miserably.

It was almost time for her to leave and she said goodbye to Beth before Dudley drove her home. 'May I come again?'

'Of course. Whenever you like.' Beth pressed her gloved hand warmly. 'Thank you, Eva. What you've done today has made us very happy, and, in time, many, many women will benefit tremendously. We want to help them to produce healthy babies that are loved and wanted. We'll be condemned for it, no doubt, but I can't believe that we are wrong.'

'Do you want me to keep your name out of it, Eva?' Dudley asked as the mean streets receded, to be replaced by broad thoroughfares.

It was lunch-time, and the centre of London was busy. So prosperous with its cars, cabs, horse-buses, motor-buses, the well-dressed crowds strolling along the wide pavements. Another life, almost another planet, from the one they had just left. She turned in the passenger seat to study his profile as he concentrated on driving.

'There's no need for that, particularly as you intend to go slowly, ostensibly opening the clinic for ordinary medical treatment. It should be well established by the time the die-hards realise its other purpose. You're in for a tough fight then, Dudley, for they'll call your work an abomination against God and man, sinful, wicked, encouraging illicit sex. You can't afford to lose fee-paying clients, and I can't afford to offend influential people who contribute to my charity fund.'

'We'll play it by ear, shall we?' he suggested, following her directions and turning into the cul-de-sac dominated by Albion House.

'I've seen your project,' she said as she alighted. 'Won't you return the compliment and visit our shop in Bond Street? Come and meet Alice Brooker, who is in charge there.'

'I certainly will.' He was standing beside her, looking down, so large and genial, with his rugged good looks and strong body.

Beth is fortunate, she thought. I wish I could find a man like him. Maybe I'd be willing to renounce spinsterhood then. For the first time in many a moon she remembered her bedroom with something akin to loathing, so vast, with its wide, empty bed. How would it be to lie there at night, whispering of love, of plans, of ambitions, with a man's arms around her? With a man similar to Dudley, unselfish, loyal, burning to ease the lot of suffering humanity.

'Come when you've a spare moment,' she suggested, getting a grip on her wayward imagination. She suddenly swung round as he was about to get into the driver's seat again. 'Oh, by the way, you don't happen to be any good with a camera, do you? I want to have some photographs taken of the shop, Alice and the other women who work there. Maybe even the designs.'

'I've a box-Brownie, and snap away at Beth and the kids, but you want a professional.' He clapped himself on the brow. 'Hang on a minute, I know one. He's a friend of mine, called Richard Sinclair. I'll bring him along, shall I?'

'Do that,' she answered. 'And make it soon.'

Alice Booker awoke early on the morning that the photographer was due to arrive in the shop. She lay in bed for a moment, savouring the luxury of it. The baby was still asleep. Yawning and stretching, she got up, glancing into the crib, a tender smile on her features. Dear little poppet. It wasn't his fault that he had no father. He was hers, and hers alone, and this made him doubly precious to her. Her body might be frail but she had the heart of a tigress, fighting to keep her child, working all the hours that God sent so that he might survive.

The tiny bedroom led out into the single living-room which doubled as a kitchen. It smelt of damp and stale cooking. There was a rope line stretched above the fireplace, with babys' napkins pegged to it. Alice had no bathroom, and shared the communal lavatory in the back yard. Her home was shabby, the window holding a view of drab houses, but the glass was clean and so were the Nottingham lace curtains. A strip of linoleum graced the floor, with a rag-rug on the hearth where a tabby cat curled up in a ball against the polished fender. Alice took pride in the fact that she was not destitute, inclined to look down her nose at those who were. Her state was one of respectable poverty, poverty kept at bay – but no more – by dint of unremitting toil and struggle.

She never allowed anything to weigh on her spirits for long, neither a childhood where she had been regularly beaten by a drunken father, nor desertion by a feckless husband. She had met him on an ill-fated Bank Holiday excursion to the fair on Hampstead Heath, and had been swept off her feet. Impressed when he had told her he was a commercial traveller, she had been blissfully unaware of the existence of no less than three Mrs Cyril Brookers up and down the countryside. By the time she found out it was too late. They were married, she was pregnant, and Cyril had vanished.

Despite this cruel adversity which would have floored anyone less resilient, she was always unchangingly gay, an even-tempered girl who believed in God and remembered Eva Pendral in her prayers each night.

She was thinking about her as she raked the coals in the black kitchen range, added a few more knubs, blew on them till the tiny flames flickered greedily, and put a saucer of milk down for the cat. Life had been hard before that blessed day on which Eva had discovered her. Jimmy had been newly-born then, and Alice had resumed work, having never really stopped, save for a week after the confinement. Her narrow hands had crocheted endlessly, anything from elaborate borders for table-cloths to duchesse sets for rich ladies' boudoirs, or worked exquisite stitching on silk undergarments the like of which she could never hope to own. It was her only way of contributing to the common exchequer she shared with her widowed mother, Mrs Mills, who lived in the room next-door. She was a charwoman, and one of her jobs was cleaning St Mark's church, which she did in the evenings when Alice got home from work.

Alice had been introduced to Eva by Stephen Savill for, sincerely devout, she regularly attended the services and had had Jimmy christened there. From the moment they met her life had changed for the better and she was now manageress of Number 12 Bond Street. Jimmy, soon weaned on to the bottle, was left with his grandmother daily and, for the first time ever, they could now afford the necessities, with a few, a very few, little luxuries thrown in besides.

She hummed to herself as she got dressed, an anaemic girl with a waxen skin and bloodless lips. Pretty in a very delicate way, with large dark eyes and long, glossy black hair, she was thin as a lathe but possessed an inner strength which carried her through a nine-hour working day, sleepless nights when the baby was teething, and tiresome bus journeys to and from Bond Street.

I hope I can be ready before Jimmy wakes, she thought, tingling with anticipation. This is a red-letter day! I'm going to have my photograph taken. Pictures of my designs, too. Eva talked of them being printed in a fashion magazine! She had one regret: Charlotte would not be there to see it. They were friends, close in age though worlds apart in experience. Alice was not sure that she approved of her gadding off to Italy. She could tell that Eva did not like it either, and anything that bothered her patroness, bothered her, too. She looked upon Eva as little less than a saint, her heart overflowing with love and gratitude towards her. She would not hear a word said against her, or Charlotte for that matter. If her embittered mother grumbled about long hours and slave-labour, then she got short shrift and the rough edge of Alice's tongue.

'It's regular money, isn't it?' she would shout, plonking down the jug of supper beer. 'I'm working in a smart shop up West now, and you always wanted that, didn't you? We eat regularly, and baby gets his milk. He's the bonniest little lad hereabouts. Honestly, Mother, we could be a sight worse off, as well you know!'

She was sorry for her mother who had once seen better days, till she married a man who promised her much but ended up drinking away all hopes of a good life. Mrs Mills had sent her to school, insisted that she spoke properly, set great store by learning, was sure that Alice would make something of herself, perhaps even become a teacher. Her father had ensured that there was no likelihood of this ambition coming to fruition. Alice had forfeited her chance, leaving school when fourteen and putting her skill at needlework to good use so that they might meet the bills. When he died under the wheels of a brewers' dray, she thought it a fitting end, though racked with guilt because she was glad.

When she met Cyril it had seemed for a short while that he would support her, take her away from the slums, even settle with her in one of those new houses that were springing up like mushrooms in the fast expanding suburbs. He was dashing, handsome, with a smooth tongue, and had boasted of his success with the tea firm for whom he worked, promised her the earth. He had been the only man she had ever walked out with and she had loved him with every fibre of her being. Even now, she made excuses for his irresponsible conduct, and was entirely without rancour. Perhaps it was some fault in herself that had made Cyril deceive her. God had looked after her, hadn't he? Sending little Jimmy to comfort her, and then working through the Reverend Savill to bring Lady Eva to her side. There was no need to be angry or blame Cyril. He was misguided, that was all. Mrs Mills frequently lost patience with such a forgiving attitude, shaking her head in perplexity over her only child, wondering how she had managed to produce such an angel in the midst of the squalor, misery and downright wickedness in which they were trapped.

Whatever the weather, come rain, snow or sunshine, Alice's heart always lifted when she stood outside the shop. Habitually the first person there each morning, she would pause for a second, holding the keys, the cold metal warmed by the touch of her fingers. They symbolised her status, underlined her importance, and she never failed to be aware of Eva's trust in her, resolving never to fail her.

Bond Street was an even more magical place to her on that particular day, *her* shop surrounded by other small, select establishments selling hats, robes, shoes. Only the discerning took their custom there, ladies who sought the very highest quality of merchandise. Although Alice did not know this, every building in the block belonged to the Pendral Bank.

She glanced up at the gaily painted sign hanging above the door. It bore the inscription *Pour Femme* in gilt lettering on a crimson background. The windows were bow-fronted, and it looked more like a private dwelling than a shop, with its central door flanked by tubs holding the spring smile of daffodils and narcissi. This was the effect that Eva artfully projected. Customers immediately relaxed when they set foot inside, the white walls, willowy furniture, and dreamy paintings conjuring up an impression of feminine mystique.

Eva had trained her assistants herself, selecting modestly dressed, quiet-spoken young women, unconsciously copying the example set by the bank when choosing staff. Because they dealt exclusively in undergarments it was necessary to maintain an even more decorous atmosphere. The work-room was at the back, a light, airy space always filled with the whirr of sewing-machines and chatter as the girls stitched away at the rarest silks and satins, needles flashing in and out as intricate embroideries appeared on gossamer nightgowns, peignoirs, petticoats and chemises.

Alice hung her coat on a hanger in the cupboard, removed her hat and fluffed out the sides of her hair, making certain that no unsightly strands had escaped from the bun-shaped knot at the crown. It was not yet eight, and the photographer was not due till ten, but Alice picked up a duster and gave the counter a final polish – an unnecessary action for the cleaner had made a thorough job of it last evening, but it gave her something to do. At eight sharp the sewing women arrived. Each one had made a special effort with her appearance, and they were twittering with excitement. Alice controlled them, and herself, with great difficulty but by the time Eva walked through the door they were making a show of being busy.

Following her customary habit, Eva entered the work-room and talked with each girl, giving instructions. An important order had come through from no less a person than Princess Mary. She was off on a foreign tour and Eva had persuaded her to give her skilled seamstresses the responsibility for making a complete set of underwear. The Princess was a humane lady who took a lively interest in Eva's charities, and she had graciously agreed. This was a feather in their cap, and Eva was content. Let the scoffers say what they liked, her shop was under Royal patronage now.

The minutes crawled by but at last a commotion at the door heralded the arrival of Dudley and his friend. The doctor's arms were full of cumbersome photographic equipment, and he was followed by a tall, bearded man carrying a box-shaped camera. His hand shot out, gripping hers firmly as they were introduced. Eva found herself staring into a pair of deep blue eyes. There was something in them, an intentness, that gripped her with a force amounting to positive pain.

The impression lasted no more than a split second, but it was something she was never to forget. It was beyond her experience. Far from being the windows of the soul, as a rule most people's eyes were no more illuminating than any other feature. Tired eyes, shallow eyes, blank, expressionless eyes ... she had encountered them at every turn, but never once had she met eyes like his, alive, magnetic, which not only looked straight from his heart, but pierced straight into her own.

For the count of ten, Eva stood motionless, almost without breath, gazing into the stranger's eyes. Then she said, 'This is quite a day for *Pour Femme*, Mr Sinclair – the first time our shop has been photographed.'

'I'll take some interior pictures to begin with,' he answered, immensely professional. 'Then you can relax while I concentrate on the outside. All right?'

'Will there be enough light in here?' she asked, making a determined effort to regain her composure and talk in a natural, easy fashion.

Richard had already thought of this. 'The walls are white which is good, light will bounce off them, and I've brought along some really powerful electric bulbs.'

'You'll not use a flash?'

He smiled, and she noticed his white teeth, the attractive shape of his pleasant mouth. 'No, Lady Eva, I think not. The magnesium powder makes a mess. That wouldn't be very good for those lovely garments on the stands, would it? I've used that method on several occasions at banquets and dinners, and always found it wise to make a quick exit during the smoke cloud, before the black specks start to settle on the guests' hair, and in their soup.'

After that, she left the entire process to him, standing where she was told, letting him take complete charge of the girls, grouping them as he thought fit. His camera was set up on a tripod, and he was extremely particular, taking his time, gazing through the view-finder, adjusting this and that before clicking the shutter.

'That's fine. Now can we have an informal setting – try to imagine that it's an ordinary working day, ladies. Shall we move into the sewing-room? Alice, could you stand by that machinist over there, as if you were watching her at work and giving advice? Lovely. That's very good.'

'He seems to know what he's doing,' she murmured to Dudley, catching him in the shop as he rushed through to get yet another vital piece of paraphernalia from the car. 'Wherever did you two meet?'

'Round and about the artists' studios,' he answered, an amused quirk to his lips at her thinly veiled interest. 'Several of them are patients of mine. He's brilliant. Takes photography very seriously, and is a clever painter, too. You should see some of his stuff. He portrays street-scenes, people at work and play, the homeless, gypsies – his photos are full of life and compassion. He's a professional, though he comes from the upper echelon – Lady Sinclair's son.'

It did not end when the work was over. Dudley and Richard insisted on fetching cream cakes from the nearest baker, while Alice brewed tea, then they sat around in *Pour Femme*, eating, laughing, talking. Eva could see that all hope of getting any sensible work out of the girls had fled, so she announced that they could have the rest of the day off, with pay.

'You're kind to them,' Richard said, hitching his chair a trifle closer to hers when everyone except Dudley had gone. His eyes dwelt on her face with thoughtful scrutiny.

'They deserve it,' she said simply. 'And helping them gives me a great deal of happiness.'

Dudley rose, stretched his large body till the joints cracked. 'Time we were going, Richard. I've a surgery to take in an hour. Don't forget, I want you round at Canyard Street soon. It will be interesting to have before and after pictures of the property.'

Eva followed them as they went to pack the gear in the car. It was afternoon by now, the hint of spring in the air drawing out shoppers. Ladies wandered through the street, parasols raised to protect their complexions from the pale sunshine, maid-servants following behind, carrying parcels. They turned curious eyes in the direction of the two men and one woman standing near the car.

'Can I give you a lift, Eva?' Dudley offered, 'I think I can squeeze you in.'

She had thought of taking a hansom cab, for her chauffeur

expected to collect her after five, but was reluctant to leave the company of these refreshingly natural men. They talked so easily and unaffectedly, treating her as one of themselves, including her in their conversation, listening attentively to what she had to say in a most heart-warming manner. So, she was Lady Eva, owner of the Pendral Bank. It made no difference to them, and she was certain they respected her for what she was, not who she was.

She was not quite sure how it happened, but within half an hour she was in Richard's studio. Dudley had gone, and Richard had led her up through the rambling Holland Park house, to his apartment at the top.

'Sorry about all those stairs,' he said as he opened the door. 'Blame it on the north light. That's why artists live in such inaccessible eyries. It's not that they're particularly anti-social, indeed most of them revel in company when the mood takes them, but the light is all-important. This room was designed for the job. Look at the windows.'

She did, and understood. A vast fan-light occupied a quarter of the ceiling, and the big room was flooded with clear, cold, undiluted radiance.

'You paint as well?' Somehow, in spite of what Dudley had told her, she had only thought of him as being a photographer.

'Of course. The camera is an extension of my brushes.' He set a metal coffee-infuser on the top of the elegant green enamelled stove. The mica windows in the convoluted floral ironwork of the door glowed crimson.

She saw the easel with a half-worked canvas standing on it, marvelled at this representation of a riverside landscape with the dome of St Paul's shining like a mirage through the haze. Then, while he concentrated on filtering the coffee, she paced slowly round the walls where framed photographs and unframed paintings hung side by side. A multitude of subjects had been covered. As Dudley had said, they were not formal pictures of wealthy people. Her eyes went from one to another; slum scenes with care-worn mothers; scruffy children staring at the camera with dull eyes and runny noses; flinty-eyed prostitutes on street-corners; drunks lolling outside public houses; tramps asleep in the gutter.

'These should go on exhibition,' she said at length, joining him where he stood, waiting for her to be seated at a round table. 'What an indictment against our cock-eyed society!'

They talked for a long time, and Eva was aware of a link being forged between them that neither time nor distance could break. It was as if two souls had met, and mutely acknowledged their kinship.

They did not only speak of serious matters, of slum clearance, prison reforms and the problem of alcoholism that marred so many lives, but laughed as well, amused by the idiosyncratic behaviour of human beings – laughed into each other's eyes with a sense of intimacy that sent Eva's spirits soaring to the skies.

The afternoon was drawing to a close and Richard hailed a cab for her in the roadway outside. 'I've enjoyed today,' he said simply.

'So have I.' She gave him her hand.

'You'll come again, Eva?' he asked.

'Visit me, Richard.' Suddenly Holland Park sparkled in the sunset, the fine houses, gardens, trees taking a special lustre – and the cause was the leggy, dark-haired man smiling down at her. 'We must talk about arranging that exhibition. Dudley and Beth are coming to dinner next Wednesday. May I expect you, too?'

She handed him an address card as the cabby waited at the kerb. 'I hope you'll find it.'

'I'm sure I shall. And why don't we all go to the theatre afterwards?'

She laughed, a soft, girlish little laugh which struck strangely on her own ears. 'Oh, yes! That will be nice – what shall we see?'

'Leave it to Dudley and me. We'll book seats and surprise you, shall we?'

Chapter Eight

In a peculiar way it felt almost comfortable to be destitute again, as if to have money, to be able to buy food and pay for a roof over one's head, was somehow unnatural. Jennie had always been used to a hand-to-mouth existence, interspersed with periods of tentative security. Now she was once more reduced to living off her wits.

Time was running out. She was five months pregnant and had no idea what to do or where to go. Since the awful truth of her condition had been borne upon her, she had hardly left her room. To return to Ford Dobbs' studio was unthinkable. She was deeply ashamed of the changes taking place in her body and could no longer bear to expose it or have Albert suspect what was wrong.

He came looking for her several times but she kept quiet and still behind her locked door. Eventually he gave up. If she had to go out, then she did so under cover of darkness. Whether the cause was anxiety or her physical condition, she was ill, unable to keep anything down, vomiting frequently and utterly drained, emotionally, bodily and spiritually.

At first, she had gone to the chemist and purchased quinine tablets which she swallowed with a tumbler of gin, then squatted over a bowl of boiling turpentine water in an attempt to bring on a miscarriage. She had experienced agonising stomach cramps, a violent purging and an increase in nausea, but the embryo stubbornly refused to be ejected by its reluctant host. Jennie hated it passionately, hated her enlarged breasts preparing themselves to give it suck, hated her swelling belly that housed it. She felt no pity for it, that tiny, insidious thing, an alien growing daily bigger, stronger, compelled to develop by the uncaring laws of nature.

What about me? she would scream into the chaos of her mind. Who cares about me? I may die giving birth to it! And if I don't, my life will be in ruins. How can I keep it? I don't *want* to keep it! And those men who did this to me are getting off scot-free.

Now the last of her money had gone, the landlord was demanding his rent, there was nothing left to pawn and she recognised that she had reached the end of the road. On a sullen, stormy day which exactly matched her mood, she flung a shawl about her head and shoulders, bundled her few remaining possessions in a scarf, took a last look about the room that had become her prison, and left the lodging-house before anyone else was up. The landlord could whistle for his rent.

The capricious English weather had made March warm and April cold. Buds had opened hopefully, only to be blasted by unexpected and sharp frosts. People did not linger on their way to work as they had done a few days before but hurried by, heads bent, hunched into themselves. No one heeded the solitary girl wandering aimlessly along. All day she tramped the streets, walking, walking, as if by doing so she could escape her own tormented thoughts. She was hungry, desperately so, but had not even the price of a cup of tea. The factory closures were over, workers employed again, so the majority of soup-kitchens had shut their doors pending the next disaster.

The markets offered no solution and only accentuated her poverty, the streets thick with stalls selling meat, fish, pies, fruit. The noise was continuous: tradesmen bawling their wares, people thrusting thier way through the crowds seeking a particular purchase. There were cheap-jacks hawking watches; quack doctors extolling the virtues of their cure-alls; beggar-boys strumming banjos to get a few coins; shoe-sellers haggling; cloth-sellers walking up and down with lengths of material over their shoulders. Those dealing in secondhand garments were doing a roaring trade. There were book-stalls, junk-stalls, antique-stalls. Almost anything and everything could be bought in the London markets for a few coppers, from a pair of kippers to an Egyptian mummy.

Dusk was settling when Jennie left, though trade was still brisk. A grocer's store on the street corner was open, its lamps like ripe oranges in the eerie half light. The succulent smell of frying batter carried an illusion of warmth, coming from the fish shop next door. Jennie joined the gang of ragged children pressing their noses longingly against the window, looking in to where olive green tiles gleamed, glasses of jellied eels stood on the wooden counter and a big pan of mashed potatoes steamed on the stove, close to a pot of mushy emerald peas.

I'm hungry! Jennie could think of nothing else. She had not eaten for two days, and then it had only been a slice of stale bread and a scrape of margarine. She could beg, she supposed, but was too proud. In any case, this was a poor area and it was unlikely that anyone would notice her outstretched hand. As she left the spot, a man sidled up to her. He seemed barely human, with a great beak of a nose above a thin mouth. He had heavy, hanging jowls, and eyes hooded by deep, fleshy folds.

'I'm lookin' for a nice girl,' he grunted. 'What about it, ducks? You got somewhere we can go? Want to come to the pub for a drink first?'

Jennie shrank back. Her self-worth might have reached an all time low, but there were still things she would never do. She turned her back on him, and quickened her pace, terrified that he might follow her but, when she glanced over her shoulder, he was nowhere to be seen.

Was prostitution all that remained for her? What price her dreams and ambitions now? A Gaiety star? She almost laughed at the impossibility of it. She was so tired that she seemed to be seeing things through undulating fog, having no idea where she was heading until a melancholy horn giving a banshee wail downstream made her aware that she was standing on the river bank, not far from where she had awakened after that foolhardy visit to the Café Royal. She was the only person in this desolate spot, though a huge rat, startled by her arrival, leapt into the water and swam away. Sinister steps led down to the exposed ooze, gleaming like polished silver, and beyond that the moon made a pattern on the water, each oily, dancing ripple crowned with light.

Jennie stood on the bottom step. The mud was disappearing, gradually covered by the rising tide. It was so quiet there, tranquil as the grave. And why shouldn't I do it? she thought. I'm alone. There's not a damned soul in the world who belongs to me. No one to mourn me. No one to care. She forgot that at one time she had dreaded becoming a decomposing, saturated corpse. Now the idea was enticing. No more pain, hunger and fear. Nothing at all. Oblivion.

Frightened? Oh, yes, very frightened. How would it be to have the murky water closing over her, to choke, to struggle, to weaken and give up? But a trancelike feeling enmeshed her, urging her to do it, and she answered the siren-call of death.

The shock of icy water around her ankles. It crept up, soaking her skirt to the knees. The current tugged at her clothing, urged her to yield herself to it, as so many had done in the past. She raised her eyes to the moon. The fretful night wind sent clouds scudding across it, and it seemed that she heard a voice. She forgot the troubles of her soul, seeing in memory's mirror the face of Zena the gypsy, and caught the echo of her voice, saying, 'All will come to you – wealth, power, the stage, the limelight – even love.'

'How can this be?' Jennie protested, standing shivering in the river.

'It will. Trust me. I warned you that you were your own worst enemy, didn't I? But you're a survivor, nothing can hold you back – not even the most dreadful adversity.'

A survivor! Yes, I *am* a survivor! Jennie shook herself awake. The river gurgled around her feet and she stepped back, shuddering with revulsion. It had now acquired a special terror, its evil vapours foetid and clammy as henbane leaves, its surface glowing with the lurid purple of deadly nightshade flowers.

Strength poured through Jennie's limbs, and fury lit up her brain. I'll find Everett Braithwaite! He should be made to pay for what he's done. He was the ring-leader, even if this isn't his little by-blow I'm carrying. That bugger will foot the bill!

It was wonderful to regain her fighting spirit. Hunger, cold, meant nothing. She ran up the steps and walked as briskly as her water-logged shoes and wet skirt would allow, through the streets toward the Café Royal. Why didn't you do this before? she lectured herself crossly. Why did you hide? You're not the guilty party. You should rub *all* their noses in it. Every single one of those bastards! They won't get away with it.

She felt well, sickness gone, energy flooding every part of her body and mind. This buoyancy lasted until she reached the great curve of Regent Street. The stores were closed, Liberty's, Jay's, Swan and Edgar, but their windows were fully lit and, because this was the time of the Season and Regent Street its artery of fashion and society, the road was filled with vehicles taking the wealthy to theatres, clubs or restaurants. Had it been July, when no member of the élite was supposed to linger in town, it would have been practically deserted, the places of entertainment closed down until the dusks of autumn brought them back again.

Jennie passed the alluring windows, the stately façade of Oddenino's Hotel, and finally reached her destination. Some of her courage deserted her, to be replaced by apprehension. Rather than walking boldly through the doors as she had imagined, she hid in the shadows. The beefy, puce-uniformed major-domo on guard would hardly let a bedraggled scarcrow like her approach within yards of that select threshold. So she waited, a dark figure half concealed behind a pillar, watching as carriage after carriage rolled up to disgorge their svelte passengers on the pavement outside the café's impressive frontage.

She was taking a chance, acting on a hunch, knowing little about Everett or his habits except for what Albert had told her when he was persuading her to pose for him. 'Likes the smart cafés,' he had said. 'Thinks 'imself no end of a swell. The Café Royal's 'is favourite stamping-ground.'

That was five months ago. Was it still Everett's haunt? Was he even in London? Yes, he was bound to be now that the Season was in full swing. So she waited with the patience granted to women as one of their weapons. A woman could wait, for years if need be, to see justice done.

An hour passed. Jennie could hardly feel her frozen feet, but she refused to give up. Then a coach – smart-painted, swift-running, with a team of sleek, high-stepping horses – appeared under the streetlight. It rocked, was still, and a man got out. It was Everett, wearing a long cape over his evening-suit, a top hat set at a rakish angle on his head. He exchanged sallies with the driver, gave a deep-bellied laugh, then sauntered towards the café's entrance, swinging his cane jauntily. His coachman clicked his tongue and drove the team round to the rear to wait his master's orders.

Jennie gathered her cramped limbs and sprang, catching Everett by the back of his cloak before he reached the door. He swung round, startled, raising his cane in a threatening gesture.

'What the devil – ?

'You've got to 'elp me! You remember me, don't you? I'm Jennie, the girl you and your mates raped.'

He stood motionless, his mouth half-open, his fingers strangely rigid. Then, with a violent movement, he flung her from him. 'Get away from me! I've never seen you before in my life.'

'Liar!' she hissed. 'Look at me, Everett Braithwaite! Look at my belly! See what you and your bloody friends did!'

Everett recognised her at once. No one could forget her hair, or those burning amber eyes. He had asked Albert what had happened to her, but the Cockney had shrugged, seemed uneasy, said she had vanished. Everett had been relieved, trying to blot out her memory, and now she was there, accusing him. He was as guilty as hell, and he knew it. His face worked; it knotted menacingly, then became smooth again; the thick beard jerked with the trembling of his lips, but he was not prepared to admit to anything.

'Stubbins! Come over here!' he shouted imperiously to the commissionaire who was already staring in their direction.

The man leapt to attention. 'Is she bothering you, sir?' he asked, glaring at Jennie.

'She is. Don't stand there gaping, man. Do as I say!'

'You've got to give me some money.' Jennie stood her ground stubbornly. 'I ain't got nothing – you must 'elp me. It's only right.'

'I don't know you – never had any dealings with you! If you don't leave me alone, I'll have the law on you.'

'You bastard!' The contempt in her voice cut like a lash.

'Are you going to get out of here or do I call the police?' Everett was mortified, for a crowd had begun to gather and he was being scrutinised by curious eyes.

Stubbins, his waxed moustache quivering with indignation, seized Jennie by the arm and tried to force her into the gutter, while an underling ran off down the street to find a policeman. Jennie defended herself with wildcat vehemence, satisfied to hear Stubbins grunt as her heels made contact with his shins, hitching up her skirt as she tried to knee him in the crotch. She fought savagely, slapping, scratching, biting, cursing, her shrieks of rage resounding through the confines of the Café Royal.

Richard came out to see what the commotion was about at the same moment that the page-boy arrived with a constable, who immediately put a half-nelson on Jennie. She sagged in his grip, looking small and defenceless in the massive clutch of the law.

'What's going on, Everett?' Richard asked, not recognising her at first.

'She threatened me. Used abusive language. Claimed that she knew me. She's a liar!'

'It's not true.' Jennie shouted, wriggling in the policeman's grasp. ''Ee does know me! I swear 'ee does!'

'Now then, my girl. Enough of this. We'll soon find out what your game is when we gets you down to the station,' the officer warned heavily.

Richard could see now who she was. He had never forgotten the beautiful girl that Everett had displayed so proudly. He had wondered what had become of her and why Everett had not brought her to the café again, but had assumed that he had paid her and sent her on her way when he was done with her. Everett was not one of his close friends. Indeed, he didn't much like the man, and was far too busy to concern himself with his business, moral or immoral. Yet from what little he knew of Everett's mode of life, he was inclined to believe him capable of twisting any situation to suit himself. So why was he denying Jennie? Was he ashamed to be approached in public by such a draggle-tailed slut? Was it bad for his image, or was there something more unpleasant behind it?

He shot Everett a steely, questioning look, and muttered. 'It's your friend, Jennie Blossom, isn't it? What's all this about?'

'She's no friend of mine,' Everett growled. 'Hounding me, making wild accusations! The girl's mad!'

'What d'you want me to do with her, sir?' The officer said, his raw-boned fingers fastened round her wrist like a hand-cuff. 'Did she steal from you?'

Everett wanted nothing more than to shrug off the embarrassing incident and pursue his evening's entertainment. 'She was importuning me. She's a street-walker.'

'Is she, indeed. Well, lass, what have you got to say for yourself?' The policeman was tired. His feet ached in the heavy black boots. It had been a long beat and he wanted to get back to the station, make his report and go home.

Jennie stared up at him, hostility in her viciously cold eyes. He was one of the enemy. He'd not listen to her, no matter what she said. So she refused to speak.

He was becoming more and more exasperated. 'This won't do you any good, you know. Were you soliciting?'

Soliciting? Good God! What a thing to suggest! Is that all men can think about? she raged inside, but she kept her lips stubbornly closed, staring him silent.

'It's all right, sergeant,' Everett snapped.

Good God, but this was awkward. There were people in the café who knew him. His evening was set fair to be spoilt and he had been looking forward to enjoying a drink or two before going backstage at the Empire Theatre, Leicester Square, and taking one of the leading dancers out to supper.

'Are you sure, sir?' The constable looked at him dubiously.

'Yes, yes.' Everett waved an impatient hand. 'Let her go. Perhaps I was mistaken and she was only begging. I won't press charges.'

The policeman pushed back his helmet, perplexed. 'I dunno whether I can do that, sir. Someone should be responsible for her good behaviour.'

Richard was not in the least given to sentimentality or grandiose gestures, but he was profoundly moved to see Jennie standing there, beaten but defiant. 'I'll vouch for her,' he said firmly. 'I'm associated with the Pendral Charity Fund. I can probably find her a place to stay.'

Jennie woke to life at this, pulling herself up to her full height, arms akimbo as she stared at Everett and Richard contemptuously.

'That won't do,' she shouted loudly. 'You can stuff your charity. I want justice – that bugger should be made to pay!'

The constable was looking uncertainly from her to Everett, unsure of the correct procedure in such a case. Richard took her by the arm, keeping his voice low. 'Shut up, Jennie! D'you want to spend the night in a cell?'

Taking no heed of her protests, he marched her to where a cab stood beside the kerbstone, slung between two huge wheels with the horse fretting in the collar and the driver perched high at the back, his long whip in a metal slot near his right hand.

'Cab, sir?' he asked casually, as if he had not been watching every moment of the scene with avid interest.

'Holland Park,' Richard answered, bundling her on to the footrest and leaping up behind.

Jennie sat glowering at him through the gloom of the stuffy interior. 'Why did you 'ave to stick your nose in?' she grated harshly. 'One of 'is pals, I suppose. You bloody nobs all 'ang together!'

Richard did not deign to reply, wondering why he was bothering with such an ungrateful little bitch. He lit a cigarette and stared out of the window in front. He could see the horse's flanks moving in a steady rhythm. The whip-lash waved in the air and touched the animal's back encouragingly, not unkindly, almost caressingly.

A fetid odour crept into his nostrils and it was nothing to do with the fusty smell of the cab. 'You stink,' he said to Jennie.

'I 'spect I do. You'd stink too, if you'd been in the bleeding river.' There was a wealth of resentment in her tone.

'And what were you doing in the river?' It was difficult to keep his patience with such a surly person, but he tried.

'Well, I weren't going for a swim! I was trying to drown myself, that's wat!' she said with asperity.

'Why were you going to do that?' he asked after a short silence during which he considered the possibility that she was exaggerating for dramatic effect.

'You got eyes in your 'ead, ain't you? Can't you see? I'm up the duff – in the club – up the spout!'

'You're pregnant?'

She heaved a sigh. 'Blimey! Do I 'ave to spell it out? Yes, I'm pregnant.'

Daylight dawned on Richard, and with realisation came thunderous rage. 'Is it Everett's? Is that what the row was about?'

Her voice was subdued now, and shaky with sobs. 'I dunno if it's 'is. That night – you remember? When I came to the Café Royal. Don't you know what 'appened back at 'is 'ouse? Ain't they told you about it, laughed about it? They got me drunk and then 'ad their way with me. There were several of 'em, and Albert Baggot, too.'

'I see.' Richard passed a hand across his eyes, riven with pity for her, furious with Everett and his unprincipled crew. 'I'm sorry, Jennie. No, I didn't know anything about it, and they're not particular pals of mine. I don't spend much time with those sort of people.'

'Where are you taking me? What are you going to do? I 'spect you're the same as them really. If you think I'm easy meat now I'm in trouble, then you can think again, mister.'

'That's not what I think. I want to help you, Jennie,' he said softly, trying to reassure this tormented, desperate creature. He shuddered mentally as he visualised the anguish that had forced her to contemplate suicide.

Eva will know what to do, he thought. He had become very close to her during the past weeks, admiring her more than any woman he had ever met. They had spent hours together, simply talking, planning his exhibition of photographs and drawings which were such a glaring exposé of conditions that brought shame to England. He had learned so much from her.

Among other things, he had talked to the girls in Eva's workshop who were full of praise for what she had done for them, and had studied pamphlets waging war on the plight of shop assistants, that class known as the aristocracy of labour, slightly more refined young men and women. They suffered the hated living-in system, board and lodging being provided by their employer which kept them in a state of servitude where their hours were, on average, seventy-nine per week for a wage of between five and ten shillings, their lives made a misery by petty rules and restrictions, both during working-time and out. Dudley had introduced him to Stephen Savill, and the three men, doctor, vicar and artist, had leant their strength to the tasks involved in re-building the house in Canyard Street.

The cab pulled up in Holland Park. Jennie resisted at first and then, bone-weary, allowed him to conduct her inside. The studio was bright and warm, dizzyingly so. She was shivering so much she could hardly stand, her teeth chattering. Richard took one look at her and said,

'I'll run a bath. You must get out of those wet things.'

The apartment consisted of one large studio-cum-living room partitioned to provide a bedroom leading from it, complete with bathroom en-suite. A kitchen had been sectioned off on the other side, and Richard had rigged up a darkroom in a large cupboard.

Jennie registered everything, impressed by the exotic rugs, drapes and furniture, for Richard had a penchant for Oriental decor.

'Cor!' was all she could say when she entered the bathroom.

It was small but very elaborate, and she could not take her eyes from the bath itself, made of mottled green marble and cocooned in a beautifully carved oaken frame. The foot-end terminated in a stand-up shower cubicle, and there were porcelain taps along the side to control both the spigot and the shower-jets. The walls surrounding both bath and shower were lined with Islamic tiles, and the woodwork finished off with railings of turned wood. It reminded Jennie of a cross between a four-poster bed and the entrance to a mausoleum.

Richard was shrouded in steam, bending over the water, testing it. He straightened up when she came in. 'Get a move on, Jennie. You'll catch pneumonia if you don't hurry.'

She was immediately on the defensive. 'I ain't taking off a stitch in front of you.'

He laughed, easy and relaxed in his shirt-sleeves. 'Don't worry, I'm not about to storm your virtue. Use that dressing-gown over there when you've finished, and we'll dry your clothes. I'll leave you to it. There's a bolt on the door.'

Still grinning, he picked up his coat and strolled out. Jennie promptly slid the bolt across, then began to undress. She could hardly believe she was really there. Such grandeur! He's a well-oiled toff, she concluded, examining the equally splendid matching wash-basin, and then, greatly daring, seating herself on the lavatory. It, too, was encased in a polished wooden chest-like frame, and the bowl was decorated with flowers, as was the high-level cistern. When she came to use the flush, her hand closed round an opulent, red-tasselled silk chain-pull.

These details imprinted themselves on her brain. I'll have everything just as posh when I'm an actress, she decided. Maybe even posher!

Lying in the warm water, her old ambitions returned. It *was* possible after all. She wasn't done for, not while she had an important friend like Richard. It was hard to credit that only a couple of hours ago she had been standing on the bank of the Thames, ready to put an end to her life. She lay there, soaping herself and scheming. So Everett wouldn't accept his responsibilities? Right, she would cross him off her list, or rather put him in abeyance for future reference. He'd pay, some way or another, she vowed, and her eyes narrowed thoughtfully.

The water was getting chilly. She turned on the hot tap with a lovely feeling of extravagance. No more inefficient old geysers for her. This was the life. This was what she wanted and was determined to get. The baby? She ran a hand over her stomach. Richard knew people, a lot of people. He must know doctors, too. He had money, that much was obvious. She would be as nice as could be to Richard . . . and somehow the idea of being nice to him did not fill her with revulsion. She had fancied him in the Café Royal, and she fancied him now. The thought of him making love to her gave her a pleasant thrill, and she had never felt like that about a man before. Perhaps he'd teach her to enjoy it? There must be enjoyment in it, surely, or people wouldn't do it so much, though she failed to comprehend what this enjoyment might be.

If we do it, I'll be safe for tonight at any rate, still pregnant, she reflected. In a week's time things will be different, if I get my way.

Jennie rose from the bath and, dripping, reached for the thick pale green towels, wrapping herself in one. Then she filled the basin with water and washed her hair, using a bottle of lotion she found on a shelf. Another towel was wound turban-fashion around her head. Dry, scented with talcum powder, she scrutinised herself in the long mirror set in the wall. Full-breasted, her figure was still passable. She had been too poor and ill to put on weight. She donned the checked wool, very masculine dressing-gown, turning back the sleeves that flopped over her hands and tieing the cord around her waist. It was luxuriantly warm, and smelt of Richard.

He glanced up when she padded into the studio, then installed her in a deep armchair next to the stove and fed her with hot soup. Jenny ate and ate, soup followed by rolls and butter, and crumpets which he toasted, opening the stove doors and sticking them on a fork held out to the flames.

Like I did once in Zena's room, she remembered. Zena saved me tonight. I'm sure of it. She must have sensed that I was going to kill myself. She sent me to Richard, arranged it all. The only thing stopping me is this damned baby. Jennie had intended to wait, to woo him first in order to soften him up, but now swivelled round in the chair, her eyes enormous in her pale face as she shot at him, 'You're bound to know a doctor who'll get rid of this for me.' and she pressed a hand against her stomach.

Richard looked up and frowned, the firelight playing over his angular features. 'You can't want to destroy your child?'

'I do – oh, yes, I do! I 'ate it!' she said with stinging vehemence. 'It means nothing to me. It's a damned nuisance. I want to go on the stage, you see. I know I'd be a success, but I can't if I've got to look after this thing.'

Then she began to talk and Richard remained silent, listening to her. It was like the bursting of a dam, a savage torrent of words gushing out. She could not keep still, rising from the chair and pacing round the room, gesticulating, shouting, crying. She told him everything, from as far back as she could recall, and Richard cringed inside, head bowed under the thought of mankind's ceaseless pain, of which she was such a prime example. Roaming the slums in search of subjects, meeting Eva, and now Jennie, he had been forced to descend from the pleasant heights of idealism to the bitter, cold and dark valleys of reality.

'Jennie, Jennie,' he whispered at last, spreading his hands helplessly. 'I'm so sorry. I'll do anything for you, but I can't agree to you killing your baby. It wouldn't be right or – '

She slowly turned on him her sorrowful face, and he floundered in the middle of the sentence. Something in that face gripped him with panic, terrified him, bound him mysteriously and indissolubly. She's so beautiful, he thought, and ached to feel a pencil in his hand or, better still, his camera. To capture her expression for ever: the young, despairing mother – wronged, betrayed, abandoned.

'How old are you?' he asked.

'What's that got to do with it? If you must know, I'm sixteen next October.' She sank down, almost hugging the stove as if she would never be warm again, drained by her outburst, by so much weeping.

'So young,' he mourned, ashamed because he desired her. There were some itches it was best not to scratch. 'Only fifteen and already an old woman of a hundred in experience. Jesus, it's the time for schooling, not taking on the burden of a baby.'

'But if you won't 'elp me, I've got to 'ave it.'

Richard dropped to his heels beside her, and his arm went around her drooping shoulders. 'Listen to me, Jennie. I can take you to a doctor I know, to see if everything's going well, but forget about an abortion. You need proper medical care right now.'

'What's to become of me?' She leaned her head back against him, forgetting that she had contemplated seduction, nothing more than a pathetic child, needing comfort.

'I'm trying to think of the best way to tackle this.' He was very conscious of the thin body so close to his own, the slenderness of it, the vulnerability. Not only was he holding Jennie, but her infant as well. 'You can stay here, that goes without saying, though not for long. There are several fellows, artists and suchlike, who have rooms below this one and they won't take any notice if I have a girl with me, but Mrs Huggins lives in the basement.'

'Who's she?'

'The caretaker's wife and she 'does' for all of us – seeing to our laundry, cleaning the rooms.'

Jennie looked into his face with a cynical smile. 'Ah, so you gents are still waited on, 'and, foot and finger. You ain't left 'ome really, 'ave you?'

'I suppose not,' he agreed, thinking, Trust her to put her finger on the tender spot. Isn't it true that I live very much as I've always done, despite all this huffing and puffing about injustice? It doesn't effect me personally. I'm never cold, homeless or hungry. Obstacles are smoothed from my path because of my money and connections.

She had discarded the towel, and her tousled hair cascaded over her shoulders, its hue rended darker because it was still wet. His artist's eye noted that it was not the colour of copper, but of rust. A subtle perfume arose from it, of honey-suckle scented shampoo mingled with a personal odour all her own. It was so soft to his touch that he felt that it must melt against his hot palm as if it were fairy gold.

Since his teens, Richard had never practised celibacy for long. There had usually been some woman somewhere willing to share his bed, even if only for short periods. At the moment there was no one unless one counted Eva, and his feelings towards her were platonic. To have this lonely girl in his room, at his mercy, weakened by distress, was a strong temptation. He had to keep reminding himself that she was under age. He drew back from her, pressing his fingertips together until the nails whitened.

'So I can't stay 'ere for good,' Jennie whispered, hunching into herself. 'And I've got to 'ave the baby. Fat lot of use you've turned out to be. I might as well go back to the river.'

'Don't be stupid.' Richard was angry because she roused in him strong emotions of pity, lust, and a sense of helpless frustration.

'I ain't stupid!' She refused to back down before his anger. 'Are my things dry yet? I'd better be going, if you don't want me in your precious apartment. Mustn't let Mrs 'uggins find out you 'ad a tart 'ere, must you? She might grass you up to your mam!'

He ignored her sarcasm, surprised at how perceptive she was, but she was wrong about him worrying that his mother might find out. It was Eva Pendral who concerned him. Though genuine in his desire to aid her in her work, Richard was ambitious. The exhibition that she was eager to promote would boost his reputation, both as artist and photographer. He had a gut feeling that she would not be so enthusiastic if she discovered that he had been sheltering a pretty vagabond like Jennie.

A plan was already formulating in his mind by which he might remain in Eva's good books, yet still retain a hold over the fascinating slum-child. Besides finding her devastatingly desirable, he also yearned to use her as a model. He was concerned about her, too, and found that he wanted to see her with her baby, to look after them both.

'Listen, Jennie,' he said, resuming his place at her side, 'I have a little cottage on the coast, near Southend.'

He did not add that it was also not far from the Sinclair family seat. This was not important and he was sure that it would be safe to take her there as his mother hardly ever left London. She hated country life. His eldest brother, the Sinclair heir who had inherited the manor house, was too wrapped up in farming to bother about his brother's affairs.

'Very nice,' Jennie commented, her eyes blank and hard. 'Ain't you the lucky one? and 'ow does this 'elp me?'

'We'll go there tomorrow, after you've seen Dr Armstrong. It's only a short train-ride. You can stay till the baby comes.'

'What about my career?'

'Christ! You're one of the most difficult baggages I've ever come across, and I've met a few in my time!' he shouted, leaping to his feet. 'What d'you expect me to do? Lodge you in Buckingham Palace?'

'Keep you 'air on, Richard. No need to get wound up.' She was sitting on the floor, her arms around her knees, staring up at him with those wide, feline eyes of hers.

He was moved because this was the first time she had used his name, but her accent made him wince. 'And another thing,' he went on. 'You think you stand a chance of appearing at the Gaiety Theatre? You're crazy! From what I hear, George Edwardes is very particular about who he employs. To become one of his Girls, you've got to be lovely, talented, and appear to be ladylike. You don't stand a hope in hell on the last requirement. First of all, it'll take elocution lessons to get rid of that awful, nasal whine of yours. You'll have to learn not to cuss and drop your aitches. You'll have to study deportment, fashion, good manners.'

'And acting, singing and dancing.' Jennie clapped her hands, her face flushed with excitement.

'Yes,' he nodded slowly, drawing on his cigarette as he studied her. 'Are you prepared to work like a black in order to get where you want to be?'

'You bet I am!'

'And the baby?'

'Seems like I ain't got no choice, but if I get a good job on the stage, then I'll be able to pay someone to look after it, won't I?'

Richard frowned. 'I don't know. A mother's place is with her child.'

'Let's jump that fence when we comes to it, shall we?' Jennie was sure she would not change her mind, but there was no point in upsetting him at this precise moment.

'You'll come to the cottage? Do exactly as I tell you and behave yourself?'

'I suppose so.' She lifted her shoulders in a shrug.

Still unconvinced, Richard went to the cabinet, taking out a bottle of whisky and two glasses. 'D'you want a drink?'

'Yes.' Jennie had not touched a drop since the gin, but hope was blossoming in her heart, hope and a growing trust in Richard. She sensed that he would not try to take advantage of her. A drink could do no harm, a single tot by way of celebration.

Two drinks later she was feeling extremely mellow. It was pleasant in the studio, lit by shaded electric lamps, warmed by the stove which sent out heat into every corner. Jennie's urchin-eye missed nothing and she had already assessed the value of the contents, and prowled the studio's length like a curious cat, asking him about his work. It was rather disconcerting to discover his interest in photography, reminding her of Dobbs, but there were no pictures of naked girls hanging on Richard's walls – a nude oil-painting or two, maybe, but these were tastefully posed and not in the least salacious.

Then there was Richard himself. Jennie wondered about him, his motives, his own ambitions. She was interested, but suspicious. A good-looker, he was certainly that, the sort of man on whose arm any girl would be proud to be seen. But Jennie was wary of her own emotions, bewildered because one half of her longed for him to kiss her, and the other half was scared to death.

It was growing late, and still they sat on in the fire-light, Richard smoking and Jennie revelling in the luxury of cleanliness, comfort and a full stomach. 'You're nodding off,' he said, stirring at last.

'Where am I to sleep?' Now for it, she thought. Now's the time when, if that's his intention, he'll suggest I share his bed.

'In my room,' he answered.

Jennie froze. Did she want this or did she not? What I'd like best of all is to be on my own for a bit, she thought, to digest what's happened. She hugged her arms around herself in an unconsciously defensive gesture.

'I see,' she faltered.

'No, you don't.' His voice was deep and full of laughter. 'You'll have my room and I'll settle for the couch out here. Give me a moment to fetch some blankets and a pillow.'

He disappeared into the bedroom and Jennie could feel herself blushing bright red. God, what must he think of me? He'll imagine that I was throwing myself at him, won't he? And the bugger's rejected me! Why? Maybe he takes me for a whore and is afraid of catching a disease. Maybe he doesn't want me. Her newly found confidence took a plunge, and anger sparked within her. She had been sitting there daydreaming of lying in his arms, tentative, unformed dreams, yet they had pleased her. His reaction had been a shock. She did not know whether to be glad or sorry.

He came back, and busied himself with turning the couch into a make-shift bed. Jennie watched him with growing admiration: his long legs in the snug-fitting trousers, the broad shoulders straining against the thin white shirt as he moved, the smile that lit up his face when he glanced across at her.

'You'll be snug as a bug in a rug there,' she commented to hide her embarrassment, afraid that something in her face had given her away.

'Yes, it'll do me fine.' He straightened up, pulled a small table closer and removed his wristwatch, laying it beside his lighter and cigarettes. 'I'll show you where the light switches are. Give me a shout in the night if you want anything.'

I'm not likely to do that, she thought, when all I want is you – that would do nothing but pile up trouble.

Richard turned on the lamps and the bedroom sprung into focus, proving to be every bit as luxurious as the rest of the apartment, filled with rich-textured fabrics and antique furniture.

'I'm an avid collector of anything old and interesting,' he explained when she remarked on this. 'Can't resist auction sales. There's nothing of great value here. I pick up odds and ends in my travels, items that appeal to me.'

'It's lovely,' Jennie breathed. 'I ain't never seen nothing like it.'

'I've put one of my night-shirts for you to wear.' He pointed to where it lay across the embossed velvet quilt.

'Thanks. That's kind of you.' It was all too much, and she could feel her head swimming. The bedroom was so splendid, the kind of room she had dreamed of occupying once she was a star.

He gave her a grin. 'I'm that sort of person. Can't you see my halo?'

They turned together, thinking only to say goodnight, then they paused, and he reached out and took her hand in his. She was aware of how tall he was, the top of her head level with his chin, and this made her feel good. He was big and powerful. He would protect her. And she, who had always fought her own battles, was glad to relinquish the burden. She was canny enough to accept that this might be an illusion, that he was probably insincere, that he might change his mind and kick her out on the morrow, but just for the while it was comforting to suspend disbelief.

'I'll try to be good, I promise,' she whispered, unable to stop herself from leaning into him.

'I know. Sleep well, kitten.' There was a thread of amused tenderness in his voice.

His eyes held hers for an instant, blue, penetrating eyes, then he lowered his head and Jennie closed her eyes, waiting in delicious anticipation to feel his lips on hers. She waited in vain, breathing in the scent of him, of wine and tobacco and masculinity. Then she felt the brush of his beard against her brow as he placed the kiss there, released her and left the room.

Well, what d'you make of that? she asked herself as she threw off the dressing-gown and pulled the night-shirt over her head. He's a funny customer. I've never come across anyone like him.

She forgot Richard for a moment in the novelty of pulling back the covers and slipping into the bed. It was wide, a curious sort of divan, lacking foot and headboard. The mattress was springy, the sheets of fine cotton. She sniffed the pillows. No, he hadn't changed the linen before handing his bed over to her. She could smell his hair, his beard, and it was lovely. There was another aroma in the room, too, the spicy smell of joss-sticks that made her think of Zena.

She saw a little box on the bedside table and picked it up inquisitively. She caught her breath in wonder when, on lifting the lid, a tiny ballerina began to twirl and the mechanism inside tinkled the strains of a waltz. Jennie lay back, holding it in her hands, turning the key at one side to crank it up when the musical-box ran down. Richard owned so many interesting things and she listened drowsily to the tune, thinking about him, thinking of her future. He had told her his cottage was by the seaside. Jennie had never seen the sea, had never been out of London. They were going there by train, and this, too, would be a new adventure.

Her eyelids began to droop, the room faded, and Jennie was dreaming of running along the sand with his hand in hers. Richard: her friend, her champion – maybe her lover.

Chapter Nine

It was evening in Florence and Charlotte was sure there couldn't be anywhere more perfect in the world, leaning on the balcony of the Villa Alinari as the day drew to a close.

The sun was sinking in a golden blaze, and against the sky the ilex and acacia trees stood out black as funeral plumes. The scent of fruits, flowers and spices blended on the cooling air. The wind had risen, blowing from mountain and sea across the plains, bearing with it the fragrance of pine and oak forests. It carried, too, the distant cadences of church bells chiming for evening prayers. This was what had struck her most since being in Italy, the almost constant sound of bells, and there were more than ever just now for it was the carnival season.

Charlotte drew in a deep breath, filled with a tumult of emotions; happiness, excitement, an ache in the heart that responded to so much beauty. On such a night as this why can't we lose ourselves in dreams? Why does reality and duty have to intrude? she wondered.

The moon was rising over the trees, the Mother Goddess accompanied by her acolytes, the stars. Charlotte loved the sultry Italian nights, and the sun-filled days where all around was a radiance of light that seemed to throb with intensity and yet conveyed serenity, too. This night had an especially magical quality because she was actually spending it in the villa of which Phelan had told her so much.

It had belonged to a great family for four hundred years, and the rooms were full of valuable treasures and masterpieces that would have fetched a fortune in the sale-rooms. But the Contessa's late husband, a dilettante hopelessly incapable of managing money, had refused to part with anything and had stipulated in his will that she was not to do so either. Thus the Villa Alinari dreamed on in its overgrown garden surrounded by crumbling walls, where the lemons clustered amid dark green leaves, and vines writhed upwards in the drowsy warmth, and flowers sprawled joyously, unfurling their many-hued petals in adoration of the sun.

Some of the land was cultivated, producing olives, figs, and grapes for wine, and the Contessa employed peasants to tend it, but she was even less interested in business than her husband had been and they took advantage. Phelan had announced his intention of spending time with the overseer, going through the accounts, but he had not sounded very enthusiastic. Both he and his mother were lotus-eaters, enjoying the good things of life which they expected to be handed over gratis on a golden platter.

Charlotte, drilled in economy by Eva and ever mindful of the glaring discrepanices in the system, was sometimes shocked by his attitude. She had witnessed poverty on their journey: the beggars in streets of the great cities, the cripples, the big-eyed, famished children holding out their hands for money, but somehow she had found herself slipping into his way of thinking. It was true that the suffering was less apparent in Tuscany where the climate was temperate, fruit grew in abundance, and the people seemed happier, more philosophical, devout and artistic than their London counterparts. No doubt the peasants groaned under the heels of harsh landowners, but Phelan did not bother about that, and she found herself pushing it to the back of her mind.

'We're on holiday,' he had said once, when she complained of his extravagance. 'Stop feeling so guilty, my dear. Enjoy it.'

Eva had given her a more than generous amount of spending money, and arranged with banks abroad for further cheques to be cashed should she need them. Bernice was taking care of Gwen's bills, as she had promised, and Julian seemed to have unlimited resources, though where they came from remained a mystery. Charlotte supposed his parents provided for him. Andrew was fêted by one and all, resting on his explorer's laurels, drawing royalties from the articles he wrote for magazines about his adventures in Africa. As for Phelan, he had hinted at a private income, and also had prodigious luck at the card-tables. The atmosphere of boundless enjoyment and carefree spending was tempting, and Charlotte yielded to it, pushing doubts to one side. But as for marrying him? This was quite different.

'A penny for your thoughts,' a voice suddenly whispered, and Phelan's arm came to rest about her waist.

She started, having thought herself alone for she had left him playing whist with the Contessa. She turned, her face aglow with pleasure in the glimmer of coloured lanterns slung on wire from the walls, but with no intention of sharing her thoughts with him, still unsure of the wisdom of yielding to the strong feelings he engendered. He had been a marvellous travelling companion, the journey by boat, train and car turned into an adventure, packed with events and excitement. Charming, considerate, he had booked in at the best hotels, making certain that Gwen and Charlotte wanted for nothing, while Bernice had been in a ferment of delight, surrounded by a plethora of personable escorts.

'I'm overwhelemed by Florence. This is a magnificent view,' Charlotte said, and his arms tightened about her.

'You've not seen anything yet. We've arrived in the middle of the Easter *fiera*. I'll take you on a tour first thing tomorrow,' he promised, adding casually. 'Mother likes you.'

Charlotte had had no time as yet to form an opinion of the Contessa. It had been late afternoon when their cars had swung into the open courtyard of the villa. After a brief introduction in the circular vestibule where vines curled around the stonework and wall-niches contained antique busts, the ladies had been conducted to their rooms, to freshen up and rest before dinner.

Later there had been so many people seated around the fifteenth century dining-table in the banqueting-hall, all chattering away in a variety of languages that, apart from being appraised by a pair of remarkably clear green eyes, and exchanging a nod and a smile, Charlotte had made litte contact with Phelan's mother. So, she approved of his choice, did she? This was a relief for Charlotte had been dreading the meeting, and her apprehension had increased once this had happened.

'I'm glad I meet with her approval,' she said, trying to make light of it. 'She's so sure of herself, and so beauitful.'

'Yes, she is, isn't she? The years sit easily on her. She hasn't done badly for a lady twice widowed. First there was my father, and I do believe she was in love with him, then she married Count Giuseppe Alinari, who left her only a pile of gamlbing debts and this magnificent though decaying villa, but still she manages to live in a grand manner far beyond her means.' Phelans voice was full of pride and indulgent amusement, as if this was no disgrace and the only way to be.

Charlotte had concluded early on in their wanderings that the friends to whom he presented her were a far cry from anyone she had met in England. She and Gwen had been swept into a whirl of balls, receptions, dinners and *fêtes champêtres* in whichever city they set foot. Phelan seemed to be acquainted with a large number of people of both sexes. Some were wealthy, others members of European nobility down on their luck, and then there were those who were nothing more than adventurers, surviving in this glittering world by their skill at cards, their wit, and good looks. Charlotte feared that Phelan fell into the latter category, but far from lessening his attraction, it made him all the more fascinating.

After the formality of London and Eva's dedication to work, she found it exhilarating to dash off at a moment's notice to some entertainment or other, a casino, an exhibition in a gallery, a ball arranged by art students, or end the day by going to an expensive restaurant for an impromtu supper-party, surrounded by lively foreign friends. Then there were the picnics – the drives through the spring countryside where the air was heavy with the scent of lemons and magnolia blossom.

As Gwen was fond of exclaiming, starry-eyed, 'It's all so wonderful!' But then, she found everything wonderful these days, secretly in love with Julian.

'Are you happy, darling?' One of Phelan's hands slipped up to Charlotte's shoulders, gently fondling the bare flesh.

'Oh, yes! I feel I've come home.'

'You have. We'll spend half the year in Italy when we're married, but I do want you to come to Egypt one day. You haven't lived till you've seen the moon rising over the pyramids.'

Her power to resist him was dwindling daily. It was easy to forget Eva's warnings, to convince herself that she had been wrong about him. On his home-ground, Europe, he had grown in stature, becoming the focus of attention everywhere.

The women fawned on him, stabbing envious glances at Charlotte. He was arrogant, yet respected by aristocrats and hoteliers alike, showing not the slightest trace of condenscension to those of lower rank; he was handsome, his swarthy skin rendered darker by the sun; he was always impeccably dressed, whether for a ball, or travelling, or hunting, each item of clothing perfectly suited to the occasion, and kept in immaculate order by his valet. So confident, so sure of himself in any given situation, never at a loss for words. He was weaving his web of enchantment around Charlotte, and she was content to fall under his spell, but the mention of marriage brought her down to earth.

'Nothing's settled,' she reminded him, and tried to draw away but he would have none of this. 'I must talk it over with Eva.'

'Why?' There was an urgent expression on his face, the strongly marked eyebrows frowning slightly. 'Why d'you even have to discuss it? We can be married here – very soon. Tomorrow, if you like. Mother would love the fun of a wedding at the villa.'

'She's my guardian. I'd have to have her permission.'

'Nonsense!' he brushed this aside as of no consequence. 'Continental laws are different. It will be too late once she gets to hear about it. Then what can she do? Have the marriage annulled? Have you back on her hands, probably already pregnant with my child?'

There was a cold note in his voice. Charlotte recognised it and wondered uneasily if he would be a dictatorial husband. She was seeking a tender lover, a friend, not a master. And yet his touch burned through her, and her body responded to him, welcomed that physical mastery, wanted to belong to him entirely. It was her mind, her educated, analytical mind, that proved a stumbling-block. Eva was not there but her influence was, those years of training Charlotte to be proud of her position as an independent woman. The inward battle was almost too great to endure.

'She'd be so disappointed in me. She might even cut me off. I could very well come to you penniless.'

'She won't do that.'

Phelan had made it his business to study human behaviour, Eva and her principles in particular. He was convinced that her devotion to her ward would prevent her from taking drastic action. She had too much to lose, a lonely woman who needed Charlotte more than Charlotte needed her.

'Well, I shouldn't be happy, and I don't want anything to spoil it when I finally decide to marry.' Charlotte surprised herself with her own firmness.

In a way it was satisfying to baulk Phelan of his will. He always got his way on every issue. It's bad for him, she had long ago decided. He's been dreadfully spoilt all his life. He still remained an enigma. She had known him for almost a year, laughed with him, shared music with him, exchanged kisses and caresses, and yet she still did not understand him. He had shown her nothing of himself that he did not wish her to see.

Now he looked at her expressionlessly. 'I can appreciate your loyalty to Eva, but don't I deserve a measure of consideration? I love you, Charlotte. I want you. D'you really expect to keep me dangling? I didn't think you were a flirt, the sort who leads men on and then says no.'

'I'm not like that,' she protested, stung by the suggestion. She had always despised flirts.

He was standing apart from her, keeping his distance. He smiled mockingly. 'Aren't you? Haven't you done nothing but tease and torment me ever since we met?'

'I wasn't aware that I was doing so.'

Charlotte was chilled by his withdrawal, frightened by the damage she might have done. Phelan was not the sort to take rebuffs kindly. He needed careful handling and she had been so confident that she knew how to do this, giving him so much but no more, which had not been easy for he was a skilled and seductive lover – so skilled in fact that she had sometimes brooded over the women in his past. She was convinced they had been legion, and the idea was hurtful. Perhaps this time I've pushed him too far, she reflected, worried and perplexed. I don't want to lose him, do I?

She knew that he wanted to pursue the subject and was relieved when the Countess came seeking them. 'Ah, there you are, Phelan!' she exclaimed in her rich, low voice. Because she had lived so long abroad she spoke English with a foreign accent.

Phelan swung round, taking her hands in his and raising them to his lips. 'I can tell by your face that you've been winning at cards,' he said, and they exchanged the intimate smile of two people who know each other very well, their failings as well as their virtues. 'Were you cheating again?'

'Wicked boy! What a suggestion! As if I would.' She tapped him lightly on the cheek with her closed fan. 'Your *donzella* will get a bad impression of me if you make remarks like that.' She turned the full blaze of her smile on Charlotte. 'How are you, *cara mia*? We've not yet had the chance to get to know one another. This must be remedied without delay. What we need to do is have a cosy chat without men around to interrupt.'

Augusta exuded a fragile, impractical, feminine appeal. Still a pretty woman, she had fine skin kept well protected from the sun,and her body was firmly made and plump. Her fashionably dressed hair was thick, fair and lustrous, and her gown, green satin encrusted with silver lace, cut in the latest mode. Emeralds sparkled around her throat and in her ears, family heirlooms in an intricate filigree setting, and she wore a gold cobra bracelet on one wrist, a present from Phelan who had filched it when desecrating the Egyptian tomb.

She laughed, displaying small, perfect teeth, and Charlotte realised that she had been staring rudely. 'I expect you're wondering how someone as blonde as myself could produce a great dark creature like Phelan? Well, his father was dark as could be. I've always liked dark men. Why d'you think I love Italy so?'

Charlotte assumed that she was teasing, nervously smiling in response, but then her eyes slid to Augusta's escort and the rumours she had heard returned to plague her. He could not have been much more than twenty, slender, golden-pale like the broken statues which stood among the olive-trees in the grounds.

His hair was ebony, his nose short and straight, and he looked at Augusta with hot, black eyes.

Phelan was regarding him with a sardonic smile, then he said to his mother, 'And when do you propse stealing Charlotte from me for this chance to tear my reputation to shreds? We have much to do. She wants to play the sight-seeing tourist, I believe. Our itinerary will be hectic.'

'Oh, don't worry, I'll find time.' Augusta was thoroughly enjoying herself, delighted to have him under her roof once more. He might escape her for a while, put oceans between them, but he always returned.

Now she drained her triumph to the dregs, rolling it on her tongue, savouring it. He was her only child and she had always bound him close to her, cold-bloodedly, imperceptibly, undermining him when they were together, insinuating herself into him, taking possession of him. He wanted to marry this icy English miss, did he? She would not stop him. She had her own reasons for resenting Eva Pendral and anything which he did to annoy her should be encouraged. Besides which, there was the ever important question of money.

The boy with the passionate eyes leaned closer, whispered in her ear. 'Ah, yes,' she nodded, while her hand came up as if to ward him off, modest yet alluring. 'I was coming to that. Of course I will introduce you. Phelan, meet Domenico Ricci. Domenico, this is Miss Charlotte Drummond from England.'

He bowed, flashed her a smile, stared hard at Phelan even as they murmured greetings, then his face assumed its customary sombre, even sulky, expression. Charlotte did not much like him, he was too faunlike, with his peaked eyebrows and oily curls, and was acting as if they were rather unwelcome intruders – jealous, maybe, of the attention Augusta was paying them. But she's old enough to be his mother! she thought, and experienced a chilling drop in spirits. What sort of woman was she? Friendly on the surface but with a hint of steel to her.

Suddenly Charlotte wanted Gwen's simple, straightforward company, or that of Cynthia Houston, a red-headed Scottish widow of forty whom Eva had engaged to accompany the girls. Though Bernice had said she would act as chaperon, Eva knew that she would forget about them for long stretches if something more entertaining hove into view – particularly if it was wearing trousers. Eva had been obliged to bow to convention. It really was unheard of for a genteel girl to travel abroad without a sensible, mature female companion.

There was no chance to retire yet, however. Augusta was in her element, liking to be up and doing, never missing a ball or party. There was a continuous round of merry-making in her villa, and tonight was no exception. She marched Phelan off to play for her guests and he, surprisingly, for he usually refused to perform at such gatherings, yielded to her. Charlotte joined Gwen and Cynthia in the ornate reception room that formed the centre of the house and which had a gallery around it, reached by a sweeping marble staircase from which the second-storey chambers opened.

The ceiling was domed and lavishly painted with scenes from Greek mythology. The room was huge, airy, filled with light from oil-filled lamps and branching candelabra, reflected endlessly in Venetian mirrors. There were life-size sculptures and gargantuan paintings in gilt frames, carpets that glowed like jewels, magnificent Cinquecento furniture, and hangings of sumptuous Genoese velvet. Chairs and couches had been lined up in rows at one end, facing the concert grand.

Conversation petered out and all eyes switched to Phelan as he commenced playing. Even Bernice stopped flirting for a while, though her eyes kept flickering toward Andew, seated a little away from her by a particularly resplendent sloe-eyed signorina. It seemed that she had met her match in Andrew, who appeared to be as promiscuous and incapable of fidelity as herself. Bernice covered her feelings well, only betraying her agitation by the way in which her restless hands kept fidgeting with her ostrich-feather fan. Then, as the notes of music resounded in that acoustically perfect hall, Charlotte forgot everything except Phelan.

He believed in genius. It was his religion. His contempt for mediocrity knew no bounds. The only time he was ever humble was when he talked of master composers and musicians. Charlotte had come to understand that if he was in a bad mood it was often because he had failed to come up to the high standard he demanded of himself in his interpretation of a difficult piece. He practised whenever possible. On their travels he had seized any chance to disappear into friends' music rooms on his own, fretting if he could not put in at least an hour of arpeggios and scales.

The first thing he played that evening was one of Liszt's most difficult rhapsodies. During the whole performance he appeared to be supremely detached, wearing an absorbed expression, lost in the music, concentrating on nothing but producing the sounds as the composer had intended them to be heard. It was as if the amazing skill of his fingers were carried out by some subconscious part of his complex personality, while the conscious intellect stood aside and quite independently considered and approved.

When this unforgettable display of brilliance ended there was a storm of applause which he acknowledged with a bow of the head, his eyes seeking his mother's. She was clapping louder than anyone else, her face alight with love and pride. Charlotte was struck by their similarity, though where this lay was difficult to define, she as fair as a holy angel and he dark as Lucifer.

He eased the piano-stool a little nearer, flexed his hands and a hush fell again. This time he played Chopin's *Berceuse*, a cradle song so delicate and gentle that it was scarcely audible at the back of the room. The caressing notes were so soft that the audience shared the anxiety of the mother singing gently lest she disturb the sleeping infant. There was a split-second silence as the last chords whispered away, then deafening applause that echoed under the dome.

He followed this with an *Etude*. Charlotte listened to him quietly. Listened to it all, inscribed it in her memory, stored it safely away, tears in her eyes as she heard the singing melody which was like the voice of a shepherd boy soaring clear and high above the rich accompaniment of summer wind and rain. It aroused in her a deep and profound emotion. She loved Phelan in that moment of time, with a love that almost amounted to worship.

'The past is very close to you in Florence. It's steeped in history. You touch it everywhere. Not a dim, dead, dusty past but one that lives on,' Phelan said as they jingled through the streets in an open carriage. Bells ornamented the harness of the hired vehicle, the horses were crowned with tossing crimson plumes, and it was driven by an olive-complexioned youth wearing a panama hat, a thin cheroot jammed between his lips.

The radiance of morning bathed everything in glory. There was the clang of church bells, the sound of countless feet on the cobbles, the excited voices of the townsfolk raised in eternal chatter, squabbling, bartering, gossiping, laughing and singing. Florence was more highly decorated than usual; coloured streamers, banners, people in carnival costumes, filled with excitement and gaiety. Above all and through all was the sweet smell of spring that breathed dreamily from vineyards and fields, and flowers everywhere, hanging in great baskets from balconies, standing in tubs on street corners, heaped on every stall, for thie was the Lily City – the City of Flowers.

Gwen was almost beside herself, leaning from the carriage, waving at passers-by who responded with smiles to this fresh-faced girl in her white dress and wide-brimmed hat. 'Look, Charlotte! Look!' she kept repeating as one sight after another crowded into view, forgetting her disappointment because Julian had been in bed when they left, lazily refusing to get up at such an early hour.

Phelan knew the place like the back of his hand and was an excellent guide. There was so much to see, every building, every roof, gable and tower in some way connected with the glorious, bloody past of this town that had once belonged to the powerful Medicis.

He took them to the Piazza della Signoria where Savonarola had offered up his life to the flames, a martyr to political hatred and religious fanaticism. They visited the house where Dante had lived; the Ponte Vecchio, that famous bridge over the River Arno, lined on both sides with the shops of goldsmiths, silversmiths and Florence's best jewellers; they saw where Donatello, Verrochio and Ghirlandaio had worked; the house where Benvenuto Cellini had cast his bronze Perseus; the lofty cathedral of Santa Maria del Fiore, the largest church in existence after St Peter's in Rome; they climbed the four hundred and fourteen steps of Giotto's Campanille for a superb view over the city.

When late morning came, Charlotte felt sure that she could not take in any more, stunned by the sight of many wonderfully ornate buildings, her brain reeling with historical facts which it was impossible to remember. By this time they had met up with Bernice who had driven out with Julian and Andrew. She was bursting with energy, scorning ancient monuments and wanting to shop, hustling them off to the Via dei Cerretani where the best establishments were to be found. With little shrieks of delight, she disappeared into a fashion-house, dragging Julian with her. Andrew bowed out, installing himself under the awning of an open-fronted café, inviting the others to join him for coffee and cognac, but Cynthia, mindful of the furthering of Gwen's education, decided that they simply must visit the cloisters of San Lorenzo.

'If you hurry, you'll be in time to see the cats being fed when the clock strikes noon,' Phelan drawled.

'Cats, Mr Charteris?' Cynthia gave him a level stare, an extremely direct, good-hearted person who took great trouble over her clothes and had a dashing style of dressing. She was wearing a tailored suit of cream linen and a black straw hat encircled with a wreath of yellow buttercups and white daisies.

'Cats, Mrs Houston. The cloisters have always offered asylum for homeless felines.' His eyes hardened, though his lips were smiling.

He sensed that she did not approve of him, one of the few women he knew who was impervious to his moods. She was annoyingly concerned about Charlotte's moral welfare, doing her best to make sure that she and Phelan were hardly ever left alone together.

'Indeed? How interesting,' she replied tersely. 'Come along, hinny,' and she swept a reluctant Gwen back into the carriage.

'Meet us for lunch around one o'clock, at *La Toscana*, a restaurant in the Via del Calzaioli.'

Cynthia nodded, settling herself and her charge and giving the driver brisk instructions in excruciating Italian, larded with a Scottish burr. She would have much preferred that Charlotte went along with them, but could see there was no hope of this happening. Eva Pendral's ward was showing all the disquieting signs of being infatuated with Phelan and Cynthia had concluded that, though not her type in any shape or form, he was nonetheless dangerously attractive.

'Shall we?' Phelan held out his arm, and Charlotte slipped her hand into the crook of his elbow.

'Where are we going?'

'You'll see.'

They wandered through winding, dusky, irregular streets that led towards the Mercato Nuovo. At every step Charlotte glimpsed bas-reliefs on lintels, Romanesque arches leading to shaded courtyards, Trecento windows, and marble statues. The market was filled with a tangle of people, busier than ever during carnival time. Acrobats, fire-eaters and musicians drew the crowds. Clowns with painted faces and fanciful costumes produced gales of laughter with their antics. There were masses of blossoms, piles of golden fruit, stalls filled with examples of straw-work, leather goods and finely embroidered linen brought in from the surrounding villages.

Charlotte turned her face up to Phelan. Her eyes sparkled in the purple shade of her hat brim. 'This is what you wanted me to see, isn't it? The ordinary people enjoying themselves.'

He nodded, her hand clasped in his. 'But of course. Have you ever seen such faces? Straight out of history. We could be in the time of Dante and Beatrice. The buildings are the same, so is the street life.'

The contents of the stalls were inviting, so much to see and purchase, with a confusion of noise all around, crowds coming and going, men haggling, lads arguing and wrestling, children dodging between the legs of their elders, their mothers shouting at them and waving their bare, brown arms. Charlotte stopped at a table filled with oddments – old books and prints, antique figurines, lengths of lovely, faded damask curtain. There were pieces of jewellery in a glass-fronted cabinet and her eyes were drawn to a seal ring.

The stall-owner, a portly individual with a drooping black moustache, smiled encouragingly and unlocked the case, taking the ring out for her to try on. He talked in a swift spate of words of which she could make no sense. Phelan entered into the discussion, and although she could not understand what they were saying, she guessed that they were bargaining. The ring was made of gold and was heavy, the seal comprised of two rampant lions and a lily. It was large, had probably been made for a man. It fitted the middle finger of her right hand. A big, ostentatious thing, and she was unaccustomed to flamboyant jewels, but it appealed to her, flashing as she moved. Romantic notions filled her head, inspired by her surroundings. Had it once belong to a courtier, maybe a general or a Medici prince?

'What does he want for it?' she asked.

'Too much. He says it dates from the Renaissance, and I expect he's right, but don't you dare give him what he's asking. Leave it to me.'

More talk, more gestures as the Italian threw hands and eyes heavenwards as if beseeching the aid of the Madonna against these tight-fisted tourists, but in the end a sum was agreed on, and Charlotte was wearing the ring as they left the market. It was a beautiful piece and she vowed to keep it for ever as a reminder of her holiday.

She opened her purse, wanting to pay Phelan, but he would not hear of it. 'You refused the Tsarina's jewels, so you must have this. Don't worry. I'm not suggesting that it's an engagement ring. Wrong finger anyway, and it would be a crime to have it made smaller. Oh, no, my love – nothing but diamonds will be good enough for that.'

His eyes moved over her face, lingering on her lips. A hot stab of desire made her tremble. Why not accept him? she thought, the enchantment of Florence, the madness of the carnival, rushing through her blood. He was a man in a million – talented, knowledgeable – and his longing for her was expressed in his every movement and action. He was difficult, but then what man worth his salt did not have some character flaw? Why not marry him? Why *ever* not? Eva and England seemed a hundred light years away.

But it rushed back with a vengeance when Charlotte had retired to her room in the villa for a siesta after lunch. Cynthia looked at the ring and pursed her lips. 'You shouldn't have taken it from him,' she began. 'A proper gentleman would never, never have suggested it. I wanted to say something in the restaurant, but didn't wish to embarrass you. And there was Mr Charteris sitting there looking like a cat that's been at the cream.'

'Oh, but it's lovely!' Gwen was thrilled by the sight of such a gift, wishing that Julian showed as much interest in her. He was kind, great fun to be with, but treated her as if she was his kid sister. It was most galling when she wanted to be his sweetheart.

'I agree, it's a beautiful piece, and this makes it even worse.' Cynthia stood, tapping her foot. Though she had jumped at the chance of this break from the customary dullness of her life, and had taken the two girls to her warm, motherly heart, a heart that had never been satisfied by children of her own, she had sometimes during the past weeks felt that she had bitten off more than she could chew.

'Then why shouldn't Charlotte have it?' Gwen had wriggled out of her morning dress, handing it to Tilly, and now jumped on to the bed in her cambric drawers and chemise.

Tilly and Cynthia exchanged a glance. They had become friends since leaving England, supporting each other in the difficult task of steering their young charges safely through the troubled waters of temptation that beset them on every side. Cynthia was acquainted with the Savill family. It was they who had put her forward as a suitable companion, and she took her responsibilities seriously. Tilly, though having qualms about leaving Wilkins, had never once considered refusing to go with Charlotte, but she had made certain that he proposed before her departure, wearing his ring with pride.

Cynthia was finding Gwen slightly more unmanageable than Charlotte, and now said caustically. 'It isn't done for a young lady to take presents from a man. You know that, Gwen. Don't be tiresome. Only bad girls who are no better than they should be accept expensive gifts.'

'What does 'no better than they should be' mean? Sounds like bad girls have all the fun.' Gwen knew exactly what it meant, and knew exactly how to rile Cynthia.

'And they also end up in the gutter,' Cynthia answered firmly, resisting the impulse to smack her across her impudent face.

'They're prostitutes. Fallen women. Is that it?' Gwen persisted, her frustrations momentarily eased by tormenting the chaperon.

Cynthia's already high colour deepened. 'I don't wish to discuss it, and I was talking to Charlotte, not you.'

'It really doesn't matter,' Charlotte interrupted them rather wearily, some of the exhilaration of the morning draining away. 'I'm old enough to be aware of the pitfalls, Cynthia. I offered to pay for it, but should have offended Phelan if I'd insisted.'

'We'll have to see what your guardian has to say about that when we get home, shan't we?' Cynthia was not usually so irritable, and providing the girls fell in with her ideas on comportment and manners was of an amiable disposition, but there was something about the lax atmosphere of the Villa Alinari that unnerved her.

Charlotte walked over to the window, looked at the azure blue sky, the colourful garden, which contrasted so poignantly with the tension in the room. If I was married to Phelan then I'd not have to put up with carping criticism. I'd no longer be a single girl who everyone seems to imagine has to be protected and coddled and kept away from those vile seducers, men! I'd like to be married. I'd like to be free. Yet she was haunted by the fear that she would be nothing of the sort. She might only be exchanging one master for another.

'Time you were going back to your own room, Miss Gwen.' Tilly shooed her from the bed, shook the lace-frilled pillows and turned down the crumpled cover. 'You must both rest, and you won't if you're in here together. Carnival Night, remember?'

'As if I could forget!' Gwen danced across the tiled floor. 'Carnival Night! And I'll be wearing my new fancy-dress costume, and we'll be going to a – what d'you call it?'

'A *veglione*. A masquerade ball.' Charlotte's good humour returned as she thought about it. Carnival Night with Phelan. Her heart thumped with anticipation.

'That's it – a thingumajig. Oh, dear, I'm never going to learn Italian and Dad will expect me to be able to spout at least a few phrases when I get home.'

'Lessons! That's what's needed. We must find someone to teach you.' Cynthia jumped at the idea. It would keep the lively Gwen occupied and out of trouble for a part of the time at least.

'Lessons? Ugh!' Gwen stuck out her lower lip, then brightened visibly. 'Maybe Julian will teach me. He speaks it like a native.'

Charlotte was glad when they left her, she needed time alone to think. The room was lovely, light and spacious, the furniture made of walnut, the walls and floor of cool, pink-veined Carrara marble. The large bed was draped in chiffon and spread with a white, handworked lace coverlet. Billowing curtains hung from ceiling to floor on each side of the windosw, stirring slightly in the soft breeze.

I could be happy here for ever, she thought, slipping out of her clothes and prowling, naked, into the adjoining bathroom. The walls were of turquoise blue tiles, and in the centre of the floor was a sunken marble tub, shaped like a shell, with gilt, dolphin-shaped taps. Soon she was immersed in scented water, taking her time, relaxing and thinking, and all the while Phelan's face with those mesmeric eyes filled her mind. She tried to block it out, but it was as if his features were indelibly stamped on her brain. She despised herself because she was becoming obsessed with him. What price her common sense now?

She roamed into the bedroom, the full-length wall mirror giving back her reflection. When she raised her arms to unpin her hair, her breasts lifted with the smooth action, her stomach flattening as she drew in her rib-cage. When naked, her body always seemed larger to her, as if joyfully escaping the confines of clothes. She dropped her arms, running her hands along the length of her thighs which curved into slim knees, then out again to the gentle swell of calves, dipping down to thin ankles and small-boned feet.

Oh, Phelan, what are you doing to me? she thought, unable to keep her hands off her own flesh, tingling at the touch. If I don't keep a very tight rein on this wilful body of mine, it will betray me.

The languorous warmth, that irresponsible sense of tomorrow-will-do which she suspected was the Italian philosophy, would only make the task harder. She pulled on her cotton négligée and lay on the bed. Hands laced behind her head, she stared up at the silk tester, watching it ripple with dancing shadows as the wind stirred the leaves of the fig-tree whose branches reached the balcony outside. Music floated in. Someone was playing a mandoline in the arched terrace below. Phelan? Julian, more like, Julian resting on a heap of tapestry cushions in the shade, wine glass to hand, with a collection of dark-skinned house-servants leaning on the stone balustrade, admiring his blond beauty. And where was Bernice? Was she in her room with Andrew, taking part in that fascinating ritual of the sexes which Charlotte was longing to experience?

She tossed, was too hot, opened her robe, ran her hands over her breasts, lingering on the nipples, teasing them into hard peaks, imagining that it was Phelan caressing her. This was too tormenting a vision, and she concentrated on Eva instead. Thought of London, and found it boring, discontent welling up. It was simply no use. She would never learn anything about her parents, or find Tweeny. That girl had never again come to the vicarage soup-kitchen, though Charlotte had been there every day while the crisis lasted, hoping – waiting – her heart pounding as if it would burst. Why shouldn't she forget it? Stay in this enchanted place. Marry Phelan, and no longer spend her siestas alone.

Her eyelids drooped and she was in that half world between sleep. She imagined that she was walking along the Chelsea Embankment. It was a cold, cheerless day, black overhead, rain running down her face to mingle with her tears. So lost. So lonely. There was no one to care. She saw steps shining with moisture and her feet were colder than ever, wading into icy water. She wanted to die – *intended* to take her own life. Tweeny! Don't do it!

She awoke with a jolt, finding that the shadows had moved as the sun sank lower. She was drenched in seat, yet shivering. The dream had been so vivid, so awful, and dark premonition weighted her mind. Tilly came into the room and the nightmare receded. She had brought her a tray of fancy cakes and tea. British to the backbone, she had packed her own supply of finest blend and insisted on brewing it herself, distrusting foreigners.

'Had a nice rest, Miss?' she said jovially. 'Come along, sleepy head. I'm just dying to see you in your costume. Ain't it all exciting? Those Italian blokes! A girl can't set foot in the street without them whistling after her. Such a cheek! I may not be able to speak their lingo but I know what's going on in their minds right enough. I've met their kind in London, pushing ice-cream carts. Hokey-pokey, all hot! They're a bunch of dirty Dagos. Good-looking though, some of 'em. Just as well I got myself engaged or I dread to think what I might do. Always was a muggins where blokes are concerned.'

'I was dreaming about my sister.'

'Your sister, Miss? But I thought you'd accepted that she was dead and gone?'

'I have – at least, I think I have.' Charlotte rubbed her eyes, her mind still fogged with sleep. The Thames. The dark water. The sound of a river-boat's siren echoing in her head.

'That's all in the past, Miss. Think of the future, and the good times in store for you. You're a very lucky young lady, you know. There's no need for you to accept the first chap who's come along. But don't you worry your head about it now. Up you get and let me brush your hair, then we'll get you into your dress.'

Charlotte fell quiet, listening to Tilly chattering on. Soon she stopped concentrating, shutting her mind. She closed her eyes, almost purring under the caress of the hairbrush in Tilly's hand, letting the words run like a rippling stream in the peaceful evening. The windows were wide open. She heard a sleepy bird singing somewhere in jerky notes. Outside a fountain murmured faintly. It was so quiet that these sounds were distinct, were a part, it seemed, of Tilly's endless soliloquy.

The sun sank, and on the delicate breeze night swooped out of the east, inking the sky, tossing the pale, bright moon in dark trailing nets of blue-black. Tilly's voice was part of the twilight. She sighed and laid the brush on the glassy surface of the dressing-table.

'And, Miss, just be careful tonight. Don't get carried away by

Mr Phelan and his blarney. I don't think you should marry him,' she concluded.

'You don't?' Charlotte snapped, jerked into wakeful attention.

'No,' said Tilly calmly.

This drove Charlotte mad. She did not hit Tilly, but she swore at her for not minding her own business. How dare she tell her what to do? She was only a servant. She leapt to her feet and stamped them. She nearly knocked over a small table. All her pent-up emotions burst out in a thunder-clap – her distrust of the Contessa, her worry about Eva, her grief for her lost sister. Her hands were clenched into fists, her eyes smarting with tears. She could hardly breathe, her breasts seeming alive under her négligée, rising and falling against the lace. She was in a terrible temper. Choking with it.

'Now, now, control yourself, Miss.' Tilly said firmly. 'I'm sorry if I upset you, but you've always asked me to speak my mind.'

At that, Charlotte lost control completely, the worries she had been holding back for weeks crowding in on her. She sprang at Tilly, but her wise maid caught her deftly round the waist and hugged her. Suddenly Charlotte's body loosened and crumpled. She sobbed on Tilly's shoulder, shudders racking her body. Tilly let her cry it out, then led her to a chair and brought over a cup of tea.

'I don't want it,' Charlotte sniffed.

Tilly took no notice. 'You'll drink it, Miss. It'll calm you. I know you've not been really happy for ages. Not truly happy, deep down. Don't try to tell me you have been. I know you too well – all this gadding about and putting on a false face. It doesn't fool me.'

'I wish everyone would stop trying to tell me how to run my life,' Charlotte replied coldly. 'Eva is the only one who has any right to do so.'

Tilly stared at her, recognising that look which always spelled trouble, and said nothing further. Time was passing swiftly and Charlotte must hurry if she was to be ready to mingle with the Contessa's guests.

She bathed Charlotte's tear-stained face, powdered it lightly and touched the cheekbones with rouge applied with a rabbit's foot. 'There, Miss,' she said, inspecting her closely. 'No one will know you've been crying. You'll be wearing this anyway,' and she held up a black velvet mask.

For this important ball of which Phelan had forewarned her, Charlotte had decided on a Spanish costume, and had bought one in a theatrical outfitters in Paris. It was a tight-fitting sheath of red silk, clasping her body closely to just below the knee where it flooded out into wide frills. The low neckline was finished with a flounce that matched those at the hem.

The costumier had told her that it was a flamenco dress, designed for dancing, for beating out a savage gypsy tempo with controlled feet, for arching the back and posturing with the arms while the fingers clicked castenets. Tilly swept back her hair from a centre parting and coiled it in a great knot at the crown of her head, then fixed a diamond-studded comb to support the black lace mantilla, its delicate folds dripping down to her wrists.

Leaning towards the mirror, forgetting everything in her absorption with this unfamiliar image, Charlotte tucked a crimson rose behind one ear and hooked gold hoops in her lobes. Finally, she slipped her feet into black, high-heeled shoes fastened with ribbons. She posed, a painted fan held up to her face, her eyes gazing invitingly over the top. She looked completely different, her carriage that of a great Castillian lady, sultry, mysterious, yet with something of the gypsy about her, too.

'Don't forget your mask, Miss,' Tilly reminded, holding it out.

A mask. Yes, that would be good, a great comfort if one felt insecure. Those the Contessa had provided were every bit as elaborate as the ones worn by the Venetians long ago. Charlotte's was of black velvet fringed with jet, a tiny, glittering strip that covered her nose and brow, with only her large grey eyes visible through the slits. An old, crafty device to aid illicity assignations, adding to the sense of wildness and abandon of carnival. Masquerade gave everyone licence to behave in ways quite contrary to the norm. Tonight was one of magic – tomorrow and its regrets far away. Charlotte slid the seal ring on to her finger and closed her fist around it.

People had begun to arrive as she reached the reception room. It was an informal gathering before they set off for the ball. The terrace, the gardens, the elegant chambers, were filling up with guests in fantastic costumes that had cost hundreds of pounds apiece.

Gwen and Cynthia were already there; Gwen in the panniered dress of a Dresden shepherdess, Cynthia in a tartan outfit that had little to do with a Florentine *fiera*, but gave her the opportunity to proclaim her clan. Bernice saw Charlotte, put down her champagne glass and waved.

She was wearing a silk shift fastened on one shoulder, Grecian-style. The colours were subtle, shot with blue, rose pink and yellow. The fabric seemed to float as she moved and it was obvious that she wore very little underneath. Her hair fell loosely about her face, and her jewellery consisted of a gold bracelet, six inches wide and decorated with oval agates, and a spade-shaped pendant that rested just above the deep cleft between her breasts.

'I love your costume, Charlotte,' she cried, running across to her. 'Very Spanish! What d'you think of mine? I'm Venus, the Goddess of Love. Did you know it was me, behind the mask?'

'That glorious bosom would be recognisable anywhere,' Julian remarked, shifting his shoulders from the pillar against which he had been lounging. 'Andrew should partner Charlotte. He's come as a South American gaucho.' And he nodded to where the explorer was standing surrounded by a gaggle of ladies who were cooing over his leather trousers, his striped woven poncho – himself.

'No, he shouldn't,' Bernice snapped crossly. 'He's coming with me. And what, pray, are you supposed to be?'

'Me? I should have thought it was obvious,' Julian replied, as bright and candid as a child. 'I'm a satyr, of course.'

A faun to the life, Charlotte thought, his costume cunningly made to give him hairy goat's legs. His sun-browned torso was bare, and a little pair of horns sprouted among his tousled curls. Grinning puckishly, he lifted a set of pipes to his lips and gave a mocking, birdlike trill. Gwen was at his side in an instant, drawn by the notes. He smiled at her fondly.

'Shall we go as a pair? Me as creature of myth, and you as a shepherdess. That would be nice, wouldn't it?'

Gwen was too overcome to reply, so Julian paid his respects to Cynthia, asking permission to escort her charge, adding, winningly, that he would be proud to partner *both* of them. Even Cynthia could not refuse an offer couched in such beguiling terms.

A gasp arose as Augusta walked in, attired in an amethyst velvet gown of the period when Florence was at the pinnacle of her glory. Julian winked at Gwen, murmuring. 'Here comes Lucrezia Borgia! Watch out for your wine-glasses everybody. She's quite capable of slipping poison into them if she takes a dislike to you.'

Glittering, ostentatious, almost barbaric, Augusta's bearing was one of supreme arrogance. She had Domenic on one side of her, wearing a costume of the same era consisting of parti-coloured tights, a thonged cod-piece, and a short, wide-shouldered doublet. On her other hand stalked her son.

He was exquisitely dressed as a Regency rake with buckskin breeches that fitted like a second skin, a bottle-green tail coat and high black stock. He had gone the whole hog, hair brushed forward in Byronic stle, carrying a Malacca cane in one hand and a low-crowned topper in the other. Everyone present was aware of his almost flagrant masculinity. Invitations were being cast his way from a dozen quarters. He took no notice. Charlotte was very conscious of him standing there, devouring her with those disconcerting eyes outlined by his black silk domino.

He bowed and offered her his arm, and soon the guests were tramping noisily into the grounds, seeking their cars or carriages. A single star hung against the darkening sky, gleaming like the diamond earring of a giantess gazing dreamily across the cosmos. It was breathtaking, and Charlotte wanted to linger, but carnival fever held everybody in thrall, and she found herself carried away with it. Florence seemed to have gone mad. The beauty and frivolity of the *fiera* were all about her.

Phelan drove his car with Charlotte beside him, leading the cavalcade of vehicles towards the town. There they had to walk, for entire roads were blocked off to traffic. They lost the others almost at once, and Phelan stayed close to her, having warned her not to carry money as pickpockets would be busy in the packed alleys. There were crowds hemming them in, laughing, reeling, shouting, and embracing complete strangers. In open spaces on the flagstones they were dancing to the shrill clamour of fife and drum.

It was frightening and Charlotte shrank closer to Phelan as a Punchinello leered at her, waving his jester's bauble of gilded bells. Acrobats were tumbling, musicians playing, the dancers whirling faster and faster, fire-crackers running along the stones like stars, the winners of the lottery darting about triumphantly, hugging their prizes of wine, capons and sweetmeats.

'Let's go to the ball,' Phelan said gaily, kissing her lightly on the lips.

It was being held at the palace of one of Augusta's cronies, an influential Italian prince of great wealth. Phelan, unperturbed by the confusion, found his way there with ease. Once inside, he quickly escorted Charlotte to the chairs reserved for Augusta and her friends. Seated above the ballroom, Charlotte stared at the milling crowd below. The building was fantastically decorated for the occasion, and everyone wore carnival clothes that flashed under the electric lights which were rendered even more dazzling by revolving coloured discs.

Gwen was already down there, dancing with Julian. Cynthia was watching her like a hawk, unhappy until she was delivered safely back. Phelan did not dance, seated silently at Charlotte's side, and she wondered what he was thinking. Did he wish he was alone, free to seek a more passionate woman? Was he really in love with her?

It was stiflingly hot. There was a never-ending confusion of noise and music, lights, paper streamers and balloons. Charlotte drank some more champagne, finding that this helped, acting as a blotter, soaking up sensations before they reached her. She kept recalling her dream, contrasting it with this scene which she found more unreal than her nightmare. The people seemed inhuman, grotesquely painted and powdered, grotesquely costumed as harlequins, as columbines, courtiers, monks, great figures of history, all masked, all growing more abandoned as the wine flowed and the music changed from waltz to polka, and then to the traditional folk dances of the area.

She found herself on the floor in Phelan's arms, then they became separated. Someone else held her by the waist, her feet faltering over the unfamiliar steps of the tarantella. She had the suffocating feeling of being crushed by the press of people. The wine she had drunk, far from deadening perception, now seemed to bring an extra awareness, and a conviction of the concrete presence of evil. From the height and glow produced by alcohol, she could see the people clearly and they struck her with a kind of creeping terror. They were horrible in their weird attire, masked, faces half concealed – grinning lips, shrieking voices.

Her new partner was dressed as a wolf, long, lean, bony muzzle with hollow cheeks and a pointed chin. '*Signorina, bella, bella*,' he kept repeating, squeezing her close to him.

His eyes were fierce, sharp, cruel, and there was something odd about them. Charlotte had the idea that there was nothing behind those eyes. He was like a house without a tenant, the windows empty and blank, a body without a soul. A night-bird, a servant of Satan, prowling in search of prey.

She struggled. Couldn't break free. His scarlet lips were coming closer, drawn back over vulpine teeth. She thought he wanted to kiss her, but then, panic rising, felt his hot breath on her throat. She screamed. No one heard her above the noise, or if they did they took no notice. Jerking backwards, she beat at his face, so frightened that it was a second before she realised that he had been forcibly repelled by Phelan.

He was angry, shouting at the man as he melted into the crowd, then saying to her, 'Charlotte, I lost you. Come with me.'

No time for argument or thought, just the enormous comfort of his strong arm protecting her. Out into the night air, cool, fresh, her head spinning. Her comb and mantilla had been loosened. She pulled them from her head, yanked at the hairpins, let her hair fall about her shoulders, tore off her mask. Phelan said nothing further, guiding her away from the ball, away from the crowds, through the streets until he finally stopped in a courtyard. It was deserted under the moonlight, with the dense shadows making the lustrous silver world beyond them even more magical.

Phelan gathered her in his arms and kissed her hungrily. 'Keep quiet, my love,' he whispered. 'There may be some still awake here, though I would imagine that everyone has gone to the carnival.'

'What is this place?' she asked softly, steadied now, though still feeling as if she moved through a dream.

He shrugged, his eyes glinting in his shadowed face. 'An old palace. I rent the second floor.'

This silenced her. She had not considered he might live anywhere but at the Villa Alinari. The front door stood wide open, the vast entrance hall lit only by the moon. Phelan moved quickly over the tessellated floor, leading her up the superb staircase. Reaching a gallery he paused at one of the great, frowning doors, taking a key from his pocket and slipping it into the lock. A dim room was revealed, a room which seemed to go on forever, its ceiling disappearing into the darkness. When he struck a match and touched it to several candles, shapes, form and colour sprang into being.

A dream. Yes, and this was a dream chamber. It reeked of dust, age and oleander flowers. They stood in great earthenware urns on the floor, their perfume overpowering. Though neglected, the room was still magnificent and the frescoes on the walls had managed to keep their colour, despite the ravages of time. Its proportions were magnificent, too, built by some master craftsman with an unerring instinct for symmetry. It had an indestructible beauty that refused to perish while one stone was left standing on another.

There was a sagging couch, a pair of carved chairs with upholstered seats of Spanish leather, gilt nails and gold fringing, a huge armoire with a matching chest of drawers, a bedside table on which stood the five-branched candlestick that provided the only light. The bed was fully six feet wide, with a tapestry headboard, and tester surmounted by gilded plaster feathers.

Phelan took off his jacket and filled two goblets with wine. 'You're nervous? Quite natural, but you've no need. It is the first time, of course, but I will be very gentle.'

His voice had a sweet, persuasive force to it, and lulled her into dreamy silence, listening to it as to some delicious music. She was glad that the die was cast, glad that he had taken the initiative. Now there could be no turning back. Maybe no one had seen them leave the ball, but if they had, then she was already compromised beyond redemption. To take the ultimate step of going to bed with him seemed no longer significant, and certainly not difficult. I'm drunk, she thought hazily. I must be very drunk because I feel so little, just extremely tired.

He smiled at her, put down his glass and started to undress her while she stood there as if turned to stone. When she was naked he sank to his knees and drew her to him, pressing his face against her stomach and lipping her skin. Charlotte felt her scalp tingle, felt that thrill running from the base of her skull to the bottom of her spine, drew in a moaning breath. His hands came up to cup her beasts, fingers seeking the nipples as she had imagined him doing that very afternoon. Pleasure radiated through her.

He stood, a tall, shadowy figure in the candlelight, and his lips were on hers, prising her mouth open, his tongue probing, sending stabs of fire into her loins. She shuddered, melted against him, her arms around his neck, and picking her up, he laid her on the bed. She felt cold when he left her, drawing herself into a ball, shivering with excitement and fear. He dowsed all but one candle and she could hear his rapid breathing as he stripped off his clothes.

The room was whirling to the beat of her heart, nausea in her throat. I mustn't be sick! she panicked. What a thing to do on our first night together! By an effort of will she managed to control the spinning sensation, keeping still, waiting for Phelan to come back to her.

She raised her lids, looked at him. His body gleamed in the light of the candle, muscular, firm, more hairy than she had anticipated, a thick black mat on his chest with a line running down across his navel to become more dense around his genitals. She had never seen a man completely naked before and found it shockingly strange and fascinating. Then he lay down beside her, reaching for her hand and guiding it to the hard column of his penis. He gasped as her palm closed around his flesh, groped for her breasts, sank his mouth on hers.

Charlotte could feel herself dissolving, sweetening, moistening to receive him. He had kissed and caressed her before, but never like this. Closed lips then, and censorial clothing a barrier between them. Now they were both naked and she wanted more and more of him. Her body felt boneless as she enjoyed everything he did to her, feeding on his kisses. But when he tried to slip a hand between her legs she stiffened, clenching her thighs together, unready for this just yet, unwilling that he should try to touch her in so private a place.

He paused, stared at her, and she wilted as she read a flash of anger in his eyes, her desire dying. 'What is it? Open your legs for me, darling.'

'I can't. I'm sorry, Phelan, but I'm afraid that you'll make me pregnant.'

This was not the whole reason, but a strong part of it. She was not so drunk as to forget everything Tilly had told her, the maid's warning voice ringing in her head: 'Now you take care, Miss. If you ever go with a fellow, make sure he looks after you. D'you know what I mean? Get him to pull out before he puts a baby in you, or make sure he uses a rubber what's-it.' All very well to be wise in the ways of anti-conception, but Tilly had failed to say how embarrassing it would be to mention it.

Phelan grunted with laughter, his hand smoothing her back, then he lowered his head to subject her sensitive earlobe to nibbling kisses. 'Don't worry about that. Wouldn't you like my child? Does it really matter? We'd have to get married then and no one would try to stop us, not even your precious Eva.'

It was seductive. He was seductive. The notion of bearing his baby was a seductive one. She would become his wife, with nothing to do but care for him and their child. Was this so bad a prospect? Under his assault on her senses nothing seemed important any more. But when he was above her, pressing into her, dividing her legs, she tried to deny him. Her struggles made him impatient, and the expression on the dark face hanging over her was fearsome, reminding her of the wolfman in the ballroom.

'What's the matter?' he growled. 'It will only hurt you a little, I promise.'

The cry torn from her as he forced entry into her body was silenced by his demanding mouth. He seized her by the wrists, holding her arms wide as he bore down on her with all his weight. Pain seared her, pain that seemed to go on and on as he heaved against her with shuddering sharp convulsions. He was slippery with sweat, she could smell it, sharp and salty, her own skin wet. Tears stung in her eyes and trickled across her temples. I'm a failure, she mourned. I'm not enjoying this and it's supposed to be a lovely experience, isn't it?

'Phelan, don't – you're hurting me,' she whispered, but he was beyond caring, caught up in the blind need for fulfilment.

'Shut up, bitch!' he snarled, and she could barely believe what he was saying, frigid, suffering – enduring, until his rapid movements rose to a crescendo and then ceased.

He rested, lying heavily on top of her, crushing her into the mattress. 'Now you are really mine,' he murmured breathlessly. 'No one can take you away from me. You'll learn to like it, you really will.'

'Shall I?' It was hard to believe.

'Indeed you will. In no time at all you'll be begging me to make love to you again.'

She had expected that he would lie with her, stroking her hair and whispering endearments, wanting some affirmation of love for there had been no completion for her, only pain and discomfort as he had his way. But, once satisfied, he withdrew from her, sitting on the side of the bed and saying matter-of-factly, 'Now we'll go back to the ball and announce our engagement.'

He got up and started to dress. Charlotte lay just as he had left her, bewildered by the abrupt change in him. She was sober, her mind clear and active as she tried to sort out her emotions, filled with a depressing sense of anti-climax. Was this the be all and end all of love-making? Was there nothing more? The earth-shaking thing she had been led to expect had not happened. Phelan had possessed her, but he had been far from touching the inner core of her being or bringing her anywhere near orgasm, and now he seemed to expect that she should act normally, return to the ball as if nothing had taken place.

Loneliness possessed her. She felt soiled, dishonoured and disillusioned. In the heat of the bed she had been further away from him than when they walked sedately through the streets together. And now he was so cold, looking at her impatiently, wanting to be off. Doubts stirred, tormenting her. Could it be that he wasn't really in love with her? Had she made a terrible mistake?

Chapter Ten

Richard's cottage was situated in a tiny hamlet about five miles from Southend-on-Sea. They had left Fenchurch Street Station in the morning and arrived at the seaside before lunch, stopping to eat at a restaurant on the esplanade before catching the motor-bus to Westhope.

'It's time I bought my own car,' he commented as he pushed open the creaky garden gate. 'Can't be doing with trains any more.'

'Won't you be staying here, with me?' Jennie pattered along behind him as he hefted the luggage and carried it down the straight path bordered with cockle-shells.

'Not all the time,' he grunted. 'I've work to do.'

Jennie viewed the scene with mixed feelings. It had been raining but now a watery sun was breaking through the clouds. The air smelled clean, and the silence was painful to her town-trained ears. Only a bird piped at the top of the laurel tree near the low, arched front door. Jennie found such peace unnatural. No traffic, no hawkers, no jostling crowds. What did the people who lived thereabouts do with themselves all day long? she wondered.

The train journey had been awesome, so much smoke and noise, Fenchurch Street a busy station with porters wheeling baggage trolleys, others slamming carriage doors shut, guards waving their flags and blasting on whistles, giant monsters of gleaming locomotives belching steam. She had sat quietly beside Richard on the crimson moquette seat of a First Class compartment, watching the bright metal signs sliding by as the train gathered speed – Zebo Blacking for shiny gates; Keating's Powder for lice and vermin; Beecham's Pills to cure every ailment. Then the train had plunged into a dark tunnel, the sickly stench of smoke oozing through cracks and crevices.

Out into the wet morning, houses rushing past, giving way to fields, and trees and farms, with everything so damp and fruitful.

And Southend itself, shops, cockle-stalls and boarding houses, the promenade, the pier in the distance striking out boldly into the spume crested waves. Jennie had wanted to linger there, filling her eyes with the glorious sight of the sea, her nostrils with its tang.

She had felt out of place in the sedate restaurant, so shabbily dressed, but Richard had taken no notice, his manner with the waiters lordly and confident. Then the tram-ride to the bus depot. The tram had been different to the ones in London, more friendly somehow, open-topped and operated on an overhead wire system. It had made a fascinating high note every time it rounded a corner, shrill and sustained. The bus was motorised, another novelty, and she had stared fixedly from its window as it rattled through leafy lanes and finally deposited them near the village green.

'Cat got your tongue?' Richard asked, smiling as he pushed open the cottage door, above which a gable had fallen askew owing to the age of its timbers.

'Blimey! Give us a chance!' she retorted. 'I ain't never been to the country before.'

'You'll get used to it.'

'Don't bet your bottom dollar!'

She seriously doubted whether she would ever get used to such cleanliness, fresh air and solitude, but within a second was exclaiming happily as she stepped into a big room with a low ceiling supported by heavy black beams, and casement windows in which the dimpled glass had a greenish tinge.

'Like it?' Richard sounded pleased.

'Cor! I should just say I do! Is it yours?'

He nodded. 'I bought it several years ago. It's what's known as a 'hall', which was what most of the farmhouses were called in this district. I'll show you round.'

He lifted the latch of a door near the hearth, and she saw a twisting oak staircase leading to the bedrooms. Upstairs the dormer windows were set back in the thick walls where the plaster bulged with age, while the floors sloped at a decided angle. There were two bedrooms, each decorated in a becoming chintzy style most suitable for such a residence. Jennie was disappointed not to find a bathroom.

'A tin bath set before the fire in the kitchen is a great way to wash,' he replied in answer to her question. 'And the privy is in that shed at the top of the garden. See it?'

She peered through the glass, unimpressed, having expected something grander. 'Well, you certainly believe in the simple life,' she concluded as they went down again. 'I'm sure to break my neck on this silly staircase, or knock my brains out on one of those bloody beams. D'you think there are any ghosts?'

'Hundreds of 'em,' he answered lightheartedly. 'But nice, honest ghosts of the farming variety. D'you see where the old folk used to plant their feet in the inglenook on long winter evenings? They wore the stone down during three centuries or so. They must have dozed there after a hard day's work in the fields, haymaking or harvesting. It's a friendly atmosphere, don't you think? They make us welcome.'

'Bunkum!' she snapped, unwilling to admit that he had scared her. 'I don't believe in ghosts!'

'Say that again when you've been here on your own.'

She turned away, disliking his reference to leaving her. Did he really intend that she should be stuck down here in the country by herself? We'll see about that! she resolved. He's only human after all, and I'm going to make damn sure that I'm soon indispensable.

He took her to the kitchen, another big room which proved to be the heart of the house with its open fireplace for cooking, stone sink and massive dresser whose shelves were filled with blue and white Willow Pattern crockery. After he had unpacked the box of groceries he had brought with him, she followed as he went outside to chop kindling, filled a basket with logs, and set about getting the fire alight. Soon a kettle was humming away on the trivet above the open flames. It was joined by a black, sooted saucepan filled with tomato soup from a can. They ate seated on stools at the pine table placed solidly in the centre of the stone-flagged floor.

Richard had plunged down into the cellar, returning with a dusty dark brown bottle which he uncorked with some difficulty. 'Homemade wine,' he announced. 'Made by the village postmistress who's the biggest gossip I've ever met. I'm sure she holds every letter up to the light to try and read the contents, probably even steams them open. As for telegrams! They excite her more than the most passionate lover. Don't suppose she's ever had one of those – very much the maiden-lady.'

'Don't she gossip about you?' Jennie was spreading yellow butter on her bread and topping it with honey.

'Oh, yes, she has a field-day about me.' Richard held up his glass, admiring the clarity of the wine.

'Then won't she talk – me being 'ere, pregnant and all?'

'Of course she will. You'll have the vicar calling before long, poking his solemn beak into my business.'

'You don't seem to care.'

'I don't. It's happened before.'

Jennie digested this information quietly. Where she came from people tried to hang on to their respectability. They might be hounded by the bailiffs, drunk, quarrelsome, starving, but they did not like being talked about. Richard was looking across at her, his shirt-sleeves rolled up, his bare elbows resting on the well-scrubbed boards, and he was smiling as if to be the centre of speculation was a joke. Jennie was sure then that this was not the first time a woman had crossed his threshold – and remained there.

Her suspicions were confirmed later when, after she had offered to wash-up and been told to leave it for his 'daily' who would be round tomorrow morning, she complained that she had nothing to wear and he threw open the wardrobe door of the master bedroom, pulling out a heap of female garments.

'These will do for the moment, won't they? In a couple of days I'll take you into Southend and we'll buy you some dresses of your own.'

Jennie looked at the clothes spread on the patchwork quilt, fingered the fine material, held a skirt up against her. 'I suppose this'll fit, though I'll 'ave to leave the waistband undone. Damn baby, it's making me swell up like a toad. Where did you get these?'

He shrugged, stretched his big frame out on the bed, watching her all the while. 'They belonged to a friend of mine. She left in a bit of a hurry.'

'One of your lady-loves? Did you fall out with 'er?' Jennie kept her tone casual but found that she cared. She was already possessive about Richard. He was *hers* – her protector, her provider. No one else should have him while she wanted him.

Richard propped his shoulders up against the bedhead, long legs crossed at the ankles, and she was again aware of a strong physical pull, wishing that she was a girl of his own class, then smiling to herself ruefully, knowing that had she been she would not be there, in a bedroom, alone with him.

'She was a model – I had her down here to paint her. I've turned the barn into a studio.'

Jennie lifted up a silky pink nightgown, holding it to her face, rubbing its softness against her cheek. Perfume clung to its folds. 'A model? Is that all?'

'No, that wasn't all. She was my mistress, too, but she was a slut, beautiful but coarse-mouthed. In the end I told her to get out.'

'And her feelings? Didn't you care about that?' He can be hard, she thought, like all the rotten male crew.

'She wasn't faithful, Jennie, knocking off any Tom, Dick or Harry who came to the door. All she wanted was my money. I can't stand greedy women. You're not like that, are you?' He gave a smile, regarding her fondly, as if she was an amusing child or a little animal whom he had befriended.

'I dunno. I might be.' She was not prepared to be easy on him. 'Tell me why you're looking after me. What d'you want?'

He sat up, swung his legs to the floor, sat there with his hands resting on his knees. 'I've told you, I want to paint you, to photograph you. I'm sorry for you, I suppose. Maybe I want to do my good deed for the year.'

She was not satisfied with this answer but said no more. They spent a pleasant evening sitting by the fire in the parlour, listening to records played on the horned gramophone, and when bedtime came she was in a fever, having been tantalised by his nearness for hours, tension building up in her. He lit two candles and gave her one when they parted on the little landing upstairs. Jennie watched him go into his own room and shut the door.

''Strewth, 'ee's a queer 'un!' She addressed the silent furniture, the single bed. 'Don't 'ee fancy me? Ain't I pretty enough for 'im?'

Running to the mirror she examined her face closely. She looked good, her skin clear with a healthy flush touching her cheekbones, her curls shining, the borrowed cream shantung blouse with its lacy trim hanging loosely over her thickened waistline. I'm prettier than I was when he found me, she decided. Must have looked like scrag end of mutton then, yet he seemed to be more interested in me than he does tonight. What's up with him? Is he doing the gentlemanly bit?

She undressed and slipped on the nightgown. The silk felt cool against her skin. She had never worn silk underclothing before. She thought about its previous owner, wondered why Richard had not removed the things to the spare room which she now occupied. Too lazy? Uncaring? And what had they used to do, there in his big double bed, him and his mistress? Jennie was well versed in the bald facts of life, but had never experienced love herself, never bothered about it till she met Richard.

She turned back the covers and slid between the lavender-scented linen sheets. The candle was still burning on the side-table and the room was alive with shadows. Ghosts! Jennie shivered and tried not to think about them. I don't want to live here on my own. I want him to stay. She could hear him moving about in the adjoining room, then the creak of his bed, then nothing. The moments lengthened into half an hour. Jennie listened to the silence that stretched like some monstrous yawn in the depths of the house, felt it splitting her eardrums, working herself up into a ferment of terror.

It was the mournful cry of an owl that finally tipped the balance. Part of her knew it was a bird, but the other, wilful, needing part managed to convince her that she was petrified. She leapt up and flung open the door, running across the landing into Richard's room. It was lit only by fingers of moonlight poking through the latticed casement. She saw the dark bulk of the bed, saw him rising up, dark against dark, hurled herself into his arms.

'There's a ghost outside!' she cried, forcing out a convincing sob.

She felt him laughing, felt his bare, warm flesh under her hands. 'It's an owl, Jennie. Good Lord, you'll have to be braver than this, my dear.'

'I can't stay in there by myself.' She wormed her way under the quilt, nestled close to his body. 'It'll be bad for me to be so frightened – bad for the baby.'

'And since when have you been the remotest bit concerned about that?'

There was a husky catch in his voice and she knew she had won. She squirmed against him, felt his response and was triumphant. Richard sighed and accepted his fate. This little minx was no more frightened than he was, she was merely using fear as a capital excuse to salve her own conscience. He was glad in one way, sorry in another. Complications presented themselves, while coherent thought was still possible. Then, his hands on the thin silk that covered her nudity, he forgot caution, yielding to urgent desire.

What happened had been none of his planning. He was swept up, engulfed, overcome. Maybe he had wanted it, but would not have made the first move. Now his courtship was swift and strong. No hesitation or delay – a male animal needing a mate. He pushed her nightgown aside, his hand closing on her breast, and she tipped her face up to him, yearning towards him, yearning for his kiss. His mouth closed on hers, his tongue darting between her lips, his hands moulding her to what he wanted. She began to writhe, every nerve, every drop of blood reaching out, and he turned on his back and drew her on top of him.

'Poor little girl,' he whispered hoarsely. 'You were raped – your first experience was awful for you. You've missed so much.'

'Is it good?' she asked 'Is it really good for women?'

'I'll show you how good it can be.'

He rolled her over, lay beside her, his hands roaming her body, rousing her, his fingers seeking that sensitive spot between her legs, playing with it, stroking it, till she rose to a frantic, throbbing crescendo. She knew this feeling, had often produced it for herself, and now he had done it for her. She clung to him gratefully, shaking, sobbing in earnest now. Recognising that she had achieved her release, he reared above her, his face a blur in the dimness, spreading her thighs with his knee. She moaned in pleasure, making his entrance easy, longing to be joined with him, her whole being one of fire and ecstasy and delight.

Much later, when he finally slept, she lay within the circle of his arm, her head pillowed on his broad chest. Is this love? she asked herself, looking round the room, liking everything about it. Richard's room. Hers now. Did she love him? She wasn't sure, having never known that emotion and too wary to give herself entirely into another's keeping. She enjoyed being with him, found him funny, interesting, knowledgeable, and he had promised to educate her, to turn her into a suitable candidate for the theatre. This was enough, wasn't it? I'm happy, she exulted. For the first time in my life, I'm happy.

She rested there, completely relaxed, curled into his side, then stiffened suddenly, hardly daring to let the breath slide between her lips, head tilted at an almost listening angle. Yes, there it was again, a movement within her, small, feeble, like the fluttering of a butterfly's wing. Her hand flew to her belly in an instinctive, protective gesture.

'The baby! It's alive! It's kicking me!' she shouted, digging her elbow into Richard's ribs.

'Is it? That's all right, then,' he replied sleepily. 'Well done, Jennie.'

She grabbed his hand, put it on her stomach. 'Can you feel anything.'

'Eh, what? Do go to sleep, there's a good girl. I'm whacked,' he grumbled, but obligingly let his hand rest there, though it grew heavier and heavier as he drifted off again. She cussed him roundly and pushed it away, impatient with his lack of sensitivity at this so vital a moment.

The movements had ceased, and she wondered if she had imagined them, keeping still, waiting to feel them again, the silence broken only by Richard's even breathing. My baby, my baby. Will it be perfect? Will it look like me? She was astonished to find that every trace of rancour had gone, thankful now that they had visited Dr Armstrong before they left London. He had examined her and said that, although terribly skinny and very young, there was no reason why, with good food, rest and care, she should not be safely delivered of a healthy infant.

She fell asleep almost at once, to dream about the cottage,

herself, the child and Richard living there for ever in complete harmony.

It was with a sinking heart that Eva read the telegram announcing Charlotte's engagement to Phelan. She was in her room at the bank, and Miss Jarrold brought in the official-looking envelope, then stood there expectantly. Eva scanned it, then laid that damning piece of paper on her desk and stared calmly across at her assistant, the iron control of years standing her in good stead.

'Thank you, Miss Jarrold. That will be all.'

Miss Jarrold's round face expressed disappointment, a question hovering on her lips before she remembered her position and closed them in a thin, aggrieved line. An admirable woman, but given to prying – in the nicest possible way, of course, viewing Eva as almost her own kin, someone to be cherished, cosseted, shielded from life's vicissitudes. Eva knew that as soon as the door closed behind her, Miss Jarrold would incarcerate herself with Mr Barford, there to mull over the possible contents of this mysterious communication from abroad.

She sat on at her desk once she was alone, giving way to her distress, her worst fears realised. Charlotte, her dear Charlotte, to become the wife of that man! To live under the influence of the Contessa and her disreputable cronies. It did not bear contemplating, but she could no more stop thinking about it than breathing.

She re-read the telegram, just a few lines typed on strips of paper: 'I'm engaged to Phelan. Letter to follow. Give me your blessing. Yours, Charlotte'.

So concise a missive, yet containing all manner of alarms and forebodings. There was no mention of an early wedding. Ideas flashed in quick sequence through Eva's head. Should she go to Florence at once and try to dissuade her? Should she threaten, plead, exhort? Should she take the final step of disinheriting her? But this would serve only to thrust her into complete dependency on Phelan, in the event of his carrying out his promise to make her his bride. Unfortunately, Eva could not quite make up her mind as to his motives. She was almost positive that they were mercenary ones, but there always remained the outside chance that he was sincere and, if Charlotte really loved him, then Eva did not want to be the one to hurt her.

The first person she went to was Frederick, placing the problem before him. She walked to his office which was just round the corner. The chambers of Haldane, Brigshore and Larch were impressive ones, deeply carpeted, solidly furnished, and Frederick saw her at once.

She almost flung the telegram at him, giving vent to her rage and concern.

'He's done it! He's persuaded her to accept him! What am I going to do, Freddy?'

'There's little you can do.' He scanned it, then handed it back to her, eyeing her anxiously.

She looked awful, her face drawn and white, hazel eyes bright with tears that she would not allow herself to shed. Frederick had been expecting something like this, the telegram coming as no surprise, and was a little shocked by Eva's reaction. Surely, she must have already faced this possibility? Or had she been deliberately deceiving herself? She was obviously deeply and horribly upset. Phelan Charteris, the scourge of her childhod, posed a serious threat to her, cheating her of Charlotte's attention and love, and, even worse, putting himself in the position of acquiring a share of the Pendral fortune, something for which he had always angled.

Frederick wanted to take Eva in his arms, to soothe and pet her like the child she had never allowed herself to be, but he knew that such a gesture would do nothing but add fuel to the fire. Instead, he strolled to the window, hands linked behind his coat-tails, a solid rock against which she could hurl her wrath.

'There must be something!' she stormed, screwing the telegram into a ball in her fist. 'He's always wanted to own this business, tried it on when my father died, and so did his mother, but there was nothing they could do to prevent me from taking over. He's a waster. You know that.'

Frederick turned, the sunlight touching the silver wings each side of his temples, his face calm, his voice devoid of emotion. 'My dear, he can't tamper with Charlotte's money. Thank God that the bill for the Married Women's Property Act was passed by Parliament several years ago, or else we should be in serious trouble. All Charlotte's property will belong to her, free from any right or control by her husband.'

'D'you think such a law with stop Phelan? He's totally unscrupulous. He'll use anything, including bullying and emotional blackmail, to get what he wants.' Eva sank on to a chair, her legs shaking. Anger had sustained her so far, but now, in Frederick's stalwart presence, she dared project a fraction of her despair towards him.

Frederick harboured no illusions about Eva's cousin. It was he who, years before, had handled the dispute that had arisen on Thomas Pendral's death. The Contessa and her son had arrived in England post-haste, gathering like vultures, employing rascally lawyers to contest the will. They had been unsuccessful, eventually giving up and retiring to the Continent. He had felt then that they had not seen the last of them, but could not possibly have foreseen the shape of events to come.

Eva was slumped in her chair, shoulders and head bowed. He had never seen her look so defeated, always proud and strong, taking life by the throat and shaking it, crushing every obstacle that stood in her path. What use her money now? he reflected sadly. Indeed, it was that very money which was causing the trouble.

'Aren't you rather jumping the gun?' he suggested mildly. 'They're not married yet.'

She looked up, leaning on his advice as she had always done. 'Should I go to Italy?'

He shook his head. 'There's absolutely no point. If Charlotte's in love, then she'll hear nothing against him. You'll only alienate her further.'

'What shall I do?'

'Leave it to me. I'll make certain there are no loop-holes by which he can make her part with a single penny.' His clever brain was already running through legal procedures. He was positive that Charlotte's inheritance was safe, but decided to consult with colleagues regarding a clause which stated that a husband remained liable for his wife's torts, civil wrongs in respect of which damages might be recovered against her. In such a case he was entitled to recoup himself out of her separate income, if she had any, and Charlotte would certainly be rich.

He offered to buy Eva lunch, hoping to lift her spirits, but she refused, taking a hansom cab to Columbia Square where Alice now lived. Eva had obtained an apartment for her in this large building which had been constructed in order to raise a few working class folk out of the slums. It was infinitely preferable to the basement she had occupied before, a large place with a Gothic feel to the architecture, the windows pointed, the exterior adorned with floral mouldings. There was room for forty-five families inside, and it had been designed so that light and air flowed through the well-lit corridors. Alice was renting one of the biggest flats, containing a sitting-room, a kitchen with a range, and two bedrooms. Gas and water were laid on and a resident superintendent and two porters kept the passages and staircases clean, waging war on the gangs of children who haunted them.

Alice, who had moved her mother in to take care of the baby, was ecstatic about her new home where everything had been done for the convenience of the tenants. There was a vast laundry on the top floor where eight people could do their washing at individual boilers, and also plenty of drying space. Even the discontented Mrs Mills could find little to fault in the arrangements, though she managed to carry on a running battle with her neighbours.

Eva knew that it was Alice's half-day off, and she was soon installed by the fire and drinking a cup of strong tea. Alice fussed, very pleased to see her, while her little son rolled and tumbled around in his cot, pulling himself up solemnly by the bars, and then subsiding fatly, vaguely annoyed and thrilled by the law of gravity.

'Mother's not here,' Alice said, seating herself near Eva, one eye on Jimmy. 'Gone down to the market, shopping.'

She was glad that the old lady was out of the way for she could be tactless and troublesome, though better-tempered now that Alice's fortunes were rising and she no longer had to scrub floors for a living, content to stay at home and mind Jimmy. Eva was not a frequent visitor and, although they had become good friends and working associates, Alice wondered why she had come to see her. If it was something to do with the shop, then it could have waited till the morning, couldn't it?

She noticed that Eva looked strained, and gently ventured, 'There's nothing wrong, is there?' For a ghastly moment she thought that she had come to tell her that *Pour Femme* was closing, there would be no more work and the lovely life she was building for herself was about to disappear.

Eva read this in her face and reassured her. 'Don't worry, Alice, it's nothing to do with the shop. I wanted to talk to you about something else. You're a young woman and maybe know how young women feel. Well, the truth is that I had a telegram from Italy today. Charlotte is engaged to Phelan Charteris.'

'Oh, my goodness! That was a bit of a shock, wasn't it?' Alice had met him once and been impressed by his appearance, though his haughty air had put her back up. She knew Charlotte well, and had thought her to be of an intensely practical disposition, able to make up her own mind on so important a step as marriage.

Sitting there in that humble abode where every stick of furniture had been bought cheaply and there was a total absence of luxury, Eva opened her heart to the mild, sweet-natured Alice who had herself been used and abused by a man. Alice listened to everything she had to say, picking up Jimmy to quieten him, holding him on her lap and giving him a toy to play with.

'I feel that I should go to Florence and talk to her,' Eva concluded. 'Would this be the right thing to do?'

'I don't think so,' Alice said quickly. 'Mother tried to stop me seeing Cyril, but it only made me more determined. Miss Charlotte always seems to know her own mind. If she's in love, then nothing or no one will stop her. I loved Cyril, I suppose I still do – wasn't really his fault that he couldn't resist the ladies – they chased after him, anyway. I don't regret what I did. After all, I got Jimmy out of it, didn't I?' And she kissed the top of her baby's downy head.

Eva left Columbia Square more bothered than ever. It had begun to rain, the late afternoon traffic throwing up showers of spray. The thought of returning to Albion House was depressing. She had nothing arranged for that night, gloomily contemplating the empty hours ahead. On an impulse, she ordered the cab driver to go to Holland Park.

Richard was surprised to see her. He stepped back and asked her to come into the studio. He wondered what she wanted; wondered, with a guilty pang, if she had somehow heard about Jennie.

'Eva, this is an unexpected pleasure,' he said smoothly, taking her coat, fur stole and gloves while she removed her hat and laid it on a chair.

Eva did not tell him at once what was troubling her. Instead they talked of the exhibition and the public's response. Large donations were already coming in, and several people were asking for appointments to have Richard paint their portraits, while magazines were requesting copies of his photographs for which they offered to pay generously.

He went to close the door of his darkroom where he had been developing prints he had already taken of Jennie. He hoped Eva would not ask to see his latest work for though he was more than pleased with them, they were of an intimate nature. Jennie in her dressing-gown snapped in the domesticated surroundings of the cottage, or lying on the bed, hair splayed out across the pillow. There was one where she was standing by the window, light streaming in, taken sideways on, with her robe held close about her body, very obviously pregnant and brazen about it.

'I called once before but you were't here,' Eva felt calmer in his company, the matter of Charlotte falling into perspective.

It was good to be with him again, this handsome young man who had proved to be an inspiring companion. She feasted her eyes on him: his bearded face, those blue, blue eyes, that lithe body clad in a claret velvet smoking jacket, a cravat tied carelessly around his neck, narrow grey trousers covering his muscular legs. Perhaps it was just as well that Charlotte was absent at this important juncture in Eva's life when she was forming a friendship with a man. In fact, Eva had begun to forget about her for long periods at a time, until that morning.

'I've been away – down to my cottage near Southend,' he answered casually, lighting up a cigarette.

'Really? That explains it. I, too, visited Brighton recently. The seaside is pleasant at this time of year.' How formal, she thought, aware of a restraint in his manner absent till then. Suddenly she began to worry. She really knew very little about him. Could it be that he had a girl-friend? Someone he didn't want to introduce to her?

He nodded, agreed that it was pleasant, wished he could be truthful with her but found the words sticking in his throat. She'd never understand about Jennie, would she? He didn't understand the situation himself, caught up in a sensual, physical passion that stunned him.

Jennie was irresistible, an uninhibited, demanding creature. Even to think about her made desire course through him. He stood up, made some coffee, tried to forget her, but it was impossible. He had never had such a mistress. There was nothing she had refused him, nothing they had not done, no part of her that he had not possessed. She was a delicious child-woman, fulfilling his every fantasy.

With a great effort he concentrated on Eva. He liked her tremendously, admired and respected her. He could talk to her endlessly. It was difficult to talk with Jennie. This was one of the reasons why he had had to leave her for a few days, despite her tears and temper-tantrums. He needed space to think, to work, to recoup his strength for the next sexual onslaught. He knew he'd not be able to stay away from her for long. She was too tempting.

At last Eva came to the crux of her visit. She told him about Charlotte's engagement. He was at a loss, having never met either Charlotte or Phelan, but he trusted Eva's judgement. If she thought the man a rogue, then he most probably was. Richard's advice, for what it was worth, was similar to that of Frederick and Alice. Charlotte should be left to find out about Phelan for herself. Maybe she wouldn't until it was too late. That was a risk Eva had to take.

'Let's go out and have supper,' he suggested, to calm her agitation.

She paused, touched a hand to her hair. 'I'm not dressed for it.'

'Nonsense. You look lovely.' He was absolutely sincere. She did look lovely in her distress, that rather severe manner softened.

Eva blushed, protested, was pleased. 'Nice of you to say so, but I know my limitations. I've never been lovely.'

'Don't underestimate yourself.' Richard could read her like a book, knew her shyness. Someone had hurt her badly in the past, he thought, then eased her embarrassment by adding, 'I'll take you to a small café in Fleet Street where journalists eat. The food is superb and no one expects formal dress. Give me a moment to grab a jacket and we'll be off. I want you to see my car. I bought it yesterday. I'm still learning to handle it, but think I can cope with evening traffic. Mind you, I wouldn't care to try it round Piccadilly in the middle of the day just yet.'

Though Richard had wanted a sporty two-seater, with frequent journeys between London and Westhope in mind and also the prospect of transporting Jennie, her baby and a possible nurse-maid later on, he had settled for a reliable Rover tourer, with plenty of room for passengers and luggage, mica windows and a protective hood which could be raised in bad weather. He had driven cars before, an enthusiast automobilist, and had been meaning to buy one for some time. His meeting with Jennie had booted him into action. He could see that the days of horse-drawn vehicles were numbered, and Richard loved new inventions, always the first to try out any innovation.

Eva, though beset with problems, had rarely enjoyed an evening more. Richard was so proud of his car, showing off the gleaming maroon paintwork, the brass head-lamps, the buttoned leather upholstery. He was like a child with a new toy, but drove the Rover skilfully. He continued to enthuse about it during the meal which, as he had predicted, was delectable, the surroundings quaintly Parisian, with candle-lit tables, check table-cloths and French waiters.

Some of the customers greeted him with a wave of the hand or raised eyebrows from their places at the tables where they were sitting around eating, smoking unnumerable cigarettes, carrying on heated arguments about new books, new movements in art, the new morality. Eva caught the edge of a discussion concerning politics; obviously the speaker was a Socialist. Several untidy, loud-voiced men, with beards and tweed suits, came up to their table and started to talk with Richard about his exhibition, angling to be introduced to his companion. It was altogether an exhilarating experience and the most satisfying thing about it was that they assumed she was Richard's close friend, possibly more than that.

It was nearly midnight when he drove her to Albion House. He switched off the engine and, 'Would you like to come in?' she asked, anxious to prolong this meeting.

'No thanks, I think I'll have an early night.'

He was looking at her steadily in the glow of the gas-lamp as they stood by the front door. Eva hesitated to ring the bell, wanting to linger there with this rangy, handsome intelligent man who had the ability to make her feel twenty again.

'Thank you. Going out has cheered me up no end.'

'Good. Glad to be of assistance. It's all part of the Sinclair service,' he grinned. 'Shall we meet again soon and do it again?'

'I'd like that.' She could think of no further reason for delay, but found it hard to tear herself away.

'And you'll promise to stop worrying about Charlotte?'

'I'll try.'

'See me first if you decide to hotfoot it to Florence?'

'Why?'

'Because I'll come with you. You'll need someone to face that Big Bad Wolf, Phelan Charteris. I'll knock his head off if he gets nasty.'

Eva's heart leapt and she wanted to cry. Just for a moment, she saw him as a kind of Sir Galahad, her knight in shining armour, then she pulled herself together abruptly. This was absurd. But it was while she was still wavering between commonsense and dreams that Richard leaned forward and kissed her cheek.

'Why did you do that?' she whispered.

'Because you're one of the nicest people I know, he answered seriously, then laughed. 'And I felt like it!'

'Richard –' she began, feeling herself falling apart inside.

'Goodnight, Eva. I'll phone you,' he shouted, then ran down the steps, paused at the bottom and gave her a cheerful wave before entering his car and driving off.

Jennie was bored. She loathed it when Richard was away from Westhope. The days dragged, the nights were lonely, spent in his bed, remembering his passion. Mrs Entworth came in every morning, to clean the house, attend to the washing and ironing, shop and prepare meals. She was a thin little woman, with bright, shrewd, all-seeing eyes, pretending to be at ease with Jennie but a trifle on guard. Richard paid her generously, she liked him and had worked for him ever since he bought the cottage. She enjoyed a good gossip, and was a bosom friend of Miss Ratley, the post-mistress. Every afternoon before she went home to get her husband's tea, she dropped in for a chat.

'Well, Mabel?' Miss Ratley would say, ushering her into the parlour behind the shop, leaving an underling in charge of the counter. 'And what's been happening at Laurel Cottage today?'

'Not a lot, Ivy – he's away, and the girl moping about. Town-bred, she is, doesn't like the country. I don't know where Mr Sinclair found her. She's ever so common. You should hear her language! Swears like a trooper.'

'I saw her yesterday. She came in to get a magazine. Bought a copy of *Home Chat*, though she was looking for something with romance stories. I don't stock those sort of papers, I told her. You'll have to go to Southend for trash like that.' Miss Ratley had taken great delight in this rebuttal, her manner suggesting that only servant girls and low women read tales calculated to stimulate the baser part of their imagination. Now she rivetted Mrs Entworth with gimlet eyes and added, 'She's far gone, by the looks of her.'

'The baby's due in August, and we've booked Sister Lumsden.' This was the district nurse who had already made several trips to the cottage to see Jennie. 'Of course, they'll want me there, too, as I've had six myself. I'll be the first to know when it starts to happen.'

Miss Ratley smoothed out an imaginary crease in the antimacassar at the back of one of the tightly stuffed armchairs. 'Seems that she's only a slip of a girl. Looks very young. Didn't have much to say for herself, but didn't try to hide her shame, neither. And I can't get any information from that school-teacher. Tight as a drum, she is. But then, I've always thought she was a stuck-up piece.'

She referred to a young woman who taught the village children. Richard had persuaded her to give Jennie lessons to improve her speech. Her name was Jean Reeves, and she was not a local girl, boarding in the headmaster's house and keeping herself very much to herself.

'I don't know what things are coming to, I'm sure.' Mrs Entworth sighed, pleasantly scandalised. 'Folks seem to behave as they like, these days.'

'Wicked, I call it. Care for a nip of brandy in your tea, dear?' Miss Ratley held out the squat bottle.

'I don't mind if I do. Just a drop, now, no more, or my old man will be smelling it on my breath and accusing me of I don't know what. Silly creatures, men.'

Miss Ratley sniffed, her bony hands busy with the tea-cups. 'I wouldn't know, being a spinster,' she reminded, her tone indicating that she really did not want to know anything about those strange creatures of lust and animal passions.

'Of course not. I was forgetting,' Mrs Entworth said hastily.

Miss Ratley sat back, nose twitching like a bloodhound on the scent. 'You were saying? About the girl. Is it *his* baby, d'you suppose?'

'Mr Sinclair? I can't tell you. I don't think so, from something I overheard her saying to Miss Reeves, but if this one isn't then I'll guarantee the next one will be.'

'Oh? What d'you mean?' Miss Ratley leant forward across the lace-edged cloth of the table, tendrils of grey hair escaping from the uncomely plaits coiled like headphones about each ear.

Mrs Entworth glanced around her as if hoping to catch eavesdroppers, then lowered her voice. 'She sleeps in his room, and when he's home she doesn't move to the spare bed. It's never disturbed, never so much as wrinkled. She doesn't use it. I can tell. It's one of my jobs to do the bedrooms. They don't get up till lunch time. I hear them laughing – and other noises, too.'

'What sort of noises?'

Mrs Entworth's cheeks went pink. 'I don't like to say, you being single – but I recognise them. The sort of noises couples make when they're up to no good.'

'Disgusting!' Miss Ratley exclaimed in delighted horror.

'Disgraceful!' echoed her friend.

'I don't know how you can bring yourself to work there.'

'He's a good payer. One has to be practical about these things and I need the extra money. Beggars can't be choosers,' intoned Mrs Entworth piously, then she twinkled, 'It adds a bit of spice to life, too.'

Miss Ratley pulled down her lips sternly, but could not help saying, 'You're right. It does. Have another tot of brandy, Mabel.'

Jennie lazed the days away, sleeping a lot. Sometimes she caught the bus to Southend, relieving the boredom by squandering Richard's money. Sister Lumsden advised her on a layette, saying, somewhat reprovingly, that most mothers sewed and knitted for their coming babies. Jennie had neither of these accomplishments so she took a list of things required to the most expensive haberdashers and returned to Laurel Cottage ladened with parcels. Richard would pay the bill so she was extravagant, buying fluffy toys, a muslin-draped cradle fit for royalty and a magnificent coach-built perambulator slung on leather straps above huge, slender wheels, ordering these to be delivered to the cottage. She kitted herself out with flowing, floral printed smocks and elastic-waisted cotton skirts, fringed wraps, knickers, chemises, nightdresses, anything that took her fancy.

But inside her was a stillness and waiting, her ear permanently attuned for the sound of the Rover coming down the High Street. Once she had tasted passion, her desire for Richard was insatiable. Sex was a wonderful new game; safe, too, until the child was born. She matured, grew plump with love as well as the baby. Love or lust? The line between the two emotions was narrow, and she a novice, unable to tell one from the other. All she knew was that she gloried in Richard and the beautiful sensations he gave her, missed him, thought about him constantly, ached for his body, his kisses, his tickly beard and musky, masculine smell.

He drove to Westhope every weekend, staying from Friday till Monday. Sometimes she would receive an unexpected visit in between, when he would stride in, impatient, needful, gathering her up in his arms and taking her to the bedroom, even more eager than herself for a fiery, volatile mating. She questioned him, wanting to hear every detail of what he did in London. A name occurred again and again, a woman's name, and she did not like it.

'Who's this Lady Pendral you're always on about? Some upper class bitch you're fucking?' she asked him one night as they lay in bed after love-making.

'Eva? She's a friend of mine, nothing more,' Richard answered, smiling at the perfect picture she made in the candle-light, her wild hair falling, manelike, over her shoulders, her red lips pouting, eyes shooting angry sparks at him. 'Good God, I've no energy left to hump anyone else.'

'But she'd like you to. She fancies you.' Jennie was not satisfied, unable to understand that men and women were capable of anything but physical relationships.

'She's never given any indication of it.' Now that Jennie had planted the thought in his mind it took root and began to grown, and he wondered if she was right. Eva certainly seemed ready to drop everything for the chance of meeting him. He hoped that she was not getting sentimental about him as this would complicate matters considerably.

Jennie sat up, pushing away his hand that was gently patting the bulge of her stomach. It amused him when the baby kicked. 'How d'you know what women feel? You're only a man,' she said scornfully. 'And leave my baby alone. It isn't yours.'

'I know, but I like it. Can't wait to see it once it's born.' Richard took her erratic temper in his stride, rarely irritated by her swings of mood, putting it down to her condition. He had never lived with a pregnant woman before, and the novelty of it intrigued him.

He still found her enormously entertaining, and was pleased with her progress. She was a born mimic and Miss Reeves was having little trouble in correcting her speech which was no longer full of grammatical errors. She had even mastered the art of aitches. A little more tuition and she would be able to pass as a middle-class girl, not an East End brat. Her tendency to swear was rather more difficult to check, a habit of long standing, but even this made him laugh.

'I don't like you going to London. Don't like you taking Lady Pendral out to dinner. I'll bet you never think of me when you're there,' she continued, a little girl now, upset because Daddy was neglecting her.

'Oh, Jennie – tell you what, I'll write to you, shall I? Send you postcards. What d'you say?' He drew her to him, cuddled her, stroked her hair.

'I've never had a letter. Nobody's ever written to me.' She was somewhat mollified, making no objection when his caresses became more loverlike than paternal.

'That's settled then. Now will you stop nagging me? Lady Pendral's a business associate – nothing more. Christ, I've got to make money somehow. You're costing me a packet.'

'I'm worth it, aren't I?'

'Every brass farthing.'

'Better than your la-di-dah lady?'

'Different from my la-di-dah lady.'

'That's all right then. Come on, Richard, let's do it again. We're wasting time and you've got to go back tomorrow.'

Jean Reeves had become Jennie's friend. She was twenty-five and tired of teaching village children, finding the Cockney girl a hundred times more rewarding. The summer was hot, the children on holiday, and Jean happy to accompany Jennie to Southend to shop or idle on the beach. If Jean had any qualms about being seen with what the good folk of Westhope termed a 'hussy', she never betrayed it, developing a real affection for her, appalled by the awful stories of her childhood which Jennie related with a certain amount of theatrical exaggeration. Never one to mince words, she was brutually frank regarding the circumstances which had brought about her pregnancy, and unrestrained in her praise of Richard, his kind heart, his open wallet, his prowess between the sheets.

'He's got a whopper,' she would boast as if she was an expert on the subject, liking to shock, and watching Jean's reaction. 'And he knows what to do with it.'

Jean never so much as batted an eyelid. She had read some of the works of Sigmund Freud and considered herself enlightened. She was a forthright person given to brusque speech and mannish attire who supported the Women's Suffrage Movement. In Jennie she had found an answer to her prayers. Here was a shining example of the way in which men trampled on women. She took this information along to the meetings that she regularly attended, becoming quite the star turn of the evening, actually in close contact with a victim of male oppression.

Late in July, she called to collect Jennie from Laurel Cottage and, carrying bathing costumes and towels rolled into neat bundles, they boarded the bus. Soon they were strolling along the esplanade, breathing in the pungent smell of sea-weed. Jennie decided she simply had to have some jellied eels, so they bought two tubs from a stall run by a typical, bawdy-tongued Eastender trading at the coast.

Everywhere was so busy, the trains disgorging day-tripping Londoners intent on enjoying themselves. There were families with hordes of children flourishing buckets and spades and demanding ice-cream; shop-girls on a spree in their best dresses and gigantic hats, escorted by office clerks in white flannels, striped blazers and straw boaters. Jennie rejoiced to hear their nasal accents, their ripe language, their risqué jokes. She was homesick for London, tired of the country drawl, the slow pace of existence.

She took off her shoes and stockings when they reached the beach, wandering along, entranced by the concert party performing on their small stage under its canvas awning, wishing that she stood there singing, dressed as a pierrette. She knew the popular songs word for word, and sang along with them, surprising Jean by the purity of her voice.

'That's what I'll be doing one day soon,' Jennie declared, hair flying loose in the breeze, skin tanned, back braced to counterbalance her additional weight, reminding Jean of a pagan goddess of fertility. 'Entertaining people. You just wait and see.'

They found a quiet corner where they discreetly undressed, donning their bathing suits. Jennie had insisted on having one, even though it was unheard of for expectant mothers to expose themselves in this way, many women refusing to appear in public under any circumstances once their pregnancies started to show. This was not Jennie's way and she had bought a costume of navy serge which consisted of pantalettes to the knee and a full tunic trimmed with lace and braid. She scorned the matching black woollen stockings, going bare-legged, but did add flat tie-on pumps and a frilled bathing cap.

'This is all so silly,' Jean grumbled, struggling into her suit while Jennie held up a large towel as a screen behind which she could disrobe. 'Women have always had to shroud themselves like nuns to enjoy a swim, whereas until recently men bathed mother-naked. And how much better they looked than in those hideous monstrosities they sport nowadays.'

'I'd like to swim with no clothes on,' Jennie nodded, agreeing. 'Why are people so ashamed of their bodies?'

'Conditioning and the church, my dear,' Jean answered sagaciously. 'Hopefully it'll change one day, if we women stand fast.'

The sea was icy but invigorating. Jennie hopped about in the waves, shrieking encouragement to Jean who struck out for deeper waters, her arms cleaving through effortlessly, a strong swimmer. She returned presently and started to show Jennie how to swim, a hand under her chin as she encouraged her to try the arm movements. They stayed in the water for a long time, the sun burning down hotly, and at last plodded wearily through the shallows to collapse on their beach-towels.

They had brought packets of sandwiches with them and, after they had satisfied their appetites, Jennie lay on her back, an arm flung over her eyes. She dozed, dreamed, thought hotly of Richard, then became aware of discomfort, a pain in her belly, an ache low down in her back. She sat up, prodded Jean awake.

'I don't feel well. Maybe we should go home.'

Jean woke up instantly. 'Is it the baby? You're not starting labour, are you?'

'I think maybe I am.' Jennie's eyes were round and scared.

Jean took charge. There was no way she was going to rely on public transport, so they arrived at the cottage in a taxi. By this time Jennie was in the second stage of labour, and pushing. Jean leapt on her bicycle and pedalled like fury for the midwife. Mrs Entworth got Jennie on to the bed in the spare room with all speed. She insisted that this was where the birth should take place, ignoring Jennie's cursing. And Jennie did curse, then and throughout the quick labour, reverting to her origins.

'That bastard!' she raved as Sister Lumsden arrived in the nick of time. ''Ee said 'ee'd be with me when it 'appened! Bastard! Sod! 'Ee's not 'ere. 'Ee's with that bloody bitch in London! Oh, oh – what the fuck's 'appening! I'm going to die! I *want* to die!'

'Stop that noise at once!' Sister Lumsden was strict with her, rolling up her sleeves and getting down to business. 'Stop thrashing about! Save your energy! That's it. We shan't be long now. One more big push. Come on, girl, put your back into it!'

'Jesus wept!' Jennie grunted through clenched teeth. 'It bloody 'urts!'

Grace Rosalind Blossom made her entrace into the world in a rush of amniotic fluid, to the accompaniment of her mother swearing violently. But once she was laid, naked, wriggling, on Jennie's flat stomach that voice changed to one of cooing tenderness.

'Aw, look at her! Isn't she lovely? Hello, darling – this is your ma.'

Jennie took the tiny hand in hers, looked at those little feet that had kicked inside her for so many months, saw the dark, damp hair, the wide blue eyes, the comical, wrinkled old-young face that resembled no one and belonged to Grace entirely, and fell madly in love – really in love this time – crazily in love with her own daughter.

Chapter 11

'Lovesick and can't spew,' was how Tilly described Gwen's condition. Cynthia nodded. Coarse though Tilly might sometimes be, she usually managed to knock the nail on the head.

Gwen knew what was being said behind her back, but paid no heed. Charlotte's betrothal had excited her beyond measure, and she fostered the hope that soon she might be Julian's future wife. She loftily condemned Bernice's liaison with Andrew, considering this gross and beneath contempt, sure that Julian and she had something of far greater value, a spiritual relationship. She was convinced that he loved her as champions had once loved their ladies back in the time of King Arthur, a pure love when they were willing to die in exchange for a smile, flourishing their adored one's favours on their lances when they rode into battle. Holidaying in romantic Italy did nothing to lessen this dream.

Charlotte was sure that Gwen was living in cloud-cuckoo-land, but hesitated to disillusion her. Gwen didn't know, *no one* knew, that she had been intimate with Phelan. She had an idea that Tilly suspected, unavoidably involved with her comings and goings. But nothing had been said. Riven with guilt, she was angered by her own burgeois feelings. She was a modern woman, wasn't she? Someone who supported those advocating free love. Why then, was she so anxious that no one should find out what she was doing? She told herself firmly that she was going to marry Phelan and that they were merely anticipating this event. As he had said, it was a good idea for couples to try sex first, in case they proved incompatible. There was nothing wrong in her sleeping with him, was there?

Yet these ideas were shockingly advanced, and she would be a pariah, shunned by society, if it leaked out. The finger of blame would be firmly pointed at her, whereas should it become known that she had received the justified, though premature attentions of a hot-blooded fiancé, it might even enhance Phelan's reputation. He would be thought a bit of a bounder and a cad, but the men would nudge one another and wink, and the ladies, pretending to have heard nothing of the rumours, would find him even more exciting.

She had put off sending the telegram to Eva for a full week, then, frightened that she might hear the news from someone else, had gone to the post office in Florence and dispatched it. Phelan laughed at her worries, and the Contessa was gushingly enthusiastic about the marriage, already looking upon her as a daughter, or so she kept telling her. Bernice briefly surfaced from her obsession with Andrew to offer congratulations, then sank back into that absorbing affair which, when they were not wrapped in each other's arms, consisted of jealous scenes, violent quarrels, and vitriolic insults.

A letter from Eva was awaiting Charlotte when she came back to the villa after visiting Rome, Milan and Venice. Augusta was on the terrace to welcome them, and she handed Charlotte her correspondence after she had kissed her and said how much she had been missed.

Charlotte waited until she was alone before opening the envelope. Even then she stood turning it over in her hands, putting off the moment. All the time, whether viewing the Colosseum, attending La Scala Opera House, or idling in a Venetian gondola, there had been nagging doubts at the back of her mind. What was Eva going to say?

The contents of the letter came as a complete surprise, leaving her deflated.

My dear Charlotte,

Thank you for your telegram. Of course, your news was rather a shock, though not entirely unexpected. You already know my opinion of Phelan, and this has not changed. However, after giving the matter a great deal of thought, I have come to the conclusion that it is your life, and you must decide for yourself how to direct it. So, my dearest girl, it is up to you. Marry him if you must and, while I can't honestly give the union my blessing, I want you to know that you can always rely on me for help and support, for *yourself*, no matter what happens.

I've had your letters and am glad that you're having such a marvellous time. Yes, Italy is beautiful, far more entrancing than stuffy old Brighton. Freddy wishes to be remembered to you. Alice is well and sends her regards, as do all the girls in the shop and everyone here. I wonder when you plan to marry? Will it happen in Florence? Take care of yourself, and I'm looking forward to seeing you soon.

With fondest love, from Eva.

So normal a letter when Charlotte had been expecting a storm. It quite upset her, almost as if Eva did not really care and was preoccupied in other directions. Such a cool reaction hurt, making her worry in case Eva no longer felt that deep affection they had once shared. It was a chilling thought, leaving her defenceless, and making her realise how much she had taken her guardian's love for granted.

I don't care! She flung back her head defiantly, pulled open the drawer of the escritoire and stuffed the letter inside. I have Phelan now.

It seemed that she did indeed have Phelan, but was no nearer guessing what went on in his mind than before they became lovers. Things had changed, of course. He now had a proprietorial attitude towards her. She could do nothing without consulting him. He wanted to know where she went and what she did. At first, she found this flattering, but it was beginning to irk her.

During the weeks they had spent touring, life had proved to be once again a round of entertainments. Phelan organised everything, and despite her watchdog, Cynthia, had made every opportunity for having Charlotte to himself. He had crept into her hotel room at night when everyone was asleep, had arranged trips for the others to get them out of the way whilst she pretended to have a debilitating headache, lying so that she might obey his demands that she spend time alone with him. Such clandestine trysts were thrilling, and she enjoyed them, but gradually an element of fear was souring their meetings. Not fear of discovery, but fear of him.

He had been right in predicting that she would learn to give rein to her passions. He was experienced, knowing how to rouse and familiarise her with her body and its responses. Yet some of the things he suggested in those darkened night rooms, or apartments shuttered to the glare of the afternoon, made her shudder with revulsion. Cruel things, involving whips and leather bindings used to evoke pain-pleasure. It was then that she vividly recalled Eva's warning.

There's a dark side to Cousin Phelan. Things I've heard about but don't wish to repeat.

'Darling, don't be so prudish,' he would say if she protested. 'There's no harm in these gadgets. They're simply toys to add to our enjoyment.'

'To your enjoyment, maybe,' she would retort spiritedly. 'Not mine. I don't like it.'

But she generally gave in, hating to cross him, for when Phelan was in a black mood everyone suffered, her especially. And yet, she loved him, enchanted by his pleasant side, melting when he wooed her with soft words, or serenaded her with piano music. At the base of it lay her stubborn pride which would not let her confess for a moment, even in her most secret thoughts, that all was not as it should be. She told herself that she was a callow girl, completely ignorant about male urges. Perhaps these toys, as he called them, were what every man needed to enhance his enjoyment. There was no one in whom she could confide, too shy to mention it to Bernice, the one person most likely to offer sound advice.

The wedding day was drawing near. The Contessa had planned it down to the final detail, booking the Anglican Church, ordering caterers to supply food and wine for the reception in the Villa Alinari's banqueting-hall, sending out countless invitations to all and sundry among her friends. Charlotte wrote to Eva, asking if she would consider coming. Eva sent her a substantial cheque as a wedding present, but refused to be there in person.

Much time was taken up in shopping. There was the wedding dress to be made, a gorgeous creation in white brocade and lace, the trousseau also, and Gwen was to be bridesmaid, Bernice the matron-of-honour. Caught up in the frenzy, Charlotte did not allow herself to think of Eva or permit a moment's regret. Everything was ready at last, the gown delivered to her bedchamber, waiters moving in, florists arriving to select positions for the sumptuous arrangements of blossoms ordered by the Contessa.

Phelan seemed unusually preoccupied, but Charlotte was too busy to worry about this. She did notice, however, that he was spending more time away from the villa. Once or twice she saw him in the distance with his coach-driver, Michele, talking and laughing animatedly. Sometimes she heard the young man singing as he went about his work, his voice having that clear, sonorous quality typical of an Italian tenor. Michele was handsome, his nose aquiline, dark eyes dreamy, face sombre in repose then, warmed by a smile, as frank as a child's. He often drove them out for picnics in the woods, accompanied by a lithe brown girl with beautiful eyes full of tenderness and mischief. Her name was Angelica and she worked in the kitchen. Charlotte had assumed her to be Michel's paramour until Phelan explained.

'She's his sister. I've known them since they were children. Their family has served the Alinaris for generations. Delightful pair, aren't they? Straight out of a Leonardo painting. Real Italian faces, and those eyes – sad as death, then changing to laughter in a flash.'

Charlotte had not paid them much heed. They were simply Augusta's servants, and Phelan was inclined to associate with these warm-hearted, garrulous people. He was attentive to her in the evenings, when they relaxed, eating, drinking, entertaining Augusta's numerous visitors. The talk on everyone's lips was the forthcoming wedding.

It was coming close, only one more day, and Phelan was particularly loving to Charlotte in the garden after dinner. The hillside sloped gently away, and below in the valley the lights of Florence glowed like fireflies. Climbing roses formed an arch over the stone bench on which they sat, and the garden was silver under the moon, black where cypress trees clustered. In the gloom his eyes burned into hers as he held her close. His lips touched her hands, her cheeks, her throat.

'Are you happy?' he murmured.

'Oh, yes, but I can't quite believe it,' she said, while he drew her arms up about his neck. It was such a lovely night and he was so sweet to her. How could she not be happy?

'*La forza del destino.*' His voice was low, caressing.

'Do you believe in destiny?'

'Of course. Fate brought us together.'

'Another night, a day and then one more night, and we shall be man and wife.' It was unreal, unbelievable, but joy blossomed within her, a perfect flower to cherish in wonder and delight.

He chuckled, held her away so that he might study her in the dimness. Finely marked brows, wide, honest eyes, lovely heart-shaped face framed in dusky hair. 'I shan't be a batchelor any more. This will be strange for I'm used to being alone, doing what I want when I want to.'

Over his shoulder Charlotte saw a falling star running swift and bright until it dropped into a sea of leaves. In the stillness she could hear the far-off tinkle of bells worn by the goats who grazed under the denuded vines. It was the time for wine-pressing and the breeze was spiced with the bitter-sweet odour of crushed grapes.

Later she went up to her room where discs of moonlight lay across the floor. She ran out to the balcony, could see him below, pacing about beneath the silvered foliage of the fig tree. He saw her leaning there and, agile as a panther, swung himself up by the boughs until he could touch her. The dark leaves were all about him, the moon lighting his tiptilted face. He kissed her, long and deep, the perfect night enclosing them, the stars throbbing overhead, the scent of roses powerful and dizzying.

She stayed there after he had climbed down, watching until he disappeared into the trees. She was full of dreams born of memories and anticipation. Phelan *did* love her. Their life together would be perfect, and she turned the diamond ring on the third finger of her left hand. Soon it would be joined by her gold wedding band, never to leave her till death severed her soul from her body.

The purring of an engine roused her. She leaned over as far as she dared, peering towards the drive which she was just able to discern. The full moon cast a light that was almost as clear as day, and in that unearthly, bluish radiance, she could see Phelan, unmistakable in his evening suit, taking his place at the wheel of his car. There was someone else there – blond hair gleamed momentarily as a man got in beside him. It was Julian.

At breakfast next morning she said nothing to Phelan about his nocturnal wanderings. He was composed, stunningly attractive in a white linen suit, smiling at her, and then telling her that he had business which demanded his attention, matters that had to be tidied up before he left for their honeymoon in Switzerland.

'Don't worry, I'll be awfully busy all day. Lots of things to see to,' she answered, her small hand grasped in his large, tanned one.

'I shan't come back here. Unlucky for a man to see his bride before the wedding day, so I'm staying at the palace. The next time we meet it will be at the altar.'

He squeezed her fingers, kissed her cheek and left her. At once Gwen leapt upon her, chattering incessantly. Charlotte refrained from informing her that she had seen Julian leaving the villa late at night. She soon forgot the incident herself. It was necessary to make a last-minute visit to Florence in order to collect an evening gown from the dress-maker, part of Charlotte's elaborate trousseau. Gwen and Cynthia went with her, and one of the servants drove them there in a gig.

The morning passed enjoyably. They found time for lemonade and cakes in a restaurant, teasing her about being a free woman for the very last time. Then Cynthia decided that she needed stamps and would they go to the post-office with her? Charlotte declined. She was wondering if Phelan would be having lunch at his apartment. An unexpected visit would surprise and please him and, with quickening breath, she visualised his dark eyes flaming with desire the moment she stepped inside.

It had been a week since they last made love, no chance to escape the furore of bridal preparations. She wanted him with an urgency that could not be checked and walked quickly through the narrow streets to the old palace. He had given her a key and, in the past, she had sometimes gone there to wait for him. Now she entered the courtyard, greeting the rounded, comely caretaker who was pegging washing on a line, surrounded by her brood of children who scampered about on ancient steps or clambered over broken statues.

The change from heat to the coolness of the hall was a relief. Charlotte ran lightly up the stairs, inserted the key in the lock and opened the door. It took her a second to adjust to the shade. A single ray of light, grainy with dust, slanted through the shutters, and touched a glint from one of the brass candlesticks. Charlotte gazed in fascination, trying to make sense of what her widening pupils and bewildered wits perceived.

There on the bed lay Angelica, naked as the day she was born. Phelan was beside her, equally nude, and standing stockstill, a towel knotted round his hips, his hair wet and tousled from the bath, was Michele. Their eyes were on Charlotte, and silence hung like a sword over the room.

Angelica was the first to move. She gasped, crouched against the pillows, pulled the sheet up over her body, skin almost as black as her hair in contrast with its whiteness. Her eyes were enormous, wistful, apologetic as they stared at Charlotte.

Phelan recovered his aplomb with remarkable speed. 'Close the door, my dear,' he said quietly. 'We don't want to shock our good Catholic caretaker should she chance this way.'

Charlotte leaned against it, speechless. Michele, taking his cue from his master, sauntered across to the bed, his eyes never leaving her face, sly eyes considering her as if he hoped she would join in the orgy.

Phelan rose, took a step towards her. 'Charlotte, don't look so upset. Try to understand, darling. They mean nothing to me. Nothing at all.'

She glared at his face, his mocking smile, his strong, powerful body. Snatching the engagement ring from her finger she flung it at him, then turned on her heel and fled the room.

'Isn't she wonderful? Have you ever seen anything more perfect, Richard?'

Jennie was sitting up in bed, cradling her baby. She looked radiant, astonishing Richard when, on arrival at the cottage, he crept up to the bedroom carrying a huge bouquet and a pink fur rabbit larger than the baby herself. He had expected to find her wan and exhausted.

Certainly other new mothers of his acquaintance always made the most of their lying-in, taking full advantage of the situation to be the centre of attention and wheedle costly presents out of their husbands in recompense for the agony they had supposedly endured.

'She's beautiful,' he agreed, bending over the shawl-swaddled bundle, seeing a tiny red face, wide-open blue eyes and a shock of thick black hair. 'Clever girl, Jennie,' and he planted a kiss on the top of her head.

To his horror, Jennie insisted on placing Grace in his reluctant arms. 'Here, take her. Give her a cuddle. You're the first man she's met.'

Richard had not had much to do with children, let alone one as young as this. He held her gingerly, afraid that he might inadvertently break her. Jennie giggled at his timidity, advised him to hold her firmly or she would feel insecure, and warned him to support her wobbly head.

'She's so tiny,' Richard protested, doing as he was told.

'No, she's not. Weighed in at six pounds seven ounces, so that's not really small.' Jennie's voice held a new note, rich with maternal pride, like the deep-throated purr of a mother cat guarding her nest of mewling kittens.

Grace returned his look with one of bright, unblinking regard, making him imagine she could really see him instead of having the misty sight of the new-born. Her legs moved strongly under the shawl, while her long fingers opened and closed like minuscule starfish, then formed into tight fists resting against her fat cheek, rather thoughtfully as if she was wondering about this large creature with the foreign smell and loud voice who had suddenly appeared in her female-orientated world.

'She likes you.' Jennie smiled, seeing the two of them together, her daughter, and her lover. Then her mood changed, emotions on a seesaw, for she had awakened that morning to find her breasts engorged with milk.

Grace had suckled vigorously, instinctively knowing what to do, but Jennie kept bursting into tears. It was ridiculous for she had nothing to be sad about. Her baby was healthy and she adored her, she was comfortable and well cared-for, yet the tears flowed and flowed.

'You've got the baby-blues,' Mrs Entworth pronounced sagely. 'Third day. Milk coming in. All we mothers have suffered from it. Nothing to worry about, deary. You'll get over it.'

Jennie had listened but decided that the reason for her depression was Richard's neglect. Although her great news had been cabled to him as soon as possible, he had not caught the next train down. Instead he had sent an answering, congratulatory wire, and not appeared in person till a day later. By this time she had succeeded in working herself into a froth of anger and indignation. When he finally walked through the door she had forgotten this in her relief at seeing him, but now it flooded over her again. She had gone through the birth without him when he had promised her faithfully that he would be there.

Richard frowned, bewildered and alarmed because she was sobbing so noisily. He did not know what to do with the baby. Should he give her back or lay her in the crib by the bed? He did the latter, tucking her in and setting it rocking. His action seemed to irritate Jennie beyond reason. She sobbed more violently than ever.

'What's the matter?' Richard asked, out of his depth and considering shouting for Mrs Entworth who he could hear making a deliberate clatter below, thus proclaiming that she was *not* trying desperately to overhear what was happening upstairs.

'That's right! Push her away – like you've pushed me away!' Jennie shouted, face flushed, eyes blazing through the tears.

'What d'you mean? I've never done that.'

'Yes, you have! You didn't come right away, and you keep going to London. Left me when I needed you most – left me to have her by myself. It's not fair!'

Richard blew out his cheeks and ran an exasperated hand through his hair. 'Dammit, Jennie, she wasn't due for another two weeks! How was I to know she'd decide to come early? And you weren't on your own. There was Sister Lumsden and Mrs Entworth. Miss Reeves, too, I shouldn't wonder, all fussing around you.'

'Oh, yes, so that lets you off the hook, I suppose? It was hell! Pure hell! I've never had so much pain. I thought I was going to die.'

Richard sat on the edge of the bed and raised her from the pillow so that her head rested on his shoulder. 'Poor little darling – but you didn't die, and she's a fine baby. I'm sorry I didn't come before but I couldn't get away.'

'Why not? Too busy with that bloody Lady Eva,' Jennie snivelled, blowing her nose on the handkerchief he had produced from his breast pocket.

'I had some work to complete.' Richard avoided the straight answer, uncomfortable because she was right. He had been dining with Eva while Grace was being born.

'You'll stay now?' It was more of a command than a request.

'Of course. As long as you want.'

Rash, he told himself, rash to promise her this when Eva takes up so much of my time. But he felt tremendously responsible for Jennie and her baby, wanted to look after them, come what may. I'm a fool, he thought, cracked in the head. I owe her nothing. It's not my child. Eva. Jennie. Two such different women yet each of them crying out for attention in their individual ways, and in the midst of this he had work to do, important work at this turning point in his career. He was much sought after, busy as never before, and he owed it all to Eva. It was she who had brought him to public notice, she who had proved to be a helpmate, a companion, loving, giving, sharing.

Happy with his arms around her, Jennie was kissing his cheek, playing with his beard, curling up against him in that familiar manner which sent the hot blood of recollection coursing through his veins. An adorable minx, even more so now that she was a mother, commanding his respect by the confident way in which she managed her baby. A deeper quality had been added to her personality, a maturity which enhanced her already considerable attraction.

He nodded toward Grace who had yawned widely and gone to sleep. 'At least she doesn't look like Everett Braithwaite.'

'Or any of those bastards, thank God!' Jennie beamed at her daughter. 'She looks like herself, and she's mine. No one else's.'

Richard remained at the cottage for a week, by which time Jennie was on her feet and back to normal, slim-waisted again, ready to take up the threads of her life. This alarmed him. He had hoped that she would forget her ambitions and concentrate on raising Grace.

'You can stay here, you know. It will be a fine place for a child to grow up in,' he reminded her one afternoon when they sat by the backdoor in the sun, Grace asleep in her carriage not far away.

'Can't do that.' She shook her head determinedly. 'Not all the time, anyway.'

'What's on your mind?' He already knew her answer, but still hoped he was mistaken.

'I haven't given up. I'm still set on going on the stage.'

'How can you, with her to look after?' He nodded in the direction of the perambulator and its helpless occupant.

'You'll help me, won't you, Richard?' she wound her arms round his neck, fingers slipping into the open shirt collar, stroking his chest. 'You've always helped me. My only pal. You'll think of a way.'

Richard shook her off and stood up, planting his shoulders against the door-jamb, his face clouded. 'Your place is with the child. She needs you. My God, you're breast-feeding her. How can you even think of depriving the little mite?'

Jennie looked at him, a stubborn expression on her face. 'I'm not talking about now, not right away. Of course I'll go on feeding her, for a while at any rate, and I'll never, never abandon her. But don't you see, I've got to do this, for her as well as me? I'll take it out on her eventually if I'm frustrated. I must at least have a go. If I fail, well and good. I'll accept it and be a full-time mother, but at least I should have tried. And I want to make lots of money so that I can give her everything. No skimping and scraping and poverty for my Gracie.'

'There's no need for you to work. You can live here and I'll give you what you need.' Richard had thought himself up-to-date in his ideas but was now certain that Jennie should be with her baby, not striving to carve a career on the stage.

'I want to work.' Jennie flashed back at him. 'Can't you get that into your thick head? I should have thought you, of all people, would have understood. You need to paint and take photographs. How would you feel if this was taken away from you?'

'Rotten,' he conceded. 'But then, I'm hardly likely to become a mother. You have a responsibility toward Grace.'

'And I'm taking it seriously. No doubt about that. She's all the world to me.'

This was no overstatement. Once Grace had been laid in her arms any lingering feelings of resentment were wiped away. Charlotte could not associate this little miracle-being with the men who had raped her. Grace was nothing to do with them. It was almost as if she had been an immaculate conception. This feeling had lasted. Sometimes she thought that maybe she was burying her head in the sand, but had firmly resolved that her daughter should never find out what had happened. She would fabricate some wonderful fairy-story to explain who had fathered her, when she was old enough to ask questions, fight anyone, claws spread and to the point of murder if need be to protect her innocent child. This included Albert Baggot, should she even so much as set eyes on his treacherous face again.

She failed to make Richard see her point of view and they quarrelled heatedly. He left for London in a white-lipped fury, and Jennie watched him go with tears in her eyes but equal rage in her heart. Back to Eva! she thought savagely. Back to his other life. There you are, you see, she argued with herself. He's just like the rest of 'em. He can do what he likes but I, because I'm a woman, can't! Well, we'll see about that. If he won't help me, then I'll do it alone.

She had no plan, as yet, and occupied herself with Grace during the week. Sister Lumsden called in to weight the baby and check if there were any problems. She had to admit that Jennie was proving to be a devoted and caring mother; intelligent about it, too, when she had expected to have trouble in that direction. Mrs Entworth could do nothing but agree, charmed by the baby and quite taken with Jennie, and saying so frequently to Miss Ratley. On Saturday morning Jennie had a letter from Richard in which he said that he would not be down that weekend. It was a frosty note, very different from those loving, teasing, even provocative missives that she was accustomed to receiving. She bit back her disappointment. So he was going to be stubborn, was he? Hoping to bring her to her knees, begging him to come and promising to forego her ambitions. She was thankful that she was not in love with him, for this might have tempted her to weaken.

She thought about it till the afternoon, quite cast down, and then, sick of hanging about the cottage, took one of her new skirts from the wardrobe and put it on. Made of coffee-coloured silk, it was much more suitable for attending a garden-party than going for a walk through dusty lanes, but she did not care. Once attired, she perused herself critically in the mirror. The gown fitted her perfectly, the stays she wore beneath it pinching her waist to a twenty-inch span, her full breasts adding to the fashionable, ultra-feminine look. The skirt swept out into elegant swirls, the hem deeply bordered by two wide frills, edged with narrow tobacco-brown satin ribbon. She wore a Holland lace button-fronted blouse, convenient for satisfying the noisy demands of the ever-hungry Grace, held in by a sashed waistband, and a matching bolero-jacket with a shawl collar and huge, puffing sleeves ending at the elbow and trimmed with satin flounces. Its shortness drew artful emphasis to that tiny waist and swelling bosom.

Her hat was a frothy extravaganza, a round straw creation with a wide, turned-up brim, worn on the front of her hair which she had piled high and fixed with combs. She skewered the hat firmly in place with daggerlike, cut-steel pins so that it was straight as an arrow but tilted forward on her brow. On the right-hand side was a massive coffee bow, a curly ostrich plume, and a cluster of artificial silk roses in palest cream.

Jennie posed before the glass, stiffening her back, arching her ribs, staring at herself with haughty, half-closed lids. You'll do, girl, she told herself. You could go to the bloody Derby wearing this, and all those toffee-nosed duchesses would have to look to their laurels. The stays were stiff and uncomfortable, made of pink damask and whalebone, with long suspenders holding up a pair of bronze silk stockings. They made her legs seem longer, slimmer, more shapely and seductive. She wished Richard was there to take a peek as she raised her rustling skirt and petticoats to view them, and her stilt-heeled beige kid shoes. No matter. She would parade through the village and knock the locals for six!

She put Grace in her pram, wrapped her snugly and flung a showy swansdown coverlet over the top, folded back the leatherette hood and adjusted the round broderie anglaise canopy with its dark green lining to shield her from the sun. Then she wheeled her out, proud as a peacock. It was hot. Jennie knew she would soon be sweating inelegantly in that impossibly outrageous ensemble, but gripped the porcelain handle of the pram resolutely with her gloved hands and manoeuvred it through the gate, heading in the direction of Westhope's one and only street. At first the way was bumpy, an unmade road, but the pram took the ruts like a stately galleon, beautifully sprung, with two huge, slim, spoked wheels at the front overlapping the smaller ones at the rear.

Jennie could not help feeling joyous, proud of her perambulator, proud of her baby, proud of *herself*. Calamity had struck and she had survived it. Let Richard rant and rave to his heart's content, she would get her way eventually. She walked along, scheming and plotting, working out a seduction campaign to put into operation when next he came to see her, only dimly aware of the birds twittering in the hazel trees, and the roadside bank filled with tufts of golden-rod and nettle-leaved bell-flowers.

The silence seemed deeper than ever. Jennie had never become accustomed to the country quiet, finding it frightening, long ago deciding that rural life was not for her. She was glad when she came to the church and the street, where a group of children were playing hop-scotch outside the public house, reminding her of games in which she had taken part in grimy London alleys. An enormous ginger tom-cat was basking comfortably on the window-ledge of the post-office and general store, while a lean, sour-faced woman, standing in the doorway, eyed her with suspicion.

Stare till your eyes drop out, nosy old bitch, Jennie thought, smiling sweetly at her and nodding graciously as she sailed by. Bet you're a dried-up stick of a spinster that's never had a man, never known what it's like to feel him inside you, swollen and hard and needing, never felt a baby's mouth on your nipple, clenched tight, sucking you dry of milk. She was sure that she was vastly superior to everyone she passed, amused by their glances, guessing at the gossip which seethed and flowed.

As she became less absorbed with herself and more aware of her surroundings, she sensed an unusual ambience rippling the placid waters of bucolic life. It was faint, under the surface, but undeniable. The children expressed it, noisy at their play, tearful and sparkish, wound up by an indefinable something, as if anticipating Christmas or a birthday.

Jennie skirted the village green, then paused as her attention was captured by a poster nailed to one of the mighty chestnut trees in its centre. She left the road, wheeling the pram over the springy grass as the clock on the church tower struck four. She was to remember that moment ever after; the cloudless sky glimpsed between the branches; the children parting to let her through; the gaudily printed poster in the leaf dappled shade.

'Barnaby's Famous British and All World Funfair', she read. 'Here all this week'.

That explained the disquiet fermenting in Westhope. She looked up and across, saw a set of crudely constructed arrows pointing toward the fields beyond. 'Right then, Grace, off we go to the fair,' she said to the baby who, disturbed by the lack of motion, had awakened and begun to wail. As soon as the pram moved again she closed her eyes and went back to sleep.

After Jennie had gone a short distance, her ears caught distinct sounds, a fret and bustle reaching her – horses neighing, pipe-organs playing, the chug-chug of steam-driven traction engines powering roundabouts and electric lights. Her nostrils came alive, responding to an old familiar smell, that of soot and smoke and oil – machine smells, London smells. It was good. People could keep their mawkish notions about the glories of the countryside. She was a townie, and always would be.

Her pace quickened and, through the trees, she glimpsed a helter-skelter tower, flags streaming from the top. Now she could see glittering brass and coloured lights, the prancing painted horses of carousels, the swing-boats, the flimsy chairs spinning outwards on the end of chains as a roundabout rotated. Noise dinned in her ears; blaring music; riders shrieking; the owners of shooting-ranges offering fabulous prizes from amongst the tawdry items on display; prize-fighters flexing their muscles on the stage in front of a marquee, along with a line of half a dozen flashily dressed girls kicking up their legs to the music of popular songs in order to lure punters in to watch the boxing.

Enraptured, Jennie wandered down the avenues between the side-shows, pausing to try her luck at darts, winning a particularly hideous china vase which she popped into the pram by Grace's feet before joining a queue for toffee-apples, made hungry by the variegated and delicious smells drifting from vans and stalls – fish and chips, candy, ginger-bread. Heads turned to look at this elegant young lady with her expensive clothes and even more costly baby-carriage who now peeled off her gloves and bit into the toffee-apple with gusto, but there were so many other entertainments on offer that they quickly lost interest.

Grace slept through the noise, not one whit disturbed, and Jennie was lost in delight, drinking in the crowds, the confusion, realising how much she had missed it. It was like coming home. She had money in her purse and would have liked to have mounted a gilded, gorgeously painted galloper, with flaring nostrils and tumbling carved mane, but did not like to leave Grace unattended. This would be her life from now on, she reflected, never able to go out or do anything without first finding someone to watch over the baby. At that moment being a mother did not seem to be much fun.

A peep under the canopy at the adorable sleeping face half-hidden by the too-large woollen bonnet restored her faith. It didn't really matter. All too soon Grace would no longer be a baby. Jennie's time would come, and she fell to planning once more. What she had to do was find a job, take a room somewhere in London and employ a nursemaid. Then she would have singing lessons, and go for auditions.

Lost in thought, she did not realise that she had strayed to the edge of the fair-ground, close to where the wagons were clustered. She stopped, a tent coming into focus, hardly able to believe the placard propped up outside. Just for an instant she was back in the house in Old Compton Street, avoiding Albert, entering a room, seeing a poster.

'Madame Zena, the World Renowned Fortune-teller. Patronised by the Crowned Heads of Europe'.

She was not the only one there. A couple of women were nervously waiting their turn to go in. With a sense of the inevitable Jennie waited, too. The tent flap opened and two young girls came out, giggling, half scared, half excited.

'Did you 'ear 'er tell me that I was goin' to meet a tall, dark man, and I 'ad to beware of 'im?' said one, beaming and apple-cheeked.

'I did, our Joyce, and she told me I was goin' to marry a farmer and 'ave six little 'uns.' Her friend was a slight, fair-haired thing, with a demure manner but roving eyes. 'Don't know if I wants that. Your one sounds much more of a masher.'

They departed for the fair, arms round each other's waists, whispering and giggling, two rustic temptresses about to cause mayhem among the dull-witted local lads. Jennie waited patiently, deep in dreams. Grace stirred, and she jiggled the pram. The other women took their turns in the tent. Finally, the last of them left and Zena came out. Their eyes met and it was as if no time had passed since they had sat together, drinking tea and eating toasted muffins.

'There you are,' Zena said.

'Yes, I've come.'

'I knew you would.'

The gypsy fastened the tent securely and took Jennie to her wagon. It was a large one, with high wheels, straight sides and skylights in a raised central area of the flat roof. It was six foot wide and fourteen foot in length, made by the finest manufacturer of showmans' vehicles, a Reading Wagon. The size, carved panels on the exterior, cupboards built underneath, windows at the back and sides, a central door with detachable steps, all symbolised Zena's wealth and status.

'Leave the pram there. It'll be quite safe, and bring the *chavi* in,' Zena said, leading the way. 'A girl, isn't it?'

'Yes, and her name is Grace.' Jennie picked her up and carried her into the wagon.

'I thought as much.' Zena bade her sit down on one of the locker-seats and turned to take up the kettle from its place on the Colcester stove, which had a small side oven and a trivet.

There was a curved mantelpiece above it with three brass rails to stop ornaments falling off when travelling. Set uncoiled his black body from the rag hearthrug and started to wind himself round Zena's skirts, purring loudly, ignoring Jennie's advances, huffy because she had a baby in her arms.

The wagon was stuffy, and Zena left the top half of its stable-door open for ventilation. After she had made tea in a stout brown china pot and served it in pretty gilt-edged cups, she took Grace from Jennie and looked seriously into her little face, then examined the minute, wrinkled palms for some time without speaking. Set did not approve, but she soon put him in his place.

Jennie was amazed at the neatness of Zena's home. The walls were panelled in mahogany, the ceiling painted with cabbage roses, the mirrors had bevelled edges and were etched with flowers, the shining brass oil lamps each side of the fireplace had translucent pink shades, the many vases and knick-knacks were of finest cut glass or porcelain. There were padded seats on either side which, when the lids were lifted, provided storage space, a square cupboard, a corner shelf and a chest of drawers. Both the cupboards had two compartments, with glass doors above and wooden ones below.

At the rear was the bed-place, which consisted of two berths, one above the other. There was a turned spindle-rail in front of the top one, and elaborately scrolled posts standing out from the side of the wagon and stretching from floor to ceiling. Flower-printed cretonne curtains were tied to them, convenient for drawing at night. The doors of the bottom berth were panelled and made to slide back when it was in use.

'You can stay here, with me,' Zena vouchsafed at last, still holding the sleeping infant.

'Will there be room?'

'You can have my bed. In warm weather such as this, I prefer to sleep under the *vardo*.'

'The what?'

'*Vardo*. "Wagon" in Rom.'

So it is settled, Jennie thought. Someone up there is watching over me. Zena did not ask questions but Jennie wanted to talk, recounting everything that had happened to her since they last met. Grace woke in the midst of this narrative and Jennie continued with the baby glued to her breast, Zena's all-seeing, all-knowing black eyes resting compassionately on them.

Jennie found it easy to tell Zena about it, feeling that the gypsy already knew. She was unaware of the passing of time, Grace still at her breast, dozing, sucking, while she bared her soul to the gypsy.

'Was it you who stopped me drowning myself?' she asked at one point.

'I've thought of you often, prayed for you, so it probably was,' Zena replied, rising to touch a spill to the lamps. A rosy glow penetrated the dusk. 'But I can't prevent what fate has in store for you, child. I can only advise, which I did in Soho, but you, wilful one, had to take this stony path for your own good. It was a hard lesson but you've learned much.'

'And Richard?' Jennie knew that she must leave him. There were regrets, but there was no turning back.

'He, too, is a necessary cog in the wheel. He's important in all this. I know it, but can't yet tell you why or how. The only thing I can say with any certainty is that the time has come to make a break from him.'

'So he's not the one for me?'

'No.'

They began to discuss practical matters. Zena said that this was the fair's last night in Westhope. 'They'll be pulling down after we close at midnight, and then we're moving on to set up again in Margate. This will take all of Sunday to do, and we'll open Monday afternoon.'

'Can I come with you?'

'You must.'

Mrs Entworth did not come in on Sundays, so Jennie decided to go back to Laurel Cottage without delay and pack. Zena promised to send a cart to collect her and her goods. Jennie covered the distance from the wagon pitch to the cottage in record time. She did not encounter a single soul on the way down the twilit lane. She let herself in, wheeling the pram into the living room and leaving Grace in it while she skimmed up the stairs. She pulled out a trunk and packed everything she possessed within it. Hardship had made her greedy, and she left nothing behind. Even if she did not need a particular object, then it could be sold and turned into money. When Zena's envoy arrived, a swarthy lad with black ringlets and gypsy wolf eyes, he humped down the trunk and lifted it on to the tailboard of the cart. The crib followed, and then the pram, while Jennie climbed up on the driver's seat, with Grace in her arms.

Bats were circling in the evening air, and she took a last look at the cottage as the boy cracked his whip, and the piebald horse between the shafts began to plod off up the lane. Laurel Cottage – where Richard had initiated her into the mysteries of sex, and where Grace had first seen the light of day. So many memories crowding in, but Jennie put them from her, hugging her baby and fixing her eyes on the darkening road that led to the fair – and her future.

Chapter 12

Frederick was worried about Eva. It was rather more than an older man's resentment of a younger rival. He thought too much of her to put his own feelings first and, for years, had stood back, trying to settle for his role as trusted friend. It had grown easier with the passage of time. He had been able to convince himself that she would never fall in love, and certainly never marry. Since Richard hove on the scene, however, he had witnessed a startling change in her.

It was as if she had shed a decade, acquiring a bloom that had transformed her from a plain woman to one who radiated sparkle and warmth so that one forget her physical shortcomings. She had always had a good figure, bearing and dress-sense, and lately she was using these assets to full advantage, adopting the new, less starchy modes. Till recently she had ordered her clothes from Madame Paquin who had opened a branch in London. Her creations were renowned for their elegance, but a whisper had begun to circulate among those in the know. A star was rising in Paris, so new, so innovative that it was predicted he would soon flash, meteor-like, over the world of *haute couture*. His name was Paul Poiret. His designs were revolutionary, and Eva was one of the first women to order gowns from him, after having seen photographs of them in a French magazine.

Frederick chanced to be at Albion House when they arrived, carefully packaged and shipped by ferry. Eva could not wait to rip off the paper and get at the contents: a dress-box with impressive writing on the cardboard lid, announcing that this was from the House of Poiret, Paris, France, a layer of crisp white tissue paper – then the clothes.

'Oh, Freddy, aren't they unusual!' Eva lifted out her treasures. He saw vivid colours, intricate beadwork and, horror of horrors, a trouser suit in turquoise and cyclamen with black fur trimming. 'This is the look for the emancipated woman! Poiret has dared to free us from stays. The waist is in its natural place, not squeezed into ridiculous shapes. I love them! I'll set fire to my corsets, and wear nothing but these.'

She may not have carried this out to the letter, but it was true to say that her afternoon and evening gowns were now simple yet exotic, with an arty influence. The shades were brilliant – cerise, flame, emerald, royal blue and violet – while her morning costumes consisted of simple skirts in plain, strong colours, and multi-hued Eastern inspired tops. She reserved the scandalous trousers for wearing around the house. Not even she was bold enough to appear in public in them yet.

Frederick agreed that her outfits were striking and not lacking in femininity, but inwardly sighed for the old Eva in her pastels or black velvets, accompanied by the soft frou-frou of frilled petticoats when she walked. He concluded, quite rightly, that this sudden upsurge of interest in fashion was directly connected with her desire to impress Richard.

It cut deeper than that, for every time Eva looked at his handsome, bearded face, and gazed into those deep blue eyes, she was desperately conscious that he was many years her junior. For the first time ever she envied young women, searched her cheeks anxiously for lines, stretched her neck to examine it for tell-tale wrinkles. She began to eat less to preserve her neat waistline. She wanted to be eighteen again, wary of every woman who swam into his ken. Just as well, perhaps, that Charlotte was getting married and the predatory Bernice out of the way. There was Alice, of course, but she was of the wrong class. How horrible to think like this! Eva hated herself, beset by ignoble emotions.

Richard seemed unaware of the disparity in their age. They were ideally suited, shared the same tastes and interests, were of a similar background. Not only this, both of them wanted to do something about injustice. They would talk for hours about politics, the legal system, the class system, and votes for women. But they did not spend all their time in such serious pursuits. Richard took her to concerts, plays and the opera, though insisting that they bought cheap tickets, sitting up in the 'gods' with the true enthusiasts and, afterwards, visiting street-stalls which stayed open throughout the night, drinking mugs of tea the colour of beef soup, eating sausage sandwiches and chatting with the down-and-outs, inevitably paying for hot drinks and meals for them, too.

Dudley Armstrong's clinic was proving a boon for the people of his district, open for two hours in the morning and evening. Beth worked there when she could, and Dudley employed another forward-thinking doctor as his assistant. So far, they had dealt merely with accidents, illnesses, children's ailments and the care of expectant mothers, whom they also delivered of their infants. At first, the old and tried midwives were indignant about this, considering that the doctors were poaching on their preserves, but when they saw that their many years of experience were taken into consideration, the doctors willing to listen, they gave their whole-hearted support.

Beth, on her part, held classes for mothers where they could learn about child-care, nutrition and cleanliness. Her job was a taxing one, for so many of the women who came to see her had little money to buy anything but the basics, some of them not even that. But she tried hard, devoted to her poor, often providing the wherewithal from her own slender housekeeping purse. And she started to teach them about birth control, astonished to discover that, incredible though this seemed, some were so ignorant and simple-minded that they were not even sure what caused them to become pregnant.

As she remarked indignantly to Steven, 'Good Lord, we send missionaries out to educate the Hottentots when we should be concentrating on those at home! Why waste time converting savages who probably know far more than us anyway, about life, about sex, about religion?'

Dudley offered a free service, and Eva kept the clinic going financially, keener than ever. Richard was her mentor and guide, opening her eyes to many things she had missed before, and taking her to places she would not have dared visit alone. They became very friendly with Beth and Dudley, often spending evenings at their house, where again much stimulating discussion took place. Other people began to ask them out to dinner as a couple. They were now Richard and Eva – inseparable companions. It was a warm, wonderful feeling.

She tried to ignore the occasional critical glance she met, and forget the vicious gossip that was bound to circulate among those who did not like her much, but was devastated when she overheard a conversation in the ladies room of a restaurant one night. She was in a toilet cubicle, her hand on the door handle, about to leave, when she recognised the voices of two women who had often come to parties at Albion House.

'My dear,' drawled one, 'did you see that chap Eva Pendral's got in tow?'

'Yes I did, and isn't he good-looking? Can't be more than twenty-six or seven, while she must be close on forty,' added her companion waspishly.

'Talk about cradle-snatching! Of course, it's obvious that he's after her money. Must be, or he'd choose someone younger and prettier.'

'And what on earth is Eva wearing? So gaudy and unsuitable. Talk about mutton dressed up as lamb.'

'All I can say, my dear, is that she'd better make the most of it.'

'Can't possibly last, can it? A boy like that – '

Those cruel, careless words cut Eva to the quick. There was a hollow feeling in the pit of her stomach, and she could feel herself blushing hotly. She panicked at the thought that Richard might hear something similar from his male acquaintances. Were they looking at her askance? Was it the talk of Whites? Perhaps he agreed with them. Perhaps it was a fact. *There's no fool like an old fool.* That realistic, cynical, unkind adage repeated itself in her brain. And close on its heels came another: *Love is blind.*

Love? Suddenly the bald truth could no longer be denied. She *was* madly in love with him. So much in love that nothing else was of any significance, neither the bank or Charlotte. As for her work, she was no longer selflessly interested, using it to justify seeing him so regularly. If he suddenly asked her to run away with him to some tropical island, then she would go without a second thought, abandoning everything.

Eva crept from the cubicle when the ladies had departed with a swish of silken skirts, leaving a strong smell of perfume behind them. She went to the mirror above the wash-basin, staring at herself, searching for an answer in her eyes, seeing only an aging woman clad in a gown that was too youthful. She burned with shame. Felt ridiculous. Wanted to weep with humiliation. For a moment, she contemplated finding a back way out and leaving Richard waiting for her at their table. She would do it. Write him a letter. Finish the affair before it had even started. For it hadn't started, and this had made her all the more unsure of herself.

He had kissed her, but only a brotherly kiss. He had placed his arm about her, but only to support or guide her. He had taken her hand and tucked it into the crook of his elbow, but only when they were walking. Sometimes he had smiled and touched her hair and she had longed to fling her arms around him, but feared that if she did it might drive him away. Instead she had closed her eyes, aware of that light touch causing havoc throughout her whole body, remembering it when he had gone, not so much with her mind but with her skin, her hair, her trembling, desirous senses.

The memory of those moments was so sweet and hurtful that she gripped the edge of the wash-basin fiercely, seeking physical pain to deaden the anguish inside her. It made no difference, clench her hands till the knuckles gleamed though she might. I can't do without him, she thought, despairing. He's like a potent drug. What would my days be – my nights – if he wasn't with me. Nights? She almost smiled. What did she know of nights, of darkness and passion? Precious little. It would be more correct to say 'of evenings', spent with Richard. Evenings when she had tried to still the throbbing need inside her, a struggle when every turn of his head, each gesture of his strong hands, each cadence of his voice made her want to scream: Take me! I'm yours! I don't care if you can't love me, it doesn't matter just as long as you sleep with me.

She pressed her hands over her eyes, head bent, fighting for control, heard a quiet voice behind her ask, 'Are you unwell, Madam? Is there anything I can get you?'

Eva started, spun round, saw the attendant in her dark blue dress and crisp white apron looking at her curiously. She had forgotten the woman who usually sat in her own small cubby-hole, ready to supply handkerchiefs, towels, smelling-salts, face-powder, sanitary napkins, employed to see that those wealthy, exquisitely gowned ladies who entered her domain wanted for nothing.

'I have a headache.' This was better. Now she had to put on a brave face. What was it the clown sang in Mascagni's opera *I Pagliacci* that she'd seen at Covent Garden not long ago? 'On with the motley, the paint and the powder', the message being that the show has to go on even though one's heart is breaking.

'I'm sorry to hear that, Madam. Shall I fetch you a pill? I've some in my cupboard.'

The woman was thin, whey-faced, thirtyish – polite but not obsequious. She had had much experience with her clients, listening patiently while they complained of their wrongs – a humble toilet attendant who, at times, became their confidant. They forgot themselves under duress, almost forgot her, pouring out their troubles – the unfaithful husbands, mean husbands, tyrannical husbands, ungrateful children, the secret lovers who consoled their loneliness, took what they could get out of them and, finally, proved as cruel as the men whom their families had ordered them marry.

She was so lowly that they involved her without hesitation. They might have been confiding in their dogs. But the tips they pushed into her hand when, confessions over, she sent them back to the fray freshly powdered and groomed, made it well worth her while to act out the role of priest.

They were indulged, pampered bitches who didn't know they were born but she bore them no grudge. Sorry for them, in a way. For all their lovely clothes and extravagant life-style, many of them seemed eaten up with jealousies and unhappiness. She might have little, a spinster with no one but an elderly arthritic mother waiting at home for her, but accepted her lot, thriving on small pleasures, glad to be in work, able to keep her end up in a harsh world.

Eva gave her a tearful smile. 'I have some tablets in my bag. I suffer from migraine, you see. A glass of water would be nice, to wash them down.'

Calmer now, her brain started to function rationally. Let them talk till they were blue in the face. They were envious of her. She was used to envy, had endured it all her life. Why should she deny herself the pleasure of Richard's company because of a chance remark made by a couple of acid-tongued vixens? And it *was* pleasant to be with him, no matter the torture she suffered.

Taking her courage firmly in both hands, she returned to the restaurant. The smile on Richard's face as he stood up to greet her made her thankful that she had not yielded to the cowardly impulse to turn tail and run. From the corner of her eye she could see the women who had been discussing her in the rest-room. She gave them a haughty, fleeting glance before settling down in a chair beside him.

'You were a long time,' he commented, ordering coffee and brandy from the waiter who appeared with the alacrity of a jack-in-the-box.

'I started talking to the attendant.'

'Not another of your lame-ducks?' His eyes were amused and tender.

She was glad when the coffee arrived, and hurried over drinking it, wanting to leave this place as soon as she could. Her mind darted ahead to the moment when she would be seated in his car while they decided where to go next. Would it be Albion House or his studio? Wherever they ended up, she had decided that she must talk to him. It was no use letting the matter drift. She had to know, one way or another, if he was serious about her.

Nervousness cramped her gut, and she longed to put off the fatal moment of truth. Supposing he laughed at her, told her not to be foolish, said that she was nothing more than a friend? Victor Dalbiac's face floated on her inner vision. She distinctly recalled every word he had uttered when he was tired of her.

'I don't want to hurt you. I'm very fond of you. You're the finest person I've ever met. I want to remain your friend.'

Is this what Richard would say, falling back on those lame, feeble excuses used by men time out of mind? She sincerely hoped not, wanting to retain a measure of respect for him.

Richard guessed there was something wrong. Eva was quiet and subdued, but he waited for her opening gambit, driving without speaking till they reached Albion House. Then she asked him to come in, so he turned off the engine and went round to open the passenger door for her.

She preceded him up the steps and a footman let them in. The house was silent, servants nowhere in evidence, apart from the one man on duty, and Eva dismissed him before entering the library. As Richard followed he admired the purple, subtly draped velvet cloak she wore, its stand-up collar framing her head. She moved with stately grace, always cool and collected in appearance, a fine person in every respect, devoid of the selfish motive of 'What's in it for me?' which guided the actions of most people. Honest, kind and in no way devious. He could not help contrasting her with Jennie.

His jaw set and his eyes narrowed as he thought about that little wretch, while he took the chair Eva indicated and nodded when she asked him if he would like a whisky and soda. Jennie had gone, vanished into the blue without a word of explanation.

'She's not here, sir.' Mrs Entworth had met him at the cottage door, bristling with importance at being the harbinger of such tidings.

'Not here? Has she gone for a walk?' Richard had thumped his weekend bag down on the tiles, tired from the long drive, cross with himself for being unable to stay away.

'She's scarpered.' With a satisfied, I-told-you-so, expression on her face, Mrs Entworth had folded her arms across the floral cotton pinafore that shielded her scrawny chest. 'Weren't here when I came in on Monday morning. Clothes gone, baby gone, everything gone.'

'Have you asked Miss Reeves?' A feeling of sadness had possessed him, disappointment, too. He had wanted to patch up their quarrel, bringing conciliatory gifts, a sable stole from Harrods' fur department, and a lace christening gown for Grace.

Mrs Entworth had nodded vigorously. 'Yes, sir, and she don't know nothing.'

Richard had slept badly that night, waking frequently, tormenting visions arising – Jennie abandoning the baby somewhere (she wouldn't do that, surely?), Jennie selling herself to a man with money (she might do that, particularly if he told her he was associated with the theatre). He was in turn furious and miserable, missing her, missing little Grace, but mostly frantic with worry. She was so impulsive a creature, wild as a bird, a gullible child and susceptible to flattery. She needed someone to look after her. He had imagined it would be himself. Apparently, she had had other ideas, and it was like a kick in the teeth.

Next day he had made enquiries in the village, and Miss Ratley recounted, with spiteful relish, how she had seen her walking toward the fair-ground last Saturday afternoon. He had gone there, but found nothing but trampled grass and some children picking about in the litter. The field had rung with a curious kind of emptiness. Richard had returned to London.

'You're very quiet tonight,' Eva said, drawing his thoughts back to the library.

'Sorry. Things on my mind.' He gave her a boyish grin, glad that he had never yielded to the temptation to tell her about Jennie.

'So have I.'

He wondered why she was avoiding his eyes, felt a prickle of unease. Had she discovered that he'd been keeping a girl down at his seaside cottage? It would be ironic if this had come out at a moment when it was no longer true. Sod's law, in fact. He had not consciously kept it from her, but there had never been the right opportunity. Too late he realised that he shouldn't have had any truck with Jennie, and certainly not taken her to bed. She was trouble with a capital T.

Eva's hands were wet with nerves, and she kept swallowing to try and shift that disagreeable lump in her throat. It was horribly embarrassing. She would never be able to say: I love you. Do you love me? She felt she would rather die than say it, but was between the devil and the deep, almost certain to die if she didn't, not physically, maybe, but mentally. She had to speak or let their friendship corrode into distrust and non-communication.

He was on his feet, striding across to her, pausing with his hand resting gently on her arm. 'What's the matter, Eva?'

She took a deep breath and the words came out in a rush. 'It's us – me – I don't know. Well, yes, I do. Lord, but this is awkward! The thing is – I think I'm growing too fond of you.'

In his relief because she had not accused him of consorting with a fifteen-year-old, he did not immediately take in the full import of this extraordinary statement. It dawned on him but slowly that Eva was making a declaration of love. His first reaction was pity. He could only hazard a guess as to how much this had cost her. A proud woman giving away the secrets of her soul, surrendering her future into his hands. He had the power utterly to destroy her or make her supremely happy.

For a second it occurred to him that she might be teasing him, but Eva was not the type to tease. He almost wished that she was, seeing her standing there stiffly, looking up at him with the eyes of a stricken doe. She was absolutely sincere, and he would always be able to trust her. After what he took to be Jennie's betrayal, the love that she offered was balm to his damaged ego.

Her stillness moved him, and he let his hand slide to her waist, saying with absolute sincerity, 'I love you dearly, Eva, but I'm not worthy of you.'

He was thinking of Jennie and of the many women before her, actresses, models, whores sometimes, back and back to the first instance, when he had been seduced by a chambermaid at fourteen years old. His appetites were normal. He wasn't a monster of depravity and lust, but he liked women, their soft skin, soft hair, their exciting smell, their fascinating minds. He was sure that he'd never understand them if he lived to be a hundred, but was perfectly willing to go on trying.

Her senses, delicate antennae picking up on every tiny nuance, flinched at his words. Here was her answer, but could she accept it? Would affection be enough? She tried to tell herself that she could hardly expect a grand passion at her age. Filled with anxiety, she attempted a smile though her face felt as if it was made of plaster of Paris, likely to crack across.

'Unworthy? Not true, Richard. I'm no saint myself.'

'Maybe not, but you've lived a better life than I.' He shook his head, lowering his eyes. She wanted to read them, to find out why he was shutting himself away in some private, guilty hell.

I shouldn't have started this conversation, she thought. I should have left things as they were. Now I've made him uncomfortable, and this wasn't my intention.

'Women are different,' she began, assuming he was worrying about affairs he might have had.

'Some of them. You, for one,' he muttered.

He thrust his hands in his pockets and wandered to the windows, staring out unseeingly on the dark street. Eva went over to him, put a hand through his arm and stood close to him. She wanted him to know that she understood if he had had women in the past, and that she was terribly ashamed of having confessed her feelings for him.

'I'm sorry,' she whispered, and could have wept for humiliation. 'Let's forget what I said, and be friends as before.'

He turned swiftly and his arms came about her. 'Don't be sorry, Eva. You've paid me a wonderful compliment, dearest woman.'

He pulled her close to him, feeling the strength of her body, its fierce response, even though she was limp in his arms, as if drugged with love, her mouth uplifted, begging for his kiss. She made a small sound deep in her throat as his lips met hers, and desire leapt in him. Her need was exciting, her submissiveness, her untried innocence. He thrust his fingers in her hair, deftly taking out the pins so that it slithered across her shoulders. Her eyes were half-closed, her head lolling back against his arm, pride, honour, self-respect swallowed up in the overpowering urge to give herself without reservation.

It would have been so easy to lay her down on the carpet and make love to her, but Richard held back. He respected her too much to treat her shabbily. She was a great lady, and it was true that he loved her deeply, but he knew himself well enough to recognise that he wasn't 'in love' with her. He smiled cynically into the shadows, Eva clinging to him, her head against his chest, her fingers playing with the crisp curls at the nape of his neck. Love? What did it mean? That poor, overused word that was bandied about so freely. Was it anything more than animal passion in a more acceptable guise?

He had seen others suffering, but never experienced the state which was like an illness, a dreadful, weakening hunger for the object of one's obsession. Many women had been his, but he had always stood a little apart. Jennie had delighted and wounded him, but he did not feel that his life was over because she had run away. He was not turning England upside down in order to find her. He doubted that he would ever permit himself to become fate's plaything in such an undignified way. Eva offered him love, herself and everything she owned. He would never again have such an opportunity. They could make a satisfactory life together, full of warmth and laughter and service, but marriage was a monumental step and, knowing her as he did, he doubted that she would settle for anything less.

Eva released herself, smiling like a young girl, hands at her head. 'My hair!' she said in a shaky voice. 'It's all come tumbling down. What will you think of me?'

'You look wonderful.' He was leaning against the window, smiling at her, fingers combing through his beard, amazed at the change in her, alarmed and fearful, knowing that it was his doing.

She stopped fiddling with her hair, nervous again, unsure what her next move should be. She wanted, needed, longed to be back in his arms, but said, 'It's all right, you know. Don't feel you're in any way committed just because you kissed me.'

'My dear girl, don't keep putting yourself down. I kissed you because I wanted to.' He reached out for her, and crushed her against his chest. 'And I'm about to kiss you again.'

He did, and Eva could feel herself ripening under those warm, experienced lips, gaining confidence, remembering, ah, so much –

the lessons she had learned with Victor, though somewhat rusty perhaps, returning with a vengeance. Not too bold, she warned herself. He mustn't think I make a habit of this. He didn't, though surprised to feel her lips opening voluptuously beneath his. A sensual woman under that businesslike exterior, and the situation was getting out of hand. He wanted her, roused despite his caution, aware that she was more than willing to surrender.

He took his mouth from hers. 'Eva, not yet. There's no need. I don't expect – can't expect – you wouldn't be happy about it when you woke up tomorrow.'

'I don't care, Richard.' Her voice was defiant, but his withdrawal hurt. She felt it like a slap in the face. He was rejecting her.

'But I do. You aren't a tart and I won't treat you like one. We must think about this, plan what we're going to do. I can't bear that you should be the victim of malicious gossip.' He softened the blow by running his hands over her thin back under the silk gown, relishing the feel of the spine, the shoulders.

All the time he was wondering, unsure, yet why shouldn't he commit himself? He was free and unattached. This woman loved him, and he did not want to lose her. Most men of his class were brought up with no expectation of a romantic marriage, willing to fall in with their parents' plans for suitable, sensible alliances with money and position as the prime objective. The fact that he felt such strong affection for Eva and that she obviously adored him would be an added bonus.

Jennie? He would forget her, was doing so rapidly, relieved at having got off so lightly in what could have been a tricky situation. His work? No worries on that score. Eva would help him. Her hazel eyes were wide with apprehension as she stared at him, her fate in the balance. Richard gave a mental shrug, and took the bull by the horns.

'Eva, would you consider becoming my wife?' he said, mock-formal but serious.

A little gasp escaped her lips. Colour warmed her ivory complexion, and she swayed on her feet. 'Do you mean it?'

'Yes. What d'you want me to do? Go down on bended knee? I will if you like,' he joked, a warm glow spreading through his system at having made another human being so happy. 'Well, you haven't given me an answer. D'you want time to think about it?'

Eva drew herself up, the velvet cloak draped around her like a royal robe, gazing at him with worship in her eyes. 'No, Richard, I don't need time. I'll marry you, if you're sure that's what you want, and I swear to do my best to make a success of it.'

Once on the road, there was no stopping her. She hurled herself into his arms, all loving, all giving, doubts forgotten, letting him know how much she wanted him. The darkness surrounded them, and he was caught up in her passion, but held off long enough to say,

'Not here, Eva. The servants – '

'Are all asleep,' she panted, trembling with eagerness.

'You can't be sure of that. I'll bet there's at least one creeping about, listening. They like to know what's going on, and are bound to have heard us come in.' He disengaged himself from her arms. 'Let's go to the studio. I'll bring you back before the milkman starts his rounds at dawn.'

She saw the sense in this, though dimly, impatient with anything that came between the uniting of her flesh with his. She wanted it over, done with, decided. Afterwards, she could not recall the car ride through the deserted streets, or their arrival at Holland Park. He opened the door of his rooms and lifted her inside, his lips feverish on hers, her hunger infectious.

She nestled against him as he kicked the door shut. Never anything like this before; not Victor – he had been a middle-aged roué when he plundered her childish body. Now she could know the joy of young skin under her hands, skin soft as velvet, muscles smooth and firm, silky beard brushing her face, sweet mouth taking her to the heights. She forgot the empty years of denial when she had scorned women who had lovers, was aware of nothing save this joining with another being. She had ignited his fire and now it scalded, burned and overwhelmed her.

So this is love, she thought, smiling into the darkness above his bed when he slept at last, exhausted by her demands, remembering that she had been smiling throughout, coming to herself in fits and starts, to find that wide smile pasted on her face. Other things, too – he had tried to stop once, saying, 'There may be a child.'

'I hope so,' she had purred, grinding her hips against him.

A child! It could happen. She was the right side of forty; rather old for the safe delivery of a firstborn but not beyond the realms of possibility. My own child to inherit the bank! How that would rile Phelan Charteris!

Richard was asleep but she lay there wide-awake, savouring her triumph. Thirty-eight, and she had brought ecstasy to this man in his twenties, her body a rich, sensual feast on which he could gorge to his heart's content. Those women in the restaurant ... how much she wished they could have seen her, naked, wanton, entwined with him, rousing him, playing with him, taking her pleasure from him.

She did not want to miss a moment of the nocturnal hours. He was sunk in slumber, but she kept touching him, feeling him, fondling him. Sleeping, waking, it was all the same – the comfort of his presence at her side. He's mine, all mine, this creature of flesh, blood and bone lit by an immortal soul. Mine to keep, hold, adore.

Charlotte took a hired carriage to the villa. It was deserted, sunk in afternoon somnolence. She told the driver to wait and ran up the steps, across the vestibule and up the stairs. Wrapped in ice, she woke Tilly and told her to pack.

The maid stared at her, bemused with sleep. 'But, Miss – ' she mumbled, knuckling her eyes.

'Don't argue. Just do as I say, and be quiet. I want to be gone from here without anyone knowing.'

The expression on Charlotte's ashen face was alarming and Tilly got to work. Obeying terse orders, she flung most of the contents of the wardrobe into a trunk, placed hats in hat-boxes and stripped the tallboy bare. While she put necessities in their hand-luggage, Charlotte locked and labelled the trunk. This could be sent on later.

'Your wedding-gown, Miss?' Tilly cast a woebegone glance at the beautiful dress hanging forlornly on the armoire door, a dress which she had been so much looking forward to helping her mistress don on the morrow.

'Leave it!'

'Miss, you can't. It cost a fortune.'

'I said, leave it. I never want to see it again.'

When the room was emptied of her personal effects, Charlotte gave a final glance round and then stalked out, Tilly following, carrying the bags. She had been permitted to fetch her own things and put on her hat, doing so swiftly and silently, no longer tempted to question. She already guessed the answer, if not the mode of its happening.

The driver of the fiacre was slumped in his seat, hat tipped over his eyes in the shade of a cedar tree, reins trailing while the horse, head down, cropped flowers from the border. He sat up lazily as Charlotte climbed in, then ambled round to help Tilly with the luggage. He addressed Charlotte.

'Signorina?'

'10 Via Tornabuoni,' she replied briskly.

Tilly sat beside her, robbed of speech, totally thrown by this turn of events. Charlotte opened her parasol and sat there like a graven image, face and eyes blank. There was something frightening about her. Tilly turned over in her mind all the things she might have done had her mistress been less adamant. Called Mrs Houston, perhaps? They should have left a note for the companion, at the very least. The poor thing was bound to be in a terrible state when she woke up and found that one of her charges had gone. And what about Miss Gwen? She would be so disappointed not to wear her bridesmaid dress. But it was Charlotte that concerned her most of all. She looked awful, like the victim of a shattering disaster. Tilly knew in her bones that Phelan was the cause. In the midst of her distress there lay a tiny kernel of satisfaction. She had been proved right, after all. Men were scum! She wanted to express sympathy and support, but Charlotte was unapproachable, repulsing the smallest attempt, determined to lick her wounds in private.

The fiacre dawdled down the hill, there was never any sense of urgency at that time of day, and into the sleepy town where hot sunlight sliced through indigo shadows and nothing stirred. A ghost town, and Charlotte shuddered. The heat, the garish colours, the sunshine – the place she had loved so much was now hateful to her. Corruption lay beneath that serene surface. It seemed to have lodged under her fingernails, clinging to her hair, her skin, the sweet, cloying, sickly stench of putrefaction.

The carriage drew up outside the offices of Cook & Son. Charlotte read the name of the English tour operator with an almost sobbing sense of relief. England. Respectability. Sanity. She paid the driver, refusing to return his flirtatious Italian smile, and turned her back on him, entering the office. To date, Phelan had always organised any travelling that had to be undertaken. Now she must do it herself. She had plenty of money, thanks to Eva, but needed advice on the quickest way to get home.

An Englishman rose from his desk to help her. Very correct in his dark suit, with sleekly brushed hair and a full moustache. The young lady and her companion wanted to get to London? The best route was by train to Turin, there to link up with the Rome Express. He would arrange tickets for them from Turin to Arezzo, just outside the capital. From there they would be given a *de luxe* sleeping compartment on a train leaving for Paris. She was not to worry; he would see to everything, smoothing the way from Paris to Boulogne, and from thence, via ferry, to England.

Charlotte thanked him and paid for the tickets, glad of his assistance, listening dully to his fulsome praise of the accommodation offered, the comfortable bunks, the fine restaurant car, but would have been content to ride in a cattle-truck if it was going to take her to Eva. All that she wanted was to shake the dust of Italy from her feet for ever.

It took thirteen hours for the express to cover the miles from Turin to Gare de Lyon, Paris, and a further twenty-four till Charlotte and Tilly arrived in London. During the whole of that time Tilly could get no response from her mistress. She was like an automaton, sitting or standing when told, moving from train to train, refusing to eat. Undressing and lying on the narrow bunk above her maid, but never sleeping.

Tilly was more than thankful when the taxi dropped them at Albion House. The butler let them in, his stately face betraying not the least trace of surprise, though he must have been astonished. Frederick was in the hall, about to leave, picking up his gloves, cane and hat. He strode toward Charlotte with outstretched hands.

'My dear girl, what are you doing here?'

'Where's Eva?'

He stared at her, that white face, those bleak eyes set in dark circles, aware that something was dreadfully amiss. 'She's not here. I called to see her myself but she's out.'

'Where? I need her – why isn't she here? Is she at the bank?' Charlotte's voice cracked, on the edge of hysteria, all her stern resolve abandoning her now that she had stepped into the house that was her home.

'What's happened?' Frederick's own voice was sharp with an anxiety that had nothing to do with her. He looked older, his shoulders sagging, the grooves on each side of his mouth more deeply defined, while the grey at his temples had spread.

She shook her head helplessly. 'I must see Eva.'

He placed a hand on her shoulder and, in spite of herself, she leaned against him. Dear, familiar Freddy. The tears swam up, spilled down her face. He tried to smile reassuringly but the smile did not reach his eyes; they were like cold pebbles.

'She's hardly ever here now. You may as well know, sooner as later – Eva is engaged to be married.'

Book Three

Sisters

For the Colonel's Lady an' Judy O'Grady
Are sisters under their skins!

The Ladies, Rudyard Kipling

Chapter 13

'I wish it would stop raining. Look at it! Pissing down!' Jennie grumbled, struggling to put on her spangled costume in the tent at the back of the boxing booth. Grace, in her pram parked near the flap, started to bawl. Jennie flung her an annoyed glance. 'And you can shut up and all!'

'Maybe she wants feeding. Get out your tit,' suggested Madge laconically, glancing across from the dressing-table with the single naked and glaring electric bulb suspended above it, where she was attempting to apply her stage make-up in the fly-blown mirror. She was one of the six sirens who danced on the platform daily.

'I've just fed her. She's a greedy little cow, never satisfied.' Jennie sighed, going over and picking up the sqalling baby. 'Come on then, rat-bag! But we'll have to hurry. I'm on in ten minutes.'

Once Grace was in her arms, tiny fists kneading her breast as she exposed it and offered the nipple, her irritability vanished. The feel of Grace's warm, pliable body next to hers never failed to soothe her, even now when she was worried about what she was going to do when the fair closed. She sat on a rickety stool, while the other girls attired themselves, exchanging quips, giving great yelps of laughter, their language uninhibited, their humour effervescent. Nothing ever got them down – neither rain, problems with their men, lack of punters, or the constant travelling from one pitch to another. They had proved good friends to Jennie, showing her the ropes, though there were a couple who resented this new recruit in their midst. In the beginning she had had trouble with Flo and Ivy, a back-biting pair, jealous of her looks and ability, reminding her of Vi, barmaid at the Bell and Crown where she used to work.

They had quickly been put in their places by the red-headed, big-busted Madge, the tiny, elf-like Dorinda, and the darkly lovely Trisha. All three had taken one look at Jennie and her newborn babe and promptly adopted them. Zena had found work for Jennie within the first few days of her joining the fair, putting on her silk shawl and taking herself off to visit the boss, J.P. Barnaby, that burly domineering showman who lived in the best wagon on the site. As luck would have it (was it luck, Jennie wondered, or had Zena cast a spell?) one of the troupe had sprained her ankle and they had left her behind in Southend. By dint of creative lying, Zena had managed to persuade Barnaby that Jennie was experienced and that it would be worth his while to give her a chance.

Normally both showmen and circus performers distrusted each other and hated gypsies, a feeling that was returned in full, but sometimes it was necessary for the three groups to work alongside, enmity temporarily shelved for the common good – that of screwing money out of the public. Zena knew Barnaby of old, and they shared a grudging respect and a curious sort of liking. He was a brash, hot-tempered, noisy individual, but his word was his bond. He did not believe in legal contracts, a handshake on a deal was sufficient, and he never rescinded. Sharp he might be, ruthless even, always operating just, but only just, within the boundaries of the law, yet if he made a promise he kept it. Though showmen had their own superstitions, jargon and traditions, Barnaby believed in Zena's powers as a seer, and consulted her before he made any important decision.

Zena had returned to Jennie and triumphantly announced that she was to dance that night. This had put her in a panic. The moment had come but was she ready for it? She had spent the afternoon in front of the stage, eyes glued to the girls, seeing how they danced, watching their movements. She knew the songs which they sang and, after trying on her costume and taking part in a brief rehearsal before the night's performance under the guidance of Bill Coles, the fussy little man who arranged the choreography, had trodden the boards for the first time, acquitting herself rather well.

This had happened almost a month ago, and now Jennie felt she had never lived anywhere else or done anything but dance and sing. They had visited Margate, Ramsgate and Folkstone, and were now traversing the Surrey Downs, setting-up in villages for Mop Fairs and harvest homes, 'backending', as the autumn work was called. These would be the final booking before they pulled-in for the winter for a much needed rest period. It was a breathing-space when the showmen could repair tents and roundabouts, while the circus people found engagements in vaudeville or burlesque theatres. The gypsy men turned a coin by selling scrap metal or horse-dealing, while their women, with their dark secretive faces, went 'calling' from house to house, their baskets filled with clothes-pegs or paper-flowers, pulling out their crystal balls and telling fortunes for overawed goodwives.

Jennie knew that her days were numbered and this bothered her, though Zena had told her not to fret. All was working out according to plan. She refused to say what this might be, and Jennie had to be content to leave her in charge of her destiny. Meanwhile, she was enjoying herself, taking to the organised, though seemingly disorganised, life of the fair like a duck to water.

A vagabond by nature, she liked being constantly on the move, perched high at the front of the wagon beside Sylvester who drove the team of horses, following the long train of vehicles that constituted Barnaby's Funfair. He was Zena's nephew, the boy who had collected her from Laurel Cottage. The roads, Sylvester called them *droma* as he tried to teach Jennie the Romany tongue, led over the hills and far away; dusty, baking, rutted roads; wet, muddy roads when the skies opened and rain sluiced down.

There was the rush and hustle of setting-up when they arrived in a field. Often, in the capricious English climate, it might be during a storm, tents flapping in the wind, muck and mud everywhere, on boots, on hems, on the wheels of Grace's perambulator, and soiling the fastidious Set's paws. Jennie disliked the rain as much as the cat did, but accepted it as part and parcel of her new existence. The scorching late summer days, the damp misty dawns, the fiery copper tints of autumn were a revelation. She might have scorned sleepy Westhope, but this was different. She was seeing the countryside through fresh eyes – the gypsy eyes of Zena and Sylvester.

Now there was another performance. Bill was hovering in the tent entrance, keyed-up and anxious, his body agile though he was middle-aged. He still moved like a dancer, and the lessons he had given Jennie were invaluable.

'Come on, girls,' he urged, and looked at Jennie, rolling his eyes in mock horror. 'You're not ready! Put that baby down and get on with it.'

'All right, all right. Don't nag,' she retorted, though with a wide smile for she liked Bill and knew that she was his best pupil.

Grace was asleep, her rosebud mouth still clamped around Jennie's nipple. She carefully eased her off, rocking her gently and then placing her in her pram. Sylvester appeared from the darkness outside and jiggled the baby-carriage. He always watched over Grace while Jennie was otherwise engaged. She was aware that he was more than a little in love with her, though it was against gypsy rules for a Rom to love a *gorgio*. He was seventeen and she liked everything about him, his jet mane, his tanned face, his aquiline nose and fascinating eyes, yet she did not return his love. He was a friend, nothing more. I'm too busy to fall in love, she told herself firmly. I don't think I ever will. I don't trust men.

Talking it over with Madge and the others, her distrust of males had increased. None of the girls had a good word to say about them. No matter how charming or handsome, they were deceivers, liars, seducers, after one thing only.

As Madge put it succinctly, 'All they want is to get into your knickers.'

Jennie thought about this as she pranced on to the stage in the chorus line. The audience consisted mainly of men, elbowing their way to the front, ogling the girls. She looked down at a sea of faces, fat faces, thin faces, some red and sweating, some pale and gaunt, yet each wore a similar expression – that of rampant lust. If that's what they want, then let them have it, was the policy of the dancers, so they kicked their legs high in the cancan, showing stocking tops, black suspenders, lace-trimmed drawers, frothing petticoats, finally swirling round and sticking their behinds in the air, skirts whipped up. The audience went wild, cheering, throwing their hats skywards, and it was Jennie, the youngest, prettiest and most brazen, who received the loudest applause.

Now was her chance to shine on her own, and Bill had let her have this regular spot. While the others posed archly in the background, she stepped forward and began to sing. Her repertoire was limited to the tunes imprinted on the perforated rolls fed through the pipe-organ, but most of the songs were popular ones. The drunken men hushed as the first notes tinkled out and Jennie broke into *The Honeysuckle and the Bee*, followed by *The Little Yellow Bird* and, finally, the raucous *Let's all go down the Strand* with everyone bellowing the chorus.

As she was taking her bow, she saw Barnaby watching her from the edge of the crowd. He was fingering his waxed moustache ruminatively, eye-catching in his green checked suit with a canary waistcoat, a bowler hat pushed to the back of his head. Later, when Jennie had changed and wheeled Grace to Zena's wagon, the gypsy hauled her inside saying,

'Barnaby wants to see you. Put on your best frock and leave the *tikni* with Sylvester.'

'What does he want?' Jennie was on the defensive at once. The boss kept himself apart from the riff-raff, issuing orders which were obeyed smartly or else, but he was a man, after all – one of that diabolical race who seemed determined to ruin women.

Zena smiled her slow, mysterious smile, wearing full gypsy regalia to impress those who came to her tent, her black hair braided under a scarf ornamented with silver coins, her skirts full and multi-hued, gold hoops in her ears, gold chains about her stately neck, gold bracelets on her wrists. She picked up her black-fringed shawl that was embroidered with crimson roses and tossed it round her shoulders.

'Don't worry. He's a *rye*, a gentleman in his own way. I'll come with you,' she said.

Barnaby's wagon was large, and light streamed through the windows. Inside it was every bit as luxurious as might be expected from someone in his position. Crystal glass twinkled, deep blue or red, Dresden china lined the shelves of the walnut bureau, a fire glowed between the bars of the stove that had been black-leaded to a pewter sheen, and electric light was provided by the whirring generator outside.

Joseph Phillip Barnaby rose as Zena and Jennie entered and politely invited them to sit down. His wife, Vera, eyed them coolly and remained silent and aloof throughout. She was a distant figure on the fairground, rarely seen but highly respected. It was a well-known fact that while Barnaby might be the boss, his wife bossed him. Of Junoesque build, with bleached blonde hair, Vera Barnaby was always magnificently gowned, and it was she who paid the wages and managed every aspect of the finances.

'Now then, my dear, let's get down to brass tacks. I don't believe in beating about the bush,' Barnaby commenced, his voice having that harsh, guttural quality that seemed to belong to showmen, circus people and gypsies alike. 'I can spot talent when I see it, and you've got talent.'

'Thank you, Mr Barnaby. Most kind, I'm sure,' Jennie murmured, having decided to be meek and ladylike. Though she could be very coarse when with the other dancers, she found it easy to switch from one persona to another and now spoke like a genteel lady.

He raised a sceptical eyebrow, obviously wondering what someone like her, who looked quality and spoke like quality, was doing with the fair. He was a large man who had been athletic in his youth but was running to fat, too fond of food, drink and Havana cigars, though still impressive in his loud suit, watch-chain, spats and stiff white collar. As for Mrs Barnaby, she wore burgundy taffeta and positively dripped gold. Jennie had noticed that every single traveller prized this metal above all others, acquiring sovereign rings, chains, earrings and wearing them the whole time, not simply on special occasions. It was as if they carried their wealth on their persons, a persecuted, reviled race who thumbed their noses at the world, wanting to be seen and envied.

'What are your plans for the winter?' he asked, taking a cigar from the box on the table and sticking it in his mouth.

Zena answered before Jennie had the chance. 'I'll be joining my people in the woods near Squire Garnet's place. Then I'll take my room in Soho and *dukker*. Jennie will come with me, her *chavi* staying with the Romany women, who'll take good care of her. Jennie wants to go on the stage.'

'So she should, so she should,' he rumbled, lighting the cigar and puffing out clouds of pungent blue smoke. It reminded Jennie of Richard's Turkish cigarettes. She did not think of him often, only when her blood ran hot and she needed sexual fulfillment, an urge which she could satisfy perfectly well on her own.

'We thought to try George Edwardes at the Gaiety Theatre,' Zena continued.

'Hmm, maybe. I know old George. I'll put in a word for her. He owes me a favour from way back.'

Jennie sat there bemused. This was the first she had heard of Zena's plan, and though it seemed a good one the thought of leaving Grace was extremely painful. Zena gave her a sharp glance, and Jennie realised that she was forgetting her manners.

'That's very good of you, Mr Barnaby,' she said, demure as a nun.

He harrumphed again, but his face was less severe. 'Well, girl, I think you're worth bothering about, but you'll have to clean your act up – none of this making eyes and flirting and showing everything you've got.'

'Yes, sir. Thank you, sir.' While fluttering her lashes coyly, Jennie was thinking, Silly old fool. What does he take me for – stupid or something?

'Right then. That's settled. Let me know where you're staying in London and I'll be in touch. We shall hole up in Dorking for the winter. You've got my address, haven't you, Zena? Fine. Now then, I've got this bit of a problem about next year's bookings. The Santos Brothers want us to join them, but you know circus coves – a fly bunch. Should I do it? Will you see what the cards foretell?'

Zena nodded and drew out the well-thumbed Tarot pack from her pocket. Nothing was for nothing. He was going to help Jennie, so now Zena, her *daia*, her gypsy mother, must help him. A debt repaid was better than a debt owed.

*

It took several days for Charlotte to return to anything like normal. She kept to the house, kept to her room, though sometimes wandering up to the deserted nursery where she had spent such a happy childhood. Then she would seat herself on the saddle of the dappled rocking-horse, swinging backwards and forwards, wishing herself an infant again with Nanny Pendral there to soothe aches and pains. She longed to see Nanny, even thought of visiting her, but was ashamed, certain that those old, shrewd eyes would somehow spot that she was no longer a virgin and had indulged in a passionate love-affair which had left her dishonoured and bereft.

She avoided everyone but Tilly, though she, reunited with Wilkins, was vague and scatty, going about with a silly grin on her face. Charlotte was not given to vulgar expressions but there was one which she wanted to apply every time she saw her maid, and that was 'cockstruck'. It hurt her, disgusted her, brought back that ghastly image of Phelan on the bed with Angelica, an image that she was trying desperately to forget.

By the time Eva returned from Brighton, Charlotte was calmer and more controlled, curious, too. Who was this man who had managed to capture Eva's heart? Frederick had not told her much, merely saying that he was someone she had met through Stephen. Charlotte had sensed his pain, wanted to feel sorry for him but was too wrapped up in her own unhappiness to give room to other emotions.

Eva was expected back in the afternoon, and Charlotte put on a pastel print dress and pinned up her hair, wanting to see her, but uneasy. Her pride had been deeply wounded. Now she would have to confess that Eva had been right all along. Shortly after she had finished lunch there was a flurry down in the hall, and Tilly came running up the stairs.

'She's here, miss!' she announced breathlessly, being privy to the time of the train as Wilkins had been detailed to meet the mistress in the car.

Charlotte laid down her knife and fork, dabbed her lips with a table-napkin and gathered up her wilting courage. As soon as she saw Eva, however, she flung herself into her outstretched arms, breathing in the perfume that always wafted about her, enveloped in velvet, in furs, in Eva's love. Tears burned her lids, but she choked them back. The servants were watching, all eyes and ears.

Eva took one look at her and knew something was wrong. She did not speak until they were in the library. There she unwound the long fox-tippet from around her neck and took off her cape. Seeing Charlotte had brought her down from the clouds where she had been blissfully drifting for days. Ever since Richard had asked her to be his wife and then taken her to bed, she had been living in a dream, able to think of nothing but him, shrugging aside responsibilities and insisting that they hide away in her house in Brighton. He had agreed, an easy-going person content to fall in with her suggestion. While they were away, the engagement had been officially announced in *The Times*. Now everyone knew and there was no turning back.

And here was Charlotte, so wan and lost, pricking Eva's conscience, forcing her to remember that there were others in need of her attention. 'I'm so glad to see you,' she began, and meant it, though her brain flashed warnings of a curb on her freedom, a lessening of the hours she could spend with Richard. And what about the nights? How could she slip away to the studio with Charlotte home once more?

'I had to come – left before the others. It was impossible to stay.' Charlotte was finding this more difficult than she had anticipated.

Eva seated herself on the couch, one leg crossed over the other in her long, slit skirt. Beneath it she wore a pair of tight black trousers and Charlotte registered this unusual vision with astonishment. Eva had changed almost beyond recognition. Those clothes! Modern in the extreme. Not only was her outward appearance strikingly altered but there was something about her personality, too. She exuded confidence, as content and sleek as a well-fed cat. No longer plain but lit by an inner glow that made her face translucent and lovely. Charlotte was thrown into confusion, shy of this woman she no longer knew.

'Is Phelan with you?' Eva reached for the cigarette-box and drew out a slender Rothman. Richard smoked and she had adopted the habit.

Charlotte could feel the colour running up into her cheeks. She could not sit still and got up to begin a nervous pacing. 'No!' she cracked out. 'No, he isn't with me.'

Eva said nothing for a second, her tapering fingers busy with the lighter, giving her something to do while her thoughts raced. 'He's decided to stay in Florence, to be with his mother a while longer. Is that it?'

Charlotte's face was white, her eyes burning, her body rigid. 'I've no idea what he plans to do. It no longer concerns me.'

Eva glanced at Charlotte's hands. They were naked of rings. 'But I thought you would be married by now.'

'I'm not marrying him. I'm not even engaged to him any more. I returned his ring.'

'My dear child, come and sit by me. Tell me about it.' Relief was

Eva's chief emotion. This was followed by concern for her ward and, far away in the background, a tremor of apprehension, not for Charlotte, but for herself. She could almost see the bars of the prison closing around her. No more selfish, love-filled days with Richard.

'You were right about him.' It was easy to say with Eva's arm around her, and Charlotte let the tears overwhelm her. 'He's bad – vicious, everything I'd heard but refused to accept.'

It seemed even more dreadful put into words, but Charlotte confessed everything. Eva made little comment until she had finished, then she said, 'You're not pregnant, are you?'

'No, thank God! I was worried, but I've got my 'monthly' at this moment, so that's all right.'

'Then no real harm has been done and you can put it all down to experience.' No harm? Eva thought, even as she said it. Of course there has been harm, devastating harm. Phelan needs putting up against a wall and shooting, and I'd like to be the leader of the firing-squad.

Her little girl, her precious Charlotte, had given her love to that man and been mocked. It was unbearable. He'd better not show his nose in England again, and if he dared do so she vowed to make his life a living hell. As it was there was bound to be embarrassment for Charlotte. People would want to know why she was no longer engaged, for engagement was tantamount to marriage. It was simply not done to bow out of such a commitment. Eva sighed, visualising these problems, and wanted to talk to Richard. He was so sensible, would laugh at her fears and say that public opinion didn't matter a jot. It would only be a nine day wonder. Let the gossips cackle away. They'd forget it when something more spicy turned up. Richard, darling Richard. How she loved him! They'd only been parted an hour but it already felt like a year.

Charlotte looked so dejected, face blotched by tears, twisting her damp handkerchief in her fingers. 'I never want to set eyes on him again,' she sobbed.

'Well, you don't have to, do you? Come along, cheer up, you haven't asked me about my news yet. I want you to meet my fiancé. He'll restore your faith in men.'

'I doubt it,' Charlotte sniffed, swearing inwardly that she would have nothing to do with them from now on and wind up a spinster. 'There's not much left in life for me.'

'Nonsense! You've had an awful blow, but you'll get over it.' Eva disliked the bossy, overconfident note in her voice but could not help using it. What could one do but trot our trite phrases?

No one could help Charlotte, or penetrate that desolate wasteland she now inhabited. Only time would heal her – time and a new love-affair.

She went cold as she thought of how she would feel if Richard was unfaithful. It was so horrible an idea that she could hardly bear to dwell on it. Supremely happy now, she would also be supremely miserable were they no longer promised to one another. I couldn't stand it. I'd kill myself. Though not given to histrionics, Eva accepted this as reality. She would want to die if Richard no longer loved her.

Used to control and putting matters to rights, she raged with frustrated helplessness in the face of Charlotte's grief. Get her out of herself, she thought. Offer a diversion, anything so that she doesn't sit there brooding.

'Why don't you go to the shop and have a chat with Alice?' she offered gently, determined not to be bright and breezy. 'She's been through the mill. She'll help you.'

Charlotte nodded, her eyes dull. 'I could, I suppose.'

'That's better. Go and put on a pretty hat, and I'll tell Wilkins to take you there. How about that?'

'All right.'

'Is Gwen home?'

'Not yet. She's travelling back with Bernice and Mrs Houston.'

'So you don't know the Contessa's reaction to the cancellation of the wedding? My God, I'll bet she was annoyed. No doubt I'll receive hysterical, abusive letters from her. Could Phelan sue you for breach of promise, I wonder? I'll speak to Freddy about it.'

'I don't know and I don't care.' Charlotte stood up wearily, all the light and loveliness stripped from her.

A frightening thought struck Eva as she walked with her to the door. 'You're not still in love with him, are you?'

Charlotte stopped dead and looked at her. The expression on her face was terrible to behold. 'Love him? I *hate* him.'

The afternoon was warm, though an autumn sun lay low in the heavens. Bond Street was busy, the élite having come up from the country to order their winter costumes, and *Pour Femme* stood there, solid, cosy and comforting as Charlotte opened the door, the little bell tinkling familiarly.

'Welcome home, Miss,' cried Alice. 'Was Italy marvellous? Did you visit any of the fashion houses? Italians are good dressmakers, and their tailors can't be beat.'

Charlotte's lips curved in an answering smile, and she took Alice's hands, then went into the work-room where the seamstresses looked up from their machines and chorused greetings. They assumed that she was married and the first thing she had to do was disillusion them. They were polite, affectionate and sympathetic, restraining their natural curiosity, though she could see they were agog to hear the gory details. She had prepared herself for this and, with quiet dignity, explained that she and Mr Charteris had decided they were not suited and had called off the wedding by mutual consent.

'That was a brave thing to do,' Alice said, as they returned to the reception area. 'I don't know if I'd have had the guts. All those preparations for a big do – all that money wasted.'

'It was for the best,' Charlotte murmured, her attention captured by the framed photographs that had not been there before. Some were of the staff grouped together, and others of designer underwear posed on dummies or draped over chairs.

Alice left her alone for a moment, called into the work-room to sort out an order. As Charlotte was still looking at the pictures, the door opened and someone came in. She turned and saw a tall, large-framed man wearing a Harris jacket, velvet trousers, and a paisley-patterned cravat in place of a tie. Despite this unconventional attire there was a natural, animal elegance about him. His skin was sun-browned, his hair brown, too, rather long and curling on his collar, and he had a neatly-clipped beard and moustache. His eyes were deep blue, and he smiled at her in a friendly manner, very composed when she was far from that happy state of mind.

'Hello,' he said, the timbre of his voice low and pleasant. 'Are you waiting to be served? Alice should be about somewhere. I'll give her a call, shall I? Or would you rather go on admiring my photographs?'

'Did you take them?' Charlotte was surprised. He did not look like a photographer, though she had no reason for doubting his word.

He stepped closer and adjusted one of the frames, studying it with his head on one side. 'Yes, I did. I'm rather pleased with them. They came out well. D'you like them?'

His tone indicated that he expected her praise. She was not in the mood to pander to his vanity, so replied coolly, 'I really don't know much about photographs, but, yes – I suppose they are all right.'

His brows swooped down, his eyes glittering angrily. 'All right! Is that all you can say? How very tepid.'

'I'm sorry.' She wasn't, but made the conventional response. 'Being no expert, I can't judge them.'

When his glance encompassed her again, the anger had faded and he was smiling. 'You'll think me damnably rude, but we artists are touchy brutes. Let me call Alice for you.'

'Don't trouble yourself. She'll be back in a moment. I'm a friend, not a client.'

'I see. So am I, as a matter of fact. I've popped in to fulfil a promise.' Now that his brief flash of temper was over, Charlotte had never met anyone more relaxed. She rather resented his affable air, his obvious satisfaction with himself, his work and the world. It wasn't fair when she was feeling so miserable.

'Is that so?' She could hear shards of ice tinkling in her voice.

He seemed unaware of it, resting his rangy, loose-limbed body against the counter. 'I said I'd bring them back some sweets from the seaside, and here it is.' He pulled a paper-bag from one of his pockets. 'Peppermint rock. D'you think they'll like it?'

Charlotte shrugged. 'I don't know.'

'Would you like some?'

'No, thank you.' She wanted to freeze him out. Wished he would go away so that she might have a chance to talk with Alice.

'Don't you like sweets? I thought all girls liked them, or perhaps seaside rock isn't good enough for you? Too common, maybe. You'd prefer bonbons from Fortnum and Mason's.' He was teasing her, thinking her some snobbish upper-class piece, and she flushed under the taunting regard of those deep blue eyes that pierced hers.

'I prefer fruit to sweets,' she stammered, sounding priggish when that had not been her intention.

'Every man to his taste,' he answered carelessly. 'They say too many sweets give you spots, but I shouldn't think you need worry about that. You've a lovely complexion.'

Again, that searching scrutiny and Charlotte wished the floor would open and swallow her. Who is he? she fumed, bristling at the way in which he was making himself at home. He sounded cultured and his manner was that of an aristocrat and yet, though a trifle high-handed, he had none of the stiffness and formality of that breed.

Alice came to her rescue, darting from the back room, rosy-cheeked and smiling when she saw him. 'Mr Sinclair! You're home again.'

'I am, large as life and twice as natural, and I've not forgotten the rock. Here's yours. The biggest stick of the lot,' and he handed her a length of round, bright pink confectionary.

'Thank you, and did you have a nice time?'

'Grand! I went swimming though the sea was cold as ice. Lord, for the warmth of the Mediterranean. The seas around this coast never get far above freezing point.'

'I wouldn't know, sir, having never been further than West Bay.'

Alice was prepared to go on chatting with him, but she suddenly remembered Charlotte. 'Oh, by the way, this is Miss Drummond. Very rude of me not to introduce you.'

'How d'you do, Miss Drummond?' he said, with an ironic bow from the waist.

'I thought you two might already know one another, but I suppose not, as you've only just come back from Italy, Miss,' Alice went on, rather confused.

'No, we've not met before. Should we have done?' Richard asked, puzzled, because when he first saw the girl he had been aware of something at the edge of memory, tantalising, perplexing, refusing to be located.

'Let me do it properly,' Alice insisted, vaguely worried that she had let Eva down somehow. 'Miss Charlotte, this is Mr Richard Sinclair, Lady Eva's fiancé.'

'Charlotte? Not *the* Charlotte, the one Eva's always talking about?' His face expressed the astonishment that she, herself, was experiencing.

'That's right, sir. Lady Eva's ward.' Alice glanced from one to the other, wondering why the very air seemed to be crackling about them.

He whistled silently. 'Well, I'll be damned! I didn't expect you to look like this.'

'What did you expect? A Cockney donah in a pearl-encrusted jacket? Sorry to disappoint you, but I left the East End years ago.'

'I know. Eva's told me.'

Eva – Eva! What had happened to her? This man was young, whereas Charlotte had expected him to be at least Frederick's age. It was appalling, almost obscene. The Contessa and Dominico had been bad enough but this was far too close to home. This cocksure person was almost young enough to be Eva's son, and it was he who had given her that special glow, the bloom of a woman who has just left her lover's arms.

The blood had drained from Charlotte's face and she leaned against the counter, feeling distinctly queasy. 'I must go now. Eva's expecting me,' she muttered.

Richard was at her side. 'I'll drive you. Eva will be surprised to learn we've already introduced ourselves. I believe she planned it to happen when we dine with Dudley this evening. But I think it's much better this way, don't you?' He was showing every mark of outward respect, but she sensed a certain mocking condescension that infuriated her.

Her hand shot out in self-defence. 'No, that's all right. Wilkins is waiting for me.'

She flung an imploring glance at Alice, then began to back out of the shop, averting her eyes from Richard, feeling for the door-handle. Then she was gone, out into Bond Street, blind to the shoppers, the pleasant warmth, making for the car and Wilkins' rugged, smiling face.

'Where to, Miss?' he asked blithely.

'Hyde Park. I don't feel like going home just yet,' she answered as she rested her head against the padded leather of the rear seat.

Would she ever feel like going home again? Albion House was no longer a refuge, for soon Eva would be sharing it with that man. Once he was her husband, Charlotte would have no chance of getting away from him. I'll be surplus to requirements, she thought bitterly. He is her all, her everything now. He'll be master of Greyfriars, too. Her eyes filled with tears as she thought of the manor house with its long, broad drive flanked by elms, its moat, its noble ancestral appearance.

Pictures of this beloved place had helped sustain her as the Rome Express had rattled across Europe, and the ferry pitched and tossed in the heavy seas of the English Channel. She had visualised arriving at the beautiful Tudor porchway, the heavy, iron-studded oaken door standing open to welcome her in, had intended asking Eva if they might go to Wiltshire at once, but now it seemed hopeless. Eva would want Richard to accompany them. Nothing would ever be the same again.

Chapter 14

There was no pull-down at the end of the show on the final Saturday night. Instead all concerned gathered in the biggest of the tents, which proved to be the boxing-booth, and Barnaby stood on an upturned barrel in its centre and made a farewell speech. Following tradition, he entertained them with whisky, gin and rum, ham and cold beef, slabs of fruit cake and gallons of tea – a lavish feast which many of the company were too tired to enjoy. Free bottles of beer and sandwiches were distributed to all hands, including the 'chaps', that most despised and abused of helpers, itinerants who attached themselves to the fair for a few coppers a week.

Jennie occupied a corner with the dancers around her, passing a wide-awake Grace from hand to hand. She was used to so many nursemaids, and cooed happily. An air of sadness prevailed, exacerbated by the alcohol they had consumed. Jennie was quite choked up, though excited by her prospects.

'Where are you going now?' she asked each of them in turn.

Flo was off home, so she said, back to her father's grocery shop and her dull boy-friend, but only till next year; Ivy had been offered a job in a pub; Trisha was to stay with an aging aunt; Dorinda was heading for Wales to help her widowed mother, until spring showed green shoots again.

'And you, Madge?' Jennie squinted at her in an effort to focus. She really had had rather too much to drink.

'I've managed to get a few weeks in pantomime.' Madge was still wearing her costume, a flounced emerald green skirt dotted with sequins, and a killingly tight velvet bodice over the top of which her large breasts swelled.

'Come with me,' Jennie pleaded. 'Zena won't mind. I could do with a hand with Gracie till she gets used to her new home, and then we could go to London. What a lark, eh?'

Madge gazed at her owlishly, her eyes circled with black where her mascara had run. She put her arms round Jennie, breathing gin fumes into her face. 'No, thanks, my old mate – I'd like to, but I want to make my own way, though I'll never get to the top. You will. You're good.'

Sentimental tears streaked Jennie's rouge. It was happening again, that separation which had always dogged her. She had never been able to keep friends for long. Her way of life dictated that she was a loner. She wept as she thought of Richard and Jean – they had been her friends and she had lost them. Forgetting the violent quarrels she had sometimes had, especially with Flo and Ivy, she was bursting with love for these show-folk, fellow travellers struggling to survive in the face of adversity.

'Bloody rubbish,' she scolded, leaning against Madge unsteadily. 'You've got a good voice, and you can dance a donkey's hind leg off. You'll get your chance.'

'Shut up, don't try to con me. I knows what I can do and what I can't. Stop crying. 'Ere, blow your nose. That's the ticket.'

On Sunday morning the pull-down was completed, the horse-wagons and motor-lorries loaded for the last time that year, the 'puffing-billies' stoked with coal before starting the long, smoky trundle to a variety of destinations. The 'chaps' departed for the nearest railway station, carrying their worldly goods in gladstone bags, bundles, holdalls and brown paper parcels.

At last Zena was ready to take to the road, her tent folded and stacked under the wagon, pots and pans secured, china wedged in place. Sylvester knew the way, singing as the vehicle lurched and swayed along the lanes till its wooden, iron-banded wheels hit the highway, rolling easily on the tarmac. They were journeying towards Squire Garnet's house, and the gypsy encampment. Jennie had shed a few more tears when she parted from Madge. They had exchanged addresses, promised to keep in touch, while both knew that they would probably never meet again. Once up front of the wagon, Jennie's depression lifted. A door had closed, but another was opening. All one could do was go through it and see what lay beyond.

Squire Garnet owned a sixteenth-century manor-house set on the side of a hill above the small village of Pitney. It was a lonely, inconvenient rambling old place, awkward to get at and too far from the road. Every year, like migrant birds, the Chikno tribe, with their wagons, tents, horses and dogs, descended on Gaulden Court, setting up camp in Beeches Wood which was part of the estate.

Sylvester turned off from the main road, taking a track that wound between the half-naked trees. A few more coppery-tinted leaves spiralled down to carpet the ground, and Jennie thought they drifted sadly, as if mourning the death of summer. Zena agreed, and understanding that she was worried about leaving her baby, tried to cheer her by pointing out the beauty of the freshly-washed woods attired in their autumn glory, with hues varying from russet to lemon yellow, from the vermillion of the turning ash leaf to the grey-white of firs.

Jennie listened to her, but could not shake off her gloom, shivering as they penetrated deeper into the forest. Was this where Grace would spend the next months, abandoned by her mother? Even when they reached the clearing they sought, it was still surrounded by woodland, beyond which rose further and more extensive trees. Despite the illusion of openness, Jennie had the sense of being more enclosed, more inescapably confined than in the midst of the woods themselves. The thickets produced a curious feeling of oppression, as if she was intruding at her peril on some private domain. Within a few moments of the wagon halting, she discovered that indeed she was – a stranger viewed with suspicion.

There was a huddle of painted wagons drawn together on the grass, near a cluster of low, arched tents. Several horses grazed close-by, and the newcomers were assailed by a trio of lean, wolfish-looking dogs, who growled warningly, but did not bark. Set, who always occupied a perch near Sylvester, did not stir a whisker, staring at them contemptuously through slitted, green-gold eyes.

Sylvester stuck his whip in the slot at his side and shouted at the dogs, his white teeth gleaming in his sun-burned face. They recognised him and leapt up on their long, skinny legs, licking his hand, snakelike tails lashing. This was the cue for the swarthy people seated on their haunches by the fire to rise and welcome their brethren. The men held back a little, their dusky faces impassive, but the women ran forward, children scampering after them.

Zena leapt down into the arms of a vast woman in a scarlet cloak, who was smiling all over her walnut brown, wrinkled face. Sylvester, too, was received into her embrace, and the others gabbled in their own language from which Jennie was totally excluded. She had become accustomed to Zena and Sylvester, and had listened for hours to their stories of the Romany people, so she was not dismayed by the ferocious aspect of the gypsies, their raffishness, their ragged, gaudy clothing.

The men were arrogant and taciturn, their black oily ringlets flowing to their shoulders, dirty fingers glittering with gold or silver rings. Some of the women were beautiful in a rich and vivid way, and the younger men were striking and handsome, wearing red spotted neckerchiefs, broad-brimmed black hats and mole-skin jackets. All, young or old, male or female, carried an air of insolent pride.

Jennie climbed slowly from the wagon, Grace in one arm, and stood behind Zena, forgotten for the moment, while Sylvester, after a quick check to make sure she was all right, was led away by a couple of girls of his own age, dark-browed and raven-maned. Then Zena presented her to the woman, whose eyes blazed as fiercely as if the devil looked out of them. Her name was Orlanda, and she held an important place in the gypsy hierarchy, wife of the chieftain, Piramus Chikno, who was Zena's brother. Sylvester was their son and heir-apparent, to become a Duke of Little Egypt on the death of his father.

'You're a *gorgio rakli.*' Orlanda addressed Jennie accusingly. 'What are you doing on the *drom*?'

Jennie looked her straight in the eye. Orlanda was a formidable being with her height and bulk, and grizzled hair that fell in two thick braids to her waist from under her bandana, but Jennie was not intimidated.

'I'm a singer,' she said. 'I'll sing for you in exchange for my supper.'

This could not have amused Orlanda more, and she gave a husky chuckle from somewhere deep in her enormous chest. 'A singer, eh? You look like a *Pikie* to me. Is she a *Pikie*, Zena? You know I won't take them in if they've been expelled from their own tribes.'

'I'm no *Pikie*. I'm a *gorgio*, like you said, and proud of it,' Jennie retorted.

Orlanda's eyes alighted on Grace. 'Is this your *tikni*?'

'Yes.' Jennie involuntarily clutched the baby closer.

'Where's her father?'

'I don't know.'

'No father? Are you a *lóoverni*, then?'

Zena butted in, her hand exerting a warning pressure on Jennie's arm. 'She's no prostitute, Orlanda. She's my friend. I'm looking after her and the *chavi*. She's telling the truth. Sings like a nightingale, she does. You've never heard anything so sweet.'

Orlanda planted her beefy fists on her hips, still rather disapproving of this girl her sister-in-law had brought into their close-knit circle. Then she inclined her head. 'All right. Show us what you can do, *rakli*.'

Jennie had won the gypsies' attention, her coolness and bravery a quality after their own hearts. She stepped forward, her eyes fixed seriously on Orlanda. 'Will you hold Grace for me?'

Orlanda hesitated for a fraction only, then took Grace into her arms, cradling her with amazing tenderness, an experienced mother of ten, with grandchildren as well. Jennie gazed solemnly at the people seated about the fire and, after a short, dramatic pause, opened her lips and started to sing.

Thus she became an associate member of the Chikno clan. For Zena's sake, and also recognising in her a spirit akin to their own, they took her into the fold. In no time at all she found herself seated on Orlanda's right hand, eating stew from a tin platter, and drinking a mug of steaming coffee. The stew tasted of rabbit, and other delicacies which she had never had before. Orlanda chuckled and explained that the Squire was a good 'un who never complained if the men went poaching game with their lurcher dogs, providing he was given a haunch of venison for his own table.

A gang of barefoot girls, some of whom were Orlanda's daughters, had swooped on Grace, begging Jennie's permission to play with her, carting her off to the wagons in their strong, skinny arms, knowledgeable nurses who looked after their own little brothers and sisters while their parents were out making a living. Every gypsy there admired the baby's fair skin, blue eyes and blonde hair, a novelty among so many dark complexions, and Jennie let her go without a qualm, for the love they showed her was genuine.

'*A bori odjus tikner*,' they kept exclaiming, and Zena translated this as meaning 'a big lovely baby.'

She smiled at her through the wood-smoke, while Sylvester squatted on her other side, a reassuring presence, and Jennie was content. The place no longer seemed alarming, even though twilight was spreading over the glade, and the rooks cawed and clustered in the trees, seeking nightime roosts. She was feeling sleepy, full of good food, listening to the murmur of voices as Zena related her adventures during the summer and they recounted their own wanderings.

Then the peace was disturbed as a gig came bowling into the clearing. It was driven by a short, peppery little man in corded riding breeches and sand-coloured gaiters, his shock of shining white hair swept back over his forehead. The man beside him was a complete contrast; tall, sun-scorched and black-visaged, his sheepskin, his peaked hat ornamented with a heron's feather, the gold ring glinting in his ear, the lovely gold serpent chain threaded round his waist, combining to invest him with a fearsome grandeur. Orlanda leapt to her feet, surprisingly agile for so large a woman, greeting Squire Garnet, and her husband.

Jennie came under the regard of two pairs of eyes. The Squire's were steel-grey; Piramus Chikno's black as pitch. Once again she had to state her business. The Squire paced himself squarely before her, legs spread to balance his weight, while Piramus growled at his wife and his dog, and got on with his supper, pretending indifference.

'Going on the stage?' the Squire bellowed. It seemed that he always spoke very loudly. 'Well, mercy me! Whatever next, I ask myself! Leaving your baby here with the gypsies? Will you permit this, Piramus?'

The chieftain spared Jennie a single flinty glance. 'I might. My sister says she's *tatcho*.'

'And what the devil does that mean? I wish you'd talk English, man!' Everything the Squire said was delivered double forte, but with a broad smile and twinkling eyes.

'She's true, genuine, real,' the gypsy duke explained, with a shrug of his lean, muscular shoulders. 'My sister never lies, and her word is enough for me.'

'Ah, is that so?' The Squire considered Jennie thoughtfully, taking in her lovely face, graceful movements, and air of dignity coupled with an allure that was irresistible. 'Well, Miss Drummond, are you content to sleep in a wagon or can I offer you accommodation at Gaulden Court? My wife would enjoy having a baby under the roof.'

'I'll stay here, sir, if I may,' Jennie answered politely. 'I'm among friends, you see.'

'Very well, but come and see us tomorrow. I'd like to talk with you some more, and Joan will want to see the little one.' The Squire turned on his heel and jumped into the gig, biding them all goodnight.

During the days that followed Jennie came to know the Squire and his wife well. A happy-go-lucky pair, who lived in comfortable, haphazard squalor at the manor. The first time she went there was when he collected her in the gig the morning after her arrival. It was a short journey to the house, and she saw a stone gateway and gables with latticed mullioned windows peeping over a moss-covered wall. There were farm-buildings at the back, and an enormous canopied well, a grass-grown terraced walk and a quaint old circular dove-cote.

A confirmed batchelor, Tom Garnet had astounded everyone when at the age of seventy he had turned round and married a farmer's widow thirty years his junior. 'We've not had any children, more's the pity,' he said to Jennie, as the gig rounded a corner and stopped in the courtyard. 'Joan's got grown-up lads and lasses, but nothing's happened since we've been wed. There's plenty of gun-powder in the old pistol, but I suppose it fires blanks.'

Joan was a kind, jolly, untidy woman, willing to help anyone, and it was obvious that she and her husband adored one another.

She gathered Grace to her large bosom and that was that – Jennie and she became one of the family. She got on well with the gypsy women and they liked her and did not take too much advantage of her generosity. Daily they tramped into the yard and worked the rusty pump, drawing crystal clear water from the well. She supplied them with milk, butter, cheese and eggs at a fair price which they never tried to knock down, respecting this pair who raised no objection to them using their land, when so many farmers shut and barred the gates as soon as a train of wagons appeared on the horizon. The Squire had always welcomed them, like his father and grandfather before him, relying on their skill if his horses ailed, upsetting the local veterinary surgeon by refusing his help.

'Piramus Chikno sees to my beasts. Wouldn't trust my hunters to anyone else,' he would say to both vet and village doctor. 'And his wife makes our medicines.'

So, when the gypsies arrived yearly, Joan threw open her house and kept the fire roaring on the great open hearth in the kitchen. Anyone could come in and dry off and, when the weather was exceptionally wet, there were usually long lines filled with gypsy washing stretched under the blackened beams, though the women refused the use of the scullery, preferring to get cauldrons of water boiling on the camp-fire, setting to work in the open air, scrubbing their own clothing, their children's and countless baby napkins. The men's garments were always washed separately, as it was taboo for them to be immersed in the same suds as those used by the women.

Zena had explained this to Jennie, saying that it was regarded as *mokardi*, unclean, but it had nothing to do with dirtiness. It meant unclean in the ceremonial sense only, as being dangerous to the health and strength of the men. It was then that Jennie realised she could never be a real gypsy. The men seemed to be even more dictatorial than *gorgio* males. It made her impatient, all this bowing and scraping to masculine vanity, and Piramus Chikno expecting to be treated like a god. She wanted to get away, even though it meant parting with Grace, longed for the challenge of London, for traffic and fog and shops and masses of people.

The Squire drove her to the general store in Pitney, where she purchased glass feeding-bottles and rubber teats. Part of the plan was that Grace should be weaned from the breast. Orlanda brewed a herb concoction to dry up Jennie's milk, and Grace proceeded to wax fat and bonny on the life-giving liquid provided by Joan's brown and white cows. Orlanda had taken it upon herself to care for the baby, and there was no further excuse for delay. Jennie stored the perambulator in one of the manor's many empty rooms, knowing that the gypsies would probably use it for collecting fire-wood if she left it in the camp. She did the same with the cradle, draping it in a dust-sheet, for Orlanda insisted on carrying Grace about in the fold of her shawl or tucking her into a rush basket.

Everything was ready, bags packed, Zena attired in a simple dark costume and plain hat, like a *gorgio*, and Sylvester given his instructions with regard to looking after Grace. Joan had promised to keep an eye out for her, too. Early one morning, Jennie kissed her baby and left her in Orlanda's arms. The Squire was waiting with the gig to take them to the nearest railway-station, so Zena and Jennie set off for the capital.

'What about asking Gwen to come to Greyfriars for Christmas. She loved it last year, didn't she? I'm thinking of inviting Dudley and Beth and the children. That should make a jolly party, don't you think?' Eva was sitting at her desk in the bank, as she did most mornings, dealing with business matters and the constant and pressing demands of her charities.

Charlotte shrugged. 'Do whatever you like, Eva.'

She had dropped in more for something to do than with any desire to work. Though she sometimes helped Beth at the clinic, and had been following a fresh scent supplied by Stephen regarding her ancestry, the well-spring of energy that had once flowed freely along her veins seemed to be dry. She had been back in England for weeks, Florence and Phelan an eternity away, yet her wounds were still raw.

Eva worried about her, and was at her wit's end to know what to do for the best. They had visited Greyfriars in the autumn, but this had proved a dismal failure, and she could no longer blind herself to the antipathy between Richard and her ward. She had never known Charlotte so wilful and disagreeable, finally losing patience with her rudeness. Why didn't she like Richard? she had asked, but could get no satisfactory reply. He had dismissed it in his customary tolerant fashion, suggesting the girl was jealous. After all, for years Eva and she had been inseparable, so it was only natural that she should resent him.

Resent him she did, her homecoming to Greyfriars spoilt because he was there. Eva did her best, but their old feeling of companionship was gone. They might retrace the walks which used to delight them, ride together, visit the cottagers as of yore, but Charlotte felt that Eva would rather be doing these things with Richard. She had taken to trudging off on her own for long hours at a stretch, knowing that she was being ridiculously childish, but hoping that her absence would trouble them, particularly if she stayed out after dark. She had behaved like a baby demanding to be noticed, coming in eventually, cold and often wet, to find them ensconced cosily in the study, and when Eva rose to cluck over her and kiss her cheek, she never reciprocated, stumping off to bed.

Now Eva looked at her sternly, annoyed by her lack of interest in the Christmas preparations. 'I thought you'd like to have your friend with you again.'

'All right, I'll ask her, but I doubt she'll come unless you invite Julian,' Charlotte replied off-handedly.

'Is he in London? I didn't know.'

'Oh, yes, he's back. Gwen is full of it,' she snapped, trailing to the window and staring down on the wet streets.

Eva tapped the desk-top with her pencil. There was something about Julian which set her teeth on edge, but if it would make Charlotte happy . . .'

'Very well. I'll send him an invitation, providing, of course, that he doesn't expect Phelan to come along, too.'

'Ha! I should think that highly unlikely.' Charlotte still flinched at the mention of his name. 'He won't be bothering to brave the English winter now that I'm no longer available.'

She had talked at length with both Gwen and Cynthia when they finally came home. Bernice had been forthcoming with information, though desolate because Andrew had gone back to Africa in search of a legendary lake, his expedition sponsored by the Royal Geographical Society. To console herself she was now in the King's favour once more. It seemed that Charlotte's sudden departure from Florence had caused an uproar, with Phelan disclaiming all knowledge of why she had decided to call off the wedding.

Charlotte had not enlightened her friends, even though Gwen was still annoyed because she had been unable to be a bridesmaid and Cynthia thought her a spoilt brat who needed slapping. Let them think what they would, but she suspected that Bernice guessed. She alone did not condemn her or ask questions, but had merely put her arms around her and given her a reassuring hug, murmuring, 'Don't let them get you down, darling. Men, I hate 'em!' and had left it at that.

Eva tried again, hoping to spark off a vestige of enthusiasm. 'I was thinking of including Archie. He's a nice boy who's always asking after you. He doesn't stammer as much as he did. He's been having singing lessons as a cure, I believe.'

Charlotte's mind went streaking back to her coming out ball, that fateful night when she had met Phelan. Archie had bearded her in the conservatory, and she had known then that he was keen on her. Till Eva mentioned him, she had forgotten about him, but now she recalled his diffident manner, his stutter, his admiration. He had vaguely irritated her and she was sure he would do so now, but it wasn't important. He may as well come to Greyfriars. As for herself, she dreaded spending Christmas there, for Phelan's ghost would haunt her more than ever. She would be remembering the time when she had started to fall in love with him.

'Is Richard coming?' she demanded and, made cruel by pain, added, 'What about Freddy? Or is he excluded? You have no need of him now that you've a lover, I guess.'

Eva did not rise to the bait, answering calmly, 'Freddy is going to visit his sister, near Lake Windermere.'

It was snowing when they arrived at Greyfriars, cottony flakes meandering down from white, bloated clouds. The air was breathless, inert with cold. Christmas Eve, and the cars had only just managed to get there. The snow had half melted during the morning, but by the afternoon a severe frost had set in, turning the roads to ice.

Everyone was very gay, declaring that this was wonderful, a real old-fashioned Christmas, as they stamped into the Great Hall, muffled in furs and driving capes, glad of the mulled wine which Hopkins, who had arrived with the staff several days before, had ensured was waiting to be served. The house rang with voices and laughter, the excited shrieks of Dudley's youngsters as they ignored the admonishments of Nanny Pendral who, fortunately between posts at that precise moment, had been engaged to care for them.

Archie had come down in his own fast sports car, making a grand entrance in his leather coat, helmet and goggles. Dudley had used his beat-up old vehicle, saying that it was a miracle that it hadn't broken down on route, while Charlotte, Gwen and Cynthia had travelled in the limousine. Wilkins had been hurriedly dispatched to the station to pick up Tilly and Lambert before the roads became thoroughly impassable.

Eva and Richard were the last to come, bursting in at the front door, their voices loud and fresh from the outdoors. They had made the journey in his Rover. Charlotte looked at Eva, who had her blue-fox coat flung carelessly over her shoulders, her fur hat swinging in one hand. Her face glowed.

'We had a marvellous drive. Stopped off at a hotel for lunch. Snow! Isn't this grand!'

Everyone agreed that it was, while evil thoughts nibbled at Charlotte's mind. Had they come straight there after the meal or had they taken a private room for the afternoon? She had no proof, but little things they said, the way they gazed into each other's eyes, made her certain that they were as intimate as she and Phelan had once been.

The footmen were circulating with trays of sherry and hot mincepies. Charlotte huddled by the roaring log fire. She kept her face averted though she sensed that Eva wanted to draw her into the conversation, perplexed by her attitude of sullen withdrawal. Then someone spoke behind her, and she turned her head.

'Hello, Charlotte,' Archie said, goggles pushed up on his forehead, the shoulders of his leather overcoat powdered with snow. 'It's good to see you again. I heard you were back, but I was on Exmoor, stag-hunting, or I'd have called at Albion House. How was Italy? I'm s-s-sorry to hear about your broken engagement.'

His pale blue eyes were anxious, his face pink with the cold and excitement at being with her, and embarrassment, too, obliged to mention so touchy a subject as a love-affair that had gone wrong. He had succeeded in controlling his errant tongue until he reached that bit. It was a small personal triumph, for Charlotte took his breath away, her face framed in furs, thinner than he remembered, a year older with something about her that spoke of pain and knowledge. Had she slept with Phelan Charteris? he wondered. Certainly she had lost that virginal look.

It was comforting to have someone pay her attention, a personable young man who wore the expression of a dog panting for a tidbit. A nice dog, clumsy but devoted. Charlotte held out her cold hand. 'Hello to you, Archie. Italy was fine – ' Then she changed her mind. Why lie to him? 'No, to be frank, it was awful. One day I'll tell you about it. Meanwhile, I'd like to forget.'

He held on to her fingers a shade longer than was necessary, murmuring, 'Will you let me help you forget, Charlotte?'

She could hear Eva's voice in the background, high-pitched and feverish, not her own at all but like that of a someone half her age. Richard was making everyone laugh, Dudley sharing the festive spirit. It was Cynthia's first ever sight of Greyfriars, and Gwen was proposing that Eva should show them round. Beth had already gone to the nursery wing with Nanny Pendral to settle her sons.

'How d'you like the idea of sleeping in a four-poster?' Richard asked Dudley, clapping him on the shoulder.

'Great! My wife will think she's her namesake, Queen Elizabeth!'

'Then you'll have to pretend to be the Earl of Essex!'

'Oh, Richard, you are awful. They weren't married! She was the Virgin Queen!' shrilled Gwen.

'There's a certain amount of doubt about that among scholars,' he replied, throwing back his head and laughing again.

Trust him to know that, Charlotte thought savagely. He's Eva's lover. That's plain as a pikestaff. Eva's fancy-man, her pretty-boy. Anger and envy twisted like serpents in her gut, the gorgeously decorated Hall shimmering through a veil of tears. The tinsel, the holly, the towering, shining Christmas tree were as cruel as instruments of torture, accentuating her own loneliness and disappointment. She gazed up into Archie's concerned face, groped for his arm with her fingers.

'Archie, I've been through a bad time. You'll have to bear with me, I'm not very good company at present, but if you can take me as I am, then I'd be glad if you'd help me to forget.'

Eva had never been happier, the only fly in the ointment being Charlotte, but she saw that Archie was talking with her and hoped they would become close friends. It felt as if a burden had been lifted from her shoulders and she linked her arm with Richard's as they set off on a guided tour of the house with her guests following. Even as she stopped at every portrait, explaining this or that ancestor, and took them through the spectacular apartments, so she clung to Richard, heart pounding as she remembered everything that had happened when they broke their journey.

They had driven into the forecourt of a country inn and there ordered a meal to be sent to a private room, giving their names as Mr and Mrs R. Sinclair. Hardly a lie, Eva had thought, for they were already married by common law even though they did not plan a church wedding until late in the following year. She felt that he was her husband already, thought of him as such.

Ah, that mellow, panelled room, redolent of beeswax and crackling pine-logs. They had eaten at a low table drawn close to the fire, and then Richard had made love to her on the rug before the hearth. A new form of loving, one which she had never anticipated or dreamed possible, almost shy when he had buried his face in her stomach and then started to lick her, parting her thighs, searching for the small hard core of her with his tongue.

'D'you like this?' he had asked once, smiling up at her. 'Is it nice? You must tell me.'

'Oh, Richard,' she had groaned, her eyes tightly shut. 'Richard! It's so nice. Don't stop. Please don't stop!'

And he had gone on and on until she had cried out with acute pleasure, waves of feeling washing over her, exploding with magnificent force. She had lain there tearing at his back with her nails, pulling him down on her, shuddering with need, and he had driven into her hard and fast, groaning in an agony of release.

It had been wonderful, but now she came out of her trance, realising that her guests were waiting for her to continue with her stories of Greyfriars' history, their faces turned to her, expectant, smiling, wondering why she had drifted off mid-sentence. She took her arm away from Richard's. The feel of his warm body was too distracting even though he was fully clad, not naked as at the inn.

'This is the tower,' she went on, amazed that she sounded so normal as she stood at the bottom of the flight of stone steps that spiralled upwards. 'It's believed that a Royalist lady once defended Greyfriars against the Roundheads, storing gold and silver plate up there. Legend has it that she weakened when a handsome enemy Colonel broke the seige. She didn't tell him where the treasure was hidden, but when her husband returned from the war, he found that she had fled with her rebel lover.'

Bully for her, Eva was thinking, now able to understand the wild passions that drove the most sensible of women to behave like strumpets, forgetting honour and decorum and dignity. I'd have done the same if I'd been her.

Christmas Day dawned, stiff with frost, a chilly sunrise lurking behind a sky of tarnished steel, but within the thick walls of Greyfriars the maids and footmen were at work early, lighting fires in the main rooms, dusting, polishing, finishing speedily so that they might change into clean uniforms and be down in the Great Hall to receive their gifts from the mistress at nine o'clock sharp, before forming into a crocodile and being led to church by Hopkins.

The kitchen staff, under the baton of Cook, had prepared the vegetables the night before, while she had been up to her eyes in flour for days, making pies and pastry, puddings and sweets. Mucky to the elbows, she had drawn and dressed numerous capons and three vast twenty-pound turkeys, besides pork and beef, to be served both cold and hot, during the feasting which would last four days or more.

'I vote we go tobogganing,' suggested Richard after luncheon.

Groans arose from the deep armchairs in the library where people had repaired to rest after the exertions of the morning; present giving round the tree; a brisk walk to church through the snow, followed by a light meal – the massive festive dinner would be served that evening.

'Oh, no,' Dudley protested. 'I'm a busy doctor, and this is supposed to be a holiday.'

‘I think it’s a spanking idea, don’t you, Julian?’ Gwen said, turning her flushed face up to him from her seat on a hassock by the fire.

Julian was stretched out on the Chesterfield. He had been delayed last night, and said it was because of the weather, arriving by car in time for lunch. Gwen had fretted all morning, but now she was happy, wearing a constant smile. He raised heavy eyelids. The trip down had been damned cold and he had had no sleep, having come straight from an all-night party in town. He had been reluctant to accept Eva’s invitation, remembering last Christmas at Hawksdown Hall. It was a pity that Phelan had not opened up his manor again, but he had only just arrived in London from Europe.

‘Gwen, you’re too full of energy,’ he complained. ‘It comes from being so young and sprightly. Wait till you reach the ripe old age of twenty-four, like me.’

‘I think sledging’s a splendid notion,’ Beth said from the wingchair. ‘It’ll tire the kids beautifully. Nanny says they hardly slept a wink last night, too excited about the arrival of Santa Claus, and getting out of bed continually to see if he had filled their stockings.’

Taking no notice of her husband’s moans, she went to collect the boys, while Gwen raced upstairs to fetch warm clothing. Cynthia declined, opting for a nap instead, and making for her room. Charlotte had no inclination to roll around in the snow, getting wet and cold, but Archie was persuasive. It had been a comfort to have his support during Christmas Eve and that day. He distracted her nicely from concern about what Eva and Richard might or might not be doing.

‘Get your coat on, Eva,’ Richard said, bending over her, his arms braced each side of her chair.

‘I’d rather stay here,’ she replied, meeting his blue gaze. ‘I’m rather tired, and we shall be late up tonight.’

‘Are you sure?’ he lowered his voice to a whisper. ‘Shall I stay with you, and we can nip off to bed?’

‘Lambert will be on the prowl,’ she reminded, laughter in her voice, the purring laughter of a woman who has recently been sexually satisfied.

He pulled a face. Lambert was a nuisance, always poking and prying, worse than any duenna. He never slept at Albion House with Eva’s watch-dog maid about and, when at Greyfriars, they had to resort to clandestine rendezvous with him creeping to Eva’s room after Lambert had retired for the night. He brought his alarm-clock with him for it was essential that they woke early so that he could tiptoe back to his own chamber before she came in with her mistress’s morning tray of tea.

'I'll be off, then,' he said, rising to his full height.

'I'm quite happy to stay in. I want to dip into that poetry book you gave me this morning, though I'll probably catch forty winks by the fire. See you at tea-time. You're duty-bound to try a slice of Cook's fruit cake, or she'll be mortally offended and threaten to leave my service.'

He grinned. 'We can't have that. She's too valuable. Like you, she knows that the way to a man's heart is through his stomach.'

'Indeed? I thought it was through something quite different,' she murmured.

'We'll talk about that later,' he answered, and winked at her.

It was a fine, crisp afternoon with a cold sparkle in the air. Ice crunched beneath their rubber overshoes, and the runners of the sledges made a soft swishing hiss as the men hauled them along on the end of ropes. Flakes lay like crystallised sugar on the top of every wall, and the frozen moat, sheltered from the weak sun, lay grey among the alders. The snow was densely white on the slopes above Greyfriars, as they laboured up dragging the heavy toboggans, their breath hanging about them in a cloud of vapour. A light wind blew when they reached the summit, fanning the snow into misty spray.

The head gardener had unearthed four sledges from a shed, dusting them off and greasing the runners. Charlotte remembered them from childhood winters and she soon occupied one, seated between Archie's legs, his arms round her as he held the guide rope and they waited for the others to get ready. It was to be a race to see who could reach the bottom first.

Dudley had one son before him, and Beth another, while Richard, Gwen and Julian had decided to go three-manned, rather than someone waiting his turn. A delighted, exuberant, red-cheeked Gwen took her place between them, thrilled to the core to be pressed against such handsome male bodies. Charlotte glanced at her. She was certainly maturing, no longer a school-girl, attractive in her fluffy blue tam-o'-shanter with a matching scarf round her neck, a warm navy jacket and calf-length skirt. She wondered if Julian was genuinely interested in her. What other motive could he have had for coming to Greyfriars?

She had no more time to think for, with a loud, 'Ready, steady – go!' the toboggans were off, careering down the slope. She felt the rush of icy wind stinging her cheeks, the whoosh of the runners gathering speed, the wintry landscape flashing past her, hanging on like grim death, aware of a crazy exhilaration. The sledges were neck and neck, then hers streaked ahead and slowed to a halt with a slither and crunch, reaching the target first.

She tumbled off into the snow, staggered to her feet, slipping and sliding, with Archie's arms around her. She laughed up into his face, her cheeks rosy, eyes sparkling. The others arrived just after with yelps and cries, issuing an immediate challenge to the winners. Up the slope they went, leg muscles burning, to begin all over again, and this time Dudley was in the lead, but as Charlotte followed a close second, the toboggan veered off course, crashing through some bushes and ploughing into a deep drift.

'Damn!' muttered Archie, and he was sitting in the snow holding his leg, blood seeping through his trousers. It was then that Charlotte saw a piece of galvanised iron sticking up through the drift.

'Archie!' She was on her knees beside him. 'What have you done?'

'Cut my damned shin open on that bit of metal,' he groaned. 'Lord, but it hurts.'

'Are you all right?' shouted Richard, tramping up to them, race abandoned. He saw the blood and Archie's face, white now under the wind-burn. 'Christ! We'd better get you back to the house.'

Charlotte was tying a handkerchief around the jagged rip in Archie's skin. 'Can you walk?'

He gave a wry grin. 'I can hobble.'

'Let me take a look. Just as well there's a tame doctor around.' It was good to have Dudley there. He seemed satisfied that there were no broken bones, just a deep and rather nasty gash, and he offered Archie his arm, hauling him to his feet.

'That was careless.' Richard rounded on Charlotte. 'You were out front. Couldn't you have managed the steering a bit better than that?'

'It wasn't Charlotte's fault,' Archie protested, his arm slung around Dudley's shoulders.

'Maybe not, but she couldn't bear the thought of losing, could she? Jesus, it wasn't a life or death contest, you know.' And Richard scowled at her.

'I think it was time to leave anyway,' put in Beth, ever the peace-maker. 'The boys are wet and cold. They need a nice hot bath and nursery tea.' Gathering up her young, holding each by their gloved hands, she started to walk back in the direction of the house.

'Oh, dear,' said Gwen. 'And we were having such a lovely time, too.'

'Grab one of those sledges, my girl, and let's get going.' Julian had had enough, more inclined towards lazing by the log fire than displaying Arctic sportmanship.

Charlotte stood there seething with fury. How dare Richard blame her? What right had he to speak to her like that? She turned with as much dignity as she could muster in the deep drifts and, righting the sledge, struggled up the slope, pulling it behind her.

'Where are you going? Don't be an idiot. It's getting dark,' shouted Richard but she ignored him. No skill with the sledge, eh? she muttered to herself. I'll show him, the arrogant bastard.

He was right about one thing, however. It *was* getting dark. Standing on the brow she could see the others, forlorn black specks below, crawling towards Greyfriars. To her extreme annoyance, Richard left them and was following her. She looked around frantically. To her left was a long drop, sloping but precipitous. She pushed the sledge to the edge, jumped on it and was at once in flight, skimming over the ice-encrusted surface. The speed was terrifying, and there was no way to stop it. Ahead she could see the hump of snowy bushes. She tried to swerve, but ended up in a breathless heap amongst them.

Stunned, she lay there for a moment, gathering her wits. It was growing ever darker and deadly cold. Perhaps I'll die of exposure out here, she thought. What a nice way to go, to fall asleep and never wake. The leadened sky was giving forth its burden again, large flakes swirling through the air, set to become a blizzard. She thought of the walk back. It would be exhausting, fighting against the rising wind, blinded by snow, stumbling into drifts. She would have to abandon the toboggan. She was thoroughly shaken by her tumble and, as she sat up, she felt the blood drain from her head and her stomach churned.

'That was a silly thing to do,' said a voice from above her. 'What are you trying to prove? That you're as good as the blokes?'

'Go away. I can manage,' she answered crossly, as Richard materialised out of the storm. His hat, hair, eyebrows and beard were white with snow.

He dropped to his haunches beside her, resting on his forearms, hands dangling between his knees. 'Why are you giving Eva such a hard time? If it's me you object to, then have the guts to tell me. Don't keep on sniping. What's the matter? Have I put your nose out of joint or something?'

'Nothing's the matter,' she lied, staggering to her feet and beginning the long haul back. 'Leave me alone. You've got what you wanted, so let's close the subject.'

'And you haven't, I suppose? It was your decision to

jilt Phelan. You can't go around blaming the world for that.'

'Why don't you shut up? You don't know anything about it, can't begin to understand why I did it.' She pressed on angrily, her ankles aching in the heavy boots, back aching, muscles cramping, but refusing to stop and rest.

'Maybe I would, if you took the trouble to tell me.' His arm shot out, preventing her from falling. She tried to pull away, but was too tired.

'I don't want to talk about it.' To her horror she knew that she was going to start crying. She bit her lip hard, but the cold made it smart.

'As you like. It's up to you.' The blizzard was gathering strength, but she could see that he was grinning.

After that they were too intent on making it to the top, then half walking, half sliding down the other side. Soon they were in the lee of the woods, the path leading them to the lights of the manor which glimmered between the heavy fall. This was so encouraging that Charlotte's spirits rose and she stepped out quickly, reaching the white lake of lawn which was the only thing between them and warmth and comfort.

'We made it!' she cried triumphantly.

'We did indeed!' he answered, taking her hand as they broke into a jog.

She pulled away, laughing with relief and, bending, gathered up snow balls and started to pelt him with them. Take that, you bastard, she was thinking, and that – but found that she no longer hated him.

Eva saw them from where she was kneeling on the window-seat, watching anxiously for their return. The others had come back with the wounded hero, and Dudley had attended to the cut. Now they were warming themselves in the Great Hall, speaking of their adventure, in that high, exaltant tone of people who have just conquered the elements, a bit ashamed of their foolishness, but proud of it, too.

She had been alone all the afternoon, reading the love-poems Richard had given her as a Christmas present, thinking about him, dreaming of the night to come, happy in the convivial atmosphere of the library, contrasting it with the metallic glare of the outside world, yet a little regretful that she was not there with him.

Now, looking out at that icy, spectacular view, she was aware that the snow had abated a little, hearing voices ringing across the lawn, and catching a glimpse of Charlotte hurling snowy missiles at Richard. He was laughing, retaliating, falling down with her on top of him. They were up in an instant but not before Eva experienced such a surge of jealousy that it was like a hot iron searing her.

Charlotte, so young, so vital! And I'm old, she thought bitterly, too old to play in the snow with him. In an instant she had gathered her feelings together. How ridiculous. Charlotte disliked him. She had made that very plain. But as she heard them coming into the Hall, still laughing and talking, so it seemed that the garden darkened suddenly, the entire sweeping vista empty and silent beyond the drifting whiteness and the sobbing wind.

Gwen was changing for dinner, and Charlotte, already attired in an oyster satin gown, sat on the bed and talked to her. Tilly was there, helping Gwen dress her hair. She was eighteen now and her parents could no longer prevent her hair going up and her skirt hems dropping down. She's quite beautiful, Charlotte thought, and has lost her puppy fat. When Julian arrived for lunch, Gwen had been radiant with joy, buoyant during the toboggan race, but now her light seemed slightly dim.

'What's the matter?' Charlotte asked, and Gwen's face, reflected in the mirror took on a shuttered look.

'It's Julian,' she replied, and this came as no surprise to either Charlotte or Tilly.

'What's he done?'

'Nothing. That's just the point, and I've given him plenty of encouragement.' Gwen twisted impatiently away from the maid's ministering hands.

'So I've noticed,' Charlotte said drily.

'It was the same in Italy. All those romantic evenings and he never tried anything on.'

'Maybe he has too much respect for you, Miss,' Tilly observed, ignoring Gwen's wriggling and tucking a stray curl into place.

'He thinks I'm just a kid,' Gwen said in a stifled, curiously dead voice.

Charlotte glanced at her diamond wrist-watch, a birthday gift from Eva. It was time they went down to dinner. 'I'm sure he doesn't think anything of the kind.' She went over and patted Gwen's limp hand. 'Maybe he's shy.'

'Julian – shy?' Gwen exclaimed. 'You must be joking!'

'It could be that he is, under that confident exterior,' Charlotte went on. 'People have strange ways of hiding their shortcomings. Anyway, stop worrying about it. You look so pretty tonight.'

'That's right, Miss Charlotte,' Tilly chimed in. 'Keep your pecker up!'

After dinner, the men repaired to the billiard-room, and the ladies sifted through the gramophone records. Gwen wanted to dance, and Julian, declaring that he had no desire to knock little balls into mesh pockets, said he would teach her the new ragtime steps. He had brought along a couple of recordings of his own, and soon the music-room resounded with syncopated rhythms. Even Cynthia could not keep still, her foot tapping in its elegant satin shoe, so Julian danced with her, too.

Eva listened and watched, not certain that she approved of the steps which were based on American negro dances, wishing they could listen to something more soothing, or even more seasonal; carols perhaps. She could play the piano well enough for this, and it would be pleasant if they gathered round and launched into *Silent Night* or *While Shepherds Watched.* But no, hot from dancing, Cynthia had collapsed on the couch, Gwen was monopolising Julian, and Charlotte had wandered into the games-room, anxious to take part in the play.

Beth was already there, giving Dudley moral support and, before she entered, Charlotte lingered in the doorway for a second, seeing in the golden glow of oil-lamps hanging above the smooth green baize of the table, Dudley stretching across the table for a difficult shot. Richard stood on the opposite side, balancing his cue like a rapier. He saw her and fixed her with a long look which she could not meet.

She lost interest in partnering the limping Archie, and turned back to the music-room, but met Julian in the corridor. It was the first time they had been alone together since Italy, and she wondered how he had managed to escape Gwen. She was cross with him, wishing he'd stop playing games with her friend. Either he wanted her or he didn't. It was not fair to keep her dangling. She had other causes for anger, though hardly dared voice them, but at the very moment when she had made up her mind to say nothing, she heard herself remark casually, 'Ah, there you are Julian. There's something which has been puzzling me. Where did you and Phelan go that night shortly before the wedding-day?'

'What?' He looked away, pretending not to recall the incident. 'When d'you mean?'

'I saw you both leaving the villa in his car, and it was after midnight.'

'Oh, that.' He tried to brush it off, smiling charmingly. 'I don't think it matters any more, does it? Let's go and dance.'

Charlotte refused to be side-tracked, the lamplight shining down on her determined face. 'Did you go to a brothel?'

His fair brows winged down, and his lips curved in satirical amusement. 'Tut, my dear Miss Charlotte, what a thing to suggest! I'm shocked to find that you know anything about such dens of iniquity.'

'Then where?' she insisted.

'We went to see some friends.' He was supple as an eel, adept at wriggling skilfully out of awkward situations.

'Do I know them?'

'No.'

He's an odd young man, she thought with sudden conviction. Not all that he seems, not deep down, under that witty surface. She was alarmed to realise that she was within an ace of telling him exactly what she thought of him. He brought Florence to Greyfriars and she was remembering too much for comfort. Phelan, Andrew and Julian, close as conspirators. There were many riddles concerning Phelan, dark twists and turns, excuses and half truths, but there was one question she had to ask.

'Has Phelan forgotten me?'

'How could he? He loves you,' he replied in that studied, sympathetic way which made him so popular with ladies of all ages.

'Tell me the truth, Julian. Has he forgotten me?' she repeated, fingers clenched around the tortoise-shell sticks of her fan.

His eyes were those of a faun, green behind thick, golden lashes, and his lips smiled faintly. 'Rather not! Phelan never lets go of anything that has been his.'

Chapter 15

With the help of Barnaby, Bill Coles, and a large slice of that essential ingredient – luck, Jennie had managed to secure an audition with George Edwardes. Early on a clear, fresh morning, she caught the tram from Brompton Road where she and Zena had rooms, and journeyed to Leicester Square and the Gaiety Theatre.

The woman who owned the boarding-house was one of that remarkable breed without whom stage-folk could hardly survive – the theatrical landlady. Tough, strident, vain and enormously kind, she had Titian hair that owed its colour to henna powder, and a statuesque figure, while her legs had been her fortune in the days when she played Principal Boy in pantomime. Sometimes she could be persuaded to don one of her costumes and display those shapely limbs in tights. Strutting around her parlour and slapping her thigh, she would declaim in that hearty manner reserved for actresses who aped swaggering lads at Christmas time – Prince Charming in *Cinderella*, the lead in *Jack the Giant Killer*, *Aladdin* in the show of that name. In her heyday she had been known as Gloria Robins; now she was Mrs Queensby, widow.

'Go for it, ducks,' she had encouraged, getting up at daybreak to make sure that Jennie kept her appointment. 'Don't be nervous – well, you will be of course, all good troupers suffer from nerves. Bless me, I was always running to the bog before I went on stage. Better than half a pound of senna-pods. You'll do fine, I just know it. Here, take this, it's a lucky charm. Never fails.' And she had placed a rabbit's foot in Jennie's hand.

'I'm scared stiff, Mrs Queensby. Will Mr Edwardes like me?' Jennie had been shaking so hard that she slopped her tea into the saucer, not with cold, for spring was just around the corner, but with fright.

'Oh, the Guv'nor's all right. His bark's worse than his bite,' Gloria had said, hurrying Jennie to the front door. 'Off you go. Don't want to be late or that *will* put his dander up.'

'Mr George Edwardes will see Miss Genevra Adele at nine-thirty a.m. April 2nd. Please come to the stage-door of the new Gaiety Theatre in the Strand.' Jennie had this precious document tucked into her handbag, alongside the rabbit's foot. It had come three days before, in reply to her letter.

Her name looked imposing, written down. Though once she had dreamed of being Jennie Blossom, now she was afraid of anyone from her past recognising her – Richard, perhaps, though she wouldn't have minded seeing him again, Albert or Everett or Frank Dobbs. She had managed to convince herself that she would be anonymous under a different title, with the added protection of stage make-up and costumes.

She was in a peculiar state, terrified of the ordeal ahead, but confident in the outcome. Zena had read a Tarot spread for her only last night and there had been a preponderance of Major Arcana, foretelling success. Even without this encouragement, she somehow knew that the Guv'nor would like her. Bill had been spending the winter in an apartment in Orchard Street, where his big, echoing front room was stripped of furniture, except for a row of hard chairs against one wall, and a massive mirror. There he held dancing classes daily, and Jennie had been a conscientious student. Also, one of Mrs Queensby's tenants was a retired opera singer, and Jennie had spent hours with her, practising scales and voice technique. Zena had provided Jennie with money, saying in her astute Romany way that she could pay her back later, with interest.

This is it, she said to herself, and pushed open the red-painted door. The first person she saw was a man with a sweep of dark hair, an olive, pockmarked skin and a military moustache, who stared at her with beady, pouched eyes.

''Morning, Miss,' he said, stepping from a cubby-hole that acted as his office, reminding her of a guard in a sentry-box. 'Are you expected? Can I have your name, please?' He was carrying a clip-board, and held a pencil between tobacco-stained fingers.

Jennie switched on her most ravishing smile, confident that she looked her best, her dress stylish without being tarty, her little fur jacket expensive but borrowed, her hat a confection of grey tulle and pink roses. She handed over her letter from the management. He read it, checked her name against those on his list and added a tick.

'I'm Jupp, Miss Adele, the stagedoor keeper. We have to be careful, you see. Lots of unauthorised people try to get past me, but they don't succeed.' His manner was brusque but not unkind, and she took to him at once. 'I'll show you the way, Miss. Mind you don't fall over that dress-basket there. I wish they wouldn't leave them cluttering up my corridor.'

The inside of the theatre looked unglamorous in the cold light of day. Jennie didn't think it lived up to its name at that early hour. It wasn't gay at all, but quite dull without its night-time sparkle. She had visited it as a patron, sitting with Zena in the upper circle, completely entranced, returning home when the show was over more determined than ever to become a Gaiety Girl.

Now charwomen were sweeping the aisles, and there was a sound of hammering, humping and swearing from the scene-shifters, but Jennie felt a tingle of excitement as her nose responded to the mixture of odours which, from then on, typified the theatre for her. The atmosphere was damp and chilly, probably because the auditorium was always in partial darkness, and borne on it was the stale smell that a crowd leaves behind, a conglomeration of used cigars, perfume and sweat. There was the acrid taint of size from the scenery, and above all, an undeniable hint of grease-paint. With her first sniff of this potent brew, Jennie became an incurable victim of stage-fever.

She stepped out from the wings with Jupp leading. In the orchestral pit below, a young man wearing horn-rimmed spectacles was tinkling on the piano. Jupp walked straight up to the doused footlights and shouted into the auditorium.

'Mr Edwardes? There's a young lady to see you, sir. A Miss Genevra Adele.'

There were several people seated at the back of the stalls, and one of them, a thick-set man wearing a frock coat and with a silk hat crammed firmly on his head, answered him in a voice which though clear, was softened by a faint Irish accent.

'Thank you, Jupp. Back to your post now.' He left his seat and came down to the front, where he took off his hat and stared up at Jennie. She was struck dumb to be in the presence of this giant of the theatre of whom she had heard so much.

Bill and Mrs Queensby had said he was a tyrant, a stickler for detail, settling for nothing less than perfection both in artistes and production, and he knew every trick in the book. Everyone respected him: players, carpenters, property men, and electricians. He had his cohort of lieutenants, and they were in charge in many areas, but it was the Guv'nor who had the final word on everything connected with *his* theatre.

Jennie had often pictured how he might look, dreaming of someone at least six foot four and handsome, as commanding as a general. In reality he was of medium height, inclined to stoutness, with a round face, a thick moustache above cushiony lips, light brown hair parted in the middle, beginning to grey above the ears, and perceptive ice-blue eyes under level brows. He regarded her for a full minute without speaking, then said in his curious, sleepy, somewhat fretful voice, 'Good morning, Miss Adele, and what are you going to sing for me?'

Jennie, Bill and Madame Pontelli had deliberated on her choice for a considerable time, discarding first one song after another. Of course, it had to be something from one of the Gaiety productions, this went without saying, and at last they had made their final selection.

She succeeded in keeping her voice modulated and steady as she replied, 'It's from *A Country Girl*, Mr Edwardes.'

A pleased smile warmed his face, making her sharply aware of why his people adored him so. 'Lionel Monckton's music. A wonderful show, and we still perform it here. Which song are you going to sing?'

'*Under the Deodar*.'

He turned to the pianist and gave him his orders. There was a slight pause while the young man thumbed through the heap of music on top of the piano, then he started to play the introduction. At a signal from the Guv'nor, the stage was flooded with light and the floats at Jennie's feet sprang into being. Momentarily blinded, she did not waver, keeping her eyes fixed on the dark mass of the auditorium and remembering everything Madam Pontelli had told her. She was *there*. This was the Gaiety, the here and now – and she started to sing.

Under the Deodar,
Lit by an evening star.
There I will rest,
Close to your breast,
Under the Deodar.

There was more, verse and chorus, but before she knew it, the ordeal was over. She had done her best. It was now in the lap of the gods. To her astonishment, there came a faint ripple of applause from the black area beyond the lights. The Guv'nor's lieutenants approved of her.

'Very nice, Miss Adele,' said Edwardes. 'I'd like to see you dance.'

The pianist struck up again, and Jennie took off her hat and jacket and went into a routine Bill had taught her. It was based on ballet movements, and she had deliberately chosen a full, drifting chiffon skirt in demure Quaker grey when she dressed that morning. It floated around her limbs, transforming her into a sylph with lovely arms and swanlike neck.

Later she went with Edwardes and his aides to the office in an apartment he had at his old theatre, Daly's, which was almost next door. He did not speak until they were inside, then he turned to his right-hand man.

'I think we've made a discovery, Malone. Get a contract ready.'

'Right, Guv'nor.' Malone smiled at Jennie. He was everything that she had imagined Edwardes would be. Like him, he was Irish, but whereas Edwardes was short and homely, Malone was tall and good-looking.

The office was a fine place, designed to the Guv'nor's specifications and used as his headquarters. He had moved from Daly's in 1903, but retained his suite in the older building. It was the hubb, the core, the heart of the Gaiety where every decision was made, each libretto and score discussed in depth, each set considered and approved. Emilie Reed, the secretary, took a contract from the desk.

'Sit down, my dear.' Edwardes waved Jennie into a chair, for courtesy was his cardinal rule. 'I like the name Genevra Adele. Is it your own?'

'Yes, sir,' she lied.

'And how old are you?'

'Eighteen last birthday, sir.' This, too, was a lie, for she had reached sixteen in October, but had been told that he would not take on anyone so young. She sweated a little when she thought of his reaction if he knew she had an illegitimate baby.

'Fine. Have you got all that down, Emilie?'

'Yes, sir.'

Edwardes pulled a serious face as his eyes scanned her, stubby fingers beating a light tattoo on the arm of his chair. 'I demand very high standards, Miss Adele. You already move gracefully and seem to have a good idea of dress, but my Gaiety Girls are superior to everyone else. They set the fashion. The young men may come to our shows to look at the girls, but the women come to see what they're wearing. D'you understand?'

'Yes, sir. I think so, sir.'

'You'd better be sure you do before you sign that contract. You'll behave like a lady at all times: in rehearsal, on stage and off. My girls never wear tights on stage or show their legs. I believe in the allure of skirts and frilly petticoats foaming around the ankles. Then if, on one or two occasions during the performace, they do show a bit of leg the effect is electric – on the male members of the audience at least. Expectation and anticipation are things of value in the theatre. We don't disclose our secrets lavishly – just a peep to whet the appetite. D'you get my drift?'

'Yes, sir.'

'Where are you living?'

'In Brompton Road, at Mrs Queensby's boarding-house.'

'Is it respectable?'

'Oh, very. She's a retired actress herself, and I'm staying there with a female companion.'

'Do you go out much? Are you courting? I don't intend to waste time on you if you're going to suddenly up and get married.'

'No, sir. I don't go out and haven't a young man. I study singing and dancing most of the time.'

'You're determined to get on, it seems. I like that. Dedication and hard work, that's the key-note of success. You said in your letter that you'd already had some experience. Would you care to elaborate?'

Jennie had her story all ready. She told him that she had been performing with a pierrot troupe during the summer. This seemed to satisfy him, and he clapped on his hat and left, after telling Malone to sign her up.

She scarcely bothered to read the contract, too excited to make sense of the closely printed document. All she could see was the salary offered – two pounds a week! This was a fabulously large sum, for shop-girls only earned ten shillings and maidservants were paid four pounds yearly, with board and lodgings thrown in. She would be part of the chorus to start with, and burned with ambition to rise speedily from that humble situation, having heard that the stars were given the princely sum of fifteen pounds. I'll do it! she vowed as she scrawled her name and shook hands with Malone who told her to attend her first rehearsal at nine the following morning. I'll be getting that, and more, before the year is out.

On her first free weekend she took the train to the station near Pitney, and finally arrived at Gaulden Court. She had been there several times during the winter, missing Grace dreadfully and anxious that the child should not forget her. Joan met her at the kitchen door, a print apron round her waist.

'We got your letter,' she said, drawing Jennie into the warmth of that large, cluttered room.' Congratulations! A Gaiety Girl! Well, I never.'

The Squire was seated at the table, bouncing Grace on his knee. Jennie made straight for her, and the baby held out her chubby arms. In an instant Jennie had swept her up, laughing and exclaiming, almost crying, hugging her close while Grace gurgled with pleasure. She was ten months old, and bonny. The picture of health, the darling of both the gypsies and the Garnets alike, with her flaxen hair, dimples and large blue-grey eyes.

'I'm glad you came just now,' Joan said, brandishing a wooden spoon and stirring one of the several pots simmering on the fire. 'Orlanda was getting worried. She wants to be on the road. The tribe delayed till March because of the baby, then I told her that I'd have her for you.'

'Oh, thank you. I knew this was going to happen and have been wondering what to do.'

Jennie shrugged off her coat, balancing Grace on her hip. The baby wriggled and wanted to get down, so she sat her on the floor. She rolled on to her knees and crawled towards the backdoor. Joan plodded across and closed it. 'No, you don't, young lady. Honestly, we can't keep her in now she's found she can move about. Off like a streak of lightning as soon as my back's turned. Found her sitting in a great big puddle in the yard the other day, splashing about, happy as could be. The imp!' And she gave Grace a bag of clothes pegs to play with.

Jennie sat back with a contented sigh. Gaulden Court had come to mean home for her, because her baby was there, because Joan and Tom Garnet were like the parents she had never known. It was lovely to return for brief spells, though it would quickly bore her to death full-time.

She was thrilled to be working, even though it was harder than she had ever dreamed possible. Malone, despite his attractive appearance, was a severe taskmaster; he could drive, he could bully, he could abuse, and he often did. As for the Guv'nor, he was present at each rehearsal and every performance, his hawk eye missing nothing, and he had certainly noticed Jennie, promoting her after a month to the part of a maid in his latest musical. A small part it was true, but she had a song, and her dancing had whipped the house into uncontrollable enthusiasm.

Bill, her sternest critic, said that she looked like a piece of thistledown floating in a sunbeam. It was as if her feet did not touch the stage. She was grace, she was allure, she was the spirit of the Gaiety incarnate. Praise indeed from her fussy old maestro! When she kicked, her foot went above her head without any visible effort, and that kick knocked 'em for six. They screamed for more.

Never had anyone so new to the profession so quickly danced into prominence.

Young men-about-town had begun to hang around the stage-door, top-hatted, evening-suited, carrying bouquets, bribing Jupp to deliver them to her dressing-room with supper invitations. She had not accepted any of them – yet. Far more important was the rise in wages; not star-money, but she was pointing in the right direction. She needed money as never before: money for clothes to make an impression, one of the major factors in being a Gaiety Girl; money to move to a more fashionable area; money to support Grace.

The Squire cleared his throat and scuffed the flag-stones with his riding boots. 'Joan and me wanted to talk to you about the baby,' he began and, as he saw the doting manner in which she was watching her child grubbing about among the pegs, he knew that she would not agree to his proposal, but he put it to her anyway. 'We're very fond of her, Jennie. Can't have children of our own, as I've already told you. I don't suppose you'd consider letting us adopt her, would you?'

Jennie's amber eyes switched to his, flashing with anger and fear. Instinctively she reached a hand towards Grace. 'Oh, no – I couldn't do that! She means so much to me.'

Even as she spoke, she realised that without Grace her work would amount to less than nothing. At one time she wanted success for herself, to satisfy her own ego, but now she had someone more important for whom to strive. She intended to be rich enough to rear her in the best possible way. Grace should be sent to the finest schools, polished and groomed, eventually marrying a title.

'Of course, we'd never insist,' the Squire said with wise understanding. 'And it doesn't make a bit of difference. She's welcome to remain with us for as long as you want. But there's something else which I hope you won't deny me.'

'What is it?' Jennie asked cautiously, sinking down beside Grace, who promptly grabbed at her glass bead necklace and started to haul herself up on unsteady fat legs.

'I'm worried about the fate of the Chikno tribe.' He puffed at his pipe, his ruddy face, scribbled all over with wrinkles, unusually serious. 'They've always wintered here, but I'm keen to make arrangements so that they'll be able to do so for generations to come, long after Joan and I are gone.'

His wife came over to lay a broad hand on his shoulder, entering into the conversation. 'We could leave Gaulden Court to my sons, but they're greedy farmers who'll turn the gypsies out of Beeches Woods. Tom and me wouldn't rest easy in our graves if that happened.'

'So how can I help?' Jennie managed to prevent her necklace from being wrecked, joggling Grace in her arms.

'We'd like to will the place to her, if you agree,' the Squire replied, nodding his head in the baby's direction.

Jennie was flabbergasted. 'You would? Are you sure? You don't know me, where I came from, what I've done, how I had her!'

Joan gently touched Grace's curls. 'It doesn't matter. We don't care. We want her to inherit this place we love so much, and it'll be your home, too, as long as you'll promise to see that the gypsies come here for ever and ever.'

Charlotte had agreed to attend a performance at the Royal Opera House, Covent Garden. She was to go with Eva, Richard and Archie. He had purchased tickets, begging them to come with him to help celebrate his birthday.

'Opera wasn't my cup of tea, till I heard your records,' he had confided in Charlotte. 'But now I'd like to give it a whirl. Do come. We'll have supper at Frascati's afterwards. I'll book a table.'

Charlotte was reluctant, remembering the times she had been to the opera with Phelan, but had felt better about him since Christmas, reassured because he had made no attempt to contact her. Though Julian's remarks about him never letting go had worried her for a while, week had followed week and there had been no sign of him. Perhaps he had gone back to Europe. Gwen, her information coming via Julian with whom she was still very thick, had said this wasn't so, but for whatever reason, he had left Charlotte strictly alone.

'Let's dress up and make it an occasion for Archie's sake,' Eva had suggested. 'I love Puccini's operas, though they are usually so sad, and his latest work, *Madame Butterfly*, hasn't been performed in England before. The cast is a strong one, including Enrico Caruso and Antonio Scotti.'

So, on a hot evening in July, Charlotte put on a gown of salmon pink Surah silk, and Eva appeared in a dramatic sheath of purple chiffon, richly encrusted with gold beads. Their escorts arrived, complete with opera cloaks, silk hats and white scarves, and Wilkins drove them to the theatre.

It was a glittering occasion, the first time the story of the little Japanese geisha and her handsome, feckless American naval officer was to enchant English audiences. Though those who could afford no other seats than the gallery benches had queued at the side door, enduring hours of blazing sunshine for the privilege of indulging their passion and hearing the great Caruso sing; the rich and noble alighted from limousines and carriages at the ornate entrance. The

Romanesque pillars and pediment were brightly illuminated, and footmen in powdered wigs and blue and gold livery were in attendance. Archie's party strolled into the foyer, with its red carpet and gilded friezes, and from thence, by dint of shallow Wilton-covered stairs, to the dress-circle.

On every side Charlotte saw ladies in sparkling jewels, silks and satins, and men in stiff white collars and formal black suits. The conversation buzzed as lorgnettes were raised so that fellow members of the audience could be quizzed. She glanced at the programme, and then leaned her white-gloved elbows on the brass-railed edge of the balcony, her eyes on the massive scarlet velvet curtain that draped the proscenium and the musicians gathering in the orchestra-pit.

They, too, wore evening dress as they adjusted their stands that had reading lights fixed to them, rubbing resin on violin bows, performing practice trills on woodwind, or blowing subdued chords on French horns. Timpani resonated as the drummer tuned up for the umpteenth time.

These sounds added to the anticipation rippling through the auditorium. The performance was about to start. Applause thundered out as the conductor entered and took his place on the rostrum. He turned, bowed in acknowledgement and, after adjusting his shirt-cuffs, faced the stage and raised his baton as the house-lights dimmed.

Music flooded the theatre: swift, airy music with a strangely exotic flavour conveying the quaint, fussy, doll-like world into which the hero of the drama was about to marry. The curtain lifted slowly to reveal the unusual setting of a Japanese house with paper walls. The audience clapped again as Caruso made his entrance, portly but dashing in tropical 'whites', attended by a rascally Oriental marriage-broker. Both men commenced singing, and the story started to unfold.

By the time the curtain came down on the first act, Charlotte was crying. The music of the love-scene between Butterfly and Pinkerton was so exquisite and so moving that it hurt. When the lights came up for the interval, she saw that Eva too, was fumbling in her evening bag for a handkerchief.

'You ladies! Love a good old weep, don't you?' exclaimed Archie, grinning at them.

'Didn't it make you want to cry?' Charlotte asked, a little embarrassed by her show of emotion.

'Not me. I'm made of sterner stuff,' he averred, rising so that she might precede him to the theatre bar.

'Philistine!' she chided. 'How could you not be moved to tears?'

'I was, and I don't give a damn who knows it,' Richard said, while Eva took his arm as they weaved through the crowd towards a spare table. 'Puccini's a master craftsman. I rate him above Verdi for dramatic musical effects, second only to Wagner.'

'I wish they'd sing in English,' Archie complained, pulling out chairs so that the ladies might be seated. 'Can't understand a confounded word.'

'You're just a heathen. I suppose you'd prefer one of those musical comedies at the Gaiety.' Charlotte was struggling to compose herself but her ears still vibrated with glorious remembered sounds, her eye still saw the diminutive figure of the trusting, childish Butterfly, placing her love, her life, her very soul in Pinkerton's careless hands.

That love was doomed, as she knew by reading the programme notes, and this very knowledge made it all the more poignant. Butterfly would be abandoned by her American husband, though she would never believe him capable of such baseness, loyal to the end, when the truth is finally forced upon her and she commits *hara-kiri*.

Richard and Archie went off to fetch refreshments, and while they were gone, Charlotte excused herself and sought the ladies room. It was on the way back that, her head full of the on-stage drama, she almost bumped into someone barring her way. Looking up, she saw Phelan staring at her with dark, penetrating eyes.

Shock jangled her to the very bones. She was trapped in an angle of the passage, out of sight of anyone, every avenue of escape blocked by his powerful body. Her skin crawled as she caught the odour of musky perfume that always meant Phelan to her. His saturnine face was illuminated by the single frosted glass globe above their heads. It was not fair that one man could be so handsome, and so wicked.

'I knew you'd be here tonight.' He spoke in a low, restrained voice.

How did he know? Who had told him? Then she recalled mentioning it to Gwen. She must have said something to Julian. He was a regular visitor at the vicarage these days. Charlotte shook as Phelan watched her intently, as a cat will watch a fluttering, injured bird. She had to speak, but what could they possibly have to say to one another? There was so much. Too much to make any communication simple. All the angry accusations she had longed to fling at him trembled on her tongue, but she finally blurted out, 'Let me pass. I've no wish to talk to you.'

His expression flickered and changed. He smiled, but his eyes were deadly. 'But you must, my dear. I need an explanation.

Why did you run away? You put us to a great deal of trouble.'

'How dare you?' Fear was replaced by fury.

'I dare because you were promised to me.' He looked harder, bigger, more menacing than at any time she could remember. 'We were about to be married. A few hours, and you would have been my wife. You can't just turn away, try to pretend that it never happened. You are mine. You belong to me. Have you forgotten that you were my mistress? I took your virginity, Charlotte. I branded you with my seal. You can't escape or dismiss it.'

'I wish to God that I could!' she hissed, and tried to push past him, but his hand closed on her arm, the touch turning to steel as she struggled. 'You ask me why I left? You were in the palace with Angelica and Michele. In bed with her, while her brother was watching. You're perverted! Disgusting! You were unfaithful to me. You lied to me. Told me that you loved me. You're vile! I hate you!'

'I do love you.'

'Love? You don't know the meaning of the word.'

'Don't I?' His grip intensified. 'Didn't I teach you what love meant – afternoons at the palace, nights in Venice? You must remember, must long to repeat them. You can, Charlotte – oh, yes, you can – I'm here now, and I still want you.'

The bell for Act Two started to ring imperiously, summoning the audience back to their seats. Charlotte moved, catching him off guard, and speeding down the passageway. She collided with Richard who had been sent by Eva to look for her. Phelan was close behind, pursuing her relentlessly, but he stopped dead when he saw Richard.

'Hurry, Charlotte, or we'll miss the start of the act.' Richard's blue eyes met Phelan's black ones, and the look that flashed between them was charged with masculine aggression.

'Richard,' she panted, hand on his sleeve. 'Oh, thank God!'

He frowned. 'What's going on? Is this fellow annoying you, Charlotte?' And he put her aside, addressing himself to Phelan. 'Who are you, sir?'

Phelan stared at him cooly. 'I'm Phelan Charteris, and Charlotte was my fiancée.'

'*Was* being the operative word, I suggest that you make yourself scarce.' Richard's jaw jutted belligerently.

Phelan ignored him, saying to Charlotte, 'This isn't the end, by any means. We must meet, and talk over old times, eh?'

The bell was still ringing, people leaving their drinks and hurrying to the auditorium. With an arm firmly around Charlotte's shoulders, Richard marched her away. She looked back once. Phelan was watching them go, his face dangerously impassive.

Eva was alarmed when she saw Charlotte's ashen cheeks. There was no time for anything but a very garbled explanation, then they were in their seats and Act Two began. Eva tried to concentrate on it, but the magic had gone. All she could see was Richard storming across the theatre bar with his arm round Charlotte. Phelan here? And what did that mean? More important even than this was the warning note that had clanged in her brain at the sight of her lover and her ward. Richard had been so furious and indignant. It was pointless telling herself that he was merely being considerate, as she had once prayed he would be, looking upon Charlotte as his responsibility too now that he was engaged to be married.

Since Christmas, Richard and Charlotte's attitude towards one another had changed. Eva had known it when she saw them having that snowball fight, and had begun to watch them covertly, despising herself for doing so but unable to help it. The only time she felt really secure was when she lay in Richard's arms, and this had always been so, long before Charlotte came home.

She had been distressed when they hated each other, and now part of her was glad they were friends. But that other bleak corner of her psyche which had always been empty since childhood, needed desperately to be filled – by her charities, by other people relying on her, and above all by Richard. Anything which threatened this caused her deep anguish. She was even jealous of his work, resentful if it drew his attention away from her.

The opera was drawing to its tragic conclusion, the sweep of the music dragging her into it, in spite of her other preoccupation. It spoke so clearly of unrequited love and betrayal, and she responded to it, every nerve quivering, pain like an open wound inside her, tears rising in her eyes. She gripped Richard's hand, felt the returning pressure of his fingers, was ashamed of her jealousy. Consequently, she was more loving than ever to Charlotte when they were in the restaurant later.

Frascati's was not quite so smart as Romano's or Verrey's, but the orchestra was good, there were bright lights, good food, good service, and good drinks. Many foreigners frequented it, for it had a dashing Parisian atmosphere, and served superb coffee, blended especially to order by a hawk-faced individual wearing full Turkish regalia.

Archie's table was one of those around the fringes of the great central floor. Eva encouraged Charlotte to sit on Richard's other side, deliberately turning her shoulder and entering into an animated discussion with Archie so that the two of them could talk.

And talk they did. Richard wanted to know everything that had taken place between Charlotte and Phelan, and she told him a great deal. He had already heard an outline, both from her and Eva, but this was the first time she had gone into details.

'He's a cad,' Richard said, under cover of the general noise of diners and the band playing light melodies. 'You were right to do a bunk. Living with him would have been intolerable.'

He was thinking of Everett Braithwaite and his diabolical treatment of Jennie. He had not dwelt on her for some time, apart from the occasional flash of concern, but now she was foremost in his mind. It was absurd, for they were as different as chalk from cheese, but there was something about Charlotte – a lift of the chin, a gesture, maybe her profile – that reminded him of that common, spunky East End brat.

'You don't think I was being silly? Many wives accept their husbands' indiscretions. It's quite the thing, isn't it, for men to have numerous affairs?' Charlotte was looking at him earnestly, and he thought how pretty she was. Salmon pink suited her, bringing out auburn glints in her dark hair, and her necklace and earrings of pendant pearls took on an extra lustre, nestling against her skin.

He sat back in his chair, brandy glass between his strong, artistic hands, considering her over the rim as he inhaled the bouquet. 'That wouldn't do for you, would it? Did you enjoy being Phelan's mistress? I think not. As far as I can ascertain he looks upon love-making as a bodily recreation, far removed from spiritual communication and commitment.'

How odd to be speaking of such personal matters in a crowded restaurant, she thought. He understands so much. How could I have been so foolish as to hate him? Eva must be the luckiest woman alive to have such a man in love with her. I can talk to him, *really* talk. There's nothing I can say which will shock him. And he's handsome, so very handsome.

'I learned a lot from Phelan,' she said, lowering her lashes and staring at her silken lap where her hands lay locked together. 'But it never seemed right, somehow. I detached myself at intimate moments, shut myself down. I was disappointed because his attitude was just as you've described it. I tried to please him, but I wasn't pleasing myself. I wanted to be with my heart, but couldn't. I felt that when we made love it should have been a meeting of twin souls as well as the fulfilling of sexual desires, but it never was. There was nothing there to affirm my spirit, no higher level of feeling.'

'You express yourself well,' he commented, placing his glass on the table and leaning closer.

'Do I?' She was flustered, her cheeks taking on a deeper rose. 'I've thought a great deal about it, but never put it into words before.'

'I feel the same as you do. I've had casual relationships, I'll admit, and enjoyed them for what they were. There's been at least one where I did care and was committed in a way, though not totally. but the lady didn't want to know.' Jennie, he was thinking, Jennie, where are you? Is Grace well and healthy? You silly girl. Why don't you get in touch with me?

'And then you met Eva.'

'Yes, then I met Eva.'

He withdrew a little, looking past her to where Archie and Eva were laughing. She sat with a glass in one hand, her head tipped back, filled with amusement at something the young man had just said. His lovely, generous Eva, the woman who was his present and his future. Charlotte seemed very young and inexperienced compared with her. Eva was wise and deep, her love for him like a rolling sea; and, like the sea, it could be overwhelming at times. I'm not good enough for her, he thought, and was aware that he was often thinking this. Maybe late at night in his studio when he was expecting her to arrive and really wanted to carry on working. Unworthy thoughts, and as soon as she stepped through the door he forgot them, borne along by the inflexible tide of her demanding love.

'Good lord! Look what the wind's blown in!' Archie said suddenly.

The others followed his eyes, and saw a waiter ushering Phelan to a table not far from theirs. Charlotte turned pale, and Richard's hand closed on hers. Archie was wildly indignant, having heard enough about him to have worked up a furious hatred of the man. Phelan saw them and, before he sat down, gave a slight inclination of his head. He was not alone. His companion was a comely, well-developed young woman in a low-cut gown, huge cart-wheel hat and feather boa.

'Isn't that "The Girl in the Muff"?' Charlotte answered, trying to make light of it to still her agitation. 'She's the star of the Ba-Tan-Clan Revue. I've seen posters of her wearing a muff and little else, and I've heard people who've been there say that the posters are justified. The muff is *all* she wears in the show.'

'Never mind about her!' Archie declared, flushing as he glared at Phelan, fists bunched in the way he had learned in boxing-classes at public school. 'The damned fellow's following us! First Covent Garden, and now here. What's his confounded game? D'you want me to thump him, Charlotte?'

'No. Leave it, Archie.' She cast an imploring look at him. 'D'you mind if I go? Sorry, Archie, to spoil your birthday and you've given us a lovely treat, but I can't stay here with him in the room.'

'Of course you can't.' Archie was disappointed but too much of a gentleman to object. 'I'll get a cab and take you home, shall I? Eva and Richard can hang on a bit, if they want.'

The Eva said something so foolhardy that she could hardly believe she was speaking. 'Why don't you and I stay, Archie? It is your birthday after all, and I'm sure you don't relish an early night. Richard will take Charlotte home, won't you, Richard? You can always come back later.'

She was testing him, hoping that he would insist on remaining, but he did not. Instead he got to his feet, told a waiter to order a cab, and held Charlotte's wrap for her. Then he stood for a moment looking down at Eva, his hat in his hand, his cloak open, his white waistcoat gleaming.

'Are you sure you'll be all right, my dear?' he asked, cocking an eye at Phelan. 'Don't have any truck with him, will you? I'll be back in a trice.'

'Don't worry.' She smiled at him bravely, and stamped her fears under heel, though they wriggled persistently. 'Archie will take care of me. See you shortly.'

He bent over and brushed her lips with his. Charlotte kissed her, too, and smiled vaguely at Archie, then Richard whisked her out of the restaurant and into a hansom. My God, but he accepted that with alacrity, Eva thought, trying to concentrate on what Archie was saying. The words were hardly out of my mouth, and he had leapt at the idea. Jealousy gnawed her like serpents, and she struggled to smile and reply, to be jovial and good company, encouraging Archie and letting him know that she approved of him as a suitor for her ward. He was a perfect candidate, but in that direful moment she would have accepted Old Nick himself to ensure the girl was spoken for and out of Richard's reach.

Phelan appeared to be totally at ease with his laughing companion. Champagne corks popped and fizzed, and her wide red mouth munched caviare and foie gras, while he smiled his sardonic smile, and slipped an arm around her, his lips pressed close to the curls over her ear as he whispered in it, eyeing Eva the while to make certain that she missed nothing. Archie ordered more coffee and brandy, but the time dragged. Eva tried not to look at her watch too often or too obviously. Where was Richard?

It wasn't far to Albion House. He should have returned before this.

I want him here, with me! she stormed angrily inside herself. Damn Charlotte, and damn Phelan! Richard, Richard, come back. In vain she repeated that he would come. Soon this torture would be over and they would be together at the studio, with him beside her in his wide bed, Charlotte of no consequence, forgotten in the heat of their passion. Meanwhile she was suffering the torments of the damned, her imagination, both her blessing and her curse, presenting lurid pictures of what he and Charlotte might be doing.

The girl was no longer a virgin. She had tasted desire, knew what a man required and what her own flesh needed. They had been so close at supper, ignoring her and Archie. Eva conveniently forgot that she had deliberately engineered this, trying to confound her own jealous feelings, conscience-stricken and guilty because she trusted neither of them, and yet had no cause to doubt their sincerity.

The after-theatre crowd was thick in Frascati's. The band was playing and waltzers revolved on the floor; moustached men, in tails and white waistcoats; ladies in the full array of flowing skirts and trains, hitched up to their little fingers by loops so that they might dance, jewels gleamed in their hair.

'Would you like to waltz?' Archie asked politely, though he was missing Charlotte.

'I think I'll sit this one out,' Eva said, nervously waving her fan, eyes on the entrance. There were plenty of gentlemen coming in, but not the one she wanted. 'Maybe we should think about going home. It's getting rather late.'

Supposing she reached Albion House and Richard wasn't there? Supposing Charlotte wasn't either? What would she do? She imagined running up the stairs, looking in Charlotte's room and finding it empty. She'd change, of course, getting into something more suitable for action, but, on thinking it over, perhaps she wouldn't delay to do this. Then she'd take a cab to Holland Park. How awful it would be to enter his room where once she had been so happy and find them in bed together – '

'Ah, here's Richard!' Archie shouted, much relieved for Eva had been so fraught and edgy.

She came to herself, came to her senses, saw him elbowing his way towards her, and then his hands were holding hers, and she was smiling – what a fool she was to doubt him. He loved her. He was hers.

'Hello, darling,' she said.

Chapter 16

'Good night, Jupp,' Jennie shouted, as she headed towards the stage-door.

'Good night, Miss Adele.' Jupp stuck his head through the window of his cubby-hole, like a booking clerk at a railway station. 'Full house tonight,' he added, with evident satisfaction. 'You're pulling 'em in, Miss, and that's a fact.'

'It's the show, Jupp. *The Spring Chicken* is a winner.'

I wish I was playing the lead, she thought, but Gertie Miller's got the starring role, and quite rightly – she's superb. Never mind. I'm not doing badly for a beginner. She had to remind herself that she was on the second rung of the ladder, had only been a member of the Gaiety for half a year, but already the Guv'nor was talking of a major part in his next production.

Some of the girls had been met at the stage-door by dapper young gentlemen in full evening rig who had arranged to take them to supper at fashionable Romano's. The stars had their own carriages, and dressed very expensively. Nasty-minded people said they lived far beyond their means, hinting that it was rich admirers who provided the ropes of pearls that lay against their alabaster throats, the bracelets that flashed on their wrists, the luxurious furs that wrapped them in cold weather, the lavish apartments where they lived.

Jennie went home alone, back to Mrs Queensby and the boarding-house. She missed Zena a great deal, for she was visiting Spain, her destination Andalusia and her home-town of Granada where, in the Albaicin, hundreds of gypsies lived in caves burrowed into the face of the mountain. Though Jennie had formed tentative friendships with several of the chorus-girls, she kept to herself, afraid that if she became too involved with them she might let something slip concerning her past.

At the moment, she was quite content to watch others receiving the adulation of dashing blades from the upper echelon who booked seats in the stalls and boxes, night after night, to watch, admire, and woo their favourite dancers. Her turn would come. So, every evening when the curtain came down, she wiped off the grease-paint, changed into her outdoor clothes, left the theatre and took a tram bound for Brompton Road.

As she was about to go out of the door, a neatly dressed lad appeared from the gloom, doffing his peaked cap. 'Hello, Lou,' she said, while he stood there grinning in sheepish admiration. 'Come to walk me to the tram-stop?'

'Yes, Miss Adele,' he answered promptly. They had this little conversation every night.

He was a nice boy of around fourteen, and was one of a group of youngsters recruited into the chorus when the plot called for juveniles. He had taken to Jennie early on, and had become her cavalier, insisting that she should not wander the streets on her own. His devotion was disinterested and sweet, and she liked him. His name was Louis Field, and he came from a long line of musicians, telling her that he was learning the violin, and acting to supplement his pocket-money, encouraged by his father who was a harpist. Though he lived in Finsbury Park, Louis went out of his way to insure that she boarded her tram safely.

A dark haired, well-spoken boy, small and slim, his features had a slightly foreign cast, French maybe. He had soulful greenish-grey eyes shaded by curling black lashes, and would be a handsome man when he grew up. Jennie left the theatre with her arm linked through his, stepping out confidently. But they had hardly reached the edge of the pavement when a man suddenly blocked their path.

''ello, Jennie,' he said, and her heart skipped a beat, then raced on madly as she recognised Albert Baggot.

'What d'you want?' she demanded, going into the attack, and the street seemed to grow darker, the lamps dim, as she looked into his ugly face.

He gave a self-satisfied smirk. 'That's not a very nice way to greet me,' he scoffed. 'What's up, Jen? To 'oity-toity now you're a Gaiety Girl to have a chat with an old pal?'

'You're no pal of mine,' she announced and, head up, back stiff, she tried to walk past him.

Albert grabbed her arm. Louis, slight though he was, spoke up bravely. 'Oi! What's your game? Let go of the lady!'

Albert rounded on him, fist raised threateningly. 'You bloody little whippersnapper! Mind your own damn business! Go on! 'op it! Before I tan your 'ide!'

Jennie could see that Louis might get hurt, so she said, 'Off you go, Lou. I know him.'

'But, Miss – ' Louis was prepared to stand his ground.

'Go home, Lou,' she insisted. Whatever Albert wanted, there was no escaping him. It was a nightmare which she had known would become reality one day. 'I'll see you at rehearsal tomorrow.'

'Are you sure?'

'Yes.'

He left reluctantly, dragging his heels and looking back over his shoulder, still defiant. For two pins he would have whaled into Albert. As he rounded the corner and vanished from sight, Jennie felt terribly alone. So Albert had tracked her down. What scheme was fermenting in his cunning, animal brain now? she wondered.

'That's better, Jen – or should I say *Genevra*?' he mocked, refusing to relinquish his hold on her arm. 'Why don't we go and 'ave a drink?'

He gave her no alternative, frog-marching her towards the Café de L'Europe. She had never been there before, though had heard it talked about. It was not the kind of place the Guv'nor approved of as a venue for his girls. Through the doorway they went, and down some stairs to the German lager hall. Lager was not the only drink served there, but English beer as well – vast amounts of it. The atmosphere was smoky and noisy. A band was playing on a balcony midway up one wall, but it could hardly be heard above the din.

Albert found them seats on a wooden bench at a trestle table, while waiters hurried about carrying trays filled with foaming glasses. Albert orderd a pint for himself and half a pint for Jennie. She could see why George Edwardes forbade his artistes to patronise the café. The lower half of the underworld were gathered there, the women mostly prostitutes, the men consisting of their clients and pimps, touts and criminals. There was a dreadful racket going on, everyone talking, shouting, making love and quarrelling. Jennie prayed that no one would recognise her, sinking down in her seat, turning up her fur collar and trying to hide her face in it.

'Jesus Christ,' she muttered. 'Coming here with you will cost me my job if anyone sees me and reports back to the Guv'nor.'

Albert was at ease in these surroundings, tipping his bowler forward on his sandy head. 'We can't 'ave that, Jennie, now can we? You're doing very nicely, thank you, and this 'as got to continue.'

'Damn right it has,' she snarled, leaving her beer untouched.

'Oh, yes, indeed. I'll drink to that,' he nodded, and took a great slurp of lager.

Jennie's slanting amber eyes glared at him ferociously. She had not seen him for nearly two years and time had not improved his appearance or temperament. He was a little rat, would always be a little rat, devious, cunning, manipulative and amoral. She hated him, and cursed the day she had allowed him to persuade her to have anything to do with him. He can't be Grace's father, surely to God? she thought despairingly. But he could be. It was impossible to know for sure who had made her pregnant.

As if reading her thoughts, he edged closer and peered into her face. His breath was sour with alcohol and rotting teeth. 'How's the baby?'

Jennie went cold inside. 'What baby?'

He squeezed her thigh under the table, dropping an eyelid in a sly wink. 'Your baby, Jennie.'

'I don't know what you're talking about.' If looks could kill, he would have been the late Albert Baggot, dead at her feet.

'Don't you?'

'No, I don't.'

He rested his elbows on the wooden strut of the bench, a coarse figure in his suit of cheap cloth and even cheaper cut. His shirt collar was grubby, his cuffs frayed, and the watchchain looped across his yellow and red checked waistcoat was too flashy to be gold. He needed a shave, ginger stubble sprouting on his jaw.

He wagged a scolding finger at her. 'I think you're telling porky-pies. I saw Everett Braithwaite a while back and 'ee told me you'd attacked 'im outside the Café Royal, and that you was big-bellied, demanding that 'ee do something about it.'

Jennie would have like to see him hanged, but she managed a tight smile. 'It was a trick. I had a cushion stuffed up my skirt, but I was skint and trying to con him. You should know all about conning people.'

Some of the wind went out of Albert's sails. He sat up, glowering at her, half believing the lie. 'Is that so? Then I'll 'ave to play my ace, I suppose. Someway or another, I'm going to share in your fame and fortune, Jennie, my gal.'

'I'm not "your girl". Far from it.' She made to rise, but he detained her, pulling her back to her seat.

'Ain't you? We'll see about that. The Guv'nor's a strict old codger, ain't 'ee? Likes 'is girls to be bloody nuns. I could drop a few 'ints 'is way, maybe speak to Malone about you.'

'You seem very familiar with these people, or is it another of your tricks?' His grin, his air of false affability, made Jennie extremely apprehensive. He had something up his sleeve, of that she had no doubt, something which could destroy her if she didn't play the game his way.

'I've met 'em. Oh, yes, your Mr Edwardes likes the gee-gees, or didn't you know that? He's often at Kempton Park Races, putting 'is money on the nags. Loves the Turf as much as 'ee loves the theatre. A betting man if ever there was one, like all the Paddys. Malone likes a flutter, too, and I've often given 'em racing tips, so it wouldn't be 'ard for me to 'ave a private little talk with 'em, tip 'em off about your lovely self.'

Jennie never knew, thinking about it afterwards, how she stopped herself from slapping him across his leering face. Instead she remained outwardly unmoved, saying crisply, 'Tell me what you want. Spit it out and be done with it.'

The crowd were getting more obstreporous, horseplay giving way to earnest warfare. Drinks were being flung in enraged faces. The neck of a bottle was deliberately smashed, turning it into a murderous, jagged weapon. Women screamed and joined in the fray, using their hatpins, nails and fists, more vicious fighters than the men. Jennie could feel the drunken frenzy spreading towards her like an evil miasma. She should leave, *must* get out of there before the police arrived, as they assuredly would. One of the men was bleeding badly, and the landlord was attempting, unsuccessfully, to control the mêlée which was rapidly turning into a fullscale battle. The last thing Jennie needed was to be arrested along with the rest and wind up at Bow Street Police Station. Fat chance of becoming a Gaiety star if this happened!

Albert knew it, too, so he laid his cards on the table. 'I want money from you, a regular sum, and later, when you make it big, I want to be your manager.'

'Sod off!' Jennie succeeded in shaking herself free and standing up.

'Now, now, that's not the right attitude.' He spread his hands placatingly, one eye on the riot taking place around him. 'I don't want to 'urt you, Jennie, or stop you getting to the top. Far from it – the bigger you gets the better it'll be for me.'

'I'm not prepared to give you a penny-piece,' she declared firmly. 'There's no baby, so you can't hold that over me.'

'Maybe not, though I've got my doubts on that score, but there's something else I can use.' His eyes glinted, small and mean in his pallid, acne-pitted face.

'What?' Jennie had intended to end the conversation and make for the stairs, but he was still as a rattlesnake, watching her keenly.

‘Photographs,’ he said, and the single word brought instant recall: Frank Dobbs and his studio.

‘You wouldn’t dare!’ She stopped in her tracks.

‘I would. If you don’t do what I tells you, I’ll take those pictures and show ’em to Mr Edwardes. Lovely they are, Jennie. You came out a treat. Old Dobbs didn’t sell ’em, he kept ’em to look at. Drooled over ’em, tossed ’isself off, I shouldn’t wonder.’

‘God, you’re a disgusting little runt!’ Jennie’s voice was thick with loathing. That awful café and its customers symbolising all that was base in mankind, and Albert was its rightful king.

‘I’ve got copies of those pictures, and Dobbs ’as got the glass plates, but ’ee’ll let me ’ave ’em, for a price.’

‘You’ll destroy them?’

‘I may. I may not. You’ll never know, unless you see me smash ’em up, and I shan’t do that yet. I look on ’em as a nest-egg for my old age. But I’ll let you ’ave the pictures, one at a time. There’s twelve in all, twelve little beauties of you at your best, Jennie girl, showing off your pussy.’

‘How much?’

He pretended to cogitate, though she knew very well that he had come to meet her with a sum already worked out. ‘Shall we say one hundred quid for starters?’

‘You’re potty! I can’t lay my hands on that sort of money.’

‘Then find a rich geezer who can. All you’ve got to do is open your legs.’

‘Bastard! I’m no whore.’

‘That you ain’t, I know it. Blimey, you’re a corker on the stage, a regular stunner. All the blokes in the audience are dying to fuck you.’

‘Shut your dirty mouth!’ Jennie felt sick at the thought of him being out there, in the auditorium, watching her – once, twice, any number of times, and she hadn’t even known it.

‘I’m a generous sort of cove, Jen,’ he went on smoothly, unconcerned by her insults. ‘I’ll give you a week to find the first instalment. One photo for a hundred quid. That’s the deal.’

He stood up, for a sudden hush had fallen on the crowd as a police inspector and a sergeant walked down the stairs. They were at once engaged in a heated argument with the landlord. During the hiatus, Jennie and Albert made their escape.

It was cold and dark in the street, late, too, and she wondered if she had missed the last tram. If so, Albert was already costing her money, for she would have to hire a hackney cab. She had never felt more angry, fearful and despondent.

This squalid, low-grade person had succeeded in blighting all her hopes.

'You're a blackmailer,' she ground out.

'That's right,' he answered breezily. 'Don't forget, Jen. I'll be round backstage to collect, same time next week.'

Alice knew, long before they had even recognised it themselves, that Charlotte and Richard were falling in love. It was nothing they did or said. Indeed, whenever they came in the shop, their behaviour was as casual and natural as could be but, super-sensitive to the slightest thing that might concern Eva, she was filled with alarm for her dear patron.

There was nothing she could do, in that unenviable position of a friend who has to stand by and watch events take their inevitable course. I'll be there to pick up the pieces, she would tell herself as she went about her daily work. I'll be there for Lady Eva when she needs me. As for Charlotte, I'm very fond of her, but she and Richard can go take a running jump at themselves if they hurt her!

They had no intention of hurting her, and it was weeks after Archie's birthday and the meal at Frascati's before they finally faced up to what was happening. Richard continued to be Eva's lover. They talked of their impending marriage but he had put it off, telling her that he wanted to be in the position of being able to pay his way.

'I need to be financially secure in my own right, Eva,' he said whenever she broached the subject. 'Give me credit for a bit of masculine pride. I don't want people to say that I'm living off my rich wife.'

Eva accepted this. Though disappointed, she could see his point of view and admired him for it. She had seemingly limitless resources at her command, and was perfectly happy to share them with him, but if he wanted to wait until he could contribute to the running of their several households, then she would comply. Secretly, she hoped that she would become pregnant. An early marriage would then be essential, but month after month went by and she wept every time she had a period, though in private. No one knew how much this flow of menstrual blood devastated her.

I'm too old, she would think, panicking. I can't conceive. Now her conversations with Dudley and Beth about infertility gained an ominous significance. She tried not to brood about it, for Beth said that this in itself could make a person barren, citing cases where women had adopted babies after years of trying for their own and, tension released, had almost immediately started a pregnancy.

Time and again, Eva was able to convince herself that she had nothing to worry about. Richard loved her, she was sure. The rapport between him and Charlotte was a blessing. He was playing the surrogate father, that was all. The girl needed such a staunch man in her life after her experiences with Phelan. To prove that she was not the slightest bit jealous or concerned, she encouraged them to spend time together – playing tennis on the court at Greyfriars, riding on the Wiltshire downland, swimming in the lake. And there was so much they could do in London, taking some of the burden from Eva by attending meetings with those who ran charities – helping with the business side of *Pour Femme*, and Dudley's clinic.

She made excuses not to accompany them, migraines were good ones, but after they had crept from her darkened room, full of concern and solicitude, she would get up and run to the window, concealing herself behind the curtains and peering out, her hands clenching with anguish when she saw them getting into Richard's car and driving away.

Now it was the fall of the year, one of those days that a reluctant summer drops into the lap of autumn, a day of still air and high, vaulted skies, faintly but exquisitely blue. The red and yellow leaves in Hyde Park clung tremulously to the boughs, and when they fell it was as if with a sigh.

Eva had one of her headaches, and Richard had taken Charlotte to see Alice concerning a batch of satin expected from the manufacturers in France, over which there had been an annoying delay. Having sorted out the problem, they had left Alice in control and decided to drive through the park. There was no point in hurrying back to Albion House for Eva would be incarcerated in her room, and unlikely to put in an appearance till dinner at the earliest.

Richard had folded back the soft top of the Rover, and Charlotte took off her hat and rested her head against the leather passenger-seat, staring up at the cloudless sky glimpsed amongst the tangle of branches bordering the tree-lined avenue. There had been an overnight frost that had laid white fingers everywhere, but now it would be unguessed but for the delicate tart purity of the air which the sunshine, warm though it was, could not quite eliminate.

'It could almost be spring,' she remarked, glancing at Richard's profile which always reminded her of a falcon.

'Don't be deceived,' he replied, his eyes on the road ahead. 'The leaves are falling, the roses are nearly over, and there are precious few birds about, except the sparrows that never give up the ghost and fly south.' Then he glanced at her momentarily. 'Care to come to the studio? I've some photographs I want to show you.'

He could not quite explain, even to himself, and he was usually brutally honest about his own motives, just why he needed Charlotte to see the pictures of Jennie. He unearthed them from a drawer in the darkroom while she was removing her gloves and coat and making herself comfortable on the couch.

Silently, he placed the sheaf of prints in her hands and she studied them carefully. 'They're good,' she said at last, returning to them, examining them, her head tilted in a considering way. 'But who is she?'

'Her name's Jennie. I rescued her from an impossible situation. Befriended her, if you like.'

'She's pregnant in these. Was the child yours?' This was an accusation that carried enormous implications, but Charlotte could not resist making it.

He laughed as he lit two cigarettes and passed one to her. 'Good God, no! She didn't know who the father was.'

'A prostitute?' It would be like him to espouse the cause of a Magdalen.

'No, just an unfortunate.'

A sudden suspicion struck her. 'Eva doesn't know about her.'

'No, and I suppose that's why I wanted to show you. You're the only person who has seen them.'

'Why didn't you tell her?' Charlotte knew the answer to this. Eva was not aware of it, but her possessiveness was obvious to those around her.

'I met Jennie just about the time I was introduced to Eva. I'd already committed myself to helping the girl, and it was after this that my relationship with Eva developed into something other than friendship.'

'I see.' Charlotte laid the photographs on the couch beside her, and rested against the feather cushions, drawing on her cigarette. 'You felt that she wouldn't understand.'

'You've got it in one.'

She placed a hand on the pictures. 'These are the best things you've ever done. You should exhibit them.'

He lifted his shoulders and spread his hands ruefully. 'I can't. Eva would go up the wall.'

'How could she object if you supported a girl in trouble? Isn't this precisely what she's always doing herself?'

'She would. You know Eva.'

He seemed so uncharacteristically troubled that she said, 'I don't think you're being frank with me. This girl – you merely took care of her?'

He picked up the pictures, stared at them, and flung them down on the table. 'Hell, no! That wasn't all.'

'You slept with her?'

He tossed up his head, looked her full in the eyes, defiance and a faint thread of amusement in his voice. 'Yes, yes. I took her to live in Laurel Cottage. She was very young and I didn't intend to seduce her. As it happened, she seduced *me*. But this was before I made love to Eva. This occurred when Jennie had left me.'

'She left *you*?' What an extraordinary girl, Charlotte was thinking. He had offered her a home, security, himself, and she had abandoned it all.

'That's it. She gave birth to her baby and then ran off with it, taking everything she could lay hands on.'

'Did you mind? Have you tried to find her?'

'I wasn't in love with her, if that's what you mean. She was fun, lively, courageous – a survivor. No, I didn't look for her. She'll battle through on her own. That's Jennie all over.'

'She's pretty.' Charlotte nodded to the heap of black and white prints, wondering about the girl. 'I take it you don't want me to say anything about this to Eva?'

'I'd rather you didn't.'

'She doesn't trust you?'

He shook his head and stroked his beard, his face troubled. 'I don't think she does.'

'But she lets us go all over the place alone.'

'Maybe she feels differently about you. Aren't you her daughter, almost?'

'I wish I wasn't!'

The words leapt from her lips – ungrateful, angry words. Words that she had been repeating to herself often lately, resenting Eva's domination and her own dependence on her. And the cause was the man standing before her, making his confession about some shameless, wanton bit of a girl in his past.

She gnawed her lip, close to tears. He saw that she was distressed, and could not bear it. Charlotte must not cry because of him. For weeks he had been fighting his feelings, denying them with every vestige of his considerable will. Now he saw things clearly. He was in love with Charlotte, desired her, but must not have her. He loved Eva, and could have her whenever he wanted; desired her when they were together, held her, comforted her, knowing that one day he would hurt her beyond all imagining.

He saw that one of his reasons for showing Charlotte the photos had been to make her despise him. He could have coped with that, settled for what he had, seen her marry someone else, Archie maybe, would have even welcomed it, for then she would have been beyond temptation. The plan had backfired. Far from hating him, it seemed that she was moved to tears. He was wrong about this, for what she was experiencing was jealous rage.

Two women had had Richard and she was not one of them. She envied Jennie but that was over; her envy of Eva was more acute for it was she who, more nights than not, was the recipient of his passion. This studio! Charlotte hated it, rising to pace its length, staring through the opened bedroom door, seeing the divan where Eva often slept. That perfectly ordinary inanimate object now became a thing of terror and pain, as she visualised them there together.

'I've upset you, Charlotte. Clumsy of me. I'm sorry.' He was perched on the arm of the couch, one leg braced on the floor, the other bent at the knee, a cigarette held to his lips.

'Sorry? You're sorry! Well, so am I – sorry I ever met you.'

'You don't mean that.' He stubbed out the cigarette in the pottery ashtray, stood up, did what she dreaded and came over to her.

She put up her hands, palms outwards. 'Please, don't. I can't endure any more.'

He ignored her. Took those rigid hands in his, caressed them with his thumbs, warmed them into response. 'Charlotte, I love you,' he said. 'What are we going to do about it?'

'Nothing.' Her voice was a small, miserable sound. 'I love you, too, but we must forget we ever said it.'

His arms were round her, and she pressed her face into the rough wool of his jacket, breathing in the scent of him, filled with a longing which was likely to torment her to the end of her days. He stroked her hair, his lips against her forehead, knowing that this moment was more precious to him than any amount of hours spent with Jennie, Eva, or anyone else, for that matter.

'We can't hurt her, can we?' he whispered. 'She's a wonderful woman, and we both love her.'

'I know. I owe her everything. I can't take you away from her.' She clasped her arms tightly around his back, pressing closer and closer till she could get no nearer.

'That's right,' he said sadly. 'She loves me so much that I think it would kill her.'

Somehow they were on the couch, wrapped in each other's arms to keep fear at bay, like two forlorn children lost in a gloomy wood. Both recognised their duty: Richard must keep up the pretence and carry out his obligations; Charlotte must withdraw as much as possible, occupy herself in other directions, leave the path clear for Eva to marry him, enjoy him, live in her blissful fool's paradise.

Less honourable people would have played the game of deceit, but they did not dare make love, for this would have rendered their task impossible, so, after a while, he helped her into her coat and took her back to Albion House.

'Hello, Richard, it's been a long time,' Jennie said, as he opened the door of the studio.

He did a double take. It was as if yesterday's conversation with Charlotte had conjured her up. It was Jennie all right, but vastly different from the girl he had sheltered at Laurel Cottage. A young lady stood before him, amused by his surprise. She was wearing an exquisitely cut afternoon costume made of finest beige wool, the skirt very tight at the waist and swirling out into a full circle at the velvet banded hem. The jacket was edged with fur, and she wore a matching hat with an osprey plume, while one kid-gloved hand was buried in a huge muff, the other stretched out towards him. He took it automatically and she stepped inside.

He was wearing his shabby paint-smeared smock, for he had been busy putting the finishing touches to the portrait of a social beauty whose father had not flinched at the high price named. Jennie was sharply aware of his attraction, had come there to ask him for money, and the prospect of having to pay for it in the age-old way was not in the least disagreeable.

'Where have you sprung from?' he growled, knocked off kilter.

'I've just left the theatre after a morning of rehearsal,' she answered cooly, glad to let him know that she was already making her mark, against all his predictions to the contrary.

'You've done it, then? Got yourself on the stage?'

He was more in command now, controlling the stab of alarm that had shocked through him at the sight of her, though he was sure that she was up to no good and that her reappearance in his life boded ill. He offered her a seat, almost shy of this gorgeous creature, shaking his head in amazement.

'I'm a Gaiety Girl, just like I wanted,' she said, draping herself elegantly on the couch and permitting her coney stole to slide off her shoulders.

He grinned despite himself, and wanted to sketch her. 'I suppose congratulations are in order. Would you care for a drink?'

She was thoughtfully working her fingers out of her coffee-coloured gloves. 'A glass of sherry, please.'

He fetched the decanter and some glasses, then sat in the armchair opposite her. 'How's Grace?'

Jennie's eyes lit up. 'Wonderful. She's over a year old now, walking and starting to talk. She says quite a lot in her own baby language.'

'Is she with you?' He was wondering when she was going to come to the point of her visit. What was she after? Him? He doubted it, understanding that the Gaiety ladies did not want for followers.

'No, she's staying with friends in the country. I'm too busy to care for her, but I go and see her quite often.'

Her manners were perfect, her speech, too. A complete transformation from the drab he had picked out of the gutter. Satisfied, he took credit for his part in her rise from obscurity. 'Do you ever hear from Jean Reeves?'

'I've not contacted anyone from my old life,' she answered brightly, then a shadow passed across her lovely, subtly painted face. 'Until recently, that is.'

'I don't blame you. Making a fresh start doesn't need complications.'

'That's right.' She fell silent, not very proud of herself for coming to the studio.

But she had a career to foster, a child to protect, and the only way she could do this was by paying Albert his hundred pounds. She knew this was only the start and that he would keep on demanding further sums until all those damning pictures were in her possession. Soon she hoped to be in the position to pay him herself. The future looked bright. Quite recently the Guv'nor had promoted her to the coveted position of standing in front of the backdrop before the show and between acts, dressed as the Spirit of the Gaiety. She wore revealing black through which her limbs shimmered, and struck a classical pose, the glowing Sacred Lamp held aloft.

Richard was at a loss how to continue this rather stilted conversation. He cleared his throat, offered her a cigarette which she refused, lit one himself and then ventured, 'I really must come and see you perform. What d'you call yourself? Is it Jennie Blossom?'

'No. Genevra Adele.'

'That has a fine ring to it. And how is it going? What are you doing? Tell me everything, Jennie.'

She related some of her adventures, concluding with, 'And you've got yourself engaged, Richard, to that lady you were courting when you were with me,' she said acidly. She had never quite forgiven him for not being with her when Grace was born, and blamed Eva Pendral for it.

'How did you know that?' He smiled a little uncertainly. She was making him decidedly nervous.

'A friend read about it in the newspaper.'

It was Jupp who had mentioned it to her apropos of nothing in particular, remarking one day, 'I see that Lady Eva Pendral who owns the bank has got herself engaged to Mr Richard Sinclair. Funny that, I never thought she'd get married.'

Jupp was a mine of information about the doings of the mighty. He studied *The Times* from cover to cover, the Guv'nor's faithful watchdog, making it his business to vet the men who hovered around the stage-door. Toffs, most of them, so he found out all about that particular breed, their backgrounds, their romances, their marriages.

'Are you happy, Richard?' Jennie enquired, sipping her glass of sherry.

He was looking at her intently, his hands on the arms of his chair, long legs crossed. 'Yes, very happy.'

'You've done well for yourself, haven't you? Lady Pendral's supposed to be very rich.' Now was the time to strike. If Albert could hold a gun to her head with those photographs, then she had something with which to pressurize Richard, should he prove reluctant to come forth with monetary aid.

'She is, but more important than that, she loves me,' he said with utmost caution. He had not felt like this with Jennie in the old days, but she was hard now, hard as steel, with an edge that could cut to the bone.

'I'm glad you're well off, Richard, because I've come to ask a favour.'

I knew it, he thought, knew that she was up to something. She'd hardly be likely to pay me a social visit if she's keen to blot out her past. He remained still, only a muscle quivering at the side of his jaw betraying his tension.

'What sort of favour, Jennie?'

'I need a hundred pounds.' She leaned forward, no longer languid and relaxed, her eyes lynx-keen.

'That's a lot of money. What is it? Pressing dress-bills?' His eyes went over her expensive outfit, one dark brow lifted quizzically.

'I'd rather not say at the present moment, but my career could be affected, and Grace indirectly harmed, if I don't have it.'

Richard was nobody's fool. 'Someone's blackmailing you,' he said.

She flushed, looked away. 'Yes.'

'Is it Albert Baggot?'

'Yes.'

'So he's found you, has he? Let me deal with him, Jennie.'

'No!' Her eyes sparked warningly. 'Keep out of it. He's too dangerous. Threatens to tell Mr Edwardes things which I'd hate him to know. It'll finish me, and I'll not let that happen. I'd rather kill Albert with my bare hands!'

He believed her capable of it, but said, 'If you won't let me knock some sense into him, then you should go to the police.'

He was up now, towering over her, so tall and angry that her heart did a strange flip over in her breast. God, but he's a handsome beast, she thought. Why am I quarrelling with him? We should be in bed.

'I can't. I won't. Just give me the money. I'll pay you back one day.' Baulked desire made her angrier than ever.

'Pigs might fly!' he rejoined with heavy sarcasm. 'No, Jennie. I refuse. Blackmail is a dirty business and I'll have nothing to do with it.'

'Is that your final word?'

'It is.'

She rose, slender, lovely and menacing. 'In that case, you give me no alternative but to visit your fiancée.'

'What d'you mean?'

'I'll talk to Lady Eva. Tell her a few home truths about you and me.' She strolled towards the door, the picture of beauty and innocence.

'She'll never believe you,' he shouted.

'I'm not stupid, Richard. I have proof.' The eyes under the edge of her absurd, frothy hat were hard as agates.

'What proof can you possibly offer? She's never been to the cottage, and even if she did, Mrs Entworth would never breathe a word.'

Jennie paused, her hand on the door, and her smile was more alarming than her words. 'I have letters. The ones you wrote to me from London. I expect they would interest her a great deal. You weren't very discreet. They could be classed as love-letters, I suppose. They're decidedly fruity, Richard, not the kind of things a man writes to anyone – except his whore.'

Chapter 17

'And how is the delightfully girlish Gwen? Have you been successful in corrupting her yet?' Phelan asked, supine on the cushioned couch in the drawing-room of his Sloane Square establishment.

The object of this ironic interrogation was Julian who, dressed in a double-breasted Savile Row suit of grey worsted, was helping himself to coffee from the steaming pot on the low, marble-topped table drawn close to the fire. It was a cold morning, and there had been a fall of snow in the night. Already the traffic had churned it into sooty slush.

'You know perfectly well that I've not attempted to bed the oh-so charming Gwendoline,' he replied, with a lop-sided smile, his green eyes speaking volumes as they met Phelan's. 'The mere idea brings me out in a cold sweat.'

'A useful lass though, so earnest and well-intentioned. What would we do without her, eh?'

'What indeed?' Julian agreed and, coffee cup in hand, occupied a footstool, leaning his shoulders against the couch.

Phelan shifted position slightly, reaching out and idly ruffling Julian's blond curls. 'It's fortunate that she's taken such a shine to you. I thought at one time that Bernice would be the one, but it's as well things have worked out this way. She's much too shrewd.'

'A bitch – a positive bitch. Gwen's nice, but so terribly robust. Wants me to go cycling with her. Can you imagine it? And I must say I'm bored with that tedious vicarage household. How much longer do I have to go there, Phelan? It's really too bad of you. So many brats swarming all over the place. Absolute bedlam! And Gwen's pa and ma, so wrapped up in the doings of their wretched flock. When can we go back to Florence?' Julian's face was petulant, lower lip pouting, and Phelan's fingers stopped caressing and turned into talons as he gripped him by the back of the neck.

'Never, unless I get hold of some money pretty damn quick,' he replied with passion, and shook him roughly. 'You know it, so stop whining. Just get on with what I tell you to do. Now then, you've met Dr Armstrong?'

'God, yes, and he's another one who wants to put the world to rights.' Julian remained passive under Phelan's hand, eyes half-closed, stretching an arm backwards and running tender fingertips over his freshly shaven face.

'And the clinic? It's flourishing?' Phelan's voice was thoughtful now, and filled with dark, swirling undercurrents that Julian picked up on and thrilled to.

'Going like a bomb, so they tell me. Of course, I pretend to be ever so enthusiastic about family limitation. You'd be proud of me, darling. I always thought I should be on the stage.'

'The directors of the Pendral bank will be interested to hear about it, when the right moment comes. Not yet, of course. I've other fish to fry.' Phelan sat up and swung his legs to the floor, leaning over Julian and smiling into his face. 'I came across someone the other day who I think may help us. I'm going to meet him this morning.'

'Can I come?'

'No.' Phelan's expression changed swiftly from indulgence to anger. 'You know the rules. We're not to be seen out together. Not alone, that is. I've got Charlotte rattled, and she deserves to be punished. I appear when she's least expecting me, then vanish for days on end so that she thinks she's safe. Eva knows I'm in the vicinity, too, and she must be wondering what, if anything, I intend to do.'

Julian was staring at him seriously. 'It's all a game to you, isn't it, Phelan? You don't care about people's feelings, not even mine.'

'Ah, but I do. You're my Achilles heel. Hasn't this always been so, from the day we first met?' His eyes were mesmeric as they penetrated Julian's, then he rested his hand briefly against his cheek and, leaning forward, kissed him lingeringly on the lips. 'Off you go. Back to Gwen. Find out what's happening at Albion House. Report in tonight, late. I'll tell Carlo to leave the door on the latch.'

'You've given me a key, remember?'

'So I have. Don't lose it.'

Phelan had first come across Albert Baggot in The Providence, a public house of ill-repute, situated in Leicester Square. Like George Edwardes and most of his contemporaries, including the King, he was obsessed with horse-racing, and it was in these less than salubrious hostelries that betting men gathered to study form, exchange tips and place their money with bookies.

Albert had sidled up to him, having already done his homework and found out the identity of this prosperous-looking gentleman. Most people had heard of Lady Pendral and Charlotte. There had also been much talk when the girl jilted Phelan Charteris. Those less fortunate than the élite enjoyed gossiping about them, their interest complicated by envy, prejudices and sheer ignorance.

Sometimes Albert was subject to revelations, mostly hell-sent, and he always acted on these hunches. He had a hunch about Eva Pendral's ward. It was hazy, unformed as yet, but he was working on it. His motive for making Phelan's acquaintance had to do with this. He wanted to sound him out, see how much he knew.

At first he had sat himself down beside him and started to chat about horses, offering a couple of tips for the next race at Kempton Park. Phelan had been haughty and stand-offish, until Albert mentioned Lady Eva. It had been neither the time nor the place to pursue the subject, but Albert had roused Phelan's interest enough to make him suggest a further meeting.

Around the corner from the Strand, in Bear Street, was a pub with a room on the first floor called The Cosy. It was always packed with street-walkers and their followers. Not the kind of habitat that Phelan would have patronised from choice, but Albert had insisted. He was too smartly dressed for a dump like that, his black overcoat with its astrakhan collar, his black Homburg hat and silver-topped cane standing out like a sore thumb.

The bold-faced women eyed him, flipping back their capes to display half-naked breasts, stalking him with their hands on their swaying hips, mouthing open invitations. He ignored them, seeing Albert through the fog of cigarette smoke, seated at a table to one side, the high back of its settle partly screening him from the rest of the room.

Phelan joined him, and ordered two gins. He wanted the fellow to state his business, aching to get out of this atmosphere which was full of cheap perfume mingled with the aroma of hot humanity and alcohol. Albert's face was less than reassuring. If ever a man looked like a villain it was him, but Phelan was accustomed to villains, never one to despise low company if he could use it to his advantage.

Albert was confident, dressed to kill. He had already received three hundred pounds from Jennie and had kitted himself out accordingly. But, no matter how much he spent or how fine the clothing he put on his back, Albert would never look anything but common. Phelan could see right through him to the shrivelled soul that lurked somewhere in the nethermost region of his being.

'Well, my man, what's this matter you wish to discuss with me?

Be brief. I haven't got all day,' he said brusquely, tapping the top of his cane lightly against his lips and staring at Albert in a way that made him ill at ease.

'It's to do with Lady Pendral and that girl what she took in,' he began, looking pointedly at his empty glass. Phelan ordered another round.

'Charlotte? What about her?'

'Well, I've got some documents at 'ome that might interest you.' The gin was taking effect and Albert's eyes kept straying towards the flamboyant women.

Phelan laid his cane aside and steepled his fingers together, never taking his eyes from Albert's sweating face. 'What makes you think I'd be interested?'

'She threw you over, didn't she?'

'We parted, yes.'

'Wouldn't you like to rub her nose in it?'

Phelan answered the question with one of his own. 'Will you let me see these documents?'

One of the women had read Albert's signals and strolled over, winding her arms about his neck and murmuring in his ear. He shrugged her off, muttering, 'Later, later. Can't you see I'm busy?' She withdrew, but not far, keeping her eyes on Albert, her next meal-ticket, warning others off.

Phelan gathered up his gloves and fastened his coat. 'It seems you're keener on chasing skirts than doing business with me.'

Albert took fright, putting a hand on his sleeve. 'Oh, no, sir – no! First things first, right? I'll bring the papers – got 'em from my old mother, I did. She used to take in lodgers, and there was this ladybird and 'er two kids, name of Margaret Drummond. She died, and the eldest girl, Lottie, ran off.'

'What happened to the other one?'

'She died, too, naught but a tot, sir.' Albert was keeping the relationship between Jennie and Charlotte to himself. With a bit of luck and careful manipulation, he could be sitting pretty for the rest of his life.

'Ma kept Meg Drummond's things,' he continued, 'to 'elp pay rent owing – wedding lines, birth certificates, that sort of caper. There was a diary as well. As I say, there may be no connection, but it's worth a go, ain't it? Wouldn't you like to know for sure that Lady Pendral's ward was a slum brat whose mother was on the game?'

'How much is this going to cost me?' Phelan rose, unsure if this unsavoury character was telling the truth.

Even if he was, then could this be of use? Thousands of children were abandoned in London yearly, and the chance that the girl he spoke of could be Charlotte was remote. It was a long shot, but Phelan was familiar with bluff and counter-bluff, and the odd coincidences that led him to risk all in the realms of gambling that were his hunting-ground.

'Cost, sir, cost? You insults me,' Albert protested indignantly. 'I wants to 'elp you, that's all. I'd not see any girl do the dirt on a fine gent like you, but if, out of generosity, you saw your way clear to slip me a few quid, then I'd not say no.'

'Naturally,' Phelan said reasonably, but if Julian had been present he would have shivered, for when Phelan was being reasonable he was at his most dangerous. 'Come and see me later this week.'

'Will you give me your address?' Albert had already found this out, but was not prepared to let on.

'No. I'll meet you at the Café Royal, eight o'clock on Saturday night.'

There it was at last. Her name at the top of the posters outside the Gaiety: *The Sailor Girl*, starring Genevra Adele. Every time Jennie walked past she tried not to look, but was never able to resist a quick peek. George Edwardes' new show, and he had chosen *her* for the lead.

It had opened in February, after the Christmas extravaganza *Two Naughty Boys* had finished its run. She had not had a part in this for it was a vehicle for the comedians, Edmund Payne and William Spray, and the rest of the players were mainly children. While this was performed nightly, with matinées on Wednesdays and Saturdays, the Guv'nor had drilled the cast of *The Sailor Girl*, calling rehearsal after rehearsal.

The show was a sell-out. Everyone was whistling or singing tunes from that slightly dotty, very frothy, light-hearted musical with a strong emphasis on comedy. Jennie played Lady Cora, a typical dainty English rose who, determined to marry against her Daddy's wishes, followed her young man to sea, disguised as a midshipman.

There was a lavish garden-party scene, where Jennie appeared in an organza dress and a picture hat and sang two songs; a scene on board the *H.M.S. Polly Sue*, where she wore trousers, danced the hornpipe, and sang a patriotic ditty which always brought the house down; an exotic scene on a tropical island where she was required to put on a grass-skirt; and a grand finale at Daddy's country seat. True love triumphed in the end, and she performed the closing duet with her leading man.

I've made it, she thought every night as she stood in the wings nervously awaiting her first cue. Thank God! Thank Zena! Thank my lucky stars!

Even the regular visits from Albert could not quench her joy. He was a menace, and Richard kept telling her that it was difficult for him to find more money, but had not failed her yet. She was looking for a house, knowing that she had to have a better address than Brompton Road. Louis, proud of her success, came up with a suggestion.

'There's one to rent in Finsbury Park, not far from Princess Road where we live. Will you come and see it?'

Finsbury Park was an area of substantial semi-detached dwellings built in the last quarter of Victoria's reign, and occupied by solid, respectable, middle-class citizens. Jennie took the house, furnished it and moved in. From then on she and Louis shared a hansom cab in the morning and at night. A star could not possibly travel by tram. Neither could a star do her own washing, ironing, cooking and cleaning, so she hired a maid and a daily. She could afford all this, with her rise in salary, could afford the extravagant clothes she was expected to wear, but could not afford to pay a blackmailer. She considered asking her bank for a loan, but was not yet established enough to make this practicable. The Squire and Joan? Wild horses would not have made her tell her troubles to them.

Part of her promotion included a dressing-room of her own, and the services of a dresser. It was a tiny room, but a palace compared to the one she had shared with half a dozen others. The dresser was a lady called Mrs Fipps, who had been in the business since she was a girl. She was always going on about former 'greats' whom she had served, and had a habit of repeating herself.

After the evening performances came the procession of flowers and invitations. Jennie always accepted the former, keeping some and sending the rest to cheer hospital wards, but was selective about the latter. She would examine the enclosed cards, consult with Jupp and Louis, those stalwart guardians of her reputation and, subject to their approval, might go out to supper with this young man or that, but always returned to Finsbury Park. Catching up on sleep was a fine excuse.

'I have my career to think of,' she would say, ever so kindly if one of her beaux became too pressing. 'An early bird, me. Rehearsals, you know.' And they usually took it like the gentlemen they were, happy for an hour in her company, considering the money for the expensive champagne suppers, the bouquets and Cartier jewellery had been well spent. At least they could boast to their friends that they had actually been out with Genevra Adele.

One night, when she was almost ready to leave, having decided that she really must go straight home, Louis tapped on the dressing-room door. He was almost swamped by the biggest basket of flowers Jennie had ever seen. He spoke from behind a great, jungly spray of ferns and orchids.

'Here you are, Miss. Present from a Stagedoor Johnny who's begging to be introduced.'

He dumped the basket on the floor near her chair and she dipped into it, drawing out a tiny envelope containing a card. On it was written in a black, scrawling hand: 'I must meet you. Won't accept a refusal. I'll park my butt here till I do. Yours ever, Max'.

No surname, no title, nothing but the Christian name. 'Who is he, Lou?' she asked, smiling to herself. Max. She liked that. Max sounded exciting, impetuous and forceful.

Louis was still in his sailor's costume, white and navy blue. Taller than when she had first met him, but still so boyish-looking that she tended to forget he was only two years younger than herself. A box of chocolates lay on the dressing-table, amongst the pots, pansticks, cleansing-cream, eye-liners and brushes.

'Can I have one?' he asked, and promptly gobbled several when she nodded assent.

'Lou, who is this masher?' she said again.

'A Yankie,' he replied through a mouthful of chocolate. 'A great bloke, been talking to Jupp and me for ages.'

'Jupp likes him?' Jupp was the keeper of secrets, the stern critic of suitors. It was he who decided if the men who presented themselves at his door were worthy of the Gaiety Girls.

'Sure does, honey.' Lou gave a passable imitation of an American accent. Obviously his time spent with this Max person had not been wasted. 'The dude parted with a fistful of dollars.'

'Dollars?'

Lou reverted to his normal tone. 'Sovereigns, Miss. And he gave me one to deliver the flowers. Will you see him? He's dead keen.'

Jennie smiled at him, putting her hand to her hair. 'Do you think I should?'

'Yes, Miss.'

Maxwell Whitney came into the dressing-room like a whirlwind. It was not that he was rude, far from it – he won Fipps over straight away with his politeness – but there was a fire and force about him that burned bright as day. Later Jennie was to learn that he was supremely confident, in himself and his abilities, a confidence that was limitless, not brash or arrogant, just rocklike.

Having placated Fipps, he grinned at Jennie, a big, broad, comfortable man who, despite his conventional evening attire, managed to look rumpled. He had thick, unruly fairish hair, a full mouth, cleft chin and bright brown eyes. Handsome in a craggy way, and certainly impressive.

'Miss Adele, would you care to have supper with me?' he asked without preamble, contemplating her with delighted written all over his face.

'I don't know.' For once Jennie couldn't think of a single reason why not.

'Sure, you do. You'd like to, huh? I know this little Italian place in Soho where they serve mighty fine pasta. I've only been on vacation here for a couple of weeks, but I know my way around.'

Louis was goggling in admiration. Fipps was chuckling and, to Jennie's amazement, behaving almost coquettishly. They liked him! They really did! It's just because he's American, she thought briskly, a glamorous visitor from the New World. Well, he's not going to take me in, with his soft drawl and old-fashioned courtesy.

But almost before she knew it, her hat and coat were on, her bag and gloves in her hand, and they were bidding Jupp good-night. 'See that Louis goes home in my cab,' she said to him, as an afterthought.

'Right you are, Miss Adele,' Jupp replied, pleased to have obliged the open-handed American, shouting cheerio to him.

Parked at the kerb was the largest motor-car she had ever seen. 'It's a Whitney Flier,' Max said as he held the door open for her.

'Did you bring it with you?' Jennie climbed in and found it very well appointed, with deep leather seats, shiny brass fittings and walnut woodwork.

'No, it's a demonstration model, but Pop arranged for me to use it for the duration of my stay.'

'How so?'

'He makes them. Has a factory in Detroit.'

The car purred into motion and covered the short journey through the busy streets to Soho. The restaurant was all that he had said it would be, small, select, run by Italians who prided themselves on the traditional cuisine. There was a man playing sentimental Neopolitan songs on an accordion. Max nodded to the waiters, who seemed to know him. A bottle of Chianti appeared as if by magic, along with the menu. Jennie admitted that she knew very little about pasta dishes, so he ordered for both of them.

While they waited, he drew out a gold cigarette-case and offered her one. 'Now then, what can I call you? Will Genevra be OK? I'm just Max.'

'My friends call me Jennie,' she said, overwhelmed by his direct approach.

'Jennie . . . I kind of like that,' he grinned, undisguised admiration in his sparkling eyes. 'Well, Jennie, I saw you in the show tonight and I think you're swell. Gee, I've been in London for days, and I've only just found you! Isn't that awful? Friends kept saying, you must go to *The Sailor Girl*, it's the hottest thing in town, and I put it off, went sightseeing instead, but if I'd only known about you the Tower, Madame Tussaud's and Buckingham Palace could have gone hang! I'd have hoofed it to the Gaiety – pronto.'

They smiled at each other across the candlelit table, and found it all perfectly enchanting. Jennie took a deep breath, hardly daring to believe her good fortune. Throughout the meal Max did not let the conversation flag for a moment, dipping into his fund of stories and anecdotes, telling her about his life in America so that she soon felt that she knew his family – brothers, sisters, cousins. His mother had been a Southern belle, a member of the 'Quality' from Virginia, while his father, born of a wealthy industrialist, had drifted to Michigan where he had started up his own concern, manufacturing automobiles. Max had graduated from Harvard, joined the firm, but was restless.

'I've been staying with friends in California – in Los Angeles,' he concluded, wiping traces of bolognese sauce from his lips with a blue and white checked napkin. 'I like it there, and some of my buddies are going into the movie business, and I want to get involved. You know – motion pictures. D'you get them here? They're the up and coming thing in the States.'

'Yes, I've been to a picture-show,' she replied, fascinated by his face, his bright, intelligent eyes, the relaxed way in which he moved, his square hands, his long limbs.

'We'll go together. Tomorrow.'

'I can't. I'm on at seven.'

'In the afternoon then. Surely we can find someone who's doing a matinée?'

'I don't know much about it. The theatre's my world.'

'Not all the time? I won't let it be – not now I've found you. You haven't told me much about yourself, but then I don't suppose I've given you the chance. Tell me to shut up if I talk too much.' He laughed, a thing he did often and loudly, with a flash of perfect white teeth.

Jennie was not very truthful, inclining towards fabrication. She simply enlarged on details she had given the press. But even as the glib lies tripped off her tongue, she was wishing that she could be frank, recognising him as someone who would give good advice, his judgement sound and unbiased. Should she confess that she had a daughter? She wanted to, but dared not. Then there was the matter of Albert, and her own descent into blackmail. Max wouldn't like that, she was sure, would be angry with her for following Albert's example. She did not want him to despise her, for already she was in thrall.

Max listened quietly, and she had no way of knowing if he believed her or not. The café was empty now, the waiters hiding yawns and glancing at them. The accordionist soldiered on and Max tipped him handsomely as he and Jennie finally left.

'I'm staying at the Westminster Palace Hotel,' he said, as they sat in the car, the engine thrumming, a powerful beast waiting to be unleashed. 'Let's skip the movies, but come and have tea with me tomorrow. I like the idea of English tea at four o'clock – used to it in a funny kind of way, for Virginians follow the traditions of the Old Country. And my mother, even now, is still very much the grand Southern lady.'

'Thank you. I'd like that.' Jennie was alarmed to discover that she did not want to be parted from him, sneaking furtive glances at him as he drove her to Finsbury Park. Those big hands placed so confidently on the wheel, his ease with the machine brought about by intimate knowledge of its inner workings. He wore the air of a gentleman, had been reared a gentleman, but had the practical skills and down-to-earth philosophy of a labourer. It was an intriguing combination.

The car stopped at the kerbside, Max helped her out and walked her through the tiny iron gate and up the path of the little front garden with its neatly clipped privet hedge. As usual, her maid had left the light on in the hall, and it was shining through the stained glass of the porch. They paused there, and Max took her hands in his. He was so tall, making her feel tiny and fragile, and she had to look up to see the expression on his face.

It had changed, no longer smiling, serious now, and intent. He wants to kiss me, she thought, and felt hot inside, wanting him to do it, wanting more than just kisses. He had taken off his hat, his hair glinting with red and green lights from the coloured glass.

She felt his hand at the back of her waist, drawing her slowly towards him, and tipped back her head, receiving his kiss like a benediction. It was a long kiss, but chaste. He did not try to open her lips with his, or drive his tongue into her mouth. She liked him for that. She knew it was too soon, and so, apparently, did he. A very mannerly gentleman from the Deep South.

He held her close for a moment more, then released her and stood back. 'Till tomorrow, Jennie.'

'Yes, tomorrow.' She was dazed, and watched him go down the path till suddenly remembering that they had not agreed on a meeting place. 'I'll be at the theatre,' she shouted after him.

'OK. Tell that guy on the door that I'm expected.' He waved and jumped into his car.

Jennie paused with her key in the lock, eyes on the long, ostentatious vehicle disappearing down the tree-lined avenue, then she let herself quietly into the house.

The Westminster Palace Hotel was very grand and very expensive, most conveniently situated opposite the Abbey and the Houses of Parliament, an American tourist's paradise. Max was delighted with it, finding it different from anything at home, except perhaps for the Waldorf-Astoria in New York, and Jennie was most impressed when she walked through the revolving glass door.

'I've asked for tea to be sent up to my suite,' he said. 'Let's go up in the elevator.'

Jennie's life to date had consisted of the theatre, the occasional outing to a restaurant, and her own cosy home, which she considered to be rather fine, but the hotel was beyond her wildest expectations. The atmosphere was hushed, as if they were in church; as she passed through the vestibule towards the lifts, she glimpsed spacious reading-rooms, writing, dining and drawing-rooms, all equipped for the comfort of hotel visitors and their guests. A page-boy in a round pill-box hat and tight maroon uniform glittering with silver buttons, bowed them into the lift.

Max fished in his pocket and produced a coin when the lift stopped and they alighted. Deep carpet covered the wide corridor ahead, and there were potted plants on stands at regular intervals between shaded light fixtures along the walls, and handsome prints of the most renowned beauty spots in England.

Max halted before a pair of double-doors and opened them with a flourish, standing aside so that she might precede him into the room. It was magnificent, a large lounge with a bedroom leading from it and an adjoining bathroom. She had hardly had a chance to look round when a tap on the door announced the arrival of the tea-trolley. Again, Max was generous with his tips, and the waiter retired well satisfied.

Max and she stood there, the trolley between them, still wearing their outdoor garments. 'We'd better drink the tea before it gets cold,' he said, without moving, just staring at her.

'Yes,' she answered, weak at the knees. She had not slept much last night for thinking about him.

'Is that what you want?' As he spoke, Max pushed the trolley away, and gently placed his hands each side of Jennie's face, then ran them lightly down her neck and along her shoulders.

She watched him with quiet concentration as he traced over her back, her breasts and her thighs. Weak with desire, she knew that she had to have him. 'Max – Max – ' she whispered, and put her arms up around his neck, pulling his mouth down to hers.

The fire that leapt into being between them was all consuming and impatient. Her hat came off, falling to the carpet. Her hands were tugging at his overcoat. He lifted her into his arms, his mouth still locked on hers, and carried her into the bedroom. Their violence contained faint elements of rapine, but who raped who it was impossible to tell. Neither fought, both yielded, madness possessing them, and certainly their clothing suffered from the mutual attack, until scattered about the floor like discarded skin.

Then they quietened, suddenly certain of one another. 'You're gorgeous,' Max said, his eyes and hands exploring her nakedness.

'So are you.' She trailed her fingers over his deeply tanned and muscular body.

He put a hand on her breast, seeing her nipple stand out under his caressing thumb, lowering his head and fastening his mouth on the dark, proud flesh. Her fingers were in his hair, holding him close, wanting him there. Though needing to enter her quite desperately, he schooled his impatience, rousing her fully first, mouthing her skin, breathing in its fragrance, hearing her moans of pleasure, aware of her quickened pulse as his fingers found the damp, sweet centre of her, moving gently, exquisitely, till she dug her nails into his back, her head twisted to one side against his chest, crying out as she reached orgasm.

He had never been so much wanted or needed and he rolled her over on to her back, urged on by her hands, and she parted her legs and pulled him down, moving smoothly beneath him to meet his need, eager to give him the same sensations as she had just experienced. She gave herself completely, holding nothing back, hands on his buttocks, grinding her hips against his, until he could no longer control the wave of feeling rushing up his legs, through his spine, into his loins. With a strangled groan he spent himself within her, her tears and his intermingling on her face, even as their bodily fluids mingled between her thighs.

Jennie lay there blissfully in the aftermath of love-making. Max was on his back, one arm flung across his eyes, breathing more evenly now. He was the second man whom she had made love with – Richard and Max. And I've been lucky, she realised, both of them expert and selfless. Yet this time it was different, for she was in love with Max. Just for a while, in that oasis of tranquility, she allowed herself to wallow luxuriantly in the feeling. Love. She was really, truly in love.

Dark shadows jostled for admittance, hammering at the sacred portals of her happiness. Go away, she said. I don't want to think about Grace, or Albert or Richard. I don't even want to remember my responsibility to the Guv'nor. I want nothing but to stay here in bed with Max for ever and a day. Damn you, shadows, sling your hook!

Max was equally confused and happy. He was not sure what he had expected. Maybe, at first, he had anticipated a quick, delicious flutter with the pretty actress he had seen on stage, a wonderful, holiday interlude, when he would have remained free. Now he knew this was impossible. Jennie had already woven her fingers around his heart. He could not imagine life without her. A strange and unexpected twist of fate, for he had enjoyed a number of lovely women, but never before found one with whom he wanted to stay till death claimed him.

He moved suddenly, propping himself up on one elbow and grabbing a fistful of her long hair. 'Marry me, Jennie.'

Her eyes snapped open. They widened under the curling lashes, stared into his face, terror in their depths of the widely dilated pupils. 'I can't.'

His hold slackened but he did not let go, bending over to kiss her. 'You can – you *know* you can. You can do anything you damn want. You're not married already, are you?'

'No.'

He snuggled down beside her, content as a child. 'That's all right, then. When shall we do it? Tomorrow? The next day? You name it and we'll do it, honey.'

The shadows had succeeded in forcing entry. Seeking comfort, Jennie coiled her legs around his, stroked his face, his hair, her lips closing his eyelids with light kisses, but said, 'Max, I can't leave the stage. You've no idea what it's cost me to get where I am. I can't chuck it up, not yet.'

'You don't have to, babe. I've got to go to the States next week, but I'll hop on a liner and come back just as soon as I can. You carry on at the Gaiety while I'm gone, but let's get married first. What d'you say?'

'Max, please – it's a dream, a lovely dream, but impossible.'

Jennie's brain was working furiously. What was she to do? There was Albert calling in a few days, greedy hand outstretched; there was Grace. How would Max react to a ready-made family? There was her career which was genuinely important to her. But was she prepared to sacrifice her love for a mess of grease-paint and spangles? Bleakly, she knew that she might have to.

She pressed close to her lover and her lips were sealed. He mustn't find out about Grace. She couldn't ask him for money to settle with Albert. Her soul withered at the thought of telling him any of these things. He loved her, and she wanted him to keep an idealistic picture of her always. He must never find out that she had been born in poverty, a thief, an orphanage child, the mother of a bastard; her pride would not permit it. Let him think her hard, ambitious, cold, self-seeking – anything but the truth.

She flung back the covers and got out of bed. Max lay there, watching her closely. 'Where are you going?' he said.

'I've a performance at seven-thirty.' She kept her face turned away as she gathered up her clothes.

'I'll meet you after the show.'

'If you like.' She managed to sound indifferent.

He reached for his shirt, swung his legs over the edge of the mattress. 'I do like. Jennie, what's the matter with you? I only asked you to marry me, goddammit!'

'I'm in a hurry, that's all.' How easy it was to lie to him, the man with whom she wanted to share everything.

He seized her wrists, made her stop fussing with her blouse, made her look him in the eye. 'I don't believe you. I love you. I mean it. I want to marry you.'

Tears blurred her vision and thickened her voice. I can't let myself be upset, she thought. I've a show to get through tonight. 'Max, this has been fun. I like you a lot, and I'll go on seeing you till you leave, but I can't marry you.'

His lips curved in a confident smile. 'Jennie, you like me a heap more than a lot. Sure, we'll go on meeting, or I'll burn down the damn theatre! And you *will* marry me, one day.'

*

Richard had been behaving oddly lately, becoming quiet, withdrawn, unlike his usual high-spirited self. To begin with Charlotte had thought it concerned herself, Eva, and his worry about that old, eternal triangle in which they were enmeshed. She had gone away for a long weekend with Gwen to her grandparents' manor in the country and, on her return, had made sure that she left Richard and Eva alone as much as was humanly possible. It was hard, and she suffered, but it was the only way. To her dismay, she discovered that he seemed no better, quite desperately unhappy and, when she was able to ask him the reason, had begged her to come to the studio so that he might explain.

She had lied to Eva, giving a visit to the dentist as an excuse for an afternoon's absence, while in reality she had taken a cab to Holland Park. It was February, that dull month between winter and spring, when the excitements of Christmas are over and the summer seems a century away. Even the usually cheerful cab driver was depressed, complaining of bills, and his children's colds, the lack of customers, the difficulties of making ends meet. She listened, nodded, sympathised, while inside her burned a forbidden, feverish fire, as she thought of being with Richard for a stolen hour. In an agony of nerves and guilt, she climbed the stairs to his apartment. He opened the door with such speed that she could only assume he had been listening for her step. It was horrible to be alone with him and not able to touch him. She dared not, doubting her self-control.

'Come in, Charlotte.' He stood there stiffly, and did not take her hand. 'I'm so glad you came.'

Her face was pink with the cold, and her beauty was torture to him. Her simple green skirt and short coat with a velvet collar emphasised her slender waist and hips. It was deliberately businesslike and practical. Her dark hair was coiled neatly around her head, the front softened by a wispy fringe, and her hat was of black straw, modest in size, the crown banded by a piece of green ribbon. She looked like a governess or a school-teacher, and Richard smiled.

'How very severe. Makes me feel I should call you Miss Drummond.'

'Maybe you should.' She sat in the edge of a chair, knees and feet together, handbag on her lap.

Richard was in his shirtsleeves and waistcoat, and had been preparing coffee. Charlotte was being so stiffly formal that he wondered if he should put on his coat and tie, then dismissed the idea. He set the pot on top of the stove, folded his arms across his chest and contemplated her for a moment.

'What are we going to do about this?' he said.

She looked up, startled, her features set in hard lines. 'We aren't going to do anything about it. We're going to carry on loving each other but love Eva more, that's all.' Then, fearing she was about to break down, she added firmly, 'What did you want to see me about? Not this, I take it.'

'No, not this, though I'm finding being noble and self-sacrificing a terrible strain.' He concentrated on the percolating coffee, lest he should go to her, take her in his arms and do something they would both regret.

'Then what is it?' She clutched the handle of her snakeskin bag. As long as she remained remote and aloof, he could not penetrate her armour.

'Jennie's turned up again.'

'The girl in the photographs?'

'Yes, but she's not like that any more. Have you heard of Genevra Adele?'

'The Gaiety Girl? Who hasn't heard of her? Musical comedy isn't my choice of entertainment but, yes, of course I've heard of her.' What now? Charlotte was thinking.

'That's Jennie, and she's been here to see me, demanding money.'

'Why?'

Richard told her about it, knowing that his weakness in giving in to Jennie sounded more than just lame. 'I can't keep it up,' he concluded. 'I'm not made of money and she's draining my resources.'

Charlotte longed to draw his head down to her breast and kiss away the worry lines. She ached with tenderness and desire.

She grabbed at the tattered remnants of control, but it was useless and anger overcame her. How dare this scheming bitch make him so miserable? 'Tell her to go to hell! Good God, she must be rich. Actresses earn a packet, don't they?'

'She says not, has to live in style apparently. Can't meet the blackmailer's demands. Those bloody letters! What a fool I was to write them!' He slumped down on a chair, his head in his hands.

It was awful to see him brought low; that man who would never willingly harm any one, so fiercely proud that he liked to tell the truth and be damned to the consequences. But we've stopped him doing that, Charlotte thought, myself and Jennie. She moved to his side, stretched out her hands to him, then remembered in time and let them drop.

'Explain it to Eva,' she advised, thinking, It will be best for all of us if she finishes with him because of this.

'She'll offer money, and I can't have that.'

'Then tell this woman that you have photos of her, too. Threaten to sell them to the press if she keeps on.'

'You don't understand – my pictures are quite artistic. The ones the blackmailer has are pornographic. There's a difference.'

'Really? She was pregnant when she posed for you. I should think they'd tarnish her precious reputation if placed in the wrong hands.'

'I can't do it, Charlotte. I won't descend to her level, and there's the child to consider.'

She threw her hands up in despair. 'The child! The child! My God, she knws how to tug at your heart-strings, doesn't she, Richard?'

Furious with Jennie, Richard, and even more with herself, Charlotte stormed out and passed the rest of the day in torment. Evening brought a plan, and after supper which she ate alone at Albion House, Eva having gone out with Richard, she told Tilly not to wait up for her and ordered a cab.

She got out in Leicester Square, and picked her way through the traffic, where crossing-sweepers in regulation cockaded hats went to work with bucket and broom, clearing away horse manure. The rowdy clamour of late-night London swirled about her; blind beggars tapped on the pavement with their white sticks, flower-girls shouted, harlots in gaudy dresses flocked out of the public houses, and hansom cabs vied for trade with the motor-taxis. Charlotte was having second thoughts about her mission, but when she saw the hoarding outside the Gaiety, she knew she had to carry it through.

The stage-door was at the back of the theatre, and when she got there it was to find a crowd of well-dressed men hanging about outside. She walked boldly up to the red door and pushed it open. Inside she was accosted by a person of sergeant major bearing, who demanded to know her business.

'I want to see Miss Adele,' she said haughtily, refusing to be intimidated by his bristling moustache and fierce eyes.

'So do lots of people,' he declared. 'Who are you?'

'A friend.' Charlotte took half a crown from her purse. 'Please tell her that I've been sent by Mr Sinclair.'

Jupp was mystified by her quiet clothing and ladylike mein. The situation smacked of intrigue, so he instructed Louis to give Jennie the message. Charlotte waited in the chilly passage, listening to the unfamiliar sounds of a theatre after the performance, smelling the unfamiliar smells, wishing she was anywhere but there.

The boy returned and asked her to go with him. Soon they stopped outside a door with a notice pinned to it, saying

Miss Genevra Adele. Charlotte knocked, and a voice told her to enter.

The first thing she saw was a young woman, framed dramatically against the electric bulbs of the dressing-table mirror. She stood facing the door, smoke wreathing from a cigarette in a long jade holder. She still wore the ornate ballgown which was her costume for the finale. A paste tiara glittered on her mahogany hair. Paste earrings flashed as she moved her head. Paste bracelets scintillated as she indicated a chair.

'Sit down,' she said, her voice low and rich, its accent cultured. 'You've come from Richard?'

'Yes – or rather no. He doesn't know I'm here.'

Jennie frowned and, sitting on the stool, one silk-stockinged knee crossed over the other, began to strip off the artificial gems, tossing them into a jewel-box. Her dresser ventured to help her, but she said sharply, 'Leave us, Fipps. I can manage.'

They were alone, and the atmosphere was far from congenial. Charlotte had arrived at an inopportune moment, for Jennie was in a foul mood. Max had caught the boat-train that morning after they had had a monumental row. He had been wild with anger at Jennie's refusal to marry him, and she had been shattered because he was going, but neither would yield an inch.

'It's the last you'll see of me!' he had roared, standing at the door of his suite, raincoat over one arm, a suitcase in the other hand.

'That's fine! I don't care!' she had retorted, but when he had gone she'd flung herself across the bed, beating at the pillows and sobbing noisily, beside herself with grief.

Her head thumped, and it had taken every iota of professionalism to face the audience that night, but she had done it, the many curtain-calls an acclaim to her artistry. She had intended to drag herself back to her lair at Finsbury Park, but now this girl was delaying her.

'How come you're here if Richard didn't send you?' Her eyes were outlined with black, her lids shadowed deep blue, her cheeks and mouth rouged. Without stage-lighting which rendered them soft and appealing, the cosmetics looked garish, reducing her to the status of a sixpenny drab.

It was what Charlotte had expected. She had never met any actresses, but they had a bad reputation as a whole, despite George Edwardes' successful attempts to present his girls in a different light. She had come there prepared to dislike Jennie, Genevra Adele or whatever else she cared to call herself, and she did, most heartily.

'I want you to stop pestering him,' she said coldly.

Everything that was common and vulgar in Jennie rose to the surface as she cast her a sneering glance. 'Oh, you do, do you? And what the hell do you know about it?'

'He was good to you once, sheltered you, helped you. How can you treat him so shabbily? Have you no heart, no conscience, no feelings? What harm has he ever done you?'

Jennie had heard enough. She stood up, an inch taller than Charlotte, or maybe it was not simply height; it was a stature, a presence, bequeathed by stage training. 'Now you listen to me!' she shouted, hands on her hips. 'It's nothing to do with you. Who sent you? Eva Pendral? Well, she can keep her nose out of it, too. It's between Richard and me and no other bugger.'

'Eva doesn't know about it,' Charlotte protested, while angry thoughts buzzed in her head. How could Richard have taken such a woman to bed? She was coarse. She was loud. She might be a famous actress, but as a person she was despicable.

Jennie's eyes narrowed to golden slits and her carmined lips twisted unpleasantly. 'She'd better bloody not know about it or it'll be the worst for him. How did you get mixed up in it? Are you in love with him? Jesus, that's it, isn't it? You're in love with him and he's knocking you off behind Lady Pendral's back.'

Charlotte's cheeks had been pale, but now they flamed. 'How dare you! He's a friend, and I want to help him. I'll give you money if you let me have those letters.'

Jennie was eyeing her suspiciously. 'Why should you do that? Trying to buy your way into his favour? Want to oust the older woman, do you? Is that it?'

'No, it's not. Don't you believe in friendship? Haven't you ever had someone who was prepared to help you selflessly?'

Jennie immediately thought of Zena, dipping into memory's storehouse and remembering her kindness and support. Her heart ached and she longed to see her, but she had not returned from Spain. Just as well, maybe, for she would never have countenanced Jennie becoming an extortionist. She'd have found some other means of dealing with Albert Baggot, a curse, perhaps, or a dose of poison slipped into his ale.

'I've got friends, very good friends,' she replied sullenly.

'Then you know what I mean,' Charlotte said.

She had money of her own, but not vast sums, and had decided to take the Renaissance ring to Hatton Garden Market and see how much a jeweller would offer for it. This would be a start, and she could add to it from her bank account. She knew that Richard would be very angry when he found out, but hoped by that time to have her hands on the incriminating letters.

As Jennie's eyes raked over Charlotte, she deliberately fed her resentment. What a genteel young lady! She'd never had to fight, starve, crawl her way out of the mire. She hadn't given birth to a child and then had to leave it for others to rear. When she spoke again her voice was defensive and hard.

'You're wasting your time, and mine, and I'm tired. Good night, Miss Whoever-you-are.' And she began to unlace her gown.

'That's your last word?' Charlotte saw the determined set of her shoulders, her dismissive back, and her spirits plummeted.

'Yes. Close the door as you go out.'

As Charlotte made her exit, she looked back over her shoulder and saw Jennie's face in the mirror. She was staring at her, not a muscle stirring, stripped to the waist, the wet-white ending in a startling harsh line just above the nipples, her own darker skin tone taking over. Her breasts were like magnets, drawing Charlotte's eyes against her will. This woman had been Richard's mistress. It was a horrible thought. When she glanced up she saw that a taunting smile played about Jennie's red lips, like a gash in her heavily powdered face.

Charlotte stiffened her spine and stalked from the dressing-room, scorned and humiliated by a vicious strumpet who had Richard exactly where she wanted him and had no intention of letting go.

Chapter 18

'I wonder how many we'll have in tonight?' Beth said, touching her husband's shoulder affectionately as she passed him on the way to her section of the clinic.

'Dozens, I expect. Saturday night, when the booze is in and the wits are out.' Dudley spoke to her retreating back while he opened the door of his consulting room.

'Is Ron coming to assist?' She stood by the mirror in the hall and pinned up the bib of the pristine white apron that covered the front of her navy blue dress. Ronald Carfax was a doctor sympathetic to their ideas who volunteered his services when he could get away from his own busy practice.

'It's his night off. So it's down to us, though I'm expecting Charlotte to lend a hand.' He switched on the desk light and, after sitting down in his leather chair, pressed a buzzer which connected with the area where his patients waited.

It was humid, and the sash windows were open on to the shrub-filled garden that had transformed the rear of the building. There was even a pocket-handkerchief sized lawn, complete with sun-dial, something green and restful to look at after gruelling hours spent with sickly slum-dwellers. Not that Dudley was discouraged, far from it. The Canyard Street Clinic was more successful than even he, with his boundless enthusiasm, could have anticipated. He was doing a worthwhile job, and this compensated for the extra work involved.

Saturday was the busiest night of all in the environs of Poplar, when the workmen drank their wages away, got into fights and then staggered home to beat hell out of their wives if they so much as looked askance. Throughout London the hospital casualty departments would be working flat out, too, dealing with razor slashes, knife wounds, black eyes and abrasions, and the police stations hard at it, their officers risking life and limb as they tried to keep order in streets and pubs and dubious clubs.

Drink, Dudley mused, chewing his pencil while he awaited his first patient. The devil's brew. All right in moderation and he was partial to a drop of Scotch himself but, as the Greeks had carved over the entrance to the Oracle at Delphi: Nothing in excess. That was the trouble with the human race, lack of moderation. A timid knock on the door, and work commenced.

He could not tell whether it was the June heat or other causes, but there did seem to be an awful lot of head colds about. Several children, brought in by their harrassed mothers, had hacking coughs. He dispatched them to the dispensary with prescriptions for linctus. The boredom of colds was varied by a stinkingly dirty old man with a leg ulcer; a woman with mastitis; a sailor whose skin eruptions in private places looked suspiciously like venereal disease; and an elderly body who complained bitterly when she saw Dudley behind his desk.

'Ain't there a lady doctor?' she declared loudly. 'I'm not 'aving a man looking at my departments!'

Wearily, Dudley summoned Beth as a chaperon. When the woman had gone, he said, 'How many more bottoms are plonked on seats out there?'

'About half a dozen.' She looked at the fob-watch dangling from her bib. 'It's nearly ten o'clock. Almost time to shut up shop.'

He stretched his arms, then pressed the heels of both palms into the small of his back. 'Thank God for small mercies. How are you doing?'

'Charlotte's here, so I've put her in charge of medicine bottles. I've had three women come in to ask about preventing pregnancy, and have examined them and issued caps and chemicals,' she answered, standing by the window and breathing deeply of the fresh air. It was a clear, starry night, with the moon hanging over London like a great, pale globe. 'I don't know if they'll use them, but I've done my best.'

She started and Dudley leapt from his seat at an almighty crash from the direction of the waiting-room. They could hear voices raised in anger, a man shouting, a woman screaming. Dudley burst out of his room and into the next, Beth close behind. Charlotte stopped dead, her hands immersed in soapy water, a line of dimpled green or brown bottles upended on the dispensary draining-board. Still dripping, she dashed into the hall.

The waiting-room was in an uproar, chairs flying, children wailing, people leaping for the door to avoid the couple locked in combat in the centre of the floor. She was a little, game woman who was trying to hit her husband, a bulky, hollow-cheeked, unshaven navvy who swore fluently as he wrestled with her.

'You filthy mare! Coming in 'ere to get those things what'll stop us 'aving another kid!'

'Sod you, Bert! Sod you! I'll do what I bloody likes! You ain't got to feed 'em, you bugger! Spending all our money down that fuckin' pub!'

'You ain't doing it, gal! You ain't! I'll beat the shit outter you!'

He had his heavy leather belt in his hand, buckle-end swinging. It caught her across the face and she yelped, blood starting to gush from the deep welt. She crumpled, arms around her head to protect it from those punishing blows.

Dudley grabbed at him. The man spun round with a bellow, and smashed into him with his fists. The impact drove the breath from his body, and he hit the floor with a spine-jarring thump. Beth made a beeline for the telephone, and it was then that Charlotte caught the acrid smell of smoke. It was billowing out of Dudley's consulting room.

Flames were leaping upwards, roaring and crackling as they greedily devoured the papers and files on desk and bookcase. Charlotte and Beth filled buckets and hurled water through the door but it was useless, the fire taking hold, smoke and flames beating them back.

'The police will be here soon, and the fire-brigade,' Beth panted. 'We must get out!'

The waiting-room was empty, except for Dudley who was slowly recovering. He shook his head, dazed and uncomprehending. Beth grabbed him, and pulled him to his feet, supporting him as they went out into the street. A large crowd had already gathered, rushing to see the fire-engines as soon as they heard the clattering of hooves and the clanging of bells. The police were there, too, helmets silhouetted against the glare, for the whole house was going up like a tinder-box. The flames soared into the night sky, huge blazing fragments hurtling down. The crowd gasped, retreated slightly, those behind in danger of being crushed.

Dudley, Beth and Charlotte, smoke-blackened and stunned, stared silently at the great black clouds pouring from every window, the scarlet fire-demons devouring the house in Canyard Street and taking two years of their lives with it.

*

In an alley not far away, two men were also watching the red glow over the rooftops. It resembled an unnatural dawn. They were standing in a doorway while people raced by, the fire providing the inhabitants with a splendid free spectacle. Maybe there would be the chance of looting.

'Well done, Albert,' said Phelan, his well-manicured hand holding out a cache of sovereigns.

'It went like clockwork, sir.' Albert was proud of himself. He'd shown this cold, arrogant geezer that he was capable of any treacherous business he cared to put his way. 'I made sure Nobbie got good and sloshed, then hinted that 'is missus was at the clinic. Old Nob didn't like that, didn't care for it at all, sir. Sort of 'urt his pride like. They got nine kids and 'ee reckons it proves 'ee's a man, 'specially as most of 'em is girls. Takes a real man to 'ave daughters, so they say.'

'You sent him there to cause a diversion?' Phelan liked that. Albert, nasty creature that he was, had his uses.

'I did. And while they was busy with the fight, I nipped in through the window, made a pile of the doctor's papers, and put a match to 'em.'

'Nobody saw you?'

'Not a single fucking soul. I weren't born yesterday, nor the day before. I knows my way around.'

'You do, there's no doubt about that. Good night, Albert.' Phelan turned away.

He did not want to linger anywhere near the fire, and he had things to do, a reporter from the gutter-press to contact. The man would be pleased to hear about this, and Lady Eva's connection with the clinic – so would the shareholders of the Pendral Bank. Their respectable money being used to run one of those sinful places that advocated anti-conception devices! They wouldn't care for that.

He had read the documents that Albert had in his possession, and there was little doubt in his mind that the Charlotte Drummond mentioned as being born on December 22nd, 1885 in the Parish of St Giles, was *his* Charlotte. Albert had refused to part with the papers, but Phelan knew that if a large enough sum was offered he would eventually capitulate. He had dismissed the other birth certificate. It did not interest him. It was of Jennifer Drummond, born October 17th, 1888, and this time it had been stamped in Bow. Albert had assured him that the child had died.

There had also been letters and a diary. Margaret Drummond, though no scholar, had poured the sorrows of her heart into it: her grief at her husband's death, her descent into destitution, her illness and fear for her children. The letters, tied up with a bit of faded pink ribbon, had been of scant interest, merely love-letters between herself and the man who had wooed her, married her, and then left her a penniless widow, Simon Drummond.

Phelan was willing to bide his time. Like a black spider in the middle of his web, he responded to the slightest tug at the edge of that sticky gossamer mesh, luring victims into it. Let the board at the bank cope with the upsets and alarms caused by this latest evidence of Eva's folly, before he dropped the other bombshell concerning the girl whom she intended to make her heir. His solicitor had already been informed, the same man who had worked for him and the Contessa years ago when they had suffered a crippling defeat. He would be more than pleased to triumph over Eva, collecting a fat fee should Phelan be considered more worthy and responsible to head such a noted organisation.

Phelan took a growler home, relaxing in the interior, content to use a horse-drawn vehicle in preference to a taxi. He needed time to savour the evening's success. His valet, Carlo, was nowhere in evidence when he reached Sloane Square, but Julian was there. He had just got out of the bath, his slim body wrapped in one of Phelan's silk dressing-gowns. He had towel-dried his hair, the strong thick curls springing up about his head, his skin summer-kissed, reminding Phelan of days spent on the Greek islands.

Good days, sensuous days of golden beaches and turquoise sea, of a tiny white villa and lithe, tanned peasant lads who had adored Julian, and done anything Phelan asked of them. Nights swimming naked in the moonlit sea, and making love to Julian in the sandy hollows below the villa.

They had met through Andrew, both of them related to an aristocratic English family, so that although Tyler was an explorer and Julian a drifter, they were accepted in society without demur. Julian, somewhat of a problem to his parents who did not begin to understand him, alarmed by his total lack of interest in having either a mistress or a wife, had been glad when Andrew collected him during one of his rare rests from ranging uncharted regions of the world, and took him to Italy to stay with Phelan. Thus their affair had begun, a love-affair that had endured, despite Phelan's ambitious plans for marrying into money. Andrew knew all about it, of course, but didn't turn a hair; an experienced, broad-minded man (some said amoral), nothing people did surprised him any more.

One had to be so careful in England, Phelan thought as he allowed himself the enjoyment of admiring his lover who now graced his bedroom. He loathed the place, with its rain and cold, its pettifogging rules and regulations, where homosexuality was a criminal offence and driven underground. He was forced to keep Julian at arm's-length in public, and be very circumspect as to what he did in private, lest it be found out. He had no desire to live here permanently, and it was only his quest for money that had brought him back.

Women? Phelan was attracted to them, provided he could ill-treat them, though Julian was not. He had never had a woman in his life, but he made friends with them and liked their company, as any other female might. He was a member of the sisterhood. Beautiful, sensitive, dependent on Phelan, a loyal, loving boy who performed the tasks he was set without argument, though there had been one or two scenes when Phelan became engaged to Charlotte. Julian did not like the idea of him having a wife, even though Phelan had carefully explained that it was a financial necessity and would not make the slightest difference to their relationship. Julian was delighted when Charlotte left Florence but, used to obeying Phelan, had done his duty in London, cultivating Gwen in order to spy on his rival.

Phelan made his anonymous call using the ornate brass and porcelain telephone in his bedroom, and Julian came straight across to him when he replaced the receiver on its hook. His eyes, green as the sea around Crete, brimmed with devotion as he asked, 'Well? How did it go?'

'No problem.' Phelan tossed his coat over the back of a brocaded chair. 'There's one hell of a fire in Poplar at the moment.'

'Oh, dear, is there? You are terribly naughty, you know.' Julian had spent the evening sick with worry. Phelan was so ruthlessly determined to get his own way, and he feared for him sometimes.

Phelan sat down on the bed and began to unlace his shoes. 'Eva's as good as done for. Kaput!' he exclaimed. 'A little while longer, and then we can pay a visit to Florence.' His eyes narrowed as he glanced up at Julian, flame in their dark depths. 'Come here, I'm feeling good. I've succeeded, and want to celebrate. What better way than with you, eh?'

Julian looked down at him for an instant, lips parted, his eyes shining with love. Phelan reached out and took his face between his palms. The silk dressing-gown slithered to the floor.

The news was terribly exciting. The Gaiety folk, actors and stagehands alike, could talk of little else. An impressario from America had seen *The Sailor Girl* and arranged with the Guv'nor for the show to go to New York.

That means me, Jennie had thought, when she heard. Oh God, why does it have to be America? How far away is Los Angeles from

New York? I don't want to see Max ever again! I hope he doesn't try to find me. I'm glad I tore up his address. America's a big place. There's not much chance of us bumping into one another.

After he had left she had gone back to work with a vengeance, resolving never to fall in love again. It was fatal; robbed her of her single-minded drive, made her vague and dreamy, filled her with the tormenting ache of desire. I don't want it! she screamed within herself. I don't want anyone! I don't want Max!

George Edwardes was pleased as Punch, going about with a happy smile on his chubby face, rubbing his hands with glee. It was not the first time a Gaiety show had appeared on Broadway, and he hoped it would not be the last. He took off *The Sailor Girl* and put on a re-run of *The Toreador*. He was most tremendously busy, organising scenery, props, costumes and artistes, booking tickets, and overseeing the packing of everything into huge crates loaded on to lorries which took them to the docks. Jennie paid six months' rent on her house, left her maid there as caretaker, went on a shopping spree and then spent a weekend at Gaulden Hall with the Garnets and Grace.

Louis, and some of the less fortunate members of the theatre who had to soldier on at home, were at Southampton to say goodbye. The Guv'nor and Malone paced the decks and buttonholed the captain, ensuring that their children wanted for nothing before abandoning them to his tender mercies. Jennie's stateroom aboard the liner was awash with flowers. Louis shook her hand manfully and tried not to cry. She hugged and kissed him and promised to bring him back a present. Then visitors were called ashore, the gangplanks raised, the graceful liner quivered to the thrum of her engines, and the fussy little tug-boats blasted on their hooters as they piloted her out of the harbour.

The Atlantic crossing was choppy and several of her companions were laid low with sea-sickness, but not Jennie. Every evening she entertained passengers in the saloon, and became extremely popular. She enjoyed shipboard life; the liner was like a floating hotel and its very size staggered her. Though travelling first-class, she promised herself that one day she would occupy one of those *crème de la crème* 'millionaire suites' which were the pride of the shipping line. She realised that, very soon, she would have to employ a personal maid who would accompany her everywhere, instead of relying on help from stewardessess. Her clothes were numerous and elaborate, and she needed someone to keep them spic and span.

The time passed quickly. In the day she could amuse herself on the raquet court, or might stroll on the Promenade Deck with fellow-actors. There was a luxuriously appointed pool, and she donned a racy costume and rediscovered the delights of swimming, progressing further than she had done on that day in July, two years before, when she had entered the sea at Southend with Jane Reeves, and brought on her labour.

In the evenings, she swanned about trailing silks and perfume in the Verandah Café where vines grew upon the lattice work of windows through which streamed artificial sunlight, or strolled throught the Café Parisian on the arm of some doting petty officer, maybe dancing the night away to French tangos and rag-time melodies. It was an enchanted week that culminated in her first breathtaking glimpse of the shoreline of New York, dominated by the colossal Statue of Liberty.

When they had disembarked and gone through the formalities of customs, the company were met by a cluster of chatty gentlemen who represented the management of the Casino Theatre. An English musical with an English cast was guaranteed to sell seats, and the lovely dancers, handsome actors and droll comedians inspired fanatic fervour in the breasts of hundreds of Anglophiles.

Jennie faced a battery of cameras on the quayside, and the attentions of pushy reporters asking impertinent questions. She was rescued by Danny Monroe, chief assistant to the producer, a dapper man in a grey pin-striped suit and a large glittering tie-pin, whose accent reminded her of Max. On all sides she was beseiged by American voices that brought him poignantly to mind. She almost wished she had never come, but this was only momentary. Soon she was engulfed in the vitality and force of the city.

It was like London, but bigger – bigger streets, bigger shops, towering blocks that Monroe told her were called skyscrapers, the latest thing in architecture, and the tallest of these was the Flatiron Building near Madison Square. Taxis took the cast to the Malborough Hotel, much favoured by stars of the stage. Jennie craned out of the window, overwhelmed by the crowds where everyone hurried. There was haste in the air, Broadway a jumble of drays, wagons and cars, the sidewalks thick with people and lined with shops, hotels, theatres and offices. There was a bewildering array of electric signs of all sizes and descriptions.

The city hummed ceaselessly, a continual sound to which her ears soon became accustomed so that she was no longer aware of it. The Malborough was larger and more impressive than the hotel where Max had stayed in London, but Jennie, playing the great actress to the hilt, did not bat an eyelid as she swept into the reception foyer where rich golden drapes and tall vases of Sèvres porcelain were offset by soaring cream and coral marble pillars.

Monroe's aides accompanied the male actors to the bar, and the other ladies wanted to go to their rooms, but Jennie consented to being ushered to the lounge which had reproduction Louis Quatorze furniture, and murals in the style of Watteau. Crystal chandeliers hung from the sky-blue ceiling, picked out with angels and cherubs. A string quartet played soothingly in the background.

'I just love hearing you speak, Miss Adele,' Monroe said, as a waitress brought coffee and cakes. 'I could listen to you all day.'

'My accent, you mean?' Jennie, every bit the lady in her cream lace dress, huge brimmed hat ornamented with tea-roses, long white gloves and furled silk parasol, was the personification of charm and grace. The Guv'nor would have applauded, had he been there. A Gaiety Girl to the very life!

'Yea, that's it!' Monroe was an even-featured man with a silky moustache, younger than Jennie had expected, but it seemed that youth was admired in America and given every opportunity.

'Have you ever visited England, Mr Monroe?' Jennie enquired, giving him a cool, but not too cool, glance.

'No, Ma'am, but I'd sure like to. My ancestors came from Scotland.' And he proceeded to tell her about them, very proud of the connection.

How friendly they are, Jennie thought, rolling back her glove, tapering fingers with pink oval nails holding a pastry fork with which she delicately cut into the cream cake on her plate. Even though she had only been in New York for a short time, she felt at home, responding to the energy surging through the city, to the smiles and warmth she encountered on every side. It was Max's country, and he had displayed the best characteristics of this polyglot race. What would she do if he were to suddenly appear in the doorway? she mused, as Monroe rattled on.

It was a question that was to plague her often during the hectic weeks that followed, her feelings ambiguous. Most times she hated Max, but occasionally she would suddenly think of him, in the middle of the show or during the matutinal hours after curtain-call, when with the other actors and a sprinkling of the *demi-monde* who always lingered around the theatres, she would be whisked off to Rector's or The Rooftop or some other hugely expensive and smart eating-place. She was wooed by many men – handsome men, plain men, all of them rich – willing to lay their hearts and fortunes at her feet, yet she remained charming but distant. She was the fashion, all the rage, but would experience bouts of acute anxiety, haunted by a vivid mental picture of Max banging at her dressing-room door, begging to be let in, or else accosting her in the street. When this happened, she would try to get away, returning to her hotel, suffering a sickening sense of loss mingled with relief – for he was never there.

The Sailor Girl ran for weeks, threatening to outdo the earlier box-office hit, *Floradora*. The hallmark of its success was the way in which delivery boys could be heard whistling its tunes in every quarter of New York. A phonograph company recorded Jennie singing, promising that this would add a further string to her bow. Several producers from other theatres were propositioning her to leave the Gaiety and work for them, offering fantastic sums. As it was, she was receiving six times the amount paid by George Edwardes.

Should she stay in America? It was tempting and, as the weeks stretched into months, it seemed that Max had forgotten her and it would be safe to do so. But she could never abandon the Guv'nor who had taken a chance on her and made her what she was. Also the best part of Jennie, the warm, tender, generous and loving part, had been left in the safe keeping of a little girl who lived in a rundown old farmhouse in Surrey. With every beat of her heart, Jennie longed to see her daughter again.

One night she returned to the Marlborough directly after the last call, refusing all invitations. She was tired, for New York sweltered under the August heat, and even the large electric fans in the wings had failed to relieve the hot waves beating at her from glaring spotlights and floats. Her dressing-room was large, as was everything about the Casino Theatre, that beautiful, Saracenic structure with its green and gold plush and fantastic Moorish arches. But this grandeur, adulation and continual partying was beginning to sour, and she thought nostalgically of her tiny room in the Gaiety, of Fipps and Jupp and Louis.

With this came the remembrance of that girl who had called on her. She had been so angry at the time, filled with pain at Max's departure, wanting to vent her spleen, and her unfortunate visitor had borne the brunt of it. Now, looking back, she was sorry that she had been so rude, for she had seemed a nice girl, so earnest in her desire to help Richard. Never mind, Jennie thought, as she left the theatre and hailed a taxi, I shall be quite well off when I get back to London, able to pay Albert myself, though it sticks in my craw to put a single farthing in that greedy sod's paw.

The hotel was still busy, for New Yorkers were night-birds. Their energy was astounding, and Jennie liked the absence of class-system, the fact that any man, or woman for that matter, could get to the top of the tree no matter how humble their origins, if they were prepared to work. They worshipped success, and gave unlimited support to the person who acquired it. More for the Guv'nor's sake than her own, Jennie had kept her secret, but she knew that had she openly confessed that she came from the East End slums, the public would have loved her even more.

She let herself into her suite. The shaded wall lights were on and this was a surprise for the maid she had hired should have left long before this. Jennie never insisted that she wait up for her, knowing her own erratic hours. She shrugged, kicking off her high heels with a sigh of relief, at the same time pulling the hat-pins from the creation that crowned her hair, and beginning to uncoil the long locks. What she needed more than anything else was a cool, relaxing bath.

It was then that she heard a movement through the half opened bedroom door. Her heart leapt with fear. A prowler? A thief? She looked round frantically for a weapon and picked up a heavy brass poker that lay beside the marble fireplace. Holding this tightly, she crept towards the door, reaching it just as someone stepped out. With a fierce yell she brandished it above her head, but her wrist was gripped and held in an iron fist.

'Hey, baby! That's no way to greet me!' said Max, grinning from ear to ear.

'You bloody bastard! Where have you been? Why didn't you come before?' And she was in his arms and he was covering her face with kisses.

Eva felt that she had aged inside. On the surface she appeared serene, but the traumas of the last weeks had taken their toll. If it wasn't for Richard, she kept repeating to herself, if it wasn't for him, I should have gone mad.

It was not only the sorrow she had felt when visiting Canyard Street the day after the fire, though it had been bad enough, it was the newspaper reports, the castigation she received both in the boardroom and from some of her acquaintances, that had ripped her to shreds. How could people be so bigoted, so lacking in understanding of the problems of having more children than one could afford? It was quite beyond her comprehension. Some of those who had been generous to her other endeavours had now withdrawn their support. Though not all; there still remained a precious nucleus of true friends as advanced in their outlook as herself.

Frederick had been at her side during every unpleasant and embarrassing meeting of directors – putting her case, couching his arguments in legal terms that carried a good deal of weight – but, despite this, they had still lost a percentage of shareholders. The directors had been divided. Those who had resented a woman's intrusion into a strictly masculine area had seized upon this as an excuse to mutter that it was high time someone else was considered as chairman.

Yet another meeting had been called and, seated at the head of the long table within whose rich dark sheen every solemn face was reflected, she had known who that someone might be. Phelan Charteris was lingering in England, had been for months, quite contrary to his customary inclinations toward Mediterranean society and climate.

'What are you suggesting, My Lord?' she stared down its length at the elderly nobleman who had been on the board since her father's time and who had just finished expounding on the inadvisability of some of Eva's policies.

He had the veined cheeks and purple nose of a man too fond of port, full of grandiose notions but unable to frame his thoughts with any force or clarity. He cleared his throat and polished his monacle, replaced it in his left eye and then mumbled, 'Seems like it may all be a bit too much for you, Lady Eva. Damn me if it don't. You get gerrymandered, my dear, talked into putting the bank's money at the disposal of any rascal who comes to you with a hard-luck story.'

Eva bridled at his patronising tone, though she replied with apparent composure, 'I'm perfectly capable of deciding whether the cause is genuine. Don't forget that a large proportion of the money I use is my own. I don't have to answer to anyone.'

'Oh, but you do. You don't run the bank single-handed.' This came from Sir Martin Evesham, who had been a thorn in her side ever since he took his father's place. He had a sneering voice and a scornful way of looking at people. 'Maybe we should seriously consider having another member of the Pendral family here.'

'Who?' Eva gave him an oblique glance from under half-closed lids, well aware of what his reply would be.

He and Phelan were members of the same club. Her cousin would have had ample opportunity to get Sir Martin on his side, pressing the advantage given him by the fire and the ensuing scandal. Eva was beginning to harbour suspicions about that devastating conflagration and the speed with which it had been reported in the newspapers.

Sir Martin stared at her down his aquiline nose, and confirmed her worst fears. 'It's time a man was in charge,' he said. 'Why don't we invite Mr Charteris to become a director?'

Freddy took up the gauntlet on Eva's behalf. 'This was gone into years ago, when Lady Eva inherited. Charteris contested the will but his case was thrown out of court.'

'He might have better luck this time,' Sir Martin replied meaningfully.

This started an argument that went on for an hour and was inconclusive. It left Eva trembling with nervous strain and fatigue. Frederick took her to lunch at a quiet restaurant where they continued to study the problem from all angles.

'Don't worry too much,' he said, spreading a damask napkin over his knees as the meal arrived.

'The board doesn't trust me any more.' Eva pushed the food about her plate, having no appetite.

He laid down his fork, and said earnestly, 'Look here, Eva, it'll soon be forgotten. This sort of muck-raking always is. The press want their wrists slapped, they really do! It's them you can thank for this hullaballoo.'

'The press, and Phelan!'

'You think he's at the bottom of it?'

'Don't you? Hasn't it occurred to you that the fire was just too providential, coming at a time when he'd lost Charlotte?'

'We need proof.' Frederick rarely allowed himself to get carried away, the habits of a lifetime standing him in good stead in almost any circumstance.

'And that's impossible, I should think.'

'Maybe not. I'll put out feelers. One of the perks of my profession is that several members of the criminal class are indebted to me.' He raised his glass to her, thinking, it really is an ill wind that blows no one any good. She's leaning on me, just like in pre-Richard days.

Eva gave him a faint smile. 'You always make me feel better, Freddy.'

'Someone has to,' he answered gruffly, never taking his eyes from her face, more than just concerned. She was far too pale for the summery weather, and dark smudges rimmed her eyes. He poured Moselle into her glass, adding as casually as he could, 'Where's Richard?'

'Helping Dudley clear up. The clinic can be re-built, and open again in the autumn.'

'But it will take a good deal of money.'

'Yes.'

'And you'll invest it?'

'Of course. You don't think I'm going to let anyone stop me, do you?' There was a flash of the old fighting spirit in her yet. 'Phelan can go to the devil! He's not sitting in my chair at the head of the boardroom table.'

*

Richard was glad that the work with Dudley took up so much of his time. He was finding Eva irksome, though hating himself for his disloyalty. She was simply too good to him, never reproaching him if he broke engagements or disappeared for days on end, always helpful, considerate and even-tempered. They never quarrelled because she would not oppose him, but the truth was that such docility irritated him, and there were times when he had to get away from her clinging arms, her welcoming body, her blind adoration. She had put him on a pedestal and it was impossible to live up to this idealistic image that had little to do with the real person.

Like most men, he avoided scenes, tears and confrontations, and until Charlotte came back from Italy, had been content to go along with whatever Eva wanted. He valued a quiet life when he could work undisturbed, but now he fretted under the yoke of her possessiveness and passivity. It was stifling him.

He was as sweet and loving to her as ever, especially so after the fire, when a distraught Charlotte had come to him and they had agreed, rather grimly, that it had made it even more impossible for him to break away. With the world against her, Eva needed him as never before. So he put his energies into clearing up the charred mess in Canyard Street, falling into bed at night so exhausted that he slept straight away, giving himself no time to dwell on either of the two women who loved him, and whom he loved in entirely different ways.

Greyfriars dozed in the glorious autumnal weather, dreaming away like some ancient hermit in the midst of its gardens filled with rose-bushes, velvety sward and age-old trees. Charlotte, weekending there, welcomed the peace that soothed her bruised soul. She lay in a hammock slung between a pair of oaks, listening to the hum of a mowing-machine cutting the croquet lawn.

Half-asleep, she could hear the others taking tea on the terrace where the french windows were hung with trailing garlands of late blooming wistaria. Bernice's voice rose above everyone else's. She had joined them for the weekend, having dispatched her husband to Scotland for the grouse-shooting. King Edward had gone, too, his destination Balmoral, so she was in the rare position of not having a man to worry about.

Charlotte had hoped she was forgotten, but Bernice hailed her from the balustrade edging the terrace, the breeze ruffling the ends of the chiffon scarf thrown negligently round her neck. 'Don't you want something to eat? Cucumber sandwiches, my dear. Delicious!'

Charlotte performed the difficult feat of getting from the hammock without turning turtle, then smoothed down her white skirt and walked up the wide steps towards the group seated at the round, green-painted wrought-iron table. Richard was wearing an open-necked shirt and cream flannels, having just trounced Frederick at tennis. The older man was mopping his face, pleased with himself for having put up a good fight.

'Richard darling, put on your pullover,' Eva said, indicating the V-necked garment draped across the wall. 'You'll get a chill.'

Dear me, thought Bernice, he doesn't look too happy about being treated like a child. She had met Richard several times before, though had not seen as much of Eva as of yore, and now she was aware of tension in the air, which increased when Charlotte took her place at the table.

Bernice leaned forward, her lips slightly parted, her experienced eyes narrowed as she considered the members of the group. She picked up curious and interesting ripples and undertows. She had tried to warn Eva of the dangers of becoming engaged to a man years younger than her, advising that she kept him as her lover, but Eva, besotted, had turned a deaf ear to her warning.

One of the reasons why Bernice had withdrawn from her had been this total obsession with Richard. It worried her to see her old friend behaving like a doormat, and she was sure that it was not healthy for him either. She liked him, few people did not, for he was pleasant and intelligent, but she had qualms about this alliance and sensed that Frederick shared them. She had only just arrived, and had not had time for a chat with the lawyer, but made a mental note to remedy this at the earliest opportunity.

Of course, she had read about the clinic fire and had rows with several people who condemned Eva. Birth control? My God, she had thought at the time, where should I be without my Mensinga cap? Up the creek and no mistake! Family limitation is the finest thing ever invented. Her finger on the pulse of everything that happened in her select circle, Bernice had also heard about the rumblings at the bank, and had seen Phelan several times at functions, taking great pleasure in cutting him dead. There was no doubt where her loyalties lay, but she feared that Eva was her own worst enemy, and was genuinely concerned about her.

That concern took on an edge of panic when Charlotte, who had been staring across the grass, watching someone or something in the distance, suddenly said, 'We have a visitor.'

She instinctively drew closer to Richard, recognising who it was even from afar. A black figure on a black stallion, riding fast and with dreadful purpose from the direction of Hawksdown Hall – one of the four horsemen of the

Apocalypse, trailing doom and disaster like swirling grey smoke.

'What does he want?' Eva recognised him, too, frozen in her seat, the colour leaving her cheeks, her fist clenched on the table.

'We'll soon find out.' Bernice settled down to watch. This was more entertaining than any stage-play, her adrenalin pumping with anticipation.

Time seemed to be playing tricks, the stallion's powerful legs rising and falling with agonising slowness, silent, like a phantom – then everything speeded up, and Phelan was drawing on the bit at the terrace steps, tall in the saddle, his eyes almost level with Charlotte's. He was attired entirely in black: black jacket, black breeches and boots, black stock around his throat, black hat on his night-black hair. He touched the top of his silver-mounted crop to his lips where a smile lurked.

'Good afternoon,' he said, bowing ironically across the saddle pommel at Eva, Bernice and Charlotte.

'Why are you here?' Eva was on her feet, impressive in a stamped velvet cloak, the satin part red and the velvet part gold, her latest acquisition from the House of Poiret, worn over a trouser suit.

Charlotte stood beside her, closing ranks against the enemy, but Bernice remained seated, inhaling cigarette smoke nervously, then quickly crushing out the butt with a flicker of diamonds on white fingers.

'Dear Eva, I'm always sure of such a warm welcome in your house,' Phelan answered, his voice pregnant with menace.

'State your business and then go away.' Eva could feel hatred flooding through her. She wanted him off her land. His very presence blighted the sunlight, and would surely blast every living blade of grass if he lingered.

He gave a soft laugh. 'Ah, my business. Yes, it is rather important and I'm sure you'll want to hear it, as it concerns you and the bank.' His horse shifted restlessly and he laid a calming hand on its lustrous ebony mane. Then in the same terrifyingly casual and conversational tone, he continued, 'I understand from Sir Mark Evesham that the directors are restless. There are certain matters I intend to put before them, but thought it only common courtesy to inform you first.'

'What is it?' Eva took a pace nearer, her cloak scintillating. She looked taller, more authoritative, the mistress of Greyfriars questioning an intruder.

His eyes shifted from her to Charlotte. 'Some documents have come my way recently. They are to do with your ward, Eva. That girl there, whom you intend to make your heir. There's a birth certificate, letters, and a diary that belonged to her mother.'

'My mother!' Charlotte's hands flew to her breast to still the sudden wild pounding. 'Where are they? Let me see them!'

Phelan was motionless, his eyes never leaving her, though he addressed Eva. 'You'll find them interesting reading, Eva, as will the directors. I suggest that you keep a close watch on your fiancé, and don't leave him alone with Charlotte.'

'What is all this?' The cold paving of the terrace seemed to penetrate the soles of Eva's slippers, creeping up her legs and through her body, a chill that entered her soul. Charlotte and Richard ... How often had she wondered, dreaded, tried to be level-headed though every instinct told her to beware. She distrusted Phelan, yet her jealousy blazed afresh. Did he know something that would confirm her fears?

He flicked the side of his booted leg with his whip, keeping her waiting, protracting the agony. 'They say that blood is thicker than water, don't they, Eva? Family traits carrying on – the sins of the fathers, et cetera. Or the mothers, in this case. Charlotte's mother was a prostitute.'

Chapter 19

'Welcome 'ome, Jen,' Albert said, without bothering to get up from the couch in the dressing-room. He was lounging indolently, head resting on the scroll back, booted feet crossed at the ankles and propped high on a cushion. 'I missed you, gal. Missed our little chats, but Fipps 'as been filling me in with all the latest about you.'

He was grinning like the Cheshire Cat, though Lewis Carroll's fictional animal had been benign compared to Albert. Fipps was watching him guardedly as she held out Jennie's cotton kimono. She slipped her arms into it; the stage had been hot, but out back it was icy. A draughty theatre, and she missed the luxuries of the Casino, but was thankful to be in England again.

In the past, Fipps had viewed Albert with suspicion, and so had Jupp. Jennie had invented a cock and bull story about him being a distant cousin, and they had reluctantly admitted him. Tonight, however, things were different. Jupp had greeted him at the stage-door like a long-lost brother, and Fipps had been positively effusive. Albert, in his conceited way, had assumed they had accepted him at last. What could be more natural than that he, Jennie's proud and loving relative, should be there when *The Sailor Girl* re-opened at the Gaiety after its triumph in New York?

Jennie, seated at the dressing-table, strained her hair away from her brow and secured it with a wide bandeau, before starting to remove her make-up with a pad of cotton wool smeared with cleansing cream. Her eyes met Fipps' in the mirror. She nodded almost imperceptibly, and said, 'I'll call you when I want my dress unfastened.'

'Don't bother about that, Fipps. I can unlace the lady,' Albert offered jovially.

When Fipps had gone, Jennie swivelled round on the stool. Her eyes, slanted up at the outer corners by the bandeau's pull, regarding him steadily. 'You've come for money, I suppose?'

'That's right.' He stirred himself, sitting up, all attempt at humour banished. 'You're rich now. Done very well. I knew you would, could feel it in my water.'

'How much for the whole bag? Every one of those bloody photos, and the negatives?' Jennie reached for a cigarette and lit it. She did not offer Albert one, though he was looking hungrily at the pack.

He eased back, stuck his thumbs in his waistcoat pockets and screwed up his eyes, as if giving the matter his deepest consideration. 'Well now, I dunno – I've got you by the short and curlies, ain't I?'

'How much?' she insisted.

'I couldn't let them go for less than a couple of thousand quid, and that'd be cheap at the price.'

Bastard, she was thinking, greedy bastard, but she smiled calmly. 'And that would be the end of it? No more visits? No more blackmail? I wouldn't have to see your poxy mug ever again?'

This did not amuse him for Albert fancied himself, and liked to think that every woman he met harboured a burning passion for him. He looked at Jennie with active dislike but, another scheme foremost in his mind, tempered both expression and voice, adopting a wheedling tone that was more nauseating than his usual hectoring one.

'The end of the photos, yes, but there's something else, and I'd let you in on this one, Jen. We could be partners, for you'd 'ave no trouble meeting the person I'm thinking about. You could call on 'er easily, a famous actress like you.'

Jennie had feared all along that even if she paid him the earth, Albert would still have some other dirty deal in the offing. She inhaled deeply of the bluish smoke and let it coil slowly through her nostrils, giving herself time to think. Now was the moment to draw him out.

She gave him a sharp stare. 'Tell me more,' she said.

He stood up, came over to her, put an intimate hand on her shoulder. She sat rock-still, conquering the urge to pull away. 'You and me, Jen. What a team! We'll make the bastards dip deep into their pockets.'

'Why should I help you? I'm rich, aren't I? You've just said so.' She even allowed herself to lean against him, feeling his body harden, hating him like poison.

'Yes, but I know you, Jen. You're extravagant. Like to live in style. And why shouldn't you? You'll always need extra money, a woman like you. And I can get it – *we* can get it. Wouldn't you like to walk into the Café Royal dripping with diamonds when Everett Braithwaite and 'is mates are there? 'Ee wouldn't be sure it was you, but 'ee'd suspect, and you could snub 'im.'

The idea was appealing and she already intended to do it, wearing the diamonds that Max had bought her. Albert, Everett and their kind could not hurt her any more. She remained passive as Albert traced along the opening of her kimono with one finger.

'Tell me your plan,' she said.

'You remember my mother?' he began, and she nodded. 'The old girl was an 'ard woman, 'ad to be to stay alive. She took things from your ma's room when she died. You don't remember anything about it, do you?'

'Maybe. I'm not sure.'

Sometimes certain memories stirred, a Pandora's box with locked lid, stored in the deepest dungeon of her mind. The key was rusted. It did not turn at the bidding of any fingers, and the box remained mostly closed. Now the lid lifted, and she looked into that fearful space, seeing a colourless room – feeling cold flesh under her hands, flesh that should have been comforting and warm, hearing a girl's voice, and then a loud, angry adult one. A tiny child was sobbing bitterly. It was herself.

Albert was still talking. 'Ma fed you, made you work. Remember? You worked alongside of me. But there was things – papers and a book what your mother wrote in.'

'You've got them?' Jennie came alive, her nails digging into his hand. 'I want them.'

'Just a tick, gal, let me finish.' Albert was delighted to have made such an impression on her. His partner, yes, that would be fine, and not only that. He had always wanted her. Maybe now she'd – ?

'Go on.' Her intensity frightened and excited him.

'I've got your birth certificate.'

'The original? I had to get a copy from the Records Office when I needed a passport.'

'Yes, the original, and I've also got your sister's.'

'My sister!' Jennie froze. 'I have a sister?'

'You 'ave. Her name's Charlotte and she's the ward of one of the richest women in England.'

Charlotte! The name flashed against the blackness of her brain. Lottie! She remembered now – Lottie who had abandoned her when Ma died. The pain had been so bad that she had shut it out, blanked it off, forgotten it. All these years and she had never once thought of Lottie. She sat there stupefied, gripping the edge of the dressing-table, the brilliant lights swirling madly.

Albert garnered information like a squirrel hoarding nuts against a severe winter. Now he handed them out, one by cautious one. 'She's quite a lass, this sister of yours, a bit of a rebel. Gets mixed up in things what you'd think she wouldn't bother abaht, with all that money. She could be 'aving a bloody good time, but she don't seem interested. A serious sort of girl, like the woman what adopted 'er – Lady Eva Pendral.'

'Lady Pendral!' Would the surprises of this night never cease?

'Aye, didn't little Lottie do well?'

'What is it you're after?' Jennie was thinking of the girl who had begged her to stop pestering Richard. She had not given her name, but Jennie was positive that it had been her sister – and neither of them had known.

'You'll go and see her, and threaten to tell Lady Eva that she's 'aving it off with Richard Sinclair. That's the bloke Her Ladyship's going to marry.'

'Charlotte and he are in love?' Of course they were. Jennie recalled the girl's intense desire to help him.

He grinned and put an arm around her, unaware of her resistance. 'I dunno about love, but they're seen out and abaht, and she goes to his place in 'olland Park a lot. It's got to be worth money.'

'You've spied on them?' Jennie felt sick to her stomach.

He shrugged. 'A chap's got to live. You can tell 'er who you are, see 'ow she likes the idea of 'aving a sister what's on the stage, and who was an artist's model once upon a time. That won't do 'er reputation much good. See if she's prepared to pay to 'ave it 'ushed up. It don't matter 'ow you does it, so long as she 'ands over the cash.'

'Does anyone else know about this?'

'I'm working for a Mr Charteris. Charlotte was promised to 'im not long ago, but she give 'im the push. 'Ee was after her money – Lady Eva's cousin what's got the 'ump 'cause she in'erited the bank and 'ee didn't. Yes, 'ee knows, and 'ee's paid me well for a few little jobs I've done for 'im. 'Ee's puttin' the squeeze on Lady Eva right now on account of those papers. You see – your ma was a street-walker, a lady of the night – an 'ore.'

Poor Mother. A great deep well of tears that Jennie had not known she possessed threatened to overflow and drown her. She wanted to see Charlotte so much, but also knew that if she did, it might complicate both their lives. Perhaps things were best left as they were.

'I can't do it. I won't harm Charlotte,' she said, staring at Albert with such hostility that even he, thick-skinned as he was, felt its force.

'You will, my gal, or I'll be straight up to George Edwardes' office.'

'No, you won't! You'll deal with me!' Max pushed aside the screen that had concealed him and was on Albert before he had time to blink.

Albert cringed, knocked over several scent bottles on the dressing-table as he tried to run for the door, but Max had him, arms pinnioned to his sides. Jennie got out of their way. She had laid a trap for Albert and he had walked into it. For once, the biter had been bit.

'Who the 'ell are you?' Albert blustered, struggling helplessly. He was fine at bullying women, but could do nothing against this broad, strong man.

'I'm Jennie's husband, you lowdown skunk!'

'I don't believe it.' Albert had managed to free one hand and was beating ineffectually at Max's chest.

'You'd better believe it, and you'd better believe that I'm going to kill you if you don't leave her alone.' Max shook him ferociously, then dumped him in a chair and loomed over him. 'Listen to me, and listen good. I want those pictures and the negs, and I want them tonight. D'you hear?'

Albert gulped, nodded, his eyes bulging with astonishment and terror, but he could not help mumbling. 'What about the money?'

'You won't get another cent. If you don't do as I say, I'll call the police, OK? Now, where d'you live?'

'Why d'you want to know?' Albert's wits had not entirely deserted him.

'Because I'm coming with you to get the photos, and those other things you were on about.'

'You can't have those. I've promised 'em to Phelan Charteris and 'ee's a cold-blooded killer, guv'nor. I'll end up in the Thames with my throat cut if I cross 'im!' Albert's face was a ghastly hue, beads of sweat breaking out on forehead and upper lip.

'I don't give a damn what happens to you!' Max stood before him, head thrust forward belligerently, shoulders squared, his hands clenched into hard-knuckled fists.

'But, guv'nor – Jennie!' Albert's eyes turned to her, filled with crawling entreaty.

'Don't even speak to her!' Max thundered, then his arm shot out and he dragged him up by his tie. 'March! Get going!' As he strode to the door, dragging the writhing Albert along with him, he looked at Jennie and said, 'I'll take him in the car. Get a cab home, honey. I shan't be long.'

Fipps came in, and Jennie threw her arms round her, not knowing whether to laugh or cry. 'There, there, ducks, it's all right,' Fipps said, patting and soothing her. 'You've got a good 'un there. I'm glad for you, honest I am.'

'I have, haven't I? The best in the world. Oh, Fipps, I've been so lucky.'

Lucky she had been in every sense, for not only did Max adore her, protect her, and give her amazing confidence in herself, he was also the son of a multi-millionaire. Independent, rich in his own right, he was forming a film company in Los Angeles which he was certain would be a runaway success. Though he had delayed coming to her in New York, fighting his own feelings, respecting her need for freedom, once he had arrived at the Malborough Hotel, he had not left her side.

On that first glorious night of reunion, she had lain in his arms and told him everything about herself, holding nothing back. It had taken courage, for he might well have rejected her, but instead he had listened and, though angry with those who had abused her, his love had intensified. They had been married very quietly a few days after, telling no one, for she wanted to speak with George Edwardes before it became public knowledge. One of the Guv'nor's rules was that his girls should be single. However, by the time she arrived home she was such a valuable asset that Edwardes had taken it like a lamb, knowing that it would make little difference to her popularity. The news was only just beginning to trickle through theatreland, but soon there would be an announcement in the papers and then the whole world would be able to share her happiness, not just the Guv'nor, Jupp, Fipps and Louis.

When she reached Finsbury Park, she made herself a cup of cocoa and went up to bed, listening for Max's return. It was lovely to be home, and she still found herself going round the house, touching objects, just to remind them that they belonged to her. She was planning to visit Gaulden Court on her first free weekend, impatient to see Grace and eager to introduce Max to her. Acting did not seem so important at the moment, especially when he talked of adding to their family. In fact, though she had been careful when first making love to him in London, since they had met again she had forgotten about this, but hoped it would not happen quite yet. She had things to do, her life to put in order, before she presented him with an heir.

She snuggled down in the feather mattress, for it was autumn and although she had set light to the fire left ready in the bedroom grate, the room was cold. Watching the wood catch, the flames leaping and dancing, throwing shadows across the ceiling, she lay and thought about Max, willing him to come back quickly, her body aching for his. She could not get enough of him, feeling half alive unless in the presence of this forceful man with his warm smile, his amusing way of talking, his vivid personality.

Before long, she heard the car outside, then the slam of its door and Max coming in. He took the stairs two at a time and erupted into the bedroom. She held out her arms, and the mattress sagged under his weight as he hauled her up against him.

'It's over, baby,' he whispered into her hair.

'You've got the photos?'

He released her long enough to untie the string round the cardboard box he had brought with him. 'Sure thing, every damned one, and the glass plates.' He unwrapped the pictures and scanned them, whistling softly. 'Phew! They're hot, honey! No wonder you didn't want anyone seeing them. I can look at them, can't I? Whenever I want? After all, you are my wife, and they make me horny as hell.'

'Yes, but only you. Put them away safely, Max,' she managed to say before he re-established his claim on her.

Whether it was his brush with Albert or the photos it was impossible to tell, but his love-making was fierce and possessive. He was tearing at her nightgown and his own clothes, and kissing her everywhere. She met his passion with a fire of her own, straining against him, swept into a beautiful oneness that lifted her far away from the brass four-poster in the snug, fire-lit room. Later, when she nestled against his chest, she asked him what they should do about Charlotte, filled with wonder at having a sister of her own.

'Just think, Max,' she murmured. 'Gracie's got an auntie – Aunt Charlotte! What d'you think of that?'

He rumbled with laughter. 'I've got dozens of 'em, and they're no help to me at all, mostly.'

She sat up, bare and beautiful, her long hair tickling his face as she bent over him. 'You've been spoilt, my lad. That's your trouble. If you lived like me – been through the shit I have, then you'd be glad to have a family behind you.'

He sobered, stroked her cheek. 'I know, baby, I know. It's great that you've found your sister. I'm glad, I really am.'

'Then what are we going to do?'

'I think we'll pay a call on Richard Sinclair,' he said, one broad hand resting on her naked hip. 'There're a few loose ends, and it's down to the men to sort them out.'

Charlotte felt guilty every time she saw Richard. It was even worse since Phelan had ridden over to Greyfriars at the weekend. Eva had been so angry, but impotent while Phelan was privy to those documents which gave him an advantage. They had talked of nothing else when he had taken his departure, and curtailed their stay, back in London on Sunday evening. Eva could take no chances. She did not know when Phelan proposed to act, but guessed that it would be soon.

In stubborn negation of her own instincts, Eva had commissioned Richard to paint Charlotte's portrait, thus bringing them together even more. Sometimes she accompanied Charlotte, watching while she posed, but there was never any indication that either of them had more than a friendly interest in one another. He was engaged on filling in background details when Charlotte arrived for a sitting.

'The door's not locked,' he called out at her knock.

He was standing back from the canvas on the easel, rocking on his heels, eyes slitted as he considered his work, a palette hooked over his left thumb, a sable brush, thick with paint in his other hand. He did not turn his head, and she joined him in studying the painting. He had cleverly captured her likeness as she sat in a thronelike chair, her head slightly tilted, her hair unbound and falling over her shoulders.

'It's good,' she commented, though finding it hard to think of anything but him.

'Not bad,' he agreed. 'I'll enter it for the Royal Academy Exhibition.'

So prosaic a conversation which they were using to throw up barriers between them. This isn't fair. I love him so much, she grieved. He put down the tools of his trade and wiped his hands on a turpentine soaked rag. She had come prepared to pose, wearing the same dress as the one in the painting, but was reluctant to do so. The meeting with Phelan had upset her deeply. Every time she saw him it re-opened old wounds. Now they were bleeding freely inside her.

'Can I have a coffee before we start?' she asked, laying her coat and hat on the chair, and giving her wet umbrella a shake.

He anxiously searched her face. 'We don't have to work this morning, if you're not up to it. The light's bad anyway.'

'I'm fine. Really.'

'You're not. That bloody Phelan!' He flexed his hands as if

wanting to strangle him. 'Threatening you and Eva! What's he hoping to achieve?'

'Taking over the bank, of course.' She had been controlling her emotions for Eva's sake, but now she could let go, safe with Richard.

'He won't succeed.'

'I'm not so sure. Eva may be forced to relinquish control, and disinherit me. They're hardly likely to want a prostitute's daughter in an executive position.'

Phelan's words had struck her a mortal blow. She had found out about her mother as she had yearned to do, but only to discover that she had been a harlot. As yet he had not shown them the evidence, but was negotiating with Eva about this. Charlotte was certain that it was true, and had spent hours since raking over the bits of her past that she could recall. Though only five when Eva found her, she could see her mother and sister quite clearly though not in living colour, the visions were in mono chrome.

At one time she would have been able to speak freely about it to Eva, but they had grown apart and this saddened her. Their old intimacy had never returned since the time when Charlotte went to Europe and Eva met Richard. It's partly my fault, she thought. I resent her claim on him, am jealous every time she looks at him or plans to do something with him that excludes me. He's living a lie, and this doesn't help. Surely, if he really loved me he would find the courage to tell her the truth? But I've begged him not to, haven't I? I can't bear to hurt her any more than he can.

Silence filled the huge, echoing studio, grey light pouring down from the wide windows in the roof, the glass overlaid by streaming patterns of rain. The effect was eerie, as if they stood at the bottom of the ocean. She shuddered and Richard stepped closer.

'Are you cold? I'll put some more coal on the stove.' But he did not move, looking at her intently, that greenish luminosity like a mist, enclosing them in a secret world of their own. Then he said, 'Ah, Charlotte, you are the love of my life.'

She made a helpless gesture with her hands. 'Don't say any more, please.'

'Dammit, I must! I can't stand this situation. I'm going away!'

'Away?' The strength drained from her limbs. 'Where?'

'I've met Bernice's friend, Andrew Tyler, the explorer. He's just come back from Africa and is getting an expedition together to go to Brazil. I'm joining it.'

'No!' It was too much to endure. Bad enough that he was with Eva daily and shared her bed at night, but at least then he was safe.

'I must, Charlotte. Don't you see?' His face was haggard, his eyes tormented. 'It's the only way out of this mess. Tyler is going deep into the rain-forests where the Portuguese slavers ill-treat the Indians. He wants me along as a photographer, needing evidence to bring them to book.'

'Have you told Eva?'

'Yes, and she doesn't like it. She wants to come with me, but she'd never stand the hardships. I've explained that, and she's very unhappy. But better this way than for her to know I love you and want to be free.'

'When are you going?'

'Next month.' His eyes held hers, and the gap between them had closed, his arms coming around her.

'Oh, Richard,' she moaned. 'How long will you be gone?'

'I can't say. It may be several years, by which time both you and Eva will have forgotten me.' He gave her a queer, twisted smile.

'I shan't,' she averred stoutly. 'I'll wait for you. Will you write to me?'

'If I can, but we'll be cut off from civilisation for most of the trip.' His grip tightened, and she could feel his heart beating heavily against her own. 'Charlotte, my love – we've so little time left together. Why should we deny ourselves? I want you, and you want me. Come to bed.'

His mouth was on hers, his kisses as she had known they would be, deep and tender and consuming, while he felt as if it was the first time he had kissed a woman, a new set of emotions taking hold of him. His hands fondled her face, her neck, the shoulders and breasts outlined by the material of her dress. He drew her to the chair by the stove, sat down and held her on his knee, still kissing her, slowly caressing her, savouring every second, till she was ready for him, head back, throat arched, limp with love.

Then he walked her towards the bedroom, their arms entwined, her face against his shoulder. At the entrance, he paused for one more kiss, then raised his head suddenly. Someone was knocking on the door. 'Damn,' he growled. 'Shall we ignore them?'

'It may be Eva.' Charlotte did not want her to find them like this, she with her bodice undone, and he in a state of arousal. Her fingers were fumbling with her buttons, her hands were tidying her hair, and then she opened the door.

Jennie stood there, a broad smile on her face. 'Hello,' she said. 'Mind if we come in?'

Charlotte gave her a freezing glare, fury sweeping through her. How dare she come there, that woman who had treated her so rudely at the theatre? What did she want now, and who was that man with her? One of her bullies?

He was a large man wearing a full-length wolf skin coat and a felt hat with a wide brim. He didn't look like a villain, radiating health and energy, his face tanned, his brown eyes sparkling, his smile all embracing. He reminded Charlotte of a big, friendly mastiff, and it confused her even more.

Richard was standing behind her and he, too, eyed the couple suspiciously. 'What d'you want?' he demanded. 'If it's more money, then you're out of luck. The well has dried up.'

'It's OK. May we come in and talk?' the man said and, when Richard nodded, he stepped inside, Jennie with him. 'You must be Richard Sinclair. I'm Maxwell Whitney, and Jennie's my wife.'

'What's going on?' Richard frowned at his unwelcome guests.

'Give me a minute and I'll tell you.' Jennie could not take her eyes from Charlotte. 'You're Charlotte, aren't you? Charlotte Drummond?'

'That's right,' she answered slowly, not even wishing to exchange words with her.

'I know this is going to be a terrible shock to you – but you're my sister. I'm Tweeny.' Jennie was standing there before her, looking as if someone had just presented her with the moon and stars.

'Oh, my God!' Charlotte staggered and would have fallen had not Richard's arm come about her. 'I thought you were dead!'

'And I'd forgotten that you existed, till yesterday.' Jennie was calmer, she had had a night to get used to the idea, whereas for Charlotte it was a bolt from the blue. Her face white, she stared at Jennie as if she was a ghost.

'My sister,' she faltered.

Max broke the tension, giving his booming laugh. 'She sure is, little lady. Why, you even look the same. Ain't that so, Richard? Alike as two peas in a pod.'

He was exaggerating to make them feel better, but Richard now knew why he had always felt that Charlotte reminded him of someone else, and he could never remember who. It was not an out and out resemblance; Charlotte's hair was dark, showing only a few reddish tints, while Jennie's was rich auburn. Charlotte's eyes were grey, Jennie's amber, yet their build, the way they moved, something about their expressions betrayed kinship.

'Lottie, dear Lottie,' said Jennie, opening her arms, and Charlotte went to her and held on as if she would never let her go.

It was Tweeny, it really was! Tweeny grown up and talented and beautiful. At last Charlotte had someone who belonged to her and made her feel truly whole. Looking into Jennie's smiling face, the ice that had always lodged in her heart, melted away. This was *family*, a force to be reckoned with, never condemning of one another, backing each other to the hilt against any outsider, loyal, invincible, faithful until death.

And Jennie, in tears, was thinking: I've a tribe of my own now, like the gypsies. I can understand why family means so much to them – now I've got Charlotte, and Grace, and my beloved Max, though he'll never be quite one us, but our children will.

Ignoring the men, they sank down on the Chesterfield. 'I still can't quite believe it,' Jennie exclaimed. 'You came to my dressing-room and I didn't know you.'

'You were such a bitch that night.' Charlotte was happy, frightened, bewildered, all at the same time.

'I was scared. Don't you see? Albert was blackmailing me.'

'He was nasty when he was a boy. I hated him then – '

'And I hate him now. He hasn't improved with age, I can tell you,' Jennie said firmly. 'It was through him that I was raped and had a baby.'

'A baby? You've got a baby?'

Then Jennie told her all that had happened, and every last trace of suspicion, each tiny pocket of reserve, fell away from Charlotte. Poor Tweeny – poor lost little sister, how she suffered while Charlotte was living like a queen! Tears coursed down her face, and Jennie cried, too. They shared the same handkerchief, sniffing, embracing, finally laughing at their emotional behaviour.

'So, you've a lovely little niece, Lottie. Her name's Grace.'

'I want to see her.'

'So you shall. I'm so glad now that I had her, though I very nearly drowned myself when I was pregnant and desperate.'

Charlotte sat very still, her mind racing back to that time in Florence when she was resting before the carnival ball. 'I had a dream – a dream that I was drowning.'

'When was this?' Jennie asked.

'In April, the day after I reached the Villa Alinari in Florence. When did you try to kill yourself?'

'Around April, I think.' Jennie was struggling to remember. 'It was spring, but the weather was cold. Well, when I was up to my knees in the Thames, just about to plunge in and end it all, I though I heard Zena telling me not to do it, so I got out and found Richard, and he looked after me.'

They stared at each other, half fearful, half filled with wonder. 'Coincidence?' Charlotte suggested.

'Telepathy?' Jennie breathed, then added, 'You really must meet Zena one day. She has the 'second sight', and I've lived among the gypsies long enough to believe in such things.'

'I'm beginning to believe in them, too. The way we've found one another has got to be like a miracle, hasn't it?'

'Oh, Charlotte, I tried to blackmail Richard! That was an awful thing to do. I hope you don't think too badly of me?' Jennie was so distressed that Charlotte put her arms around her and held her close.

'How could I? You're my sister. You mean everything to me.'

While the women were getting to know one another, holding hands and talking as if they would never stop, Max and Richard went into a huddle as the American explained everything. They struck up an immediate rapport, cast in the same mould, men of action not words.

'What we need is a private detective,' Max said, rubbing his jaw thoughtfully. 'Someone who'll tail Phelan Charteris. Don't worry, I'll foot the bill. I want this business cleared up once and for all. I've scared the crap out of Albert Baggot, so he'll do what I tell him. But it's Charteris we've got to get. We need to find something that we can use as a weapon. Blackmail him, if you like, though it's a dirty game. What d'you know about him?'

The rain continued, the studio darkened, and the four people in it were too absorbed to notice. Their futures hung in the balance, and they were united against a common enemy. One man, one evil man was holding them to ransom, and he had to be stopped.

Eva knew her idyll was over when Richard told her that he intended to go to South America. But she was glad that it was an idea that was taking him from her, not another woman. She held this thought to her for solace; he loved her but was a young man who needed adventure before finally settling down. She'd wait and he'd come back one day, then all would be well. He would have got this restless itch out of his system. All she had to do was be patient.

She told herself bravely that this explained his coldness of late, his avoidance of her, his expressed desire to be left in peace. It wasn't that he was tired of her. It simply meant that he wanted to meet with Tyler, to talk men's talk, to plan details of the expedition. Eva was almost happy again, until Phelan appeared on her doorstep at Greyfriars.

'I'll be in touch very soon,' he had said, before he rode away, but there had been no way of telling whether he meant in touch with her or with the bank.

Eva tried to forget both her cousin's threats and her fiancé's planned departure for the tropics. She divided her time between *Pour Femme*, Alice's home, Stephen's vicarage and Dudley's ménage. She saw little of Charlotte, but this was to be expected as Richard was eager to finish the portrait before he left. Bernice was much in evidence, saying that she was bored, complaining that Andrew was neglecting her, but Eva had the feeling that she was hovering around as if she expected to be needed soon. More than once she caught her and Frederick in earnest conversation, though they stopped when they saw her, and pretended it was nothing of importance. Like a ruler who feels herself at the mercy of conspirators, Eva slept badly, wandering the house in the small hours, worrying the faithful Lambert who dourly prophesied a migraine attack if she did not rest.

There was a stirring and apprehension in the air to which Eva was acutely sensitive, and it was almost with a sense of relief that she admitted a stranger to her drawing-room one afternoon, an American who gave his name as Maxwell Whitney, and announced that he had news for her.

'Mr Whitney,' she received him graciously, and he was struck by her regal air, her plainness relieved by her extravagant and ultra-fashionable clothes.

'Good day, Ma'am. I'm sorry to intrude like this, but it really is important,' he began, removing his hat and overcoat. 'It concerns Charlotte Drummond.' And as gently and diplomatically as he could, he started to tell her the whole story.

She listened without comment, then when he paused for breath, said, 'So you've invited Mr Charteris here this evening, along with my solicitor, Charlotte and Richard?'

'Yes, Ma'am, and Jennie, too. I hope you don't mind?'

'I want the matter settled, Mr Whitney.'

Phelan was practising the piano when the messenger arrived. Julian answered the door for it was the butler's night off, and Carlo was absent. He took the note from the lad who stood on the threshold then, after tipping him, he carried it to the music-room. He knew better than to interrupt Phelan when he was playing and waited patiently till the final chords rang out.

Phelan glanced up irritably. 'I've not finished yet. Go away.'

'It's a letter, came by special delivery.' Julian brought it to him.

Phelan snorted impatiently and ripped open the envelope. He read the letter with a slow smile. 'Well, well – so Eva wants to see me, does she? Perhaps the bitch has thought better of it and decided to nominate me to a directorship?'

'Oh, dear, does this mean we'll have to stay in England?' Julian sighed, sinking down on the piano stool beside him. He was wearing full evening dress, having promised to take Gwen to the theatre.

Phelan's mood had swung to one of exultation. He put an arm around Julian's shoulders, caressed his back and kissed his mouth. 'Don't fret, my dear, I'll be most conscientious about my work and put a curb on Eva, but shall take plenty of time off, and receive a handsome yearly income. I need to go back to Egypt for a bit more tomb robbing, and you can come with me. I stayed in a splendid hotel in Luxor, you'll love it, and we'll spend a lot of time in Greece and Italy, too.'

When Phelan entered the hall at Albion House, he handed his top hat, cane and cloak to Hopkins and was conducted to the drawing-room by a footman. As he followed the man's straight back, he glanced around him, making a mental inventory of the statues, the gilt-framed water-colours, the eighteenth-century furniture and velvet hangings.

One day all this would be his. He had heard that Eva's fiancé was going off adventuring, and this was providential for it would not have suited Phelan if Eva had married and produced a child. Now it would not be too difficult to dispose of her, accidents were commonplace, and Charlotte would soon be so discredited that her claim would not be worth the paper it was written on.

The footman threw back the great double doors and Phelan entered, expecting to find Eva alone. His black brows drew together as he found himself confronted by several people, two of whom were complete strangers. He checked for a moment, then held his head high and stalked towards them.

'Lady Eva – Charlotte – good evening. And to you, Mr Sinclair, Mr Haldene – and – ?' He paused, looking enquiringly at Max and Jennie.

Max, standing behind Jennie's chair, did not extend his hand. 'I'm Maxwell Whitney, from Los Angeles, and this is my wife, Jennie.' There was a challenge in his voice, and Phelan's eyebrows shot up.

He glanced across at Eva, who was leaning against the fireplace, gorgeously attired in silver brocade and lace. 'Eva, this is a pleasant social gathering, but I was under the impression that you wished to talk with me in private.'

Frederick was straddling the hearth-rug, his hands clasped behind his back. 'I'm here as Lady Pendral's legal adviser, and the others have come at her behest. The game's up, Charteris.'

'It is indeed – Eva's game,' Phelan said smoothly, while his mind grew crystal clear.

'Not hers. *Yours*,' Max rejoined, rage surfacing on his face.

Phelan spared him hardly a glance, saying unpleasantly, 'I don't know you, sir, and can't think why you're here, interfering in family matters.'

'D'you consider Charlotte to be family?' Max had never met anyone he disliked so much, his hackles rising.

'No. She's a whore's brat, not worthy to be associated with the Pendral name.' Phelan's lips twisted in a snarling smile.

'You insult her, sir, and her mother – and my wife, who is Charlotte's sister.'

'Baggot said the sister had died,' Phelan muttered, almost to himself. 'How can this be?'

'She *is* my sister.' Charlotte addressed him for the first time, her eyes cast down, fingers toying with the silk tassels that ornamented her grey velvet gown. 'Albert was lying.'

There was a moment's hush, broken only by the settling of the logs in the fire-basket, then Phelan drew himself up to his full height, awesome in his rage. 'It makes no odds. It's you that is important. I can get hold of the documents, and your mother's diary is damning. Inherit the Pendral bank? You don't stand a hope in hell!'

Max reached into his pocket and pulled out a bundle of papers. 'Are these what you're talking about?' And he tossed them on to the low buhl table.

'Where did you get those?'

'Baggot gave them to me, and it's no use you thinking you can hurt him. When we've done with you, you'll be leaving England by the next boat.' Max was cool, he was even smiling, but his eyes held a warning impossible to avoid.

Phelan attempted a laugh that rang hollow. 'You're crazy if you think I'm giving up now.'

'I suggest you leave, while you're still able to walk.' Richard was on his feet, keeping his temper with difficulty, prepared to back the American if it came to a fight. Phelan was in a corner, and likely to fight dirty.

He stared at them contemptuously. 'Eva knows what I can do to her, even now. I shall go to the bank first thing in the morning and state my case.' His eyes met hers, and she was suddenly terrified of what she saw in their depths. Her hand reached out blindly for Richard, but he had gone across to Charlotte.

Max took command. 'You won't see the bank, sir. You'll go home tonight and pack your bags, and advise Julian Leigh to get his luggage together, too.'

'You're mad!' Phelan took a step forward. Whatever his faults, he could never be accused of cowardice.

Max's threatening grimace astonished Jennie. She had never seen him look like that before. 'We've been having some interesting conversations with someone who knows you very well. His name's Carlo.'

Phelan shot him a glance of concentrated malevolence. 'My valet! What's he been saying? How dare he? I'll fire him!'

'He's already left your service,' Richard said tersely. 'We paid him handsomely for information about you and your lover.'

'My lover? Which one?' Phelan jeered. 'There are many women who love me.'

'I'm not talking about women. I'm talking about Julian.'

'Julian? You're joking, aren't you? How ridiculous! Ask Charlotte, if you want details of my sexuality.' Phelan's mocking eyes flicked over her. He had no compunction about compromising her to save his own skin.

Charlotte lifted her head and looked at him. He was my first love, she thought, and remembered the magic of his hands on the piano keys, the thrill of his presence, the wonder and romance that had been Florence, until disillusionment had come. Even now he had an undeniable charisma, even now when she faced the truth about him, feared him, hated him – but was still fascinated.

'I wasn't surprised when Max and Richard told me about Julian,' she said quietly. 'I remembered you and that Italian boy, Michele. I don't fully understand about such things – Michele and Angelica – Julian.'

'Tshaw! How can you understand the complexities of human relationships? You've scarcely lived yet.' Phelan's voice was charged with irony, then, cooly, he turned to Richard and Max. 'As for Carlo, you know nothing, can prove nothing – the word of a foreign servant against that of a gentleman.'

'Maybe not, but mud sticks, and the board will tell you where to go if you dare approach them after we've told them what we know.' Max was enjoying himself hugely, proving his worth to his lady, meeting Jennie's smiling approval.

'Prove it!' Phelan challenged. 'They'll want proof!'

'They can have it. Carlo stole letters from your house, ones that Julian wrote to you. The police will take action if we inform them, and you and Julian will go to gaol.'

Phelan put a hand to his face, stayed in that position for a second, and then raised his head to sweep them with a terrible glance.

'All right. You win,' he said quietly. 'I'll go, back to a country where the love between men can bloom freely. You don't understand, can't comprehend how beautiful such a thing can be. It surpasses anything you'll ever experience in your paltry little lives. Julian loves me, has been with me through thick and thin. Keep your bank, keep your damned country, keep your hidebound ideas, and may you have joy of them!'

He turned on his heel and walked to the door, a tall, handsome man, arrogant and sure of himself. He's a devil, thought Jennie, but there's something about him ... She was the least shocked of all of them by the revelation concerning his private life. People of the theatre accepted relationships which were condemned by outsiders – men and women, man and man, woman with woman – it didn't matter as long as love and respect were part of the ingredients. She was not much concerned about his love-life, but relieved that Eva and Charlotte had been saved from his selfish determination to ruin them.

'We did it, Jennie! We did it!' Max shouted and swung her in his arms, whirling her round. She laughed up at him, and then put her free arm round Charlotte, joining in the celebrations as champagne was borne in by a smiling, though still stately, Hopkins. The danger was over.

Bernice took upon herself the sad duty of telling Eva the truth about Charlotte and Richard. Frederick had wanted to leave it, letting her believe that Richard would come back to her after his travels.

'No,' Bernice had said briskly. 'That's not a good idea, Freddy. Don't be such a lily-livered coward. She'll merely sit around for months, waiting, and then be disappointed at the end of it. If you won't tell her, then I shall, but I expect you to be there afterwards. She's going to need you.'

She and Eva had been to *Pour Femme*, where Bernice had ordered yet another set of lovely underclothes, and had then gone to Albion House for lunch. It was served in the library, and they sat at a small table in the bay window, the meal dished up on Crown Derby china, the cosy room so serene that Bernice almost hated it, knowing that she was about to shatter that tranquillity.

'So, Phelan's gone, and good riddance,' she said, helping herself to water biscuits and Stilton from the cheese-board.

Eva nodded. 'Did you know about him and Julian? You must have suspected, living with them all those months in Europe.'

'Well, not exactly. I'd heard rumours, but he seemed so wrapped up in Charlotte, and I wasn't thinking about anything much except Andrew.' Bernice was adept at steering conversations in the direction she wanted them to go. 'Dear Andrew, such a restless soul, and now he's off to Brazil, kidnapping Richard. What d'you think of it?'

Eva's face betrayed nothing of her inner torment. God, she's strong, Bernice thought, I'd never have the courage, not if I loved a man as deeply as she does Richard. And that malicious gossip of a while back. She defies them all, bless her, ever more outrageous in dress, cocking a snook at every damned one of her critics. And I, who are supposed to be her friend, am about to crucify her.

'Richard is his own boss. I don't own him,' Eva said, sipping her glass of white wine. 'In fact, I rather admire him for going on such an adventure. I'll miss him dreadfully, of course, but it won't be for ever.'

'You're sure he'll come back?' Now for it, thought Bernice, and fortified herself by selecting a cigarette from a silver case and inserting the end in her ivory holder.

Eva sat there with a Sphinx-like expression on her features. 'Of course. Why shouldn't he?'

Bernice took a deep breath. 'Eva, darling, please listen to me. You're wrong.'

'What d'you mean, wrong?' Eva said, her eyes darkening.

'Because he's not in love with you. Because he hasn't the guts to tell you.'

Eva sat quite still, but her face grew pale. 'It's not true,' she said, though she knew that it was.

'My dear, dear Eva. I'm your friend. I love you. I'd not be saying this if I didn't. It's not easy for me. But you must listen. Richard is very fond of you, but he couldn't help himself. He met Charlotte, and they fell in love.'

'No,' Eva whispered. 'Please – no!' Her hands were before her face as if she prayed, her eyes closed.

'I went to see him, and he wept, Eva. It's terrible to see a man cry, but he did.'

'How could he do such a thing to me?' Eva said quietly. 'And as for her – I knew there was something going on, and she's been with me, day after day, and butter wouldn't melt in her mouth she's so damned pure, but all the time she was going to the studio, sleeping with him – Richard, who is mine!'

Her face was contorted, eyes wide and tearless. Bernice watched her in silence and, after a while, went over to sit by her. Such control was terrible. Grief and anger were far better expressed as loudly and violently as possible.

'Eva,' she said, though unsure if she was being heard, 'I wish it was otherwise, I truly do, but it's not, so there you are. There's not a thing you can do about it. They're going to be married and then leave for Brazil together in three weeks' time.'

'She's going, too? But he wouldn't take me, said it would be impossible for a white woman to survive in the jungle.'

'Good God, Eva, you've had a narrow escape,' Bernice laughed shakily. 'Nothing would drag me to such a god-forsaken hole, not even Andrew. Would you really want to be eaten by mosquitoes, chased by head-hunters, subject to a thousand and one horrors and discomforts? Charlotte's welcome to it.'

'I would have gone, suffered anything but this. I can't bear it.' Eva cried, her whole body shaking. 'For the first time in my life I was happy. I'd never felt like that before. He's so lovely, so strong, I felt safe. I can't live without him. I can't.'

Bernice sat stroking her friend's frozen hands, and thinking sadly that she would have given anything she had in the world to have saved her this agony. 'You can survive, Eva. I know you can. It will be dark and terrible now, but you'll come out into the sunshine again.'

Eva pulled away from her. She looked old, her eyes sunken, her cheeks like wax. 'Save yourself the platitudes. I know I'll live through it. What else can one do?'

Bernice, more upset than she had imagined she could be and indignant that Richard had not had the courage to speak to Eva himself, went to the studio. She had done his dirty work for him, but thought him weak, cowardly and lacking in backbone, and she told him so.

Eva was still sitting as Bernice had left her. She resembled a graven image, motionless, her eyes blank. The ringing of the telephone roused her from her trance. She moved stiffly, the blood flowing back into her cramped limbs, walked to the side-table and picked up the receiver.

'Yes?' She was surprised that she could speak, and that it was so normal a sound.

'Eva. It's Richard.' His voice awoke her numbed heart and hope rushed in. He's going to tell me that Bernice was wrong, she thought.

She leaned against the wall, the receiver pressed tightly to her ear. 'Yes, Richard?'

'Bernice said she'd been to see you.' The line was crackly, but she could tell that he was anxious.

'Yes.'

'And she told you about Charlotte and me?' She must havc made some sort of noise – a sigh? A sob? His voice sharpened. 'Eva, are you still there?'

'Yes.' She spoke clearly. 'I'm here, Richard.'

'Do you want me to come over?'

To see him! Maybe convince him that he was making a terrible mistake. To look at him, fall into his arms – he wouldn't reject her, she knew that, but nothing would change his mind. He was too kind, too cruel, a man. She was silent for a moment, and he spoke again, fearing that she was going to cry.

'Eva, answer me. Shall I come?'

Only her pride remained. She was lonely, panic-stricken, there was nothing more to say, but she could not hang up, prolonging the contact, gripping the receiver like a lifeline.

'What is there to talk about?' she said, the tears running, running. She could taste them, salty and sharp on her lips. 'You want to leave me. You don't love me any more.'

'It's not like that.' He sounded desperate. 'I do love you – as a friend. D'you want to see Charlotte? Shall I bring her, or you can meet her on your own if you'd rather. We must talk about this.'

'Talk! What good is talk?' She was angry now. How dare he! How dare he suggest – Charlotte – himself – those two together bringing their stupid sympathy, their guilt. 'She's your mistress. Everyone knows and has been talking about it, laughing at me behind my back.'

'That's not true. We've not slept together. We couldn't because of you. Don't you understand? It's been platonic.'

'Platonic!' She gave a sharp laugh. 'Well, there's no need to restrain yourselves now, is there?'

'Eva, please,' he was pleading down the line, and she could imagine his expression. He'd be wildly agitated, running a hand through his hair, his blue eyes intense with misery. Let him sweat! Let him suffer! There was no way she'd make it easier for him.

'I'll send back your engagement ring.' She turned the screw a notch tighter.

'Keep it,' he begged, his voice husky.

'No, Richard, give it to Charlotte, and I never want to see you or her again. As far as I'm concerned, you're both dead.'

She replaced the phone on the hook. Walking in a dream, she fumbled her way back to her chair. Her hands were icy. A sense of unreality swamped her. The whole thing was like some ghastly nightmare from which she could not wake.

When Charlotte arrived at Albion House later that day, she found a letter from Eva asking her to move her things out straight away. It was a bitter letter, in which her benefactress accused her of disloyalty, treachery, and betrayal. She could expect nothing further from her, no money, no support. Charlotte showed it to Jennie, and then moved into the house in Finsbury Park, carrying such a load of guilt with her that she was certain she would never recover.

She went to Richard that night, and they had several drinks, talking, crying, and making love, but all the time she was seeing Eva's reproachful eyes, remembering her scornful words. Loving him, wanting him, but feeling like a criminal.

'This is terrible,' she said at last, her head pillowed on his bare chest.

'That's not very complementary,' he replied, trying to make a joke. 'No one's said that about me before.'

'Not you, silly!' She sat astride him, naked and tousle-haired, her hands moving over his eye sockets, his cheekbones, his mouth, and he turned his head and licked her fingers, one by one, slowly, appreciatively. Then he pulled her down on top of him, and she shed more tears into his neck, sobbing, 'I feel such a bitch! Why is it that lovely happenings are always marred by something bad?'

'It's not your fault.' He tried to comfort her. 'Be happy, Charlotte, don't grieve.'

He was caressing her, seeking to use their bodies as solace, to pleasure her again as he had recently done, whispering love-words, cherishing her, but passion spent, there were too many thoughts intruding and she lay like a stone in his arms ... thinking, thinking. He had lain with Eva and Jennie. How did she compare with them?

'You've made love to my sister,' she said helplessly, sensing that he did not want to talk about that.

'And you made love with Phelan.' She was ashamed because his voice lacked the reproach of hers.

She rolled over on her back, arms behind her head, looking up at the ceiling above the divan. 'Don't remind me. It was nothing like this.'

Richard had practised the controlled passion of an expert lover, tender, loving, demanding, all at the right moment in each stage of her arousal. Now she realised that Phelan had been selfish, concerned only with his own pleasure, using hers as an adjunct to it, often leaving her unsatisfied and responsible for her own orgasm. It would never be like that with Richard, and she thanked God for him. But, even so –

'Was Eva good to go to bed with?' she asked, turning her face toward him on the pillow.

He had propped himself up on a pillow, staring at her in the pink glow of the bedside lamp. 'Yes,' he answered truthfully.

'And Jennie?' Every time they had been together, Jennie and Max, herself and Richard, she had wondered about this, picturing Jennie half-naked as she had seen her in the dressing-room, trying to push the jealous thoughts from her mind, but unsuccessfully.

'Darling, don't,' he groaned. 'I never think of her now, or Eva. It's gone, done with, in the past. Jennie and I weren't in love. Forget it, please.'

Then he used his strength to extinguish her fears, his hands tugging at her hair, forcefully determined to show her how much he loved her. Despite herself, he conquered, and she whirled into a sensual world where the ghosts of other lovers were exorcised. She gripped him in a fury of passion, and then there was nothing but the night, and Richard.

Eva felt that she was going mad; her hatred of Charlotte and her rage against Richard accompanied her wherever she went. It was as if she was suffering from a terminal illness. She avoided going to any places where she had been with him, or seeing anyone who had known them. Mostly, she stayed in her room where Alice eventually found her, worried because she had not put in an appearance at the shop for several days.

It was Alice who brought her back from the dead, Alice with her gentle simplicity, her faith in a higher power, Alice who reawakened her interest in the things she had once held dear – the shop, the clinic, her charities. She became Eva's constant companion, either at Albion House or at the flat in Columbia Square, and tempted her back to *Pour Femme* where the welcome of the girls, primed by Alice to say nothing about her broken romance, was sincere and reassuring.

Eva's sense of purpose returned, and she accepted Frederick's invitations. He had been totally at a loss, wanting to help her but denied access. Alice patted herself on the back, thinking that Eva was beginning to see sense at last and would finally accept him. Sentimental and romantic, she laboured under the illusion that his patience, kindness and loyalty would soften Eva's heart.

She was wrong, for only one thing shone crystal clear through Eva's torment. She was determined to have a baby, and Frederick was as good a man as any to father it. Married to him, her child would be given every advantage that life could offer. She would have someone born of her own flesh on whom to lavish her love, but, more important even than this – someone who would eventually inherit the bank and every single one of its assets.

Neither Phelan nor Charlotte would see a penny of the Pendral fortune.

Chapter 20

Orlanda picked up the child and carried her towards the manor house. 'Come on, Grace. You're going to see your ma today. Got to get you cleaned up and dressed like a *gorgio chavi*.'

Joan had a bowl of warm water ready on the kitchen table, and the two women undressed the sturdy little girl, sponged away the dirt and washed her mop of curls. Grace, at two years and four months old, objected to this treatment. She wanted to stay at the camp in the woods, where no one curbed her lust for life, her curiosity and adventurous spirit. She loved Joan, trusted and relied on her, but had been glad when the gypsies returned in the autumn. She'd not forgotten them; they were her friends.

She squirmed and shouted while she was being washed, struggled when a vest was popped over her head, made her legs stiff and awkward when they tried to put on a pair of linen drawers. They were strong women, used to carrying loads and working hard, but it took their combined efforts to complete her attire – the liberty bodice, the flounced petticoat, the plaid dress with its huge skirt, puffed sleeves and ribbon sash.

'She's a demon,' Orlanda said fondly, shaking her greying ringlets. 'A *beng's chavi* – a devil's brat!'

'No you aren't, are you, Gracie?' Joan was working a comb through the damp curls. 'You're my little angel girl. And Mummy's coming today. What d'you think of that? Lots of people are coming from London especially to see you, my pet.'

'They don't want to take her, do they?' The big gypsy woman managed to look fierce and anxious all at the same time. 'Not our *chavi*.'

'I don't think so.' Joan popped a sweet into Grace's mouth as an inducement to sitting still. 'I had a letter from Jennie and she didn't mention that.'

'She'll tell us about America.' Orlanda wrapped a flannel holder round the kettle handle and poured boiling water into the brown glazed tea pot. 'Some of the Chiknos went to America, doing well, so I hear.' She fixed her black eyes on Grace, while waiting for the tea to brew. 'She'll go one day. I've seen it in the cards. That one's going to have many ups and downs in her life, but she has a golden future.'

'Golden fiddlesticks!' Joan did not hold with the art of *dukkering*. Of the earth earthy, she only believed in what she could see, taste, hear and touch. 'We haven't got time for that now. There's a table to be laid, and food to be put out. They'll be here for tea.' She strode to an inner door, stuck her head through and shouted. 'Tom! Look after Grace, will you? See she doesn't get herself dirty again.'

Grace liked Uncle Tom. He carried an exciting aroma of tobacco and horses, ancient tweeds and tanned leather. His den was an untidy, dusty wonderland, with books, months' old newspapers and periodicals on every chair and shelf, dogs sprawled before the hearth, a tabby cat on the window-sill, paintings hanging askew on the walls and a fox's mask in the centre of the overmantel.

He dunked gingernuts in his tea and held them to her mouth, though careful to tie his handkerchief under her chin to catch the dribbles. Grace crunched the hard, sweet biscuits and slowly sucked their juices, sitting on his knee in the armchair where the worn brocade had stuffing poking out of it. This was good, almost as good as crawling through the undergrowth with Priam, her favourite among the gypsy boys.

The logs flared on the hearth and Tom told her to look into those glowing peaks and caverns and find Loke, the god of fire. She stared, thumb in mouth, leaning against him for safety, and yes, there he was, Loke himself with his hair ablaze, his sharp pointed features, his scarlet cloak floating up the chimney. Her chubby hand slid down against her chest, her head nodded and her eyes closed, her jaw still working away at her thumb even though she was asleep.

'They're here! Quick, get the kettle on!' Joan yelled, tearing off her apron and running to the back door.

The chickens in the yard scattered with indignant squawks as the automobiles rumbled over the cobbles. A pig, one of Joan's household pets, gave a shrill squeal, and collided with her in his frantic attempt to get into the kitchen.

'Silly creature!' she scolded. 'Out of my way!'

Jennie turned in the tulip-shaped, red morocco leather seat of their new car and said to Max, 'This is it! Gaulden Court! Bet there's nothing like this in the States.'

'You can say that again,' he agreed, through the cigar held between his lips. 'Pure medieval! Great! I love it.'

Then she was jumping down, careless of her shoes, her hem dragging in the mire, running to the following car, shouting to Charlotte: 'Hurry, come on! You must see her – your niece – little Miss Grace Blossom.'

She was embracing Joan and Orlanda, wrapping them in her furs, her perfume, amazing them by her beautiful travelling costume of finest wool, her big, flat muff, chinchilla coat and hat which got in the way of kisses, till she tore it from her head, tossing it to the man who stood behind her, smiling at them. They were enthralled by his American accent.

Then they had to meet her sister, Charlotte, and the man she was about to marry. Orlanda stored up every detail about them to relate to the gypsies later. Fine, rich-looking *gorgios*, little Grace's relations. They were in the kitchen now, filling it, talking endlessly, and there was so much to tell. But first the Squire appeared with Grace in his arms. She was big-eyed, still half asleep, on the verge of tears, until her mother took her.

Grace did not see her very often but she never forgot her, dreaming of her sometimes, though still too close to babyhood to differentiate between dreams and reality. Her mother was like one of those princesses in the story books that Uncle Tom read aloud to her. Her clothes were so silky, her furs so soft, and she smelled like wild roses and herbs and the violets that grew in the hedgerow.

Grace was silent, staring at the strangers, the men so big and noisy, the other woman who they said was her Aunt Charlotte, so lovely, another princess, who looked like her mother. One of the men, she was told to call him Papa Max, dropped on his hunkers by her side, a large parcel in his hands. It was a doll with a china face, jointed limbs, real hair and pretty clothes.

'D'you want to come and see my car?' he asked in a deep, chuckling voice.

Grace burrowed into her mother, hid her face in her lacy jabot.

'I'll come with you, Max,' said Jennie. 'She's a bit shy. Give her time. She doesn't see many people, only the gypsies when they come in the winter. Mostly it's just her and the Squire and Joan.'

'And this place is really going to be hers one day?' he said, as they walked into the yard. 'It's great! Needs money spending on it, but that's OK.'

Charlotte sat by the fire, Richard's hand in hers, and sifted through her impressions. So much had happened recently, happy things, sad things. Eva's complete rejection had wounded her deeply, though she still felt that she richly deserved it. I shan't be truly happy until she's forgiven me, she thought, even as she smiled at Joan and Orlanda, accepted a cup of tea, and chatted with them. Richard was a treasure on such occasions, so easy with everyone, genuinely interested in all aspects of the human condition. He asked Orlanda if the Chiknos would object if he photographed them. He carried a camera about him always, in the same way that other people wore clothes. Orlanda carted him off to the camp, while Charlotte remained in the kitchen, delighted with Grace, that quaint, wild little thing.

She had no qualms about undertaking the journey to South America, having met Andrew and won him over, for at first he was dubious about taking a woman along. She was impatient to leave her old life far behind her. Maybe, in time, Eva would find happiness and be her friend once more. It grieved her to part from Jennie so soon after finding her, the child, too. It was strange to have kith and kin when, for so long, she had believed herself alone. She and Jennie had had much to discuss, spending every free moment together, reading their mother's diary and crying over it, her love-letters as well, on a voyage of discovery as they saw their own birth certificates and the marriage lines of Margaret and Simon Drummond. It was no wonder that Charlotte had not been able to trace them, for they had been married in Wales, migrating to London later.

She and Richard had gone to a performance of *The Sailor Girl*, where she had marvelled that the glittering figure on the stage was really her sister, listening to the applause, the shouts for encores, tingling with pride. She had invited Gwen and Archie along, glad to see that her friend was recovering from the shock of Julian's abrupt departure. Charlotte had explained the situation, and Gwen had readily grasped the significance of the friendship between Phelan and Julian, finding it quite amusing, not shocked but just annoyed that he had not told her. Her heart had mended with amazing rapidity and she was now happily receiving Archie's attentions. This comforted Charlotte; now there was one person less for her to feel guilty about, for he had been distressed when he realised that she was engaged to Richard.

When Jennie and Max returned, Grace was riding on his shoulders, her fingers clenched in his hair. Joan had prepared a typical farmhouse high-tea where the table groaned under massive fruit cakes, apple pies, plates of ham, homemade bread, dairy butter and great wedges of cheese. Max swore that this was just like teatime down South, praising Joan's cooking and stuffing delicacies into Grace's mouth.

This is my home, Jennie thought. This is where my roots are now, no matter how far I roam. I'm like Orlanda, and will always drift back here; so will Zena one day. I hope she's not away too long. I want her to meet Max and Charlotte, though I suspect they won't be strangers to her. She'll have seen them in the crystal, in the cards, as she did on that long-ago day in Soho. She knew there was someone looking for me, and it must have been my sister. She also knew that Richard was not the man who would be my husband.

It was strange to recall that he had once been her lover – Richard, the link between three women, Eva, Charlotte and herself. Fate worked in mysterious ways, and she shared the gypsies' belief in destiny. Now, Jennie was happy with Max, needing no other man. Richard would soon be her brother-in-law, and she saw him in an entirely different light. He bore no grudge against her, liked Max, and was good-naturedly prepared to let bygones be bygones.

'I want you to come to London soon,' Jennie said when it was time to leave, one arm round Joan and the other round the Squire. 'Get the train and stay at my house. I've heaps of room. You must see me in the show. Please come, and bring Grace. I'd like her to get used to living at Finsbury Park.'

She was anxious about Grace, reluctant to leave her, especially since Max had taken to her so readily, but not wishing to disrupt her. Max must return to Los Angeles before long, and she was prepared to give up her place at the Gaiety and go with him. She could act in America, if she wanted, and he was talking about making movies with her starring in them, but what was best for her daughter? Joan and Tom would be miserable without her, yet Jennie felt that she should be with Max and herself.

I'll think about it later, she decided, and kissed her child goodbye. Charlotte kissed her, too, hugging the little one close, knowing that it would be a long time till she saw her again. The wedding and their departure date drew ever closer, and she had already purchased tropical kit, stout snake-boots, linen shirts, divided skirts and floppy hats for the Amazon jungle heat.

The headlights of the cars joined the hurricane lamps which Joan and the Squire held high; Orlanda, a dark bulky figure in the background, raising her hand in a gesture resembling a blessing. Max parped his horn, and the cars swung out through the broken gateway of the manor where the gypsy children had been waiting to see them go, running along by their sides, cheering and yelping.

Grace wriggled down from Joan's arms, let her doll drop into the mud, and escaped into the twilight to join her friends. Priam was there, older than her, a creature to be admired with his rough hair, dirty, roguish face, and slim naked feet, like a monkey's.

'Look at her,' Jennie exclaimed, glancing back over her shoulder, intending to wave but stiffening to attention. 'It's cold and she isn't wearing a coat.'

'Who? Grace? I can't look,' Max answered. 'I'm driving, remember? What's she doing?'

As Jennie watched, she saw Grace tear the ribbon from her hair and speed away, heedless of Joan's angry voice behind her. Jennie was half amused, half anxious. 'Jesus Christ, the little demon! I think she's heading for the gypsy camp.'

'Don't worry. She'll be OK,' said her husband calmly. 'She's the spitting image of you, Jennie. A tough cookie! A survivor.'

Jennie's final glimpse of her daughter was of her running through the gate, pausing to tug at her skirt that had snarled on a nail, and impatiently tearing it free. She's already forgotten me, she thought regretfully, forgotten everything but the gypsy fires beckoning through the trees.

The church hall was festive, its plain walls adorned with bunting, paper garlands and colourful balloons. There were flowers everywhere. Across the bare stage was slung a great banner, saying: 'Good Luck to the Happy Couple'.

This was the first thing Gwen saw when she entered, radiant and smiling, clad in white satin, a huge bouquet of stephanotis and orange-blossom cascading down to mingle with the lace, the silk, the trailing ends of her misty veil. Archie held her arm, spruce in a morning suit, and her bridesmaids ran ahead, rustling their pink dresses, flushed and excited – her sisters, making their debut as wedding attendants.

Everyone was there, all of the Savills' many friends, as well as Archie's relatives, some of whom she had not yet met. They could have been formidable, coming as they did from the nobility, but all were beaming and congratulatory. Her grandparents from both sides had been staying at the vicarage for the great occasion, and altogether the weeks leading up to her marriage had been exhausting ones.

Though engaged to Archie for three years, knowing that she would eventually be called upon to take the major role in such an event, she had not been prepared for the confusion and thrill of it all. There had been serious talks about where the marriage should take place. Archie's father, the Marquis, had desired that his youngest son be married in the chapel attached to his manor house in Huntingdonshire; Gwen's paternal grandfather had suggested his mansion in Shropshire; her mother's parents had opted for their home in Kent, but Gwen had been firm on this issue. She wanted her father to marry her in St Mark's, and for the reception to be held in the church hall, just down the road.

Archie, since spending so much time with the Savills, had become an ardent Socialist and was entering the political lists. Gwen supported him whole-heartedly, fully prepared to stand at his side when he put up for candidate at the next local election, but it was not her intention to be a nonentity in the background. Inspired by the example set by the Suffragette martyrs, she was determined to join the struggle for the rights of women. So, everything considered, a simple wedding in a simple setting suited her admirably.

She had been moved by the way in which her father's parishioners had packed the church, or stood outside to cheer and shower her with confetti when she walked to the be-ribboned carriage on Archie's arm. Stephen Savill had made sure that they did not miss out on the feast, arranging with the landlord of the nearest public house to provide food and drink for them. Gwen would have welcomed them into the hall, but there was not room. Archie had been secretly relieved. Though fired by his newly discovered tenets, he was not at all sure how his parents would have got on with the East End women in their best garb, all gaudy feathered hats and tatty dresses. As it was there was a tendency for the wedding party to split into factions – the Savills drifting towards the Stapleys, the Armstrongs mingling with the girls from *Pour Femme*.

Gwen was swept up by the guests, faces she knew, some she did not, all wishing her well. Her father, wearing his dog-collar, had become the Master of Ceremonies, officiating at the top table where stood the massive, three-tiered wedding-cake, while people occupied a series of smaller ones scattered around the room. The caterers were busy in the kitchen at the rear, keeping the buffet tables well stocked. There was plenty to drink, and a white-jacketed waiter served behind the bar.

'I s-say, Gwen, they've done us proud, haven't they?' murmured Archie when they bumped into one another during their circulation of their guests. 'But I'll be glad when we're in the car and off, won't you?'

She gave him a wide smile. He was such a nice person and she loved him, not with the passion she had felt for Julian, perhaps, but warmly, comfortably, knowing that their love would deepen with the passage of time. Her parents were her role models, and she saw that she would never have been happy with someone like Julian, even if he *had* been interested. She needed security, a home similar to the one she was leaving, and a strong man of principle like her father. Archie was already maturing fast, a serious person now, but they shared the same sense of humour, the same expectations and, above all, he was devoted to her.

Their courtship had been a chaste one, though not as rigidly chaperoned as some, but Gwen knew that tonight was the night for her first taste of sexual fulfilment. She was looking forward to it. Beth Armstrong had talked to her frankly and advised on contraception, so she and Archie would be able to plan their family, but she had already made up her mind that it would be a large one. She wanted Archie, had been frustrated because they had decided to wait until they were married, and armed with books on the subject and Beth's advice, she had no qualms, certain that everything was going to be wonderful.

Most of the guests had already arrived, and she welcomed Bernice who had entered at the same time as Eva. Bernice was still as lovely, though she had put on a little weight. Abreast with fashion, she was wearing a Princess style fuchsia-pink afternoon dress, the long, draped skirt ornamented by a cluster of silk tea-roses at the waist and near the hem. Her hat was dramatic, with a huge brim and high crown, covered in lace and adorned with further overblown roses.

Eva had come *en famille*, with Frederick in tow and Nanny Pendral bringing up the rear, carrying their son, a blond two year old. Gwen greeted them warmly, saying, 'How lovely to see you, and thanks for the wedding present.'

Eva kissed her cheek, her lips cool, her smile remote, while Frederick shook Archie's hand, clapped him on the shoulder and told him he was a lucky blighter. She was remembering her own wedding, a quiet affair which had taken place at Greyfriars shortly after Charlotte had left England. Once having made up her mind, Eva had acted swiftly, giving herself no time for repining, clinging to the hope that once she had given herself to another man she would forget Richard. This hadn't happened, of course. It had been impossible to push him from her mind, especially on her wedding night when Frederick had come to her, humbly, hesitantly, aware of her jumbled feelings. Surprisingly, he had partially healed her, his gentleness, his adoration making her realise that life was still worth living. He was so steady and reliable, helpful in every aspect. To all intents and purposes, her marriage was a success, and within months her prayers had been granted when she had given birth to a son.

Intensely proud of this achievement, she took him from Nanny Pendral so that Gwen might admire him. 'There, Ryder, my love – look at the balloons? Aren't they pretty?' she crooned, and her face was transformed, glowing with that inner light which comes with mother love.

'He's such a big boy now,' Gwen murmured politely, for she had not seen this wonder-child since he was a baby.

She had heard about him through Beth, Alice and Bernice who all considered Eva fortunate to have had him so easily at her age. She knew that Nanny Pendral had been engaged, and that Eva insisted that Ryder accompanied her almost everywhere. She did not like to let him out of her sight for a second. A besotted mother, and her friends predicted trouble ahead, unless she was able to have another child soon.

Eva had not altered, still elegant and given to eccentric modes of dress. She was wearing a wine red velvet skirt, tight and buttoned all down one side, a tunic of the same material, very severe in cut, and a close-fitting hat with a wrap-around scarf. Frederick, whose hair was now snowy white, fetched over glasses of champagne, a contented man married to the woman he had always loved. Ryder wriggled down from Eva's arms, sturdy in a white frilly dress and bonnet. He made for Gwen's riotous collection of brothers and sisters, soon romping with them, though both Nanny and his mother kept their eyes glued to him.

'Ah, there you are, Lady Eva,' cried Alice, bearing down on them, escorted by a young man to whom she was now engaged. She had met him at *Pour Femme* for he was the manager of a firm that made lingerie satin. 'Isn't it a wonderful wedding?'

They all agreed that it was, then Gwen, taking a quick glance round to see that everyone was eating and drinking and generally enjoying themselves, saw someone who had just come in. She clapped a hand to her mouth, her face lighting up.

'It's Charlotte!' she exclaimed, made to go towards her then stopped, remembering her manners. 'Excuse me,' she said to Eva, but could contain herself no longer, pushing through the throng.

'Gwen!' Charlotte hugged her, then stood back, holding her at arm's length. 'My word, just look at you! What a gorgeous bride!'

'You came, you came, you got here in time! This has really made my day!' Gwen cried.

'I wasn't sure if I'd be able, but we docked yesterday, stayed with Richard's mother, put on our best bibs and tuckers and shot over here.' Charlotte was finding it more than just strange, the hall, the people – so English. She wasn't yet used to it. Everything seemed so much smaller after America.

'Charlotte!' It was Bernice who, wreathed in smiles, rushed to fling her arms round her. 'Good heavens! Talk about the return of the prodigal! Where's Richard?'

'Outside in the car. We weren't sure, you see. Is Eva here?' A shadow passed across Charlotte's face.

'She is, and Freddy, and her baby boy.' Gwen hesitated, knowing what was in Charlotte's mind.

'And what sort of mood is she in?'

'My dearest girl, don't tell me you're afraid of her?' Bernice was overjoyed to see her again. 'She's a mother now, you know, so proud of her sprog you'd never believe. Spoiling him, of course. He's going to grow up to be a most awful little prig.'

'I didn't, did I?' Charlotte challenged, spirits raised by the irrepressible Bernice.

'Not you, dear, but then you came from working-class stock, and you didn't have a doting mama. Ryder, I fear, is treated like an extra special, almost divine creation – Eva's creation at that.'

'What about Freddy?' He had never struck Charlotte as a meek and mild person who'd be willing to allow his wife to ruin his son by overindulgence.

'Freddy, darling, has very little say in the matter, from what I can see.'

'Listen, Bernice, there's something I want to ask you before Richard comes in,' Charlotte said quickly, lowering her voice. 'Have you seen or heard anything of Phelan?'

Bernice shot her a glance. 'I've not seen him, but someone told me that they'd come across him in the casinos in Monte Carlo.'

'And Julian?'

'Was with him.'

So Phelan was carrying on with his customary life-style. Does he ever think of me? Charlotte wondered. Her time with him was like a dream now, fantastic, horrible, but unforgettable. More important was the present and her confrontation with Eva. They had not met since that dreadul time when Eva had found out about her and Richard.

Gwen had realised this when she sent the wedding invitations, but Archie had advised her to not worry. It was Charlotte's and Eva's problem, not hers. Gwen and Charlotte had kept in contact by letter, and the addresses she had been given over the months had been exotic ones. Thus she had learned something of Charlotte's adventures, and had known that she was going to New York to see Jennie before returning to England.

Gwen shook her head, her smile uncertain. 'What are you going to do about Eva?' she asked. 'Richard can't stay outside all afternoon. That's ridiculous. I'll send Archie to fetch him.'

Charlotte hardly recognised her former beau. He was bearded now, no longer the fresh-faced boy who had wooed her. Everyone looked older, the Savills, the Armstrongs, their children who had grown beyond belief. I shouldn't have known them, she thought, the feeling of being a stranger increasing by the minute. So long immured in the wilds of Brazil where, more than once, her life had been on the line, such gatherings where light laughter and chit-chat were the order of the day seemed artificial and totally unreal.

'I had to come, Gwen,' she said earnestly. 'I wanted to see you as a bride, but I dreaded the thought that Eva would be here. We've unfinished business, and I hate it. She was like a mother to me, and I can never forget that. But Lady Sinclair wants to be my mother now, and that's fine.'

'You get on well with her? It's always a help if one's ma-in-law approves, isn't it?' Gwen looked across to where Lady Stapley was graciously holding court. 'I was scared stiff of meeting Archie's mama, but it seems that I've been given her blessing.'

Charlotte nodded, smiling. 'Richard's mother accepted me as her daughter when he and I were married, though she was upset because we were going gallivanting off round the world, as she put it. She's told me that she had never really liked him being engaged to someone as old as Eva. But sweet though she is, she'll never take Eva's place. I must speak to her, Gwen.'

'So you shall,' she answered firmly and, chin lifted, daring anyone to spoil *her* day, she took Charlotte by the hand and led her to where Eva was talking with Stephen. Bernice went, too. She wouldn't have missed this for anything.

Eva turned and saw them, recognising Charlotte at once, though she was much thinner and her skin bore that dark tint of someone who has lived in a hot climate. For a moment neither of them spoke, then Charlotte broke the ice, saying, 'Hello, Eva.'

Eva was torn. She had hoped this would not happen, but feared that it might. Her heart, that ever vulnerable part of her, ached for her former ward. She wanted to embrace her, yet her pride forbade it. She had sworn never to forgive. She was annoyed because Stephen had excused himself, and Frederick was smiling at Charlotte. It was all very well for him, he had got what he wanted out of the situation, whereas she had been the injured party.

At that moment Ryder toddled over to her, holding out his arms, 'Mummy, me can't see,' he lisped.

Eva snatched him up, holding him tightly against her like a shield. Then, and only then, could her lips form the words, 'Charlotte. It's been a long time.'

'How are you, Eva? Is this your boy? I read in the papers that you'd had him. I'm so glad for you.' Charlotte looked over his head into Eva's eyes. They were hostile.

'I'm well, thank you, and yes, this is Ryder. I've heard of your exploits in the Amazon jungle. You've no children yet?'

'The rain-forest is hardly the place to start a family, unless you're a native,' Charlotte answered, smiling but equally formal.

'That's true, I suppose.' Eva's voice was clipped, courteous. 'How is Richard?'

'Fine, he's just fine. He had several bouts of malaria but recovered. I had it, too. It's not pleasant.'

This is terrible, Charlotte was thinking. Such distance between us – like strangers. Eva's changed, not physically but within herself. She's hard now. It's only when she looks at her son that I recognise the caring person she used to be.

'Really? I'm sorry to hear that,' Eva said untruthfully.

Bernice decided it was high time to change the drift of the conversation. 'Charlotte dear, I adore your dress. It's frightfully smart. Where did you get it?'

Charlotte was wearing sky blue silk, trimmed with coffee-coloured lace. The gown had tight sleeves, a lace gorget filling in the square neckline and hugging her throat. White lace mittens and a tasselled bag completed her attire, and her dark hair was crowned by a Gainsborough hat of natural straw with a single large ostrich feather.

'I bought it in New York, when I went to see Jennie,' Charlotte explained.

'I thought she lived in Los Angeles.'

'They've a house there, but also own an apartment in New York.'

'How is your sister?' Eva asked frostily.

'Very well indeed. She's been playing in a show on Broadway but Max is starting to film a Wild West story, and she's going to be in it.' Politeness, politeness, and all I want to do is ask her forgiveness, Charlotte mourned.

In actual fact, Jennie was blooming, a successful, happily married woman. She had been back to England several times to see Grace, and had given Charlotte strict instructions to visit the child just as soon as she reached home and, later, take her to America.

'All this dashing about from one Continent to another,' Freddy put in almost desperately, steering the women away from deep waters. 'You didn't fly, by any chance?' He was joking, of course, but Charlotte answered him seriously.

'We came by liner, but Richard and Max feel sure that one day it will be possible to cross the Atlantic by flying-machine.'

'Maybe they're right. The Germans already have the Zeppelin – '

'And Colonel Cody has succeeded in getting a heavier-than-air machine off the ground.' Charlotte smiled at Freddy gratefully. He was such an understanding person.

'Where's Andrew Tyler now?' Bernice asked brightly. He had written to her for a while and then the letters had petered out. Bernice was not one to grieve over a man, and had soon found others to take his place.

'He's still in Brazil. There's so much work to be done there.'

'And will you be returning?' Eva hoped so. England would hardly be big enough to hold both of them. She wanted no reminder of the past.

'Soon, but first Richard wants to give a public showing of the photographs he took there.'

Further talk was delayed as Gwen and Archie were summoned to cut the wedding cake. There were joking comments, laughter and cheers as, hands joined, they sliced through the thick icing. The best man made a speech, so did Stephen, and Archie replied and thanked the Savills for the wedding breakfast and for giving him their daughter, speaking confidently with hardly a trace of his former speech impediment. Then glasses were topped up and raised to toast the couple. Charlotte saw Richard at the back of the hall. So did Eva. Two spots of colour appeared on her pale cheeks.

Charlotte leaned forward and, under cover of the general noise as the bridal pair departed for the vicarage to change into their going away clothes, said, 'Eva, speak to him. He's never forgiven himself for hurting you. He spoke of it when he was delirious with fever. That shows how much it has worried him.'

'I'm astonished that you should even ask it of me.' Eva's eyes were piercing and glacier cold.

'I'm asking for the sake of what we once had. Our friendship, our closeness, our love.' I'm begging her, Charlotte thought, appalled. Begging this icy woman, and she's enjoying it.

'Love? Friendship? I'm sorry, Charlotte. What you did to me obliterated that.'

She's frightening, Charlotte thought. She bears grudges. Look how she hated Phelan. She stood there amid the crowd of merry-makers, wanting to cry. Eva cared for no one but Ryder now. Her son, her heir. Fortunate child who would inherit the bank, who had Eva to love him, and Nanny Pendral. She had already met Nanny's condemnatory eye. The old lady had deliberately snubbed her, concentrating on Ryder. Nanny hates me, too, she thought despairingly. I'm no longer their beloved little girl. That wretched child has taken my place. I'm jealous, and it hurts. She could not know of the turmoil raging through Eva, of the pain so great that only the comfort of Ryder's solid little body in her arms stopped her from breaking down.

Then Charlotte felt an arm around her and looked up into Richard's sun-browned face. Her husband, her lover, her comrade-at-arms. She was deeply comforted. They had made a life for themselves, and it had been an exciting one. The church hall and the wedding guests faded, and she saw steamy jungle, magnificent mountains, mighty rivers and the forest indians, friendly people who had been grateful for assistance against oppression. Many others had come their way – adventurers, treasure-seekers, ex-mercenaries – all respecting and admiring Richard, forming themselves into a band of loyal stalwarts.

There had been enemies to fight, greedy planters, slavers, even those higher up the tree who had made fortunes from the rubber trade. And it was Richard who had shown her these things, so much, and so many, enriching her experience beyond measure. How dare someone like Eva refuse to acknowledge the existence of a man of his stature?

'Are you all right, my love?' he murmured in her ear. She did not have to tell him that the situation was fraught.

'Yes, now that you're here,' she answered.

He bowed to Eva. 'Congratulations. I'm happy for you. You've a fine son there,' he said.

She looked at him. He seemed taller, thinner, his face gaunt, his beard long and shaggy, as was his hair, and his deep blue eyes met hers with a glance that contained so many things – apology, conciliation, the hope of friendship. She said nothing.

Frederick's hand came out and shook Richard's. 'Nice to meet you again,' he said, giving Eva a stern look, daring her to be rude. There were times when he put his foot down, and this was one of them, but even he could not force her to speak to Richard.

Dudley, alert for storm-warnings, engaged him in conversation and soon they were discussing South America. 'I hear it's a dreadful place for voracious flies, ants and venomous snakes,' he said jovially.

'That's true,' Richard replied. 'But the wild plants contain antidotes to everything. That's where quinine comes from, the cure for malaria, and I've had cause to be grateful for this. I learned a lot from the natives, but there's a great need for further investigation into their herbs.'

'So I understand.' Dudley was launched on one of his favourite topcis, and he pursued it sedulously, aware of the tension that was so thick it could have been cut with a knife. 'How do they treat their children? Are they well cared for?'

'Better than many in more civilised countries,' Richard warmed to the theme, aware that Eva was listening and watching, though appearing to be absorbed with Ryder. 'They don't go in for large families.'

'Really?' Dudley took another glass of wine from a passing, tray-bearing waiter. 'How so?'

'Many of the tribes don't permit their new-born babes to live if they're crippled or otherwise defective. It's all a question of surviving. Most couples limit their offspring to two, one each for a parent to carry if they're forced to flee from an enemy.'

'Well, well – you surprise me,' Dudley said, and gave Beth a nod, indicating that she should stop gossiping with Cynthia Houston and join him. 'Beth'll be most interested to hear about all this. And how do these people control the population?'

'There's a plant called *peri-peri*. If women eat it, then it makes them sterile. That's just one of the several methods they use.'

'Sounds fascinating. Come back to our house when this shindig's over. I want to hear more.'

When Gwen and Archie returned to the hall, she was dressed in a neat costume and he was wearing a Norfolk jacket and knickerbockers, most suitable for the long drive to Cumberland where they were spending their honeymoon. More confetti, more laughter, and Gwen throwing her bouquet so that one of the unmarried girls might catch it and be a bride herself within the year. Everyone poured out to stand on the pavement and see the couple leave.

Eva and Charlotte were the last to go. They paused in the doorway and, 'I suppose this is goodbye,' Charlotte said wistfully.

'Yes.' Eva was anxious to get away, her eyes going to where Frederick stood with Ryder lifted high so that he might see over the heads of the crowd. Nanny, a small blue-clad figure, hovered at his elbow.

'I'll be taking my niece to America.' It's nearly over, Charlotte thought. I can't make contact with her.

'Jennie's child?'

'That's right.'

Eva looked straight at her and said, 'Good luck, Charlotte.'

Charlotte drew in a deep breath, wanted to take her hand, did not do so. 'Eva, I must say something – '

'Yes?'

'Thank you for all you did for me. I hope that one day – '

Eva gave a thin smile, a ghost of the one which used to light up her face when she looked at Charlotte in the old days. 'One can always hope, Charlotte,' she said. 'Goodbye.'

Then she left the porch, her head held high as she walked towards her son. He was now her *raison d'être*, and her plans for him were legion. Charlotte watched her go, tears refusing to be checked, blinding her and wetting her cheeks. Someone put a handkerchief into her hand.

'Don't cry,' Richard said.

She went into his arms, sobbing against his shirt-front. 'I can't help it. I feel like an orphan again.'

'How can you be? I'm here.' She could feel him laughing, feel his broad chest under the conventional suit, his arms holding her tightly.

'Yes, you are, and I'm so glad.' She raised her face to his, wiped her tears away and adjusted her hat. 'You're right. I don't need her any more.'

'You don't. You're a grown woman now, Mrs Sinclair. Come along, we're to go to the *maison* Armstrong for dinner. There's a lot to do, darling, busy days ahead. Aren't you looking forward to seeing Gracie again? I know that I am.'

The crowd was thinning, the guests rather lost and aimless now. There was a general feeling of anti-climax. Some were already entering their cars or carriages, others walking away down the dusty road, the Savills collecting up various relatives and organising them, the children overtired and quarrelsome. The Armstrong boys scooped up handfuls of confetti from the gutter and tried to stuff them down the bridesmaids necks amid protesting shrieks and tears. Beth remonstrated, administering clips around the ear.

Richard cast them a wry glance. 'It's time we were off,' he announced decisively.

He accompanied her to their car, parked at the kerbside. It was a hot, dry afternoon and the street swarmed with ragged children who, losing interest in the goings-on at the church hall, were engaged in hopscotch or skipping, while the adults, replete from the entertainment provided at the Pig and Whistle, sat on their doorsteps in the sun, idly commenting on the departing guests. The river was running low, and there was a heavy exhalation of dirt, refuse and mud, the acrid smoke from the factories whose stacks pointed black fingers to the blue sky, the cooking smells from eating houses and fish-shops combining to hang over the street like a miasma.

An Italian ice-cream seller appeared, strolling beside his little pony cart with its striped awning. Hordes of children gathered, eyeing Charlotte and Richard. She took some money from her purse, and an urchin appeared beside them.

'Spare a copper, missus,' he whined, stunted and wizened, holding out a grubby palm.

'Here's enough for all of you to have some. Share it, mind. I don't want you scoffing the lot,' she warned, dropping the money into his claw-like hand.

'Thang-you, missus!' And he was off, his mates prowling round him like a pack of hungry wolves.

Richard set the car in motion, and grinned at her. 'You're a great big softie, aren't you?'

'I come from here,' she answered, as they headed for Dudley's house. 'I'll never forget that, and neither will Jennie. We've both been lucky. We got out of it. Those poor little devils may never do so.'

'Darling, I'm not criticising,' he assured her, resting his hand on her knee and squeezing it.

Charlotte watched the streets go past, the sunlight pouring down over this area where people fought to exist against all odds. Then, as they turned into an alley behind the Armstrong home, she saw a few straggly marigolds in the sour soil of a window-box outside one particularly delapidated house.

They raised their orange faces bravely heavenwards, and to her they were more beautiful than anything she had seen in the rain-forest, yet no less jungle flowers – planted by someone in defiance of misfortune, perhaps – to grow like symbols of hope in the jungle of the city.